I0680460

*   *   *

Drones Over
Machu Picchu

* * *

Drones Over Machu Picchu

An Inca Mystery

Edward D. Curry

Published by MERLIN & ASSOCIATES
Virginia Beach, VA 23452

Copyright 2016
by Edward D. Curry

Without limiting rights under the copyright reserved above, no part of this publication may be reproduced, stored in or introduced into a retrieval system, or transmitted, in any form, or by any means (electronic, mechanical, photo photocopying, recording, or otherwise), without the prior written permission of both the copyright owner and the above publisher of this book.

Library of Congress Control Number: 2016905587
ISBN: 0692031944
ISBN: 9780692031940
(E-BOOK) ISBN: 978-0-692-03194-0

Printed in the United States of America

* * *

Acknowledgments

Drones Over Machu Picchu is primarily a work of fiction based on actual Inca history. Names, characters, places, and incidents are the product of the author's imagination or research. Any resemblance to actual persons living or dead, business establishments, events, or locales is coincidental or, in some cases, entirely purposeful.

Many wonderful people have played a part in my life. I have acknowledged our friendship by weaving those individuals into the overall tapestry of this book. I would be remiss if I omitted mentioning the following persons: Charlie Finley, Holly Hartman, Carol Hodies, Elayne Weinbrecht, and Sandy Wendell. In several instances, their critiques and fusion of thoughts often prompted me to back up the truck and seek another path.

Todd Washburn of Washburn Mastering was a joy to work with, and his electronic prowess became self-evident as we created sparkling covers for each of the five books in my Maya-Inca adventure series. Jill Melichar of Synergy Associates is a jewel! In addition to her offering me her considerable astrological insights, she used her formidable editorial skills to make the story shine even brighter. Lynne Curry of LSC Editing added a deft editorial touch and editing know-how. She ensured the contents of this book meet the critical standards of today's readers.

This story is built around Pachacuti, perhaps the greatest of all Saba Incas. During his long reign, he provided his people with enlightened leadership. He did not exhibit a proclivity for sacrifices as was the norm with many other previous Inca leaders.

I often found myself sitting back and admiring the Incas' numerous mind-boggling construction feats that continue to astound people of all walks of life. They achieved much. They did so without the benefits of a written language, no road-building equipment, and no wheel or beast of burden. Their astrological and agrarian prowess was unequaled. Their knowledge and development in the field of head trauma injuries, better known as trepanning, was also a staggering, much-needed skill for the Inca were a war-like people who were not bashful when it came to expanding their territory. I sincerely hope that you enjoy, as much as I did, learning about the Inca for they were indeed a remarkable people.

Table of Contents

MAP OF PERU

Lima ●
Paracas
Ballestas
Islands

**Machu
Picchu** ●

DRONE TEST AREA ↘ Inca
Sacred Valley
Ollyantaytambo

Nazca
Nazca Lines

● Cuzco

Cuzco

Colca
Canyon

Lake
Titicaca

Puno

Arequipa Sillustani

Cast of Characters

ACAHUANA, son of Adan and Nusta, future leader of the Inka throughout Peru

AHAU, Mesoamerica K'iche Maya spiritual leader, husband of Elena, father of Constanza and Jumo

ALLIE LEA SHELTON KESHAW, PhD, the Smithsonian executive, vice president in charge of explorations, wife of Ryan, mother of Lynne, RK and Allison

ALLISON, daughter of Allie Lea and Ryan

ANITA, wife of señor Urgar and hostess to the Smithsonian crew

ASHLEY CLEMENS, Smithsonian Maya-Inca archaeologist, wife of Eric Clemens

ATOC, known as "the fox," also a secret leader of a splinter group of Inca

BARBARA HOOKWAY, Ken's mother and environmental lawyer

CATHERINE, Maya fortune teller and mother of the twins, Uno and Dos, and wife of Juma

DENISE WILLIAMS, Facebook drone research manager

DOUBTFUL, Ryan's imaginary worry dog

ELENA, wife of Ahau, mother of Constanza and Juma

ERIC CLEMENS, the Smithsonian's ALSM – drone specialist, husband of Ashley

FRANK JOHNSON, Smithsonian IT manager

JAMES HAMILTON, PhD and president of the Smithsonian

Jim Leachy, the Smithsonian vice president of field operations and husband of Judy

Ken Kanebti Hookway, senior at American University, son of Steve and Barbara

Lynne, daughter of Allie Lea and Ryan

Marjua, head of señor Urgar's kitchen and bakery

Pearl Estrella, Mesoamerica TV personality, WKOG anchor woman

Red O'Shaun, Smithsonian vice president, head of research and development, husband of Anna

RK, son of Allie Lea and Ryan

Ryan Keshaw, narrator, owner RK Consulting, and husband of Allie Lea

Rodrigo, señor Urgar's 'copter pilot and overseer

Roja, WKOG Director and creative vice president

Rondo, Inca police captain of the district surrounding Machu Picchu

Sandy K., executive assistant to Allie Lea

Sara, Smithsonian and Larco Museums' archaeologist, wife of Rafael

Señor Diego Fuentes, chairman, Larco Herrera Archaeological Museum of Lima

Señor Rafael, Sara's husband, president, Larco Herrera Archaeological Museum of Lima

Señor Urgar, Guatemala cattle baron, husband of Anita

Steve Hookway, Ken's father and retired ambassador

The tiara, an amorous symbol

Prologue

My interest in the Maya and Mesoamerica came about through a series of extraordinary circumstances—some real, some figments of my imagination, all of which prompted my four previous Maya-Inca adventure books. The first was the *Temple of the Two Jaguars*. I carefully researched the Maya and Inca cultures and became aware of how these two tribes evolved into such an astounding force in astronomy and how that affected their daily lives.

This was before the Spaniards arrived with their deviousness, diseases, and greed, leading to death. My research helped me to inject as-near-to-life situations as possible in each of my novels, which are set in contemporary surroundings.

The Popol Vuh is the Maya sacred book and the focus of my second and third books in the Maya adventure series. Both books were used as the foundation for my fourth book, *The Pink Bra Archaeologist*. The excitement builds along with a tender love story, riveting action, and unexpected dangers.

I had completed my research of *The Pink Bra Archaeologist* and was into the writing of my fifth book when a strange series of events spun me around. My book took a wholly unexpected turn, and I found myself involved in a scenario that centered on the Inca. They, too, were a remarkable, brilliant race, though they exhibited traits of brutality and sacrifice. These characteristics were part of their

DNA upon which their survival depended. Much of the Inca's knowledge and habits were viewed by the Spaniards as being barbaric and pagan.

A little-known fact emerged during my research: the Inca, much the same as the Maya, were traders and used the waterways as a conduit for trade.

As the scope of my research broadened, I became aware that the Inca, like the Maya, relied upon the knowledge and understanding of the cycles of the cosmos. Their survival depended on this information, for they were primarily an agrarian society.

The Inca were great communicators despite not having a written language. However, they were also great builders: witness the 10,000 miles of roads and bridges built over streams and difficult terrain, all without the benefit of metal road-building equipment or beasts of burden. And, they accomplished all this without the use of or concept of the wheel.

These roadways and the *quipu* (a series of knots on a string) allowed the Inca to communicate with other parts of their empire. Specially trained runners provided the method to move the *quipu* from one post to another, all in record time.

My goal is to create a panoramic view of the Inca, their customs, and habits, and weave them into a contemporary setting that is anything but dull. Many adventurous and often deadly twists are included, in addition to an unexpected budding romance.

The characters like to indulge in the cuisine and *chichia* (beer) of Peru and Guatemala. Should you be an adventurous chef or connoisseur of fine foods and beverages, try the dishes. They are authentic.

On to the story. Be prepared for an adventurous dipping of the archaeological toe into the roles my characters will play in lives yet to come. Fifteen years have whizzed by since our fateful venture to Nuevo Ciudad (new town) in Chichicastenango, Guatemala. The harrowing moments and the wonderful times have embedded themselves deep within my memory.

Our family is doing well. It's difficult to realize that Lynne, our oldest daughter, and RK, our son, are safely ensconced at American University. Why they picked that snobby school is beyond me. I guess they have thoughts of entering the diplomatic service.

RK is five foot nine and dreams of becoming a pro baseball player. I don't have high hopes for that dream, although I would never tell him his chances are slim. Until he learns to hit the curve on a regular basis and exceed his current .255 batting average, making the dean's list will best serve his ambition in finding a job that pays.

Regardless, they are doing their utmost to deplete what we thought would be our future financial nest egg. Allison, our youngest, is a member of the freshman class at Langley. She takes after her mother except that she is five foot four and Allie Lea is five foot one, but she insists that she is five foot two. Both are blonde beauties.

Allie Lea's well deserved promotion to vice president in charge of the Smithsonian's field operations has absorbed her. She loves the challenges of her new position, well, most of the time, despite my nibbling into her business.

I remain Ryan Keshaw, the lovable, grouchy consultant who knows that it is in my best interests to keep the money wheel turning. My weight remains the same, 174 pounds, as when I was in the Marines; my six-foot frame hasn't shrunk and I have a full head of brown hair.

When it comes to taking chances, I'm a bit more conservative than during those golden explorative years. I often long and hunger for the excitement, the past adventures, and the friends we made in Mexico and Latin America.

Little did I know or expect that hunger was about to be satiated—all because of a little phone call and an unexpected invitation which would involve what I call "the clan."

Our close friends, Rafael and Sara, were flying in from Lima, Peru, where he is president of the world famous Larco Museum and she is an experienced Inca-Maya archaeologist. Their presence was significant. They opened my mind to a most astounding Inca who was known as Pachacuti and perhaps better known in history by all Inca as **THE SABA INCA** or the number one Inca emperor. Many of his accomplishments included the expansion of the Inca empire by some three thousand miles as well as designing and overseeing the building of Machu Picchu, one of the seven wonders of the world.

Chapter 1

*   *   *

Passing the Torch Is Often Difficult, But for Whom?

ork has been somewhat slow these past months, and my family tells me I'm getting under everyone's skin. Today, upon returning from the gym, I was shocked to see a gathering of the clan. This, I knew, spelled trouble—for yours truly. Allie Lea had sprung for a catering service and it looked as if we had enough food to last a week. I asked, "What in the hell is going on? Are you pregnant, or, heaven forbid, are you thinking of changing jobs?" The room went quiet as all eyes zeroed in on Allie Lea.

Allison, our youngest, broke the awkward silence and retorted, "Good old Dad, you can always be counted on to liven up a party!"

Allie Lea put her arms around me, gave me a kiss and whispered, "Have you forgotten today is a special Maya anniversary? To celebrate the special occasion, I've invited the old gang to share and relive those happy moments. I think the caterer did an imaginative, decorating job and our great room sparkles. It's amazing how flowers can brighten up a room and, given the opportunity, bring even a little cheer to a certain grouch I know!"

I said, "The flowers really dress up the place and the food looks expensive. Wasn't it only last month that you were harping about our household expenses and the new car I was considering? I'd love to have a Tesla, but that's a little

1

out of my reach. Maybe a Porsche would be more in keeping with my status in life."

Allie Lea looked horrified. "Ryan Keshaw, you are full of it."

That quieted the room and then RK asked, "Dad, do you know what a Porsche costs? Mom, I bet I know what's Dad's problem. He's experiencing a midlife crisis."

Allison popped up and in all innocence asked, "Dad, what's a midlife crisis?"

I was saved from having to reply to her embarrassing question when the doorbell rang.

Lynne yelled, "I'll get it, Dad. Be nice to our guests and, at least, act like you're enjoying the party Mom put together."

"Young lady, just when were you appointed head of this family?" She gave me a smile, the number one finger sign, and made for the door.

Allie Lea said, "Don't sulk. The money you plan to spend on a car might be better spent on things like painting and redecorating the upper floor."

Then in trooped Jim Leachy, the Smithsonian's director of security, and his wife Judy, followed by Red, the Smithsonian's IT director, and his Russian wife, Anna, who remarked, "It looks like old times. No doubt, Ashley and Eric will be along shortly."

Allie Lea replied, "While we await their arrival, make yourselves comfortable. Ryan is in the kitchen mixing drinks. We'll eat shortly after the rest arrive."

In the meantime, RK pulled his mom aside and said, "From the looks of things, you are planning to hold a business meeting. We kids don't fit into that scenario, so count me out. I have the possibility of hanging out with a *hot* new acquaintance I just met a few days ago."

"Young man, go if you must; however, you'll miss out on something very interesting."

Jim Leahy turned his attention to me, started to laugh, and said, "Old friend, I see you've been reading your crystal ball. When we were having a spot of tea and crumpets last Thursday, you told me you were bored and asked if I had any ideas."

Allie Lea gave me a questioning look and coyly remarked, "Sweetheart, that's the first I've heard of you being bored. Perhaps we are in need of a pillow-to-pillow talk."

Hells bells, in hot water again. I looked around and saw my old friend, nemesis, and worry dog Doubtful sitting on the end of the couch. I hoped someone would say something and break the ice rapidly forming around me.

I walked over to Allie Lea, gave her a buss, and whispered, "Face, darling, face." Thankfully, there came a knock on the door! Three of us made for the door and then everyone started laughing. We looked pretty darn silly as Anna opened the door and Ashley asked, "Did Ryan lose or win the bet as to our being on time?"

I raised my hand. "Close, but your entrance was most timely."

Eric waved to the gang. "I'm sure thirsty."

Not to be outdone, Ashley yelled to Allie Lea, "When are you going to train Ryan how to stay out of hot water?"

Allie Lea giggled. "Ryan is a work in progress, but he is learning. Give me your coat, grab a drink, and I'll get the business part of this get-together over and done with. *Señor* Urgar and our friend Ahau are putting together a fifteenth anniversary celebration of our first trip to Nuevo Ciudad, and they have extended an invitation for us to join the celebration as his guests of honor. How about that?"

Judy jumped up and asked, "Does his invitation mean wives are invited? If so, we're all for it." She turned to Jim and demurely said, "I'm confident my wonderful husband would agree."

Allie Lea announced that when she spoke with señor Urgar, he extended his invitation to everyone who worked on the last two digs including their wives.

I also spoke with Jim Hamilton regarding use of the company jet. He was all for it, provided the Maya are on schedule to repay the Smithsonian for its part in the restoration of the temples and rerouting of the riverbed.

She continued, "The question of the wives attending falls in my bailiwick and Jim doesn't think bringing the wives will pose a problem as long as we're not expected to foot the bill for their expenses, other than air and room.

"However, there's a fly in the ointment! And that's bringing children under high school age. It is the Smithsonian's policy to exclude them for insurance and legal reasons. Other than that, we're good to go."

That ended the conversation on a high note with Jim Hamilton agreeing to our departure ten days from today, provided our travel people could make it happen. Jim Leachy will be our logistics expert and he will be responsible for handling all the other nitty gritty details.

Allie Lea then threw her arms into the air and exclaimed, "Hallelujah, it's a done deal. Let's drink a toast to a successful and safe visit, courtesy of señor Urgar and Ahau."

Ashley asked, "Does Rafael or Sara know?"

Allie Lea said, "I haven't spoken with señor Rafael or Sara as they've been traveling. Any questions?"

There was a moment of silence and then, of all people, Allison asked, "Mom, does that mean kids like me are invited and do we have to go?"

I made for the kitchen as I wanted no part of that little grenade Allison just tossed to her mom. Speaking of silence, it was as if all the air had been sucked out of the room. No one said a word as Allison suddenly realized she put her mom in a very delicate position.

She said, "Oops, sorry, that question would have been better asked over the dinner table. This kid is going to her room and listen to some music. Perhaps the funeral march would be appropriate."

With that retort, everyone broke into applause. Allie Lea hugged Allison!

Allie Lea remarked, "I knew that question would be at the top of the list. I just didn't expect it would come from Allison. I'll be conducting a question-and-answer session on Tuesday in our conference room. Provided there are no more questions, our feast awaits."

A feast it was: shrimp remoulade, New Orleans crawfish, salmon, fresh trout à la Normande, baked potatoes, a host of salads, corn on the cob, and a special Caesar dipping sauce that was simply delightful. Surprise! Surprise! Allie Lea ordered only one dessert. It was a huge chocolate bombe decorated with pink icing that said, "Adventurers, Friends, Always." What a dessert it turned out to be!

The question of Rafael and Sara's whereabouts came up for discussion. Allie Lea said, "As far as I know, they've been trekking somewhere near Machu Picchu. Rafael is working with a company that's experimenting with a new type of drone. I think they hope to join us later today, provided they make some tight flight connections."

Eric announced, "I, too, am working with a company that is drone-oriented. I'm convinced the use of drones is in the Smithsonian's future. They lower the cost of explorations and help avoid the wild goose chases that have dotted our past. Not to mention the instant information that formerly took days or weeks to compile. I plan to spend time with Rafael and get his take on what he has learned using these new model drones."

I pulled Eric to one side and said, "Before making yourself available for such an assignment, you might consider clearing it with the queen bee. Or, were you personally planning on springing for the expenses?"

"Are you crazy? As much as I would like to participate, I was merely musing. If a trip is in the offing and the Smithsonian is paying, I'd go in a New York heartbeat."

I said, "Eric, there is no doubt as to your knowledge and abilities. But for now, there is nothing of that sort on the horizon or the drawing board, let alone the talking stage."

Looking over my shoulder, I saw Doubtful jump onto the couch. His timing is anything but good. Without warning, a cold chill suddenly ran down my body. The next thing I knew Allie Lea was staring at me from across the room.

Before I could move out of her line of vision, she walked over, sat down beside me, and asked, "Are you not feeling well? You're as pale as a ghost."

Not wishing to worry her, I gave her a quick kiss and said, "Eric and I were remembering and reliving our first venture into the lagoon at the Maya sacrificial cavern. We didn't know who was scared the most. Despite his being a weak swimmer, he didn't hesitate to jump in and grab me when I surfaced. My fear was that I stood a good chance of being impaled on one of the earlier sacrifices or colliding with one of the stones that jutted out of the sidewalls of the sacrificial cavern."

She replied, "You have me worried. Are you sure you're okay?

There was a huge commotion on our front porch followed by a loud thump and then an incessant pounding on the front door. I jumped off the couch and asked, "Who is the rude sonofabitch making all that noise?"

I jerked open the door and there was Sara, who said, "Rafael, what did I tell you? It's the old grouch himself." Despite that, she gave me a big kiss and remarked, "Sorry we're late. As you can see, we didn't stop to change our clothes, and, even so, we almost missed the plane. Hello everybody, and for those of you who are interested, I'm not pregnant—yet!"

Red snickered. "Why not?"

Sara gave him an impish smile. "I can assure you it's not for lack of trying!"

That brought knowing looks from the adults, and Ashley said, "Hang in there, Sara; it took us two years." I stared at the large black limo and saw Rafael who gave me a brief wave and asked, "How about a hand with Sara's baggage? She brought enough for two people."

Rafael wiped the sweat off his brow. "*Saludos amigo*, I hope you have something good and cold just waiting for a thirsty soul like me."

The limo driver spoke up. "Amigo, leave luggage. I carry for señor."

Rafael smiled. "You will no doubt give him a special tip as I am without any dollars. I have only Peruvian *soles*."

The limo driver reached into the front seat, pulled out his iPad, and said, "I take credit card, small fee, señor."

I said, "No problem." I gave him his fee along with a twenty for a tip. He bowed, saying, *"Muchas gracias* amigos," and quickly backed out of our driveway.

Sara came to the door and asked, "What's taking you guys so long? I took care of his fee when I booked the limo."

Rafael and I looked at each other. I remarked, "That countryman of yours just beat me out of sixty bucks!"

Rafael smiled. "Amigo, you win some and you lose some." With that, we joined the happy throng and my stupidity was put on hold, at least for the time being.

Allie Lea was all smiles when she pulled me aside. "Forget the sixty bucks. You have a problem looming on the horizon which no doubt will rock you. You are about to inherit a business associate! The lack of which you have constantly complained. Just think, someone to do your grunt work. Isn't that wonderful?"

The air just got sucked out of the room. Angry, I replied, "What are you talking about?"

Ignoring me, she turned and walked over to join the crowd surrounding Sara and Rafael. Doubtful, ever faithful, was on the couch looking anything but happy.

Lynne bounced over and said, "Dad, a family conference is needed after our guests have departed. Now, give me a kiss, smile, and act pleasant, even if it kills you. *Ciao!*"

After the last gun was fired, I made my way to our backyard. I needed relief that would blunt the anger and anxiety that had been building. I plopped down on one of the kid's swings, and despite my size, I squeezed into one of the seats and began to swing. After a while I, felt my cares slip away and then a soft voice asked, "May I join you?"

Lynne in a very contrite manner said, "Mom thought I should talk with you before you blow a gasket. Dad, I'm in my last year of college, and I'm not aware that you have given much thought to my future. I'm working on an advanced degree in economics and business management. After I graduate, I hope to land a job in government or the corporate world. I realize my experience in business is limited. I counted on you to welcome me with open arms and teach me how to survive in the corporate world."

"Honey, I welcome you into RK Consulting. However, it would have been nice had you and mom made me a part of your discussion and decision, especially since it was my firm."

Lynne took my hand. "Mom thought it would be a good time for us to talk.

She knew you wouldn't go apeshit in front of all your friends. It's a lovely night, and after everyone is gone, we can have a nice little talk without you getting your nose out of joint."

Allie Lea joined us. "I see the tiger has met his match. I wonder who taught our mild-mannered sweetheart such an important skill? And at such an early age."

I said, "When the two of you finish carving me up, let me know what you plan to do with what's left of the carcass. Then, like the good soldier I am, just hand me my marching orders. Lynne, I gather you'll expect your name on the masthead along with an email advising my clients I have now surrendered a portion of my turf to a good-looking young lady, who, no doubt, has thoughts of taking my place in the not-too-distant future."

To quote from a rather infamous personage, the words, *Screwed Again* come to mind.

Monday zoomed up and everyone in the family was off and running. Allie Lea to the Smithsonian, the kids doing their thing, and me getting my business in order. I'm sure my clients will be thrilled to learn I will be traveling for the next few weeks. Thank goodness I am in the middle of my slow season! Who am I kidding? It's always a slow season when I'm not out beating on doors or working the phones.

Now that the house was peaceful, I had time to focus on what I hoped to be our upcoming trip to Guatemala. For some strange reason that long forgotten Inca riddle— *Puric Sinchi Huaca Chullpa Yacara Tocco*—swam up to the surface of my subconscious. Without thinking, I looked around and sure enough, Doubtful had parked himself on my easy chair. I asked to no one in particular, why are you here? After all, we're going for a good time and to renew old friendships; we're doing no exploring and not placing anyone in harm's way. As I closed my computer, I realized a snack would solve most of my immediate problems. I found some salami in the fridge, hacked up a tomato, cut a slice or two of French bread, added a touch of buttermilk dressing, and grabbed a cold mango drink before I headed for my office and plopped myself in my newly acquired Ethan Allen recliner.

It didn't take long before I found myself immersed with a most interesting client, which, sadly to say, I had to decline for he wanted an immediate on-site evaluation. I gave him the name of a friend in the business, for which he thanked me. I sat there brooding over the loss of a new client and then our house phone began an incessant ringing.

After looking at the clock, I wondered who was calling at three in the afternoon. I stopped the ringing when I stuffed the phone under one of the pillows on my couch. The ringing ceased, but five minutes later it started again. This time it was my cell. I knew it had to be Allie Lea, so in my best smarmy voice I asked, "What is it that your highness desires?"

Allie Lea said, "Cut it out, darling. I wouldn't have called unless it was important. What were you doing taking a nap? I happen to know you didn't get up until after 10 a.m."

"And, just how would you know that?"

"RK gave me a heads-up before leaving to meet his friends."

"If you must know, I've been entertaining a prospective client which I had to turn down due to our attending the fifteen-year celebration. Other than that, what's up?"

She said, "I wish to remind you that you are expected to show for tomorrow's briefing. Also, I need your help in assigning seating arrangements for our jet. Our pilot says the maximum number of passengers allowed is twenty. Their personal luggage cannot, under any circumstances, exceed one piece of regular luggage and one carry-on. He made it very plain when he said, 'Your flight will not take off unless these conditions are met!' So there you have it."

I laughed. "Really? I'll wager a buck or two the baggage limit will be tested if you don't nip it in the bud. There will be several bags sitting on the tarmac when the jet takes off."

"Ryan, should anyone need reminding, the Smithsonian is making an exception in allowing wives on the flight and small children are absolutely taboo. Are you in for an unsolicited surprise? Our lovable president has added you to the payroll for the next ninety days. He believes it best that I have a minder, and should the occasion arise, do whatever heavy lifting comes my way. In short, you are to handle unexpected problems. Don't get it in your head this unexpected windfall opens the door to a new car. How about that?"

I was quiet for so long Allie Lea asked, "Has the cat got your tongue?"

I thought I had gotten rid of Doubtful, and now this. "Allie Lea, I have been giving this trip a great deal of thought and right now I'm not so sure it's a good idea. Our experiences in Guatemala and Peru have been anything but peaceful. This cat is fearful that he has used up most, if not all, of his proverbial nine lives."

"Ryan Keshaw, you're not a cat. This trip should be anything but fearful, provided you get rid of your grouchiness. I knowingly wouldn't approve any venture that was too dangerous for me or any of our associates, let alone my husband. This trip should be a no brainer: no digs, no excavations, no unruliness.

"If you need more convincing, give Catherine, your favorite Maya fortune teller, a call and get her take. If she doesn't convince you, call Ahau. Now, get your ass in gear and get ready for tomorrow's meeting." With that she purred "meow," and hung up.

I put my feet on my desk, contemplated the lint in my navel, and began to meditate. My thoughts dwelled on wondering how many guys realize that today's women are becoming more powerful and that one day they will take over. If we men are to coexist, we will have to come up with something other than being known as the main meat gatherers. Perhaps big pharma will discover a pill that rewires us and makes us more amenable to change.

I wonder if the story of *Lysistrata* by Aristophanes, the fifth century BC Greek comic playwright, is still a required college reading course. I came out of my trance said, "horse feathers," and went down to fix dinner. I grilled hot dogs, opened up a couple cans of baked beans, chopped some slaw, made a pitcher of iced tea, set the table, and waited for the onslaught. While whisking the sugar-free chocolate jello, I had a sudden thought that came right out of the blue and it jolted me. Then the kids hit the porch and everything including my thoughts went to hell in a hand basket.

Despite that, I managed to tuck away this thought-provoking idea for future reference. I didn't plan to share it with anyone until I had worked out all of the pieces of the puzzle. This trip will no doubt help me learn the true meaning of Acahuana's riddle. It's been driving me bonkers. I needed to accomplish some high-powered research and that, I knew, would take time. I made myself a mental note to again talk with Eric after tomorrow's meeting. In my estimation, he possibly held the key to something very promising. Also, I planned to have a heart-to-heart with Ahau, I knew he could be like the Sphinx when asked.

Allie Lea and the kids made their entrance and saw that I was barbecuing and whistling. She playfully grabbed an imaginary phone and announced, "I'm calling your doctor and informing him you're sick and you have been in a shitty mood for the past few days, but now you're whistling. What I want to know is: Who died and left you a million dollars?"

"I just read *Lysistrata.*"

Lynne started to giggle, RK's mouth dropped open, and Allison asked, "Mom, what's Dad talking about?"

Allie Lea was blushing like a bright red rose when she said, "Your father, as usual, is *jackpotting.* Get washed; he has dinner ready." As she passed me, she said, "You and I are going to have a talk tonight and it's not going to be about *Lysistrata. Comprendes*, amigo?"

Allie Lea often conducts late night pillow-talk sessions, particularly when something bothers her in a big way. Was it possible she, too, was having recurring dreams about what happened on our last exploration? One thing I knew for sure: her thoughts were not about her tiara.

It was to the bedroom and the new book Allie Lea had given me. I read about forty pages and asked myself "do I really want to read, let alone carry, a 1,079-page book?" The damn thing was so heavy I was constantly having to shift it from side to side. However, the deeper I got into it, the more interesting it became. William Manchester, a famous writer, was the author, and his book was titled *The Last Lion.* Thus far, it is riveting, and for sure the authors take no prisoners.

Churchill was indeed the last lion. The author died before the book was completed and finished by Paul Reid whose masterful presentation proved that there are too few leaders who dare to stand up for their beliefs. As far as I could tell, it was a seamless transition. What a book! I drifted off at about seventy pages and shortly afterwards felt Allie Lea slide in beside me. And that was that. No discussion, no problems, just a night of blissful sleep.

Lynne figured she got the best of it last night and decided to fix breakfast to make amends. She had whipped up a batch of pancakes, heated some Surrey sausage, sliced a luscious honeydew melon, and warmed a dozen or so pecan sweet rolls. When it was all ready, she yelled, "Breakfast and the cook are available for the next fifteen minutes, so come as you are or be prepared to fix your own!"

It wasn't long before everyone came rushing down the stairs and then the chattering started. RK took one look at me and said, "Another dull day, Dad, huh?"

Allie Lea smugly remarked, "Not if I can help it. RK, your father had to make an executive decision. It was either shave or eat a prepared meal, and since pancakes with maple syrup is one of his favorites, he knew he could put off shaving. He does have a heavy day now that he is on the Smithsonian payroll. Doing what, I don't know, but I'm sure he'll find something."

RK raised his arm in a mock salute and said, "Way to go, Dad! I guess you and I will be making a trip to look at those Porsches you were telling me about. That hot girl I met last night would think I am one cool dude if I drive up in a red Porsche."

Allie Lea nearly choked when Lynne said, "Here's a news flash. Some of the guys at college think I'm pretty hot and with a Porsche, wow!"

Allison asked her sister, "How come you have never told me about your adventures? After all, I'm starting high school in the fall."

That did it. Allie Lea quickly put a stop to those wild thoughts and said, "Let's get one thing straight: there will be no Porsche in this family, now or the foreseeable future. Two of you in college and Allison awaiting her turn! Your dad and I must keep the money crank turning while all this happens, and God forbid if we experienced a medical or financial emergency. Should all go as planned each of you might just make it through college without any major student loans. So, get real guys. You, too, Ryan!"

She whipped around and in one furious motion snatched her handbag as she made for the door. Just before climbing into her car, she blew me a kiss and off she went. As she pulled out of the driveway, I uttered, "Please have mercy on those with whom she comes into contact before she has her morning coffee."

Allison put her arm around me. "I guess no new car for you means I won't be inheriting your ancient Volvo. How am I to get to school? And to think my friends were counting on me. I learned a valuable lesson today."

I laughed and asked, "To what lesson are you referring?"

Lynne paused on the porch. "This I have to hear."

Allison remarked, "It doesn't pay to talk about things that may or might happen. Above all, make sure your parents are dealing with you in facts and not pie-in-the-sky fiction. I wonder how I'll break the news to my friends. Unless a miracle happens, and since miracles in this house are in short supply, I'll be riding the bus."

Chapter 2

* * *

Control, Much Like Power, Often Proves to Be Elusive

I went into my office, checked the time zone, and called Ahau. Wouldn't you know it? He was in Chichi running errands for Elena. As the gals are wont to say, we chatted. She related all that was going on in town and on señor Urgar's fabulous *estancia* and was looking forward to our getting together. I asked her to have Ahau call when he returned from his chores.

Before getting off the phone, she commented, "Señor Ryan, we have talked about everything but what's really on your mind. I am sure Ahau will be glad to talk with you about whatever you didn't wish to tell me."

She giggled and hung up.

I wondered, am I really that transparent? On second thought, yeah, I believe I am. My thoughts were rudely interrupted with the ringing of my cell. I knew it was Allie Lea, and the first thing out of the box she asked, "How are you doing on the lists I asked you to assemble for tomorrow's meeting?"

"I'm working on it."

"In other words, you haven't given it one iota of thought! Get busy and get it done!"

"No problem. I just set the ground rules for young people the same as they do at many swim parks. No age requirement, just a height requirement, kids under five feet don't make the cut. Period, end of story, problem solved."

Allie Lea asked, "And how did you arrive at such a brilliant piece of reasoning? You didn't by chance take into consideration our Allison is just five feet, did you?

Or did you consult your crystal ball earlier this morning?"

"No, I didn't use my crystal ball. I just pulled the number outta my derrière."

The silence was deafening. Finally, she replied, "I have a hard time believing you are as crass as you are now. Have it your way Simon Legree.

"Are you up for eating out tonight? If so, round up the kids and meet me at Clyde's. The food's good, the drinks neat, and the prices somewhat reasonable. The only drawback is the noise; if it was any louder, they would have to pass out earplugs. See you at six."

I alerted the kids and, much to my surprise, they were all for it, except Lynne who politely informed me she had "plans." I laughed. "Bring him along. After all, it's a free meal and we may get a sneak preview of what our future son-in-law is all about."

"Dad, have you ever wondered how it is you so often manage to get under my skin? I have better sense than to bring my 'date' and expose him to our 'nutzy' antics. Not only would he realize we are a dysfunctional family, but he would never ask me to go out with him again."

I wondered, where were we remiss in bringing up Lynne? Allie Lea would be hurt if she was privy to Lynne's response. I decided to brave it out and said, "Young lady, don't you think dysfunctional is a bit of an overstatement?

"If you had a similar conversation with your mother, I doubt that she would be overjoyed. Bring your date along; he might be interested in observing a happy family in action. On second thought, take him to a different restaurant. I'll pick up the tab and you can spend the evening without our dysfunctional company. I'll explain it to your mother. By the way, what is your young man majoring in at those hallowed halls of American University?"

She haughtily replied, "Diplomacy, with an accent on entering the diplomatic corp when he graduates."

"It figures; I should have known." I made haste for the fridge, grabbed a cold Dos Equis, drew up a sign that said, "Knock before five-thirty and you can plan on cleaning the garage Saturday." Signed, "Your dysfunctional father." I then headed for my office.

I was so pissed off, angry, and hurt, I almost choked on my beer. The phone rang, and I decided not to answer it so I took it off the hook and said, "Screw whoever you are!"

I settled in what I call my money chair and went to work returning the eight messages awaiting my golden touch. A while later, I heard a scratching on my office door and then Lynne, in a small voice, timidly asked if the tiger was gone and informing me that it was now five-thirty.

I threw open the door and replied, "The tiger is gone; let's go eat." I tore up the sign and nothing more was made of it. We ambled slowly down Wisconsin Avenue toward Clyde's and I became aware of an unexpected event. Allie Lea and Lynne's date, Ken, had arrived early and were seated by the window looking out on Georgetown's main drag. RK, Allison, Lynne, and I slipped into the small seats without making a ripple in the ongoing conversation.

Allie Lea broke the tension when she said, "Ryan, darling, I understand you have displayed a hidden talent. I was unaware you have such a creative bent."

I knew better than to respond to such a loaded remark, so I replied, "Over time we discover skills we never knew we had. Lynne, I don't think I've met this fine-looking young man. How about an introduction?"

She looked at her mom and smiled. "Daddy, you and mom are in for a pleasant surprise."

Before Lynne or Allie Lea could go any further, for some stupid reason, I blurted out, "Are you planning on getting married?"

Lynne, in a shriek of embarrassment, broke down in tears. Her date laughingly said, "Mr. Keshaw, this is my first date with your daughter and hopefully not the last. Perhaps, at some future time, we might reach the stage you so eloquently announced."

He handed Lynne some Kleenex, dried her tears, and put his arm around her. "I guess what you told me about your family is right on target. Unlike my home, I'll bet your family life is anything but dull. I think your father and I will, at some point, become great friends as he appears to be a hip-shooting thinker."

"Mr. Keshaw, my full name is Kenneth Kanebti Hookway. My special friends and parents call me Ken. Can we order? I didn't eat lunch as I was saving my appetite for tonight."

It wasn't long before our drinks and food arrived; we settled down to devour our meal. Everyone was all ears when Ken told of his childhood and eclectic upbringing as an only child.

"My father served in the diplomatic corps and a couple of his key assignments, among others, included a stint as the US ambassador to Peru and Egypt. Now that he is retired, he's doing pretty much of nothing, other than driving the family crazy. He is prone to sticking his nose into everyone else's business."

As I sat nursing my drink, I thought that I've heard that theme expressed before tonight.

Ken continued, "Dad and Mom developed a common interest and passion for archaeology during the time he was assigned to Egypt and Peru. They managed to work on one dig a year all at their own expense.

"Because of Dad's former diplomatic service, he helped me receive a scholarship, after I passed A.U.'s diplomatic entrance tests. Without that scholarship and my parents' help, my student loan would have required a serious adjustment in my lifestyle. My father's name is Steve, although many of his friends and colleagues still call him Ambassador. Despite that, he does not stand on ceremony. My mother makes sure of that."

RK had been sitting quietly throughout the meal until he asked, "Hey Ken, what's with your middle name? It seems to be a bit unusual."

Lynne blushed. "Ken, it's time for us to get the hell out of here before my family further embarrasses you with their lack of sensitivity."

Everyone looked at Ken, who was laughing and obviously enjoying himself, when he said, "RK, the fact that I am six foot three limits the number of questions I get about my name. I find it interesting that you raised the question. When Mom was about to deliver me, we were living in Cairo, and my father was the US ambassador to Egypt.

"I was born with this mop of brown curly hair, which in ancient Egyptian translates as Kanebti. My first name, Ken means astronomer. Even today, Mom still thinks of me as her curly-headed astronomer.

"Astronomy has not been my passion despite my mother's wishes. Until I got my growth, I had to defend my name on several occasions as many of my school mates took me for an easy-going softie, which they quickly found to be anything but true. But, I sense that Lynne is ready to catapult out of here. Maybe we should leave. Goodnight all."

When it came time to split, everyone went separate ways, particularly so after the check arrived. Allie Lea asked, "How bad was the damage?"

I laughed. "Does your question mean that you are paying this $268.00 check?"

She replied, "That's a small price to pay for helping rectify your stupid question. All in all, things turned out pretty well and everyone had a good time. Don't try to wiggle out of giving a 20 percent tip.

"I know you like to squeeze 'your' money as long as possible and no moaning and groaning. Todays little get-together may work out to be something very useful."

I remarked, "Now that, to my way of thinking, puts a different spin on things. It is my understanding that this little get-together now qualifies as a legitimate, business expense."

"Pay the check, Scrooge!"

I know when I'm staring defeat in the face, so I changed the subject and said, "My day hasn't been entirely wasted."

Allie Lea ignored my reply and asked, "Do you think Ken's parents will approve of his joining our group? It would be great if he decides to come along. His coming would relieve a worry that's been bothering me ever since señor Urgar extended his invitation."

"Now what is so earth shaking about him coming?"

"Well, darling, for one thing, he could watch over Lynne!"

"He what?"

She said, "You well know Lynne tends to be, at times, somewhat impetuous, and Ken is exactly the opposite."

"Allie Lea, if either of them knew your reasoning, they would show you a side of their personality you wouldn't appreciate and tell you to stuff it. Trip or no trip! Today's young people expect and enjoy more freedom than you were raised with. Micromanaging may work well in the office world, but not in today's young peoples' world."

"Ryan Keshaw, I don't appreciate being lectured even when I am wrong. Just tell me if you think Ken would be receptive to an offer to join us on this excavation."

"Only if Lynne makes the offer," I said. Then, for some strange reason, I had the feeling that, like it or not, we were once more heading down the rabbit hole. I knew that thought wouldn't engender a vote of confidence from Allie Lea, especially when she was in such a mood.

I went to work on the flight seating list, and from the looks of things I felt we'll be okay as to the number of people. Regarding the luggage, that is a whole other thing. Later that night, I was awakened by a stream of light from Allie Lea's bedside lamp. I raised up in bed and asked, "Anything wrong?"

"Honey, I'm glad you're awake. If there is a little extra space, do you think I could get away with an extra bag or two?" With that said, she turned out the light, mumbled goodnight, and went back to sleep.

I was so out of it, I groggily replied, "Uh huh," And that was that. I had just gotten back to sleep when that damn alarm clock began its shrill sound.

After a quiet breakfast, we made for my Volvo. When we were passing the Lincoln Memorial, I asked, "Didn't you awaken me for some reason that I seem to have forgotten?"

Allie Lea asked, "You mean you don't remember me asking if I could take an extra bag or two?"

"I thought what you said wasn't that important, otherwise you would have held forth with one of your 3 a.m. conferences. So what's the big deal, sweetheart?"

"Ryan Keshaw, there are times I could choke you and this is one of them."

As we pulled into the VIP underground parking, the Smithsonian security guard opened the electronic gate and saluted, and we then made our way to the executive elevator. In a defiant manner, she informed me she had no intention of continuing our previous conversation.

By the time we reached her office, she'd cooled down, pinched my rear end, and said, "You're right; it wasn't that important. How is it that you know what button to push when you want to quiet me down?"

I gave her a lingering kiss and remarked, "Your crew awaits your presence. Don't forget to fix your lipstick; that kiss you gave me is somewhat telltale."

An air of anticipation swirled throughout the conference room as everyone eagerly awaited her remarks. Surprisingly, the questions were few and to the point.

Jim Leachy got it started when he said, "Allowing us to bring our wives is greatly appreciated. I'm sure I speak for most men when I say we are thankful there are no national shopping chains and our 'plastic' will have limited use!"

His remarks brought a round of applause, a few boos, and three hurrahs, which Allie Lea gleefully acknowledged. She exclaimed, "Ryan has worked out the logistics regarding the seating and baggage requirements, for which there will be no exceptions!

"Our president, Jim Hamilton, will not be making this trip as he is scheduled to be the keynote speaker at a special museum conference in Istanbul. I will officially represent the Smithsonian, and I've been informed that Ahau will present us with a check that will pay off the Maya's final debt to the Smithsonian.

"He is most proud that the project is being paid off some two years early. Knowing that, I was able to prevail upon Jim Hamilton and wrangle three extra days' stay.

"Plan on returning home on the Tuesday following the ceremony."

She turned the meeting over to me, and I announced the baggage limitations and seat assignments. It didn't take me long to learn I was the most unpopular person at the Smithsonian that day.

I snagged Eric as he exited the men's room, and we moved to a quiet alcove where we could talk without interruption.

"From the looks of things, we possibly have a special project brewing. Bring whatever information you have on drones and extra batteries for your electronics. Plan on staying an extra week. I'll explain after we get settled in at Urgar's *hacienda*. If possible, hold off discussing this with Ashley, or with anyone else for that matter, until we are further down the road."

"Ryan, you took your sweet time in getting around to talking with me."

I looked perplexed when he said, "You made a mistake when you spoke with my secretary."

I was somewhat angry at his choice of words and asked, "Eric where is this going? You're making me mighty uncomfortable. I don't remember talking with or even knowing your secretary."

Eric blushed. "My apologies, Ryan, but when you spoke to my secretary, you asked for any information I had regarding drones. Later in the week, I saw the four or five booklets on drones lying on her desk, plus a pamphlet outlining the URLS for information regarding drones.

"I asked who ordered these. She curtly replied, 'Dr. Shelton.' I didn't think she was into drones and that they had to be for you. Since I work in her section and she, being an officer, I couldn't ignore or question her request unless I wanted to seek employment elsewhere.'

"Uh-oh, Ryan, here comes my sweetness. If she finds out what we are talking about, we may find ourselves explaining what drones have to do with this trip."

Eric turned, took Ashley's hand, and asked, "Why is it you always appear when Ryan and I are in the middle of a juicy conversation?"

She laughed. "With Ryan, a juicy conversation, that's a joke!"

"Let's eat. We have the trip information and our babysitter asked to leave a bit early. Times as such, are rare!"

Eric broke into a trot and yelled, "I'm on the way! Meet me at the main entrance."

Ashley blushed and gave an all-knowing smile, saying, "It's nice to have a man who responds to my slightest verbal suggestions, especially when it comes to the thought of sex."

Allie Lea joined our group and whispered to Ashley, "Enjoy the rest of your day."

When Allie Lea made that remark, I too colored up and made my way to meet up with Jim and Red to join in whatever it was they were talking about. On the ride home, I asked Allie Lea which one of us is going to prompt Lynne to get her diplomatic friend to join our expedition.

She replied, "Why, me, of course!"

"Keep that seat reserved beside her. I noticed you passed out your sheet of instructions and, like Ashley, I find it delightful to have a significant other who responds to my slightest verbal suggestions. Does this mean we, too, are taking off the rest of the day to seek bliss and happiness?

"If so, I'll get the car, I knew there had to be a reason why I shined up my crystal ball. Unlike Viagra, it has no waiting time, mail or otherwise."

"Ryan, you're pushing your luck!"

Blissful days, as such, are rare. I knew when the kids get home bliss would be shoved into the corner and chaos would be the order of the day. Both RK and Lynne were delighted with the opportunity to make the trip.

Allison surprised us when she announced, "My friends and I have made applications to attend a wonderful camp in Rising Sun, Maryland. We've checked it out, and despite being an all girls' camp, everyone we talked with loved it. So that's what I wish to do."

Allie Lea said, "Young lady, did it ever occur to you and your friends that they and you would need their parents' approval?"

Allison replied, "Mom, my friends have their parents' approval. I knew you wouldn't stand in the way of your daughter having a great learning experience. Not to mention a lot of fun in a safe, well-run, boy-free, camp!"

When Allison made that plea, I exited the great room before bursting out laughing.

Allie Lea yelled, "Ryan, come back here. I have a question or two to ask you. Now, young lady, I wish to know if you discussed this plan of attack with your father, and did he give you an idea or two to help 'sweeten' the pot so good old Mom would say yes?"

Allison replied, "Mom, I thought you knew you taught me better than that."

Allie Lea threw her hands in the air and said, I plea 'mea culpa' to all charges. It appears our young *consigliere* has organized her presentation in a most compelling fashion."

RK and Lynne had taken a seat on the couch in the great room, as if to await the verdict. Meanwhile, Allie Lea paced around the room, not saying a word and finally she said, "Well done, my darling."

Then she walked up the stairs, smiling all the way as she wiped a stray tear or two. RK turned, looked at Lynne and said, "Maybe we can take a lesson or two from our not-so-little sister."

Allison's smile said it all, and off we went, proud of our daughter and her first foray in the real world. I dreaded going into our bedroom and facing Allie Lea. However, all was well. She was taking several items out of her closet when she said, "Our little one is growing up, and I am proud of her standing up to me. I notice you didn't weigh in with one of your famous non-statements."

"I know better than to get between mother and daughter dust-ups. I take it I can scratch Allison from our flight list."

Allie Lea threw a pillow at me. "Must you always be such a pain?"

With that, Lynne stuck her head into our bedroom and said, "Heads-up time. Ken's parents are delighted we asked him to visit Chichi."

"Lynne, I was amazed how quickly he agreed to join our little group. Weren't you as well?"

Without batting an eye, Lynne asked, "Why do you think I invited him to join us at Clyde's? I thought it was time to use one of your old tricks. I knew if you liked what you saw, then an offer would be forthcoming, especially since his parents are into archaeology. How 'm I doing, Dad?"

I went over to Allie Lea, put my arm around her, stroked her hair and said, "Well, darling, at least we have each other if that's any consolation. Let's go to bed and let the kids take over, which they are obviously in the process of doing. Tomorrow is another day, and come to think of it, maybe we should be proud of what we have accomplished."

Allie Lea asked, "Just what do you believe we have accomplished other than drive ourselves nuts?"

I gave her a serious look. "Freedom of thought, care for each other, and the ability of our kids to think for themselves. In the terms of horseplayer parlance, that, my dear, is a winning trifecta."

The next four days were filled with meetings at the Smithsonian and endless checking and rechecking of the supplies we would need, not to mention the numerous questions. I had been designated as the trip's quartermaster. Why, I don't know. I guess I just morphed into the job. Two days before our departure, I was in the bedroom closet packing when I heard my cell ringing. I had forgotten that I had left it in the great room. I thought, to hell with it; if the call is important, they'd call back. Bad, bad, bad, decision!

After finishing packing, I ambled downstairs to retrieve my phone. I saw that I had a text message, and it was anything but welcome and it threw me into a complete tailspin. Catherine, our favorite Maya fortune teller, had left me a cryptic bombshell saying, your visit to Chichicastenango and the following celebration will be a *grande* success. The same cannot be said for your other approved trip to Peru.

"You and your companions will be tested in ways you cannot even imagine. Lives will be placed at risk, yours in particular. Do not, under any circumstances, make your friends aware of this text! Be prepared for an unexpected turn of events. Putting off or delaying in handling life-threatening situations will cost you more trouble than you and they can possibly handle. Whenever Doubtful shows up, pay heed to his presence. Comprendes, amigo?"

I couldn't delete Catherine's text fast enough. I broke out in a cold sweat not knowing what to think or how I would handle her message. She made it very plain that the information she had given me was not to be shared. Her past messages were nowhere so terse and never before had she told me that I wasn't to share the information with Allie Lea.

In short, I was stumped, but I knew it wouldn't be for long. The kids and Allie Lea would be arriving soon and it was my turn to fix dinner. I wondered how in the hell I would get through the evening without displaying worry and concern over Catherine's text. I hustled into the kitchen and decided tonight would be a box dinner.

I opened the freezer, took out a couple packages of Trader Joe's jumbo split shrimp, two bags of frozen hash browns, and a large box of fresh organic greens. I whipped up a marinade, dumped the shrimp into it, placed the hash-browns in the oven, tossed the salad, got out the ranch dressing, plunked down a pitcher of ice water, set the table, and then the onslaught began.

I encountered a slight problem. Lynne showed up with Ken, all six foot three of him and his need to eat. I ended up having to fix myself a peanut butter and mayonnaise sandwich. Allie Lea and I retired to the swings in the backyard. The kids didn't miss us and they chattered on like young adults do. Ken indicated he would be interested in discussing his role in the upcoming trip. So much for our worry and concern.

Ken and Lynne joined us in the backyard. Allie Lea filled him in on the reason for the trip, and that he was free to take part in the celebration and Lynne would be his guide.

Ken said, "I prefer to avoid underground exploring. I have a problem with claustrophobia. Other than that, I'm open to suggestions regarding what is expected of me. By the way, I discussed your up-and-coming trip with my mom and dad.

"They think this will be an experience of a lifetime. If, in the future, there are other opportunities for outlanders and paying archaeologists, they would welcome a call."

Allie Lea's eyes brightened up when Ken said, "Paying archaeologist." I made a mental note to earmark the last two seats (just in case) for Ken's parents, despite our leaving in two days. I also anticipated one of Allie Lea's 3 a.m. conferences confirming my hunch.

I didn't see how it would be possible for the Hookways to just drop everything and in the space of two days get ready for such a trip. Oh well, that's Allie Lea's problem; at least that's what I thought when I drifted off into that large fluffy cloud surrounding my bed.

At one o'clock, I felt a gentle nudge and a soft voice said, "We need to talk."

I said, "Talking is for tomorrow; come on to bed."

With that, she turned on my bedside lamp and seductively said, "Tonight would be more productive!"

I rolled over and saw that she was sitting there in the buff, laughing. Now that she had my undivided attention, I immediately sat up and asked, "How productive and how soon?"

She replied, "That depends on how cooperative you prove to be." I pulled up the covers and said, "Give it a rest. I've got a headache!"

"Ryan Keshaw, I don't ever remember you letting a headache interfere with one of the wonderful pleasures of life. So, get out from under those covers, and let's get down to business."

"Monkey business or real business?"

Allie Lea was brimming with enthusiasm when she said, "I know what you have been up to, and this is one time I have beaten you to the punch. I managed to snag those pamphlets and books on the state of drones and read them before you got your hands on them. Eric, the dear soul, pointed me in the right direction and when I spoke with Rafael, he filled in the blank spots.

"I know for a fact you have been at odds with yourself trying to figure out the riddle that was so neatly dropped on our head when we were last in Chichicastenango. I worked with Rafael helping to secure the funding for the Larco Museum to further their knowledge of drones. All of which leads me to the question of how the Hookways fit into this puzzle without giving away the company store.

"I foresee the need for diplomatic help and advice in Peru, and that's where they come in. Last week I spoke with the personnel who will be responsible for extending the Larco's stay, should their efforts regarding drones come to pass. A-ha! I see that I have your undivided attention, and it didn't take sex to get you interested. What do you think so far?"

I hesitantly said, "For openers, I feel like I'm a fifth wheel that is unneeded. Can I please get back to sleep before you decide to drop an H-bomb on my head? I guess the partnership you speak of so glowingly just flew out the window. I realize this is your show. But, don't make the mistake of thinking you can handle it all by yourself, else you may be in for some unpleasant or nasty surprises."

Allie Lea gasped and asked, "What in the world are you talking about and why would you bring up such negative thoughts at a time like this?"

"Allie Lea, we leave tomorrow afternoon and that's enough stress for now. Remember, two can play at the game of silence and secrecy. I'm going to the spare bedroom and attempt to get back to sleep. Goodnight, and I mean goodnight."

"Darling, I had hoped my actions would be received as a pleasant surprise, and that you would be happy I took some of the load off you. I made an error in judgment not bringing you into the loop. You're right; we need a good night's sleep."

As she tip-toed out of the bedroom, she said, "You know I wouldn't do anything to upset the bond we have established. I love you, and don't you ever forget it."

Morning came all too quickly, along with the bedlam the kids generated. But, in the end it all worked out. Allison's friend and mother picked her up and promised they would look after her. Kens' father dropped him off at the executive terminal at Dulles along with his sparse baggage, and I used the opportunity to float Allie Lea's idea.

Steve made the most of the moment when he asked, "When would this trip come to fruition?"

I replied, "Next week or no later than ten days. Perhaps, I didn't make myself clear the invitation is for you and your wife."

Steve was grinning like a Cheshire cat when he pulled out his cell phone and murmured, "Well, well, well, will miracles never cease? Barbara will be out of her mind when I mention this opportunity. She might even say a prayer as she will, no doubt, consider this invitation as if it was sent from on high."

"Steve, wait a minute or two before you make that call. I suddenly remembered I overlooked what could be a deal breaker. There is a catch that might influence your decision. We would ask that you pay the initial one-way flight expense. Other than that, the Smithsonian would absorb the rest of your costs."

He grinned and said, "Our family has not lived beyond our means, due to the uncertainty of the diplomatic arm of our government. We saved for just such opportunities. When should I book our tickets?"

I guess I looked a bit incredulous and asked, "Can you be prepared to leave next Tuesday or Wednesday? Don't worry about the return flight; we will use the Smithsonian's jet for our return trip."

Steve pumped my hand. "I, or we, can be ready to leave on two day's notice. By the way, you didn't mention where we would be going!"

About that time, Jim Leachy came rushing up. "Ryan, if you don't get your ass in gear and get on board, your friends are going to throttle you."

Before boarding, I cupped my hands and yelled, "Steve, it's Lima and Machu Picchu!"

As the steward closed the door, Jim said, "I was under the impression our destination is the La Aurora International Airport in Guatemala City and then on to attend the celebration in Nuevo Ciudad. What in the hell does our flight have to do with Lima and Machu Picchu?"

I playfully punched him in the ribs and replied, "Everything and nothing!"

He squinted and asked, "Perchance does your 'everything and nothing' mean there might be something of interest that would make the lead chapter in my new book? Should that be the case then what I suspect will exceed my fondest expectations."

"Jim, old friend, I'll give you a hint, provided you keep it to yourself."

I was laughing when I replied, "*Puric Sinchi Huaca Chullpa Yacarca Tocco.* Jim, it's not Inca—it is Quechua!"

Chapter 3

* * *

Myopia Is a Disease Not Limited to Just a Select Few

Our sleek silver and blue jet whistled through the fleecy clouds as it climbed to our cruising altitude with nary a bump. The remainder of the flight was smooth and tranquil as the ocean below; inside was a different story. The atmosphere was positively electric, and the anticipation of what was to come was on the tip of everyone's tongue.

Midway through the flight, Jim sidled up and took the vacant seat beside me. He groused, "I should know better than to play poker with you. However, I'll still keep my part of the bargain, provided you level with me. What's up, or better still, what's on your mind? If secrecy is your main concern, remember I'm pretty good at keeping my mouth shut and my brain disengaged—when necessary."

I kept silent for a bit and then decided to fill him in on why Lima and Machu Picchu were destined to play a part of our lives. Not once did he interrupt or say anything.

When I concluded my tutorial, he said, "Whew! I don't know whether I'm glad to be a part of what you have in mind or fearful of what I've learned; the scenario you have laid out is fraught with peril. Have you given any thought to the idea that some of the players might turn tail and run when they realize the implications of what you have in mind and the dangers they may encounter? Should word of this venture leak before you have fully developed your plans, you could be in for a heap of trouble and that trouble might come from an unexpected source."

I interrupted, saying, "I don't get it! An unexpected source? If so, from whom, and why?"

He quickly replied, "The wives! I didn't hear you mention their role or what you plan for them while others are fulfilling your plans and dreams. Should this trip be extended, I seriously doubt that the Smithsonian will spring for the wives' expenses past our scheduled return date.

"If push comes to shove and you asked the husbands to ante up for their wives' extra expenses —forget it— regardless of how much we love them. I certainly wouldn't relish the thought of being the one elected to deliver that message. So, count me out on that part of the deal. Ryan, you are a true-blue friend and I would like to offer you another piece of advice."

About then the captain announced landing in twenty minutes. I sat there trying to make sense of Jim's remarks and finally I said, "Give it to me straight, but make it snappy, for we are being vectored into the landing pattern."

He replied, "When you discuss your plan with Allie Lea, I suggest you give consideration to finding a soundproof, uninterruptible place. She'll wonder why you didn't take her into your confidence or, at least, given her a heads-up long before now. My guess is that she will rip you a new asshole. Be prepared to duck and beware of any throwable objects within her reach. Let me know what day and time this event will take place. I'll plan to be scarce on that occasion and take Judy shopping in Chichi, despite my abhorrence to what many in our country call the all-American custom."

Our landing was smooth and without incident, and Rodrigo was there to greet and welcome us. I wondered where Urgar's 'copter was parked, and sensing my concern, Rodrigo said, "*Mucho* people and luggage, need bus. It takes only one hour." Before we got underway, there was a rush for the restrooms. Several guys made for the bar to get some of that great drink they call *cerveza* (beer) to take with them. I started to laugh, and Allie Lea looked puzzled and asked why I was laughing.

"Remember the last time we made this drive? You constantly griped about the dangerous, narrow, lousy road. Unless I miss my guess, Rodrigo will not be our driver of choice, and if we are lucky, we won't get one of the crazy kamikaze drivers. Not only will it scare the hell out of the women, but that *cerveza* on an empty stomach will require several pit stops. What should be a one-hour trip will be considerably extended."

Allie Lea said, "With that knowledge in mind, I suspect we should seek dibs on sitting as close to the front of the bus as possible."

We looked at each other, broke into a trot, and claimed the seats behind the driver. Looking very smug, we gave each other a high five. We had a few minutes before Rodrigo finished storing our luggage. I decided this was the time to bring Allie Lea up to speed. She was unaware of the problems that Jim thought we might encounter and surprised me when she suggested we spend some quiet time together before things go hectic. In fact, I surprised myself when I recommended that tomorrow we take a buckboard ride complete with a picnic lunch, blankets, and straw. As we took our seats and prepared for what I knew would be a grueling bus ride, Allie Lea gave me a close stare and said, "I'm looking forward to such an unexpected romantic affair. I hope the sun doesn't fry us, despite the neat little river close by. I know it isn't like you to offer up yourself for a picnic without being prodded, cajoled, or just plain coerced."

She continued, "I don't wish to have my day ruined all because of some hair-brained scheme you cooked up. This much I know: whatever you have in mind must be of great importance, otherwise, you wouldn't have gone to such pains to set me up."

I smiled. "You wound me deeply to think that I would exhibit such lowly feelings for the one I love. If the heat becomes too oppressive, there is that cave where we spent several hours. The Maya believe caves are the domain of *Xibalba* (underworld), so we should have it all to ourselves. After the sun goes down, the coolness might call for a light blanket and straw in case you wish to take a nap. How does that sound?

"It sounds wonderful. The question is, how big a price will I have to pay? Right this instant, I'm thinking that a dip in that cold water will bring back those traumatic memories of you and Sara being pulled out of the water looking half dead. When those memories come flooding back, there will be no swimming for me, despite the heat. As to the blankets and straw, are you sure they're just for a nap?"

I pulled my ball cap down. "Wake me when we arrive. I need to gather all my strength as tomorrow holds the promise of being a strenuous day! Uh oh! Our driver is pulling over. No doubt several of the beer drinkers are now realizing that those extra beers were not the smartest choice they ever made."

After a couple more unexpected stops, we finally pulled into the long winding drive and saw the beautiful stone fence marking the entrance to Urgar's estancia. Allie Lea looked at me and said, "Don't even think of asking me to do anything. I am on a mission. If anyone delays me, they might be surprised and I embarrassed. Do you get the picture? Taking those front seats meant we'll be the first off, a very timely move."

Rodrigo directed the bus driver to a spot near the chopper pad, and surprisingly there was no one to greet us, other than the housekeepers who were there to direct us to our rooms and assist us with our luggage. Allie scooted ahead of the crowd. I asked Rodrigo, "Where's everyone?"

He smiled. "At the beach welcoming party for a big barbecue, swimming, mariachi music, and Guatemala's Famosa Gallo beer." After making that announcement, the crowd surged around him. Someone asked, "Where are the swimsuits?"

That brought several snickers. Those who had extra suits helped work out that pressing problem. Rodrigo pointed out El Donkey's location and explained how to operate the shuttle and said, *"Andale, Andale!* (Hurry, hurry!)"

Those with suits made their way to the snazzy bathhouse, changed, and headed for the beach and the water.

Allie Lea emerged resplendent in her new emerald green suit, matching Panama hat, and bag. She turned and asked, "Are you buying or selling? I wonder if anyone else observed you catching up on the latest styles, or were you just counting heads making sure we weren't missing anyone?"

I had to laugh. "Guilty! My research paid off because I failed to see anyone who comes even close to you and your curves. I guess that diet you've on the past month is paying dividends, big time."

She smiled. "Diet, what diet? I don't remember my weight being an item of concern whenever you feel amorous. By the way, did you get a look at Catherine when you were doing your research or head count?"

I understood why Allie Lea evidenced interest in Catherine. She too was wearing a tight-fitting emerald green suit. It was obvious she didn't have her crystal ball as her suit was on the skimpy, but delightful side.

I glanced at Allie Lea, who said, "There's Catherine and does she look stunning! Are you sure you didn't see her when you were going your research?"

Allie Lea waved and remarked, "I believe she wants us to join her and Juma."

Sphinx like, I answered, "Okay" and then shut my mouth. I prayed that Catherine had no intention of discussing the contents of the text she sent me.

Allie Lea was eager to get into the water. I had no desire to jump into that river of ice cubes, so I said, "I'm going to work on my tan and then see if I can find Ahau and señor Urgar."

Catherine asked, "Allie Lea, is it okay if I join you?" As she passed me, she whispered, "Meet me in the cave behind the waterfall in about forty minutes. Try to slip away unnoticed. I have a small torch, so we don't go wandering off. Don't forget to seek out Ahau's special guest. Pay particular attention to what he has to say."

Sonofabitch, and to think I came here expecting to have a good time without having to be on guard full time. I managed to slip in a question: "Anyone else invited to this meeting?"

She shook her head as if to say no as she put on her bathing cap. Out of the corner of my eye, I saw Ahau, señor Urgar, RK, and a well-muscled young man approaching. After a few bear hugs, I caught my breath and asked, "Who might this young amigo be?"

RK said, "Dad, this is my friend I met when we were last here. Acahuana, this is my father, Ryan. I don't think you met him before now. When you get to know him, he can be a regular guy. He is still trying to solve that riddle you left us, but so far he hasn't had much luck."

Ahau and señor Urgar stood there speechless for they thought the subject was taboo especially in public. I didn't know how to approach his remarks without his losing face, so I said, "Acahuana, that's one of the reasons we made this trip. I hope you will be available to help us if things work out as planned. In the meantime, do me a favor.

"The riddle is known to a select few. Allie Lea would like to keep it that way until our plans are finalized. I see everyone is queuing up in the food line. Señor Urgar if you will lead the way, I, for one, will have some of those wonderful, barbecued ribs for which your *ranchero* is famous." After inhaling several of those mouth-watering ribs, I made for the cavern behind the water-fall. I made sure no one followed or saw me slip inside.

Should Allie Lea get a whiff of what I was about to do, she would fry me in oil and hang me out to dry, in addition to retiring her tiara. Well, maybe not that far. I saw a light flicker in the distance and it kept moving away from me further into the cavern. In my haste to catch up, I tripped and fell, and then I heard Catherine ask, "Why are you just poking along?"

I replied in a moment of pique, "Catherine, you're the one with the light, and without a torch, I can't see jack. Pray tell me, what's so important that it requires us meeting. I'll bet that Juma and Allie Lea would give a pretty penny to know what's going on between us."

She stopped and gathered her breath as the going became more arduous. When she straightened up, she dropped the light and out it went. I said, "Catherine, we need to find that light or we may be hours getting out of here. If you think we have a problem now, wait until our spouses and the rest of the crew find out where we have been and what we've been doing.

"We can find the light if we stop right here and search in quadrants. That is, if we don't panic or get overcome with guilt. By the way, that's a lovely swimsuit you are almost wearing."

"Ryan Keshaw, you are a devil! You liked it that much did you? Take a seat. The path is somewhat dry and is as good a place as any for a discussion. You and your crew are in for a difficult and extremely dangerous time should you press forward with your search in the Sacred Valley of the Incas and Intipunku, better known as the Door of the Sun.

"Do you have any idea of what you will be up against? You will be operating in an area without the support of friendly Maya and their surroundings. Many of the Inca will be hostile to your parties' efforts. Several of your staff will agree to join you in this venture. Make sure they understand that this could be a dangerous and possibly deadly mission. I cannot say any more, nor can I offer more help than what we have discussed today. Choose your partners carefully. Now let's find that damn light and join the others."

"Catherine, I thought you said we were here to discuss. So far all I've heard is bad news. I have as yet to put forward my plans, let alone discuss anything. This isn't like you, *señora*."

When I said that, she gave a little sob. "The rest is for you to figure out, amigo. Wait no longer to inform Allie Lea of our discussion. She may wish to pull the plug on the operation. Trust her judgment. I would not advise discussing this with anyone other than her. Otherwise, you may start a panic among your people. Oh, look what I found!"

With that, she clicked on her little torch, and we made our way back to the entrance and parted, each going a separate way.

Despite it being early in the afternoon, I was chilled to the bone. I wondered why.

After a short interlude, I hooked up with Allie Lea, who now had Ken and Lynne in tow. Juma and Catherine were preparing to board El Donkey when Juma yelled, "Catherine is cold. She needs a hot soaking in the tub. We'll see you tonight in the great room."

The remainder of the day turned out to be spectacular. Over and over, I heard many exclaim, "This is an adventure right out of Disneyland!" and "Can you imagine our host making his 'copter available for tours of this unbelievable *estancia*?" I knew that for many, this would be an adventure of a lifetime and I hoped nothing would mar their memories.

My morose attitude, despite a soothing, warm shower, was noticed by Allie Lea and I knew I was in for a grilling. I had no answer how to handle Catherine's remarks, and I attempted to put her ominous advice out of mind— at least for the rest of the day. Thank goodness Allie Lea received a call from Jim Hamilton, ensuring, for the time being, my ability to put off a discussion I dreaded.

Because of the festivities, *cenar* or dinner, was late and on the light side. Despite that, there was an abundance of sandwiches, tacos, soups, salads, and a wonderful selection of raspberry, strawberry and blueberry tarts. Gallo and Moza Beer were *senor* Urgar's favorite libations and plenty of each were on tap.

Halfway through the meal, Allie Lea tapped on her glass. "Plan to attend a short get-acquainted meeting at eight o'clock in señor Urgar's great room. Everyone is invited."

With that said, she asked Anita and her crew to come forward and take a bow for the wonderful welcoming reception. This is one time I was glad we were seated next to Judy and Anna. They simply chatted throughout the meal. How about that? I caught Allie Lea glancing my way several times and at one point Anna, Red's wife, mentioned to Allie Lea, "Words cannot properly convey our thoughts for the wonderful invitation you extended to us."

A thought quickly flashed through my brain. I wondered if she would be as grateful if she knew the dangers her husband would possibly encounter. Possibly not! After everyone finished dessert and after dinner coffee, Allie Lea took the opportunity to satisfy her sweet tooth with an additional dessert. I reminded her of her supposed diet. Annoyed, she retorted, "Diets are made to be broken, and tomorrow, should things go as planned, those extra calories will magically disappear." With that, she curtseyed and remarked, "It's showtime."

Despite the size of Urgar's great room, the seating was tight and someone had the foresight to place a sign by the podium which read No Smoking Inside Casa, Señor Urgar and Anita. I nudged Allie Lea and said, "I wonder how Jim will survive without his daily ration of cigars."

Allie Lea opened the meeting with a vote of thanks for our hosts and then called Jim Leachy to say a few words. He then presented a plaque to our hosts. On it, the words said, "Señor Urgar, Anita, Espiritius, Ahau and Elena, Forever in Our Hearts, James Hamilton, President, and Dr. Allie Lea Keshaw, Smithsonian Vice President of Field Operations."

Eric served as our official photographer. Ashley asked why he was taking scads of pictures. Judy commented, "Perhaps he thinks his pictures will make the Smithsonian's award- winning magazine."

All that aside, my uppermost goal was to keep Allie Lea in a good frame of mind until tomorrow rolled around.

Allie Lea continued, "Friday, will be a free day to enjoy the beach, the town, or a 'copter trip around this magnificent spread. A word of warning: do not stray too far off the beaten path and travel in pairs. Alert Jim Leachy if you run into a problem. Guatemala is the third most dangerous or deadly place in the world, and without a guide, you could find yourself in a difficult situation. Don't miss Chichi's centuries' old Maya church; it has a worldwide reputation. The marketplace is a sight to behold. Many of the most exotic, authentic Maya designs and colors are on display and for purchase. Keep your credit cards close to your heart."

That brought a groan from the male members in the audience.

"Saturday and the ribbon-cutting ceremony is a command performance," Allie Lea explained. "Ahau and his people have planned some interesting ceremonies. Those of you who are here for the first time will find the Maya a friendly people, and they'll be happy to talk with you. Make the most of your time and remember you are the Smithsonian's goodwill ambassadors.

"Now, a bit of unexpected good news! I have asked for and received approval for an exciting new project, so be ready to shift gears and take part in what could be an important archaeological discovery.

"Señor Urgar informed me he is making his 'copter available for a limited number of trips to Guatemala City. It's a great city, but I must warn you: be careful of street food. If you don't see it being washed or know that it has been well-cooked, don't eat and don't buy it, despite how good it may look or smell.

"For those interested, sign up with Ryan; get your name on the list. The 'copter holds five passengers and Guatemala City is but a thirty-minute ride. That's it. We're adjourned. Ryan and I are open to questions for the next few minutes, and then we plan to look for an empty veranda lounge and enjoy the night's changing colors; they are a sight to behold. Elena has also asked me to remind everyone smoking is not permitted anywhere indoors, but it's okay on the veranda."

As we exited the great room, I took Allie Lea's arm and said, "After listening to your presentation, I'm considering a change in plans."

Allie Lea gave me a quizzical look and said, "I believe a major adjustment is on the way. Does it mean that our buckboard ride and picnic are about to go by the wayside?"

"No! It was only a thought and despite my misgivings, it's still on."

Allie Lea gave me a punch in the ribs. "If you continue your waffling, I might decide to shove you off this veranda. Now let's get down to business."

I did my best to persuade her to postpone our discussion until tomorrow when we would be fresh and rested. She would have none of that. However, the Maya gods must have heard my prayers because Ahau, Elena, and Acahuana asked to join us as we were being seated. I found three vacant chairs just waiting to be used, and it wasn't long before Elena and Allie Lea became ensconced in an animated conversation.

After introducing Acahuana, Allie Lea said, "You have become a very handsome young man and RK has spoken of you many times. I hope you and RK continue to develop your friendship much like Ryan and Ahau. You're welcome to visit us, anytime."

Acahuana took Allie Lea's hand, gave it a tender caress, and said, "I just might do that, provided señor Rafael and Sara agree. I am living in their casa and attending the *Pontificia Universidat Catholica del Perú* and majoring in management and international finance. RK and I have much in common. The flute and music were the bonds that brought us together and I am looking forward to him visiting me. I know he likes old and ancient things, and in my spare time, I am cataloging many of the paintings that have been gathering dust in the Larco's cavernous basement.

"Uncle Rafael plans to sell or auction off several as the museum can use the soles. It would be great if RK would give me a hand; otherwise, I might be there until *Inti,* our sun god, visits the Earth.

"RK has been telling me the most interesting stories about many western American heroes in much the same manner as the stories Ahau tells.

"Ahau always uses humor or a story to make a point and one day, he remembered reading about the Lone Ranger and his amigo Tonto. They always arrived on the scene when one of their friends needed help. Several years ago they achieved celebrity status in books and movies, and on TV, and I asked Ahau, 'Was this Lone Ranger and his friend, Tonto, for real?'

"Ahau replied, 'Certainly, ask your friend RK about them. I'll bet he watched them on television when he was younger.'"

Acahuana laughed and remarked, "If there was an exit moment, I think I just heard it. I'll leave you grownups to talk out your problems. Meanwhile, I'll look up RK. Don't stay up too late." He went away humming the song, "Knock Three Times on the Ceiling."

I sat thinking of Acahuana and what he'd told us. Because he, Rafael, and Sara were to play a major role in my plans, it was imperative that I talk with Allie Lea tonight! The evening was warm; the moon full; and the ever-changing shadows blended into a giant screen highlighted by the hosts of stars that seemed to dance through the heavens.

Ahau put his arm around Elena and said, "We mustn't overstay our leave. I'm tired and it's past our bedtime. What do you amigos have planned for tomorrow?"

Allie Lea quickly answered, "Guess what? Mister romantic is taking me for a buggy ride and picnic. I hope it isn't too hot. However, that nearby infamous cave gives us an option as a backup."

Elena broke into a knowing smile. "Goodness gracious."

Ahau said nothing and got up to leave. As they were exiting the casa, Elena suddenly turned and flashed the thumbs-up sign. Allie Lea returned the gesture, and we, too, began the walk to our bedroom. Suddenly, she started humming and remarked, "That song is right catchy. We don't have a pipe in our room and perhaps it's just as well."

"Allie Lea, get serious. We need to talk and without any interruption."

She replied, "I'm not going to let anything interfere with such a wonderful, romantic night. Whatever it is that's eating at you will keep until we are in the wide open spaces. Give it a rest after you answer this question: Does what you plan to cover have anything to do with Catherine? In case you're wondering, I caught a glimpse of you making your way into that cavern behind the waterfall, and being the curious person I am, I did a quick scan of the area and guess what, she didn't pop up on my radar screen.

"For some reason, I took for granted your little clandestine meeting had to do with a part of our trip you have yet to expose. It didn't by chance have to do with the meaning of that puzzling riddle and the drone research in Peru, would it?"

I was flabbergasted and didn't know what to say other than, "How did you know? By the way, darling, I almost forgot, Lynne asked if we had plans for tomorrow. I explained what we have planned and, naturally, I invited them to come along.

"Lynne had been intently listening to our conversation and squealed with joy and exclaimed, 'How wonderful! Ken and I will be tickled to accompany you, provided Mom agrees. I well remember the wonderful times we had at the little river, the cave, the picnics, and riding through that wild countryside. Ken is an adventurous soul and loves exploring. He'll find it absolutely fascinating when I tell him of your adventures and your hair-breadth escapes.'

"She then skipped off in a simply delirious mood in anticipation of what tomorrow will bring."

Allie Lea uttered two words, "Oh, youth!" She then exhibited part of her steel when she asked, "Just when did your enlightening conversation with Catherine take place? And why, may I ask, are you so late in the game informing me, and what happened to that all important message Catherine gave you?"

I gave her my best smile and said, "Since you have already figured out the most important piece of information, and being that the veranda crowd has flown the coop, we have the place to ourselves to discuss whatever is on your mind."

"Ryan Keshaw, you are dancing and playing it by ear. Since you so magnanimously agreed with Lynne, I suppose your convoluted logic makes sense. I'm going to pee and when I return, we will have it out, even if it takes all night."

When she said that, I knew I was screwed. She returned carrying a pitcher of orange juice and a dish of fresh pastries. I saw a large couch that had a mass of pillows and a couple of beautifully decorated poncho-styled throws and we made ourselves comfortable.

After wrapping herself in one of them, she announced, "The night air has cooled and I intend to stay warm, regardless of the time it takes you to rid yourself of those troubling thoughts you've been harboring. So get to it and keep in mind: this is my project. I don't expect any spinning for or against. Are we clear on both points?"

I nodded. "This may take a while as there are two parts to this story. The first part deals with what Catherine told me."

I laid out the scenario as best I remembered, and when I got to the part concerning the dangers, Allie Lea shuddered. "I don't wish to hear any more if dire predictions are all she made, at least, not tonight."

I said, "Stay with me; the rest of the story gets better. Maybe I have unraveled the riddle which RK and Acahuana so generously presented us years ago. I wish to reserve judgment until things unfold on the drone front. The answer to that riddle could lead us to the burial spot of Pachacuti, an ancient Inca emperor who had buried with him a large supply of gold and precious jewels.

"For the last six hundred years, archaeologists and looters have searched unsuccessfully for the exact location of his burial place and that's where the drones come in. The Largo museum has a store of knowledge regarding the drones and their capabilities. Their exploratory flights indicate they haven't been searching for archaeological sites, let alone Inca burial sights.

"Their initial forays did not center around Machu Picchu. They scanned an area I would not have selected based on what I've deduced from the riddle. They should be looking no further south than the Lost City of the Incas, which is part of the Sacred Valley of the Incas. Ollantaytambo should be our demarcation point. Those wishing to visit Machu Picchu have two choices: take the five-mile uphill hike or take the train. There is no roadway between the two. Olly, as many call it, is deep in the heart of the Andes and is a popular overnight stopping point, giving many tourists time to adjust to the altitude. Altitude sickness can be very difficult and many senior citizens, despite taking advantage of the overnight stay, find the climb or the train ride beyond their capabilities.

"Those who suffer from altitude sickness will find Olly a most beautiful place to unwind, readjust their biological clock, and take advantage of the quaint hotels, restaurants, and shops. This is a town of oh's, aha's, and wow's! From what I've been told, the scenery is absolutely 360-degrees spectacular. According to my findings, the Inca living adjacent to the drone launching area consider them to be small flying gods. Most local Inca are afraid of them and others have been downright hostile. Should we make a discovery, the Peruvian government will no doubt take a greater interest in our project. They will require reams of paper to cover their asses if the drones run amuck, causing property and tourist damage to the daily twenty-five hundred cash-paying tourists.

"Anything or anyone that adversely affects that cash cow will be considered *persona non grata* and, no doubt, will be escorted out of the area after spending time in a less-than-hospitable Peruvian jail while things get sorted out.

"Machu Picchu is less than fifty miles from our proposed work site. It's time we sign Steve Hookway and ready his ambassadorship for action to represent the Smithsonian and ask how he recommends we handle the political waters. Steve's on-site presence will impress and slow down the bureaucrats in Cuzco. As to his wife's presence, she could prove to be of value as she is well into archaeology.

"Allie Lea, that's enough. Let's hit the hay unless you would rather sleep on this well- padded couch. You've had very little to say. Despite Catherine's admonition, I wonder if she is on the money this time. So far, I haven't been able to wrap my arms around that thought."

"Ryan, for the life of me, that thought has been running around in my mind as well. I *wonder* what prompted her remarks. This project is one that should be low risk, and I cannot see where we would be putting anyone in harm's way. Unless you come up with anything to the contrary, this project, on a danger scale of one to ten, would rate a two or three at worst. Let's sleep on it and make our decision tomorrow.

"Early tomorrow, I'll seek out Rafael, get his take, judge his response, and then talk with you. Let's go to bed; we are in for an exciting day despite getting off to a rocky start. How would you feel about inviting RK to join us on our little jaunt? That is, provided he and Acahuana don't have other plans. In the meantime, I'll alert Marjua as to the number making this trip so that there will be plenty to eat."

"Scheduling Friday as a free day is proving to be fortuitous as it should be a no-pressure day. Let's hope Lynne doesn't ask too many questions and that she's not getting in too deep. Ken seems to be a most unusual guy; their likes and personalities appear to mesh."

I expected Allie Lea to, at least, respond, and hearing nothing, I asked, "Are we done here?"

I gently nudged her and all she did was roll over and take up the whole couch. I wrapped the other throw around her, found an extra pillow, and tip-toed away.

Chapter 4

* * *

Flying Gods

$\mathcal{B}$reakfast was a bedlam of noise, laughter, and animated conversations. Despite that, everyone showed up at about the same time. However, the cooks, bakers, and grandmothers had everything under control.

I motioned to Marjua. "Have you seen señor Rafael and señora Sara?"

"They eat with others outside before it gets too hot. Do you and señora Allie Lea wish to join them? If so, I will have your food brought to you."

I told her there would be a couple extra hands for our buckboard ride. She started laughing and replied, "Your daughter has already given instructions."

Allie Lea shrugged her shoulders and rolled her eyes as if to say, Lynne is turning out to be quite the take-control person.

I called to Marjua, pointed to a table in the corner, and asked, "I trust she hasn't reserved that table as well?"

We had just begun to eat when Sara and Rafael waved and asked if they could join us. Sara coyly remarked, "Allie Lea, there is a rumor making the rounds that your ringmaster is going to pull another rabbit out of the proverbial hat in Machu Picchu."

I was so anxious that, without thinking, I practically shouted, "Just where is this so-called proverbial hat and why are you discussing this subject in public? Did it ever enter your mind that this was a subject best left to be discussed in private?"

Sara turned crimson and cringed a bit when I challenged her. She realized she had committed a breach of confidentiality. She took Allie Lea's hand and said, "I didn't mean any harm. I was just pulling Ryan's chain. Please forgive my faux pas. I promise you it won't happen again."

Allie Lea hesitated for a minute. "Sara, who told you of our plans and was it from a reliable source?"

Rafael spoke up. "Blame me. My source was Acahuana, who learned it from RK. One evening during dinner Acahuana told us that you were interested in drone technology. He told us RK had read about drones in the manuals and pamphlets you brought home. These young men put two-and-two together and arrived at the conclusion that Ryan was considering submitting a drone project for your approval. When we last visited your home, I had an opportunity to further the conversation with your son. That's how it got out."

Allie Lea in a rare moment of introspection sighed. "For the want of a nail."

She put her arm around Sara and gave her a big hug. "We owe you an apology. It seems as though Ryan was a bit hasty in his thoughts.

"Señor Rafael please excuse the interruption. I know Ryan will be extremely interested in your findings. Please continue.

"We have been working with a company that is on the cutting edge of this new technology. It's no secret we have been testing their drones. The test areas are adjacent to Machu Picchu. Logically, we surmised these are the places in which you would be most interested.

"Ryan, you're welcome to take advantage of Larco's command center in Olly. It is located in the Hotel La Casonade de Yucay and is a fantastic gem. The place is immaculate, the restaurant good, the staff friendly, and the owner is a friend and a Larco contributor. Let me know how things work out, and I'll make the reservations. Oh yes, Ryan even you will appreciate the prices!"

Allie Lea injected a note of caution as to the Smithsonian's participation in extending the scope of her project when she said, "All this comes with a proviso, which hinges on my securing an extension to phase one by the board and Jim Hamilton's approvals on what he, no doubt, will call another one of Ryan's harebrained ideas."

"I put in a call for Jim and was told he is in Istanbul participating in a high-level security meeting with many of the world's top museum officials. He returns Sunday or Monday; until I hear from him, any plans that involve Peru will have to be put on hold. Since today is a free day, I'm looking forward to a buckboard ride and picnic, courtesy of one Ryan Keshaw. We will be accompanied by our daughter and Ken Hookway, something I don't think Ryan anticipated. But, it is what it is, and we'll make the best of it. Perhaps we can have dinner in Chichi Saturday evening.

"Sara, Ryan's synapses have been firing more frequently of late, and I asked him to develop a scenario to use when I speak with Jim Hamilton. Regarding our Saturday night dinner, it takes four to play bridge. Let's keep it that way."

She no sooner said that when in trooped Lynne and Ken dressed in true drugstore-cowboy style: big hats, tight jeans, bandanas, boots, and the most garish shirts you have ever seen. Talk about head turnings!

Without thinking, I asked, "Where did you get those god-awful duds?"

"Dad, we ordered them online before we left home. Do they look that bad?"

All the while, Ken stood there shifting from one foot to the other and then said, "Before we donate these so-called duds to señor Urgar's favorite charity, how about taking our picture? The folks back home will get a kick out of our getups!"

Sara stood up, walked over to Lynne, who had teared up, and said, "To hell with convention. Those duds might not win you a movie contract, but you'll be remembered as the young señor and señorita who weren't afraid of what people think.

"One day, in the future when your children come across this photo, I wouldn't be surprised if they said, 'My goodness, our parents weren't always fuddy-duddies.'"

When Sara uttered those words, the tears flowed, as well as the applause from those still enjoying their breakfast.

I said, "Now that everyone's sartorial needs have been satisfied, it's time to board our magic, horse-drawn carriage and experience a once-in-a-lifetime opportunity. I don't have a silk top hat or a red carpet to welcome you, so my genuine cowboy sombrero will have to do. Please be aware that modesty may take a back seat, due to the lack of civilized facilities.

"Flora, fauna, and low-growing, thorny, bushes are readily available. Shall we delay the start of today's trip by some fifteen minutes?"

My passengers debarked without saying a word, other than Ken, who said, "Good call, kemosabe."

Ashley had been standing off to one side observing my antics; she walked over, gave me a hug, and whispered, "Must you be so devilish?"

As Ken prepared to climb aboard, he asked, "Could I drive part of the way? I may not be a cowboy, but when I was a little kid I always dreamed of riding a horse on those wide open spaces I saw in the movies!"

"Ken, this is not the movies. It takes a good bit of skill to keep the horses in line, especially if we come upon an aggressive four-legged creature who hasn't eaten in a while. On the return trip, sit beside me, and we'll share the reins."

All he said was, "Yippee!" This time he didn't climb aboard—he jumped aboard.

About then the señora and the señorita returned and asked, "What was that all about?"

"We had a bet on how long it would take before you returned from your earthly duties."

Lynne looked at Allie Lea. "Mom, it's times like these that Dad gives me the feeling he is certifiably nuts."

Allie Lea responded, "Lynne, men do have their idiosyncrasies. However, many women realize it's best to ignore times as such and craft answers that help the opposite sex realize life is much more pleasant when both partners are pulling on the wheel at the same time. I think we can enjoy the rest of the trip now that the thorny-bushes part of the trip are out of the way."

We were almost half way to the picnic area and our horses were setting a lively pace when suddenly they began to snort and buck in the traces. It was all I could do to keep them from breaking into a gallop.

Ken asked, "What the hell is bothering them?"

I yanked on the leads, pulled on the so-called brake, and said, "Lynne, hand me the blanket that's rolled up lying beside the basket of food. Do it now! Don't ask any questions!"

She handed it to me, and I pulled out a shotgun, which Rodrigo had insisted on my bringing. Just in case. The horses were working themselves into a lather, and Allie Lea asked, "Is it a mountain cat and where in the hell is it? I have looked in every direction, but I can't spot him."

Then the horses began to calm down. I handed the gun back to Lynne and said, "Keep it close. Based on the horses demeanor, I believe they are telling us the intruder has moved on."

I cracked my whip, and the horses once more picked up the pace. It wasn't long before we arrived at our destination when Ken decided to make an announcement. He put his arm around my shoulder and said, "You're right; this isn't the movies. Never in my wildest day did I ever expect to come so close to the wild kingdom. I know I am strong enough to handle the horses, but I don't know if I could handle them should another such occasion arise."

Everyone suddenly declared they were ravenous. I guess the excitement and adrenalin charged their motors. I suggested that Lynne and Ken take a walk down by the river while Allie Lea and I rub down, water, and feed the horses. They offered to help, but Allie Lea told them to go ahead, as she would give me a hand.

After finishing our chores, she remarked, "This takes me back to some of the good times we had on my Dad's farm at Swiss. I had forgotten the pleasant smells and the appreciation horses show when they are being cared for. I know you had a few unpleasant experiences with horses at the Greenbrier and the Homestead, but I thought you handled this situation and the horses just like a pro. How about a little insight on a question we've never discussed?"

I replied, "I don't know where you are taking this, but let her rip!"

She laughed. "I wondered if you would have shot that animal if it presented us with a dangerous situation."

I didn't hesitate when I said, "In a heartbeat."

Lynne helped her mom set out the food, and on an impulse, asked, "Mom were you frightened and would you have shot that creature had the occasion arisen?"

Allie Lea thought for a moment. "Certainly. I learned to shoot and handle a gun when I was in high school. Mom and Dad were crack shots, so I guess I took to it naturally. As I've grown older, I have become wary of guns, and that's why we don't have any in the house."

"Mom, Ken has grown up with guns. He was required to take small arms training, due to his dad's diplomatic assignments. He is hesitant to talk about it and I don't push it. I never saw the need to bear arms for any reason until now. In fact, before this trip is over, I am going to ask Ken to give me a few elementary lessons. I can see where that knowledge might come in handy. Do you think dad would mind?"

"Lynne, your father served in the Marines, although he never talks about it."

After we finished eating, Allie Lea said, "Lynne why don't you show Ken the lagoon and the Maya sacrificial chamber? Explain the part it played in Dad's and Ashley's lives. I imagine he will find it fascinating."

The incident with the cat unnerved me more than I cared to admit. I didn't say so, but thought it best we cut our trip short and get back before darkness set in. Allie Lea had other plans.

She announced, "I think I'll take a little nap in the buckboard. See if the kids wish to take a dip in that beautiful little river. Ryan, the straw you so conveniently thought of makes a welcome cushion for a short snooze. Care to join me?"

We started back just as darkness began to fall. I cracked the whip a time or two, and the horses responded with a brisk pace. A few minutes later, I felt a tap on my shoulder and Ken asked, "How about giving me a shot at handling this rig? I figure the creatures are home after filling themselves on some that were less fortunate. How about it?"

I handed him the reins, climbed into the back, put my head in Allie Lea's lap, and said, "Wake me when we get there." Before long, the lights of Urgar's hacienda came into view and as we pulled up into the barn, Lynne giggled, stepped out of the driver's seat, and said, "We're home, James."

Allie Lea gave me a gentle shake and asked, "Guess who shared the driving with Ken? And if you said anyone but Lynne you would be mistaken. You might unleash that hidden sign-making talent you displayed back in Georgetown and chum up an equestrian certification for each of these two young people."

When she said that, they took a long, low bow and headed for the bar, laughing all the way.

As we lay in bed contemplating tomorrow's ceremony, reality set in when Allie Lea said, "Since we are having dinner in Chichicastango with Sara and Rafael, you better be prepared to bare it all, as time is beginning to press. Jim Hamilton is supposed to give me a call tomorrow morning. God only knows how he will react to this new proposal."

I put my arm around her and said, "Oh, he'll expect an outline or a broad brush of why the Smithsonian should fund our latest and greatest project. Otherwise, be prepared to pack up and go home on Wednesday."

She turned her baby blues on me and remarked, "Now's a fine time for you to tell me that when you know damn well all I have on paper is a short synopsis. Had I known this was in the offing, we would have stayed home and not gone on a picnic, even if it was being held on the hacienda's veranda.

"I'm in dire need of a ghost-writing assistant and, properly encouraged, you're it."

She walked over to her closet, and after some intense rummaging, she pulled out her tiara. "Good things happen quickly when one is in the mood to accomplish miracles. Are you sure it will be impossible for you to complete such a task by noon tomorrow?"

I then uttered what my family calls my famous household password, "Screwed again."

I was up bright and early, long before Allie Lea stepped out of the shower. When she saw me hunched over my iMac, she said, "My goodness, I see the muse is hard at work. I didn't expect it to be finished this early."

"Allie Lea, you are a manipulator first class; but do me a favor, take your foot off the accelerator. I don't mind being had when it's for a good cause. What I've developed will require a leap of faith and trust on your and Jim Hamilton's part. So be prepared. Thus far, I am long on ideas and short of proof, but that's the purpose of our trip to Peru. I do not wish to answer any of your 'what if' questions now or after the meeting.

"When you talk to Jim, stick to the facts; don't wander and you'll do fine. Here is your copy. I'm ready for a light snack and then a short nap to make up for the all-nighter I pulled. So please keep the wolves away, at least for the time being."

Saturday arrived in all its glory and despite the festive air of excitement, I felt detached for reasons I couldn't explain. I planned to talk with Ahau, but that was a non-starter. They told me he had been at it since five a.m. making sure that all would proceed as planned. Señor Urgar's crew had two barbecue pits fired up, and the delightful aroma of roasting beef was wafting throughout the area.

I couldn't believe what I saw when Allie Lea came swishing into the breakfast room. She turned many an eye as she was dressed not to-the-nines, but in colorful señora garb.

"So this is why you wanted me to go ahead. Well, if hiding your curves was your intent, then you succeeded admirably. Then, on the other hand, if you are sending a message indicating the oneness of this project, you couldn't have done it any better. As soon as you finish your breakfast, we must get underway. Thankfully, Eric has reserved a parking spot for your little red wagon. I just hope it stays reserved, otherwise, we're in for a long walk. By the way why did you decide to change outfits?"

She replied, "My message will be anything but formal, so I thought what's the point of dressing formally? Also, I think you and Sara are in for what, I hope, will be an unexpected surprise. At least, that's what Ahau tells me. So, stay close; he wishes to talk with us after the main ceremony ends. He is expecting a crowd, in addition to the town's large number of Maya who live in and around Guatemala City.

I asked, "So, what makes this such a big deal?"

"Why don't you ask Ahau? Other than that, it beats me."

"I hope you aren't pulling my chain, since it's time to sally forth to do our duty for God and country, and in this case the Smithsonian."

The crowd and the festive mood intensified. After giving it further consideration, I realized it wasn't the ceremony that was the draw; it was the thought of free barbecue, Moza beer, music, and dancing later in the evening.

Ahau opened the ceremonies, and as MC, he saw to it that the speakers kept their remarks short. Ahau urged the stars of this event, the Urgars, to come forward and accept their due as the ones most responsible for the financing and formation of Nuevo Ciudad.

I was taken aback at how much the good señor had aged during the last fifteen years. His few remarks were well received and the large crowd gave him a tremendous ovation. The responsibility of managing such a large cattle-and-horse operation and age were beginning to tell on him. It's obvious that señor Urgar has very deep pockets; this shindig will cost him several thousand soles after all is said and done. The heat was stifling and the shortness of the ceremony was appreciated—by everyone.

As soon as the ribbon was cut, many of the Maya sought out the cool interior of the two temples and the iced drink booths. The younger set headed for—what else—the food and drinks. The two mariachi bands tuned up and the festival was off and running. Several of our crew decided not to fight the crowds and opted to take advantage of *el donkey* and a dip in that cold water.

Ahau, Anita, and señor Urgar motioned to us, asking that we join their group. After congratulating Ahau for his people's spectacular performance in paying off the Maya's share of the note held by señor Urgar, Ryan said, "Amigo we have a surprise for you and Sara. However, it takes a little walking, say ten minutes, provided you are up for it."

Sara left me no choice when she said, "Let's go!"

I quietly said, "Allie Lea, this heat is a killer and now we are expected to climb this damn hill. It's a good thing you didn't wear heels. As a matter of curiosity, did you have any advance knowledge of this little endurance test? I only hope what we are about to witness is worth all this effort."

When we crested what I remembered to be a small hill, Ahau said, "Amigo, I trust you and Sara have vivid memories of what your amigo, Ben, called their boogie board rescue in what was then a dangerous river. What do you think of our re-routing job?"

When it dawned on me, all I did was gaze at the marvelous job that his countrymen did. Sara punched me. "Answer him, dummy; he's looking for your approval!"

"Ahau, I'm overwhelmed, and to tell you the truth, I couldn't comprehend the enormity of change your people made."

We continued our cautious descent when I caught a glimpse of Catherine and Juma standing by a dock. I turned to Sara and asked, "Why in the world are they here?" Then I realized that they're here because of the major role they played in our rescue.

Allie Lea responded with a tone of understanding. "It's a shame Ben couldn't be here for he, too, played a critical part in your rescue. He informed me he couldn't make today's festivities due to an important, longstanding commitment."

I shook my head and laughed. "An important, longstanding commitment? Knowing Ben as I do, I have a hard time believing he would miss a free trip and the opportunity to broaden his social circles."

Allie Lea broke into a big grin. "I suspect that is exactly what he is doing— surfing at California's Half Moon Bay with what he termed an 'awesome' companion!"

I shook my head. "An awesome companion? I only hope she likes surfing."

Rafael remarked that maybe she has developed a passion for surfing much as I have for my new sport, rock climbing.

Sara blushed. "This hill is a bit more difficult than I remembered, and it appears our little river now makes a lovely, long, lazy S pattern."

Off in the distance I saw two or three small rafts tied up to a little jetty. I immediately turned to Sara and asked, "Are those what I think they are?"

She nodded. "The sight of those rafts and this river gives me a feeling I hoped I would never again experience in this lifetime. I never knew how Ryan felt, but I fully expected that we never would come out of that venture alive." She grew silent and then pleaded, "Help me out here, Ryan!"

All heads swiveled, focusing on me. This is one time I had no response. Ahau, as well as the rest of the group, had not anticipated Sara's reaction to what they thought would be a welcome attraction to us and many of the tourists.

He said, "Sara, I miscalculated. I should have discussed what we had in store for you and Ryan. Not once did it enter my head that either of you might have adverse feelings regarding what was once a major difficulty and then turning it into something that is now a pleasurable experience. Where the river goes underground, we removed the large stones, widened the channel, and made it so one could safely float down the river, under the temples and land near señor Urgar's electro station.

"We delayed the opening because we thought it only fitting our first passengers be you, Ryan, Juma, and Catherine."

There was a moment of silence as no one wanted any part of this discussion.

I summoned up the courage and asked, "How many amigos will these boats hold, and is the cover the new, bulletproof, neoprene plastic?"

I no sooner asked that when Sara put her arm around me and whispered: "Ryan, we've been in much worse situations. Get your ass in gear and join me; otherwise, I may take off running—back up that damn hill."

Catherine and Juma boarded one of the other rafts and began to leisurely float toward the underground entrance. As we boarded our raft, Sara said, "Ryan, give me your hand. I don't know why, but I am scared silly."

The boat moved effortlessly and quietly through the narrowest part of the cavern. Without warning, Sara exclaimed, "Ryan, I need a flashlight or a lantern."

I wondered why the hell she needed a light, but I handed her a lantern anyway. She began to play it over the cavern and pointed to a ledge and the cave behind it. "Ryan, remember this spot?"

I nodded. "Is that what spooked you? We'll soon be out of the darkness. Sara, trust me. Everything is okay and you'll be fine."

She replied, "That ledge is the exact spot where you shoved me into this god-awful river. The only thing I could think of doing was to call you something I had never, ever called anyone before or since. Whenever I am reminded of it, it makes my blood boil. I'll bet you don't even remember what I said—you were so out of it. After seeing it again, I've changed my attitude. I realize what you did saved my life. I wish to apologize for what I called you, even though fifteen years have passed since it happened."

As we emerged into daylight, she asked, "Please, please don't tell anyone how I felt and that I needed a dose of your courage to get me through that ordeal."

Before answering, I saw several of our crew milling around, shouting words of encouragement, and, of course, many had their electronics ready to shoot any selfies they thought worthwhile. As I stepped onto the dock, one of the spectators asked, "Did this trip bring back old memories, and were you scared?"

"We thought it a great experience! Yes, it brought back memories, many of which were pleasant, some not so pleasant. We surely do remember those horrible moments when the temple collapsed and that it was touch-and-go until Sara and a host of brave souls came to our rescue. Whenever I mention our travails, Sara reminds me that we must live in the present and let the past stay where it belongs."

Sara ran over, threw her arms around me, and said, "You are a wonderfully, convincing liar! Thanks for once again rescuing me. How about it? Do you forgive me?"

"Only if you tell me what you called me!"

"Not a chance! If you think I'm going to ruin a great friendship, you are delusional. Now, give me a hug, and let's get this ordeal over and done with."

I gave her a hard stare. "Sara, at that time we were under tremendous stress.

The only thing I concentrated on was making sure you got out of there alive. The rush of the water and the shouting drowned out whatever it was you said."

I gave her a peck, a hug, and said, "Sara, we will always be okay with each other!"

That brought a rain of tears and out came the tissues, which was followed by a big smile when she said, "Ryan Keshaw, you have made my day in more ways than you can ever imagine."

I walked over to where Juma and Catherine were standing. They had been taking in the drama that developed, and I gave Juma a hug. "My friend, if it hadn't been for you, Ben, Sara, and Rafael, we would never have made it out of that mess, alive.

"Catherine, without your insights, directions, and caring, our future would have been in serious doubt."

I quietly asked, "I presume green remains your favorite color?"

Much to the surprise of Juma and Allie Lea, she whacked me on the head and replied, "And I thought you were color-blind!"

As we ambled to the river, Catherine remarked, "Speaking of pulling one's chestnuts out of the fire, I loved it when you took Sara's hand and sprinted for the dock and the rafts. A large number of soles were risked in what Ahau hopes will be a popular, money-making added attraction for the temple and the town of Nuevo Ciudad. Unfortunately, he will be unable to help you in your endeavors in Peru. Make the most of your dinner tonight and remember my warning. Your toughest challenges lie ahead. Several lives will depend on your judgment. Don't make hasty decisions and remember your tendency to shoot from the hip."

Meanwhile, Allie Lea had been chugging up the hill, and between huffing and puffing, she exclaimed, "Change of plans! I'm asking all previous dig members to gather at the helio pad for a group picture. It's only proper we have a photo to remind us of how young and eager we once were, and that we had a hand in discovering an archaeological mystery, or two, that had been hidden ages ago."

After a bit of posturing, trips to the bathroom, and primping, the deed was done. She announced she'd received approval to expand the project. She was deluged with a storm of questions and several thought they could get out of her the role they would play. Little did she or anyone else know, I am counting on tonight's dinner partners to bring clarity to my ideas and fill in some of the cracks. Allie Lea will have to be well-versed regarding our recommendations when she makes her presentation to Jim Hamilton. I waded into the crowd surrounding her, put my arm around her shoulder, and said, "Enough, I think a short recess is in order."

Allie Lea retorted, "You meant a short swim and all that goes with it is in order for one Ryan Keshaw, didn't you?"

I said, "That would be nice, but I believe a private question-and-answer session is in order for the Ryan Keshaws before tonight's dinner, and for that, we need a bit of privacy."

She coyly asked, "And, why would that be señor Keshaw? Was there a problem with my presentation? I thought I handled the question-and-answer session pretty well."

I nodded my head. "Your presentation set the stage by creating an aura of expectancy. The project I have in mind is a two-part scenario, and for the life of me, I'm not sure how or what our people should be told."

She hesitantly said, "Mr. Know-It-All, it's a little late in the game to bring this to my attention. Unless you think we can pull the proverbial rabbit out of the hat, we will have an information crisis. Surely everyone doesn't expect to take part in our new project. I too am at a loss as to how we should proceed."

I spread out on our bed, sans everything but my underwear, and after a few minutes, I asked, "Do you want to take notes or do you want me to wing it?"

"Ryan, there are times when I have no idea whether you are pulling my chain or if you are deadly serious. Of course, I'll take notes. Let it flow and see how it plays. We have almost two hours before we meet Sara and Rafael for dinner, so we better get started. Stop staring at my cleavage; we're here for work. Play comes later, but that's not an iron-clad promise."

I said, "Okay, spoilsport, here goes: Since circumstances have changed, we should tell Sara and Rafael about both phases of your new project. Make your announcement fairly innocuous; refrain from making it a big deal We cannot have the local Inca and our people wondering if we are doing anything other than what was initially agreed upon.

"For starters, I recommend that Steve obtain a copy of the contract signed and approved by their Minister of Antiquities. We must be absolutely certain that the Smithsonian has the rights to conduct further drone tests. This would conclude the first phase of our project. Initiating the second phase hinges on a successful phase one. I have possibly made understandable the riddle that our Inca friend and RK have been bandying about. The drone mapping must be reconfigured to explore the area adjacent to Machu Picchu and continue along the Urubamba River for some six or seven miles.

"At some point, the Peruvian officials will ask for a report. They will no doubt take an added interest if they learn that we plan to reprogram the drones and they zero in on the area surrounding their favorite cash cow, Machu Picchu. This would not be the time for anyone in our crew to hint or talk about anything but phase one.

"Should phase one be a success, it's only natural we widen our search for the tomb of Pachacuti, who no doubt was the most famous of all Inca Sabas. Many Inca will react with pride and help us where possible. I suspect some will respond unfavorably. I've asked Rafael if Larco is willing to share their headquarters or base camp, which I understand is in a delightful but small town called Ollantaytambo. It is reasonably close to the area we seek to map and near the Urubamba River that flows through the Inca's Sacred Valley.

"Most Inca consider drones to be flying gods and regard them in awe. According to my research, there are others who not only fear them, but are always on the lookout to destroy any that fall to earth. Anyone trekking into the surrounding countryside should keep this thought in mind. Eric has a storehouse of knowledge and experience in the areas of ALSM and flight detection ranging, and he is pretty much up the learning curve concerning drones. No doubt, he will prove to be invaluable to our needs. It's up to you to handle Ashley.

"I guess you and Lynne have already worked out travel arrangements for next week. Speaking of travel arrangements, I haven't seen hide nor hair of RK and Acahuana. I presume they attended the ceremonies."

"Señor Keshaw, you just touched on a delicate matter. Early this morning, Rodrigo flew them to the La Aurora airport in Guatemala City where they had connections to fly to Lima. It seems that Acahuana and our son will be working on an important task for the Larco museum. They should have stayed for the ceremony, but they were bound and determined to leave."

I asked, "RK is our son, isn't he? The last time I looked I didn't see any evidence of his being gainfully employed. He's still on our payroll, isn't he? Me thinks that it's time to rein him in financially; then we will see how many decisions he makes on the short end of his bank balance."

Allie Lea lowered her head. "Earlier in the week, RK floated the idea of leaving early. At that time, it never entered my head that he and Acahuana planned to skip the entire ceremony. So, get out the wet noodles and give me a few lashes."

"Allie Lea, you have earned one of my favorite lines: Screwed again. Forget blaming yourself. Let's move on to the guts of my thoughts and that is phase two."

"Okay, but I need a few minutes to compose a message and then speak with Sandy. Provided I can catch her, I'll ask her to see that the crew is informed regarding the Sunday meeting."

"I'm at the most important part of my reasoning and you talk about sending a text to Sandy. Who the hell is Sandy? I was under the impression Erica is your executive assistant."

"Mr. Rip Van Winkle, several days ago I mentioned that Erica would be leaving. She has been seeing a good bit of Frank Johnson, one of the Smithsonian's up-and-coming managers, and they decided it was time to tie the knot. She gave me plenty of notice, hence Sandy.

"I'll wager that tidbit of information was nothing more than a blip on your radar screen and received only a nanosecond of your interest span. All because Erica occasionally busted your balls over some of your trivial, hip-shooting, nonsensical bull crap; she wouldn't have anything to do with it, would she? Sandy's a quick study in organization and figures, and she's filled in for Erica on several previous occasions. Erica informed me of her decision and I put in a request to promote Sandy as my executive assistant. Her manager was agreeable, despite her being his most valued associate. Sandy was appreciative of the opportunity, and I am damn glad of it. As a matter of further interest, she, too, is a mountaineer. Ryan, don't go snarky on me, because I'm not the least bit interested in one of your famous grunts. Do you get my drift, sweetheart?"

When Allie Lea is serious, I know I'd better have my A game and do away with the foolishness. Otherwise, she and Sara will team up, and that's trouble in River City—for me.

We dressed and emerged as the loving couple we are, ready to enjoy a memorable evening. Allie Lea appointed me as the assigned driver, so I dutifully made my way to into señor Urgar's cavernous garage, found her little red wagon, and picked up my three passengers. The ride into town was short; despite that, silence reigned.

Chapter 5

* * *

Despite the Best of Intentions, Plans and Parlays Often Go Awry

$\mathcal{B}$ased on Ahau's recommendation, I had reserved a small, private room in Chichi's *Mucho Grande* eatery. We pulled into the parking lot and, as we piled out, Rafael said, "I trust tonight's dinner won't be as somber as our ride."

Sara picked up the gauntlet and slyly said, "I wonder why that was."

I realized the perfect opportunity to even the score was staring me right in the face.

"Sara, our ride was like a pre-season football game. The players' thoughts are centered on impressing the coaches, performing their assigned roles, and doing damn little other than avoiding getting hurt, and expending as little energy as possible. Once the regular season starts, look out because that's when the fireworks really begin."

Sara remarked, "Ryan, I thought you were into horse racing. I don't see the correlation."

"Sara, it's all the same. The next time you visit the races, pay particular attention to how the horses react during the ten-minute post parade that precedes each race. Observing how your horse performs during the warm-up period will often keep you from betting on a horse that's not on his game, causing you to lose a bundle whenever you visit a race track."

As we were being ushered to our private dinning room, I said, "The warm-up and/or the post parade is over."

She turned to Allie Lea. "I didn't see that one coming. Ryan can be so charming and then, wham, without any warning, out jumps a different persona. I guess I'm in for it tonight, despite my thinking we were going to have a peaceful non-contentious affair."

Allie Lea put her arm around me. "Sara, Ryan may be the jockey in whatever race we run, but he knows he wouldn't go anywhere without his favorite mare."

Sara started laughing, turned to Rafael, and asked, "Well, darling, am I the jockey or the horse in the race to the finish line?"

He gazed into her eyes, gave a short "neigh, neigh," sat down, and said to the patient waiter, "We'll take a menu, and then you can get our drink order."

Dinner was great, and the Famosa beer even better. I thought I'd order another beer, but after Rafael told me that particular *cerveza* was fermented with saliva, I quickly changed my mind.

When he dropped that bit of information, Allie Lea howled. Sara stuffed her napkin into her mouth to keep the nearby patrons from hearing her give out with several belly laughs.

I felt like Willy Lump, Lump and to escape further embarrassment, I swung right into action and announced, "I've made a breakthrough which should help us solve the riddle that Acahuana gave to RK some fifteen years ago.

"Rafael, I'm unaware of the progress you've made in this area, and I don't wish to step on your toes; so feel free to dive in if you have other or conflicting thoughts. I've arranged the words in unscrambled or, what I believe to be, logical order. The first word should be *adivino,* as it stands for soothsayer. This figures, as my reasoning has to do with a recent meeting I had with Catherine, the Maya fortune teller. Her words of advice were hard to take, let alone understand. She indicated our efforts would prove to be most difficult and successful only to a degree, and that lives would be at stake. She also said,

'Ahau will not be able to provide any Maya support and the local Inca will be anything but helpful.'

"She thought that despite my impulsive nature, I've been very fortunate. And if I wish to stay that way, my decision-making must be sound and no shooting from the hip. Unlike our previous conversations, she closed with a warning I found difficult to accept."

Sara leaned forward, put both elbows on the table, and announced, "We came here for an enjoyable dinner with two dear friends. So far, all I have heard is some tough love. By the way, what was the last pearl she laid on you?"

I replied, "She thought Allie Lea should think twice before seeking the green light to proceed any further before searching Pachacuti's tomb. Sara, I agree with you and Rafael. How's that for an introduction to an already questionable undertaking?"

They stiffened, nervously shifting in their chairs.

Sara looked at Rafael when she said, "Rafael, we too were lucky once. Is it possible that Catherine and the spirit world have sent a message that applies to us as well?"

Rafael nodded. "We need a little time to discuss our reaction to what we're about to hear. But prior to that, we must hear the rest of señor Ryan's deductions. Please continue, amigo."

Allie Lea interjected, "Of course, there will be time to hear you out even if we have to stay here all night. I have been absorbing what Ryan said, thinking how I can weave his remarks into my call to Jim Hamilton. Okay, Ryan, I promise not to interrupt. On with the show."

I continued, "The second word, *Puric,* stands for head of the family and confirms that we should be looking for a male. This bit of knowledge furnishes us a most important, beginning piece of the puzzle. Female rulers in the Inca empire were in the distinct minority, thus any female internments never rivaled those of the overwhelming male majority.

"The third word, *Sinchi,* means ruler, king, or emperor. Understanding the meaning of this word is of vital importance. The one we seek would have been known as the *Sapa Inca,* which means he was known throughout the Inca empire as *the man* or the all powerful *Sapa Inca.* The burial place we seek houses a ruler of great accomplishments, one who was known as Pachacuti, the most famous ruler the Inca have ever known. His final resting place would also house his current Queen. It is the custom that the reigning king's wife be mummified along with her husband. I don't believe divorce or annulment was a part of their lexicon."

That bit of reasoning earned me a swift kick in the shins by Allie Lea and Sara glared at me and gave me the "cut it out" sign.

Thank goodness Rafael said, "I can't contain myself any longer. Señor Ryan, do you realize the significance of what you have deduced? Pachacuti rose to become the emperor of the entire Inca empire. He is the one who had Machu Picchu built for himself and his family's living quarters. I can't wait to hear how you came up with such an important bit of reasoning."

I continued, "The fourth word, *Huaca,* means sacred site. Machu Picchu is situated above the Sacred Valley of the Incas. It narrows one's search if, indeed, the person whose remains they seek is, in fact, Pachacuti. He died of a lingering terminal illness, thus giving him time to carefully choose his final resting place. I'll bet dollars to doughnuts he chose to be interred somewhere close to his beloved Machu Picchu valley and home.

"The fifth word, *Chullpa,* means burial vault. An important reminder is that the place of internment would require no above-ground digging or mounds that could be easily looted. To my way of thinking, this pretty much narrows our search to look for a cave burial site within the Sacred Valley area that borders the Urubamba River canyons.

"Much has been said about the ruler Pachacuti. During my research, one thing jumped out and got my attention—Pachacuti loved gold and jewels in abundance. No doubt, he carefully chose such a place to hide the *gifts* he expected to sustain him throughout his Inca afterlife.

"I also stumbled across a fact that not only blew my mind, but I found difficult to comprehend. Once I grasped the enormity of what I learned, I began to cross-check my results, seeking verification that I correctly understood the results of my research. Pachacuti seldom walked, even from his childhood to the day he died. He was always carried everywhere on a palanquin whenever he was out and about. His six to eight bearers received special training to make sure the Gifted One had one a smooth ride. Can you imagine he lived to be 103 years of age and ruled for many years? As his successful warring tactics grew, the palanquins on which he rode were encrusted with more and more precious jewels, and the frame itself was covered with gold. From the looks on your faces, you're, no doubt, wondering how this information will impact us.

"That bothered me as well. As his palanquin became laden down with the additional spoils of war, the frames had to be enlarged, requiring a wider entrance to his future burial vault. I paused to quench my thirst. The Moza beer tasted good as I continued.

"Despite being buried six hundred years ago, the looters and archaeologists have all drawn blanks when it came to finding his final resting place. The sixth word, *Tocco,* reinforces my thinking that my logic is on the right track; the word *Tocco* means a cave. It makes sense for us to look for grassy areas that share an outcropping of rocks along the Urubamba River somewhere within the Inca's Sacred Valley.

"The use of drones for mapping the area is vital. While others have looked, I doubt that they had a map such as the one we have. This information plus the six-word riddle together allow us to program the drones using the parameters and the algorithms that are needed to conduct such a search.

"Eric will have Larco's mainframe at his fingertips, allowing him to program each drone to complete a regression search of each area it maps. He will be able to simulate things and places exactly as they were years or centuries ago, such as looking for ancient, well-worn footpaths, in addition to mapping any anomalies on the faces of the mountains and gorges.

"However," I said, taking another sip of that smooth beer, "there is a fly in the ointment that, for once, works to our advantage. The drones the company has been testing are programmed to stay airborne for several hours per flight. Eric has worked with the Titan techies and they believe our drones' air time should not exceed thirty-five to forty-five minutes, which in the long run, saves us time and money.

"Published sources say Facebook has bought Titan Aerospace. This is a small company located in New Mexico with a deep experimental drone bench, according to *TechCrunch.* For now, Titans' brain power is working to develop a pilotless drone intended to stay in flight for five years at a stretch. They are also working with Facebook and their drone team who are taking advantage of Peru's liberal drone regulations, something they are unable to do in the US because of the difficult regulatory process. We should get our K Street lawyers and have them work out a contract that covers most contingencies, provided our exploration doesn't exceed two years."

Rafael said, "Based on your findings, I positioned the drones to map the wrong areas. I wish I had spoken with you before now; we would have saved many soles (Peruvian currency)."

Allie Lea jumped in. "Don't beat yourself up. Ryan came up with this scenario a short while ago. He ran some, but not all, of his ideas by me yesterday. I don't wish to be the one to throw cold water on what appears to be a very logical series of deductions, but how in the world will I tell Jim Hamilton, let alone sell, the idea of an addition to our existing project? Testing drones is one thing; searching for the remains of a ruler who was buried six hundred years ago is another kettle of fish, not to mention the extra cost."

Sara sat there taking it all in, and then she came out with, "I guess it won't be long before we can expect several Facebook experts to invade our little fiefdom and stick their noses into what, so far, is our project."

I remarked, "Sara, I suspect you're right. Someone had better get the Hookways' reservations secured; otherwise, they might have to camp out."

Sara asked, "Ryan, did I hear the word volunteer sail in from you? Or better yet, 'Screwed again.'"

She and Allie Lea couldn't help but giggle when they said, "Thank you, oh great leader!"

The waiter appeared with our desserts and then sang a few bars of the rock and roll hit, "Yummy, Yummy, Yummy (I Got Love in My Tummy)." Before departing, he said, "This is our way of saying you are being served a very special musical dessert. We are confident you'll sing its praises on your way home. For the señoras, I have here a copy of the ingredients in case you wish to make your señor happy."

The dessert was a light sponge cake over which the waiter sparingly poured a local wine. He spooned a thin champagne glacé over the cake and lit a match; the cake burst into a rosy glow and when the blaze died out, he cut each of us a healthy slice.

"It is best eaten before it loses its special aroma and flavor which come from the heated wine. I trust each of you will enjoy this special dessert."

Sara said, "That, my friends, was worth whatever price they charge! I wish they had a little live music to go with it. What a stimulating evening! Wouldn't you say so, Ryan? I notice you have a look of concern, but I think your worries are premature. Hold those thoughts for a minute or so. I have to take a quick pee. Care to join me, Allie Lea?"

After the señoras returned, I replied, "Sara, why the mystery?"

She laughed and said, "When I first visited the ladies room, I asked the owner, knowing how you love plastic, does Mucho Grande take plastic?

He replied, 'But of course, señorita!' Rafael and I wish to thank you for inviting us, not to mention Ryan's generosity in picking up the tab."

I winced. "Rafael, I presume you're taking lessons. Speaking of lessons, we still need to bail out Allie Lea and craft a response that Jim Hamilton will buy. I know just the spot where we can find privacy and free beer. I'll get the car."

On the way home Allie Lea hummed a few bars of "Yummy, Yummy" and then said, "I echo Sara's thoughts. That dessert was just about the best I have ever had and to think you picked up the check made it even more memorable."

"How about it honey? Anything you wish to add?"

I gritted my teeth and said, "We'll be home in about five minutes. Allie Lea, too bad you didn't get our waiter to cut another piece of that world-class dessert for carryout."

The only answer I heard was a light snicker and the response, "Not on the expense account lover boy."

I pulled up at the hacienda and, unexpectedly, Allie Lea leaned over and remarked, "You are in for a surprise and a change in plans regarding tomorrow's meeting."

She then skipped along to the door Rafael was holding for her. I thought there is only one reason for Allie Lea to be so ebullient and that's because Sara is finally pregnant."

Then I pondered, if Sara really is pregnant, this presents a new set of problems that neither Allie Lea or I ever considered. I dread thinking of how our project will be affected. In the back of my mind, I thought that if events on our project went awry, Sara's mountaineering skills would be sorely missed.

After parking the wagon, I visited the restroom, doused my face with cold water, and sought out my friends. They had staked out a spot on the far end of the hacienda and the gals were in deep conversation. Rafael patted the empty seat beside him and remarked, "Amigo, we are in for a long night. We might as well make ourselves comfortable and be prepared to listen to what the so-called weaker sex has in mind for us."

I said, "At least the temperature is comfortable and the sights from our vantage point are almost unbelievable. I didn't realize there were so many stars, and, fortunately, the bats are doing their part in keeping the bug population under control. Rafael, speaking of control, I think our señoras have arrived at a conclusion."

Allie Lea and Sara excused themselves. "Don't you guys go wandering off; we'll be back in a jiffy."

I looked at Rafael. "Is this where that special announcement will be made?"

He laughed. "I believe so. It is not in my best interest to upstage Sara; this is her show."

Suddenly, our señoras came charging onto the veranda, and they were not alone. They had rounded up most of our crew, and Sara said, "Such an occasion deserves to be shared with friends."

Allie Lea produced several glasses and, in short order, Anita followed, carrying a couple bottles of the bubbly.

Sara asked Rafael to join her and exclaimed to the assembled, after a long and exciting period of stops and starts, "I am finally pregnant!"

A beaming Allie Lea found a spoon and tapped on her glass. "Sara and Rafael may you remain as happy in the days ahead as you are now!

"It seems as though today is our good-fortune day. After speaking with Jim Hamilton, our meeting will be abbreviated due to a change in plans. I believe each of you will be pleased with the change; in fact, many of you might even say, 'Wow!'"

I meandered over to where Jim Leachy was holding court. Before I could ask him a lingering question, he said, "Based on what I've heard and observed, I'd say you are up the proverbial creek without a paddle. Whatever you're planning, count on me to be there when you need a helping hand; just don't expect me to suddenly acquire Sara's mountain-climbing skills. We'll talk later." He gave me a manly hug and went back to join the merrymakers.

I felt a light tap on my shoulder and Allie Lea whispered, "It's time for us to vamoose and turn the floor over to the 'newbies.' This is their time in the sun. You and I need to have a serious discussion regarding our change in plans. I want your input, and, yes, even some of your hip-shooting thoughts. Shall we go?"

I had to laugh when I asked, "You're that desperate, are you? I noticed how you teared up when you and Sara were first talking. I presume you are thinking it would be nice to have another child, or are you? If you are, I can see a good bit of practice awaits yours truly."

She replied, "Ryan Keshaw, at times, you can be utterly charming, and then there are moments when I could just throttle or muzzle you. Now is the time for romance!"

"Okay, I'll get the tiara." When I didn't get an answer, I saw Allie Lea in conversation with Anita. I know when it's time to change tactics; otherwise, the battle is often lost. I unlocked our bedroom door, undressed, and awaited the queen's entrance, which wasn't long in coming.

She sighed as she slipped out of her clothes and stepped into the shower saying, "This and a good old-fashioned eight hours of sleep is exactly what I need, so don't get any ideas.

"Sara's announcement took the wind out of our sails. I now know how it must feel when a fighter takes one in the gut. This shower is downright heavenly. Already, I feel more relaxed than I have in days. I'm dreading the call to Jim, because of the change in dynamics and the shuffling of assignments that Sara's condition will bring about. I realize you considered her your backup, in case unexpected problems arose."

"Little one, don't buy trouble before you are forced to face it. As far as Jim is concerned, I don't see why you have to make Sara's pregnancy an issue, other than making it a passing item. Stick to your original game plan and, for goodness' sakes, don't throw any additional monkey wrenches into his thinking.

"He's a money man, and a logical thinker. He will jump for joy, provided you paint him a compelling picture of our deceased friend. Remember, he's responsible for keeping the Smithsonian in the forefront of the archaeology field. Play that tune, and you will inflame his imagination. Before you complete your call, you will hear him heave a big sigh and then remind you, 'It's your show to handle, but watch the costs!'"

Allie Lea was now seated on the edge of the bed, smiling, and sans her shortie, when she asked, "Did you find my tiara? I don't think we need to spend any more of this glorious night talking. Jim Hamilton is the least of my concerns, lover boy."

I replied, "When you roll out the love-boat carpet so abruptly, I'll wager you have another surprise just waiting in the wings for this poor, dumb cluck to stumble into."

The rest of the night proved to be uneventful, up to five a.m., when our sleep was interrupted by the shrill ringing of Allie Lea's iPhone. She shook me, said, "Wish me luck," and sailed into her presentation with Jim.

I thought it best to give her some privacy, so I donned my running togs, and quietly made my way to the kitchen; on my way out, I grabbed a muffin and a mug of fresh orange juice.

Marjua peeked her head from behind the oven, shook her apron, and laughed as the flour flew. She asked, "Señor, what's wrong? Why are you up so early? I'm sure you didn't come to help me with the baking or were you just hungry for some of my fresh out-of-the-oven goodies?"

I replied, "As soon as I finish my orange juice and this delicious muffin, I'm yours to help in any way I can, and then I'm off for a short jog."

She surprised me when she said, "I am short a señora; it would be *bueno* if you would help set up the tables for our breakfast amigos who will soon be arriving, ready to eat."

"Marjua, that I can do. Where do you keep the silverware, plates, and glasses?"

I had just finished setting the tables when in walked a deliciously happy Allie Lea who said, "You nailed it! Jim bought my suggestions lock, stock, and barrel." She paused, looked around, and asked, "What in the world are you doing? Marjua is the boss of the food and baking areas; she will have your hide for intruding in her domain."

Marjua appeared with a plate of steaming hot goodies and said, "Señor is my number *uno* amigo. Help yourself to the raspberry *buñelos* and the fresh oatmeal on the table your *hombre* just finished setting."

Allie Lea's state of euphoria was evident when she explained how she approached Jim and heard his response. She said, "Ryan I don't know why I didn't think earlier of a change in the meeting schedule. On the spur of the moment, I recommended our jet's flight plan be altered. Sending the jet to Dulles and then returning via Lima is not cost effective. Flying our crew direct to Lima will give everyone a couple of days to explore and help with our new plans. Whatta ya' think, *compadre*?"

"As Alice said, 'Things get curiouser and curiouser?' Will our people love it? Of course they will! They would be dumb not to. Can you find enough tasks to keep them semi-busy for the two or three extra days? Evidently, Jim believes there was a genuine reason to approve our plan. I'm all for doing as you suggest. Besides, neither of us have yet to tour Machu Picchu. By chance, that thought, no doubt, entered your reasoning?"

She laughed. "You, dog, you! I knew you would jump to that conclusion. But the answer is no. I think before this is all over, Machu Picchu will figure heavily in our plans for exploration. The more we know about it and the surrounding areas, the better our chances of success.

"I can't think of a reason why we shouldn't pack up and leave on Tuesday; our work here is pretty much finished. As much as I would like to spend more time with our friends, this new project excites me, and since Jim gave us the green light, it's time for us to get at it. How about it?"

"Works for me. Now that you are in a creative mood, how about booking the Mucho Grande restaurant for a private crew party tomorrow night? Make it a real blowout. Invite Marjua, her crew, the grandmothers, Rodrigo, and all others who had a hand in helping make our archaeological dreams come true. I'll see if señor Urgar can chum up a few musicians; they will give the party a warm, rosy glow. This will be a party that won't soon be forgotten. God knows, we have been treated like royalty and our gesture will be deeply appreciated. On a more sobering thought, the expense of this farewell party should be billed to the Smithsonian. You have resisted my previous entreaties on this subject, and before I go putting our thoughts into motion, I need to know we are on the same page."

Allie Lea grinned, much like the Cheshire Cat, saying, "Need I remind you that the Mucho Grande takes plastic?" She rummaged in her purse, handed me her Smithsonian charge card, and remarked, "I think that about does it. The analytics and arrangements are now in your hands."

"Allie Lea, why throw those monkeys on my back? I realize the true meaning of what you are politely saying, 'Ryan, don't screw up!'"

She put her arm around me and purred, "I would never think that except on rare occasions."

I asked, "Is this one of those rare occasions? For if it is, you will have to do the packing for both of us; I will be much too busy to do anything other than my superior's bidding. I must make sure I don't screw up what had started out as a simple set of ideas and instructions."

She replied, "My, oh, my, aren't we testy? Here come señor Urgar and Anita; do you want me to break the news about our change of plans and the party, or do you wish to do it?"

"You're the boss, and this is one of your perks. Don't screw it up!"

I quickly moved out of her line of fire as she gave me one of those "up yours" looks, finger, and all! Out of the corner of my eye, I saw Doubtful shaking his head and the word *tonto* (dumb) popped into my mind. I knew it was time to begin making the arrangements for our big soiree. Before I could get started, Ashley waved. "Hold on, general, I have a message for your ears only. I know a little secret and I know who is responsible. Care to listen?"

I often ignore what she calls her juicy tidbits, but she got my attention when she said, "I need a slice of your valuable time, as well as some privacy to convey an exciting thought or two just for your ears!"

Before Ashley got started, I said, "In case you haven't heard, Allie Lea plans to put on a bash tomorrow night and I need help with the logistics.

"Also, she plans a welcome surprise at tonight's meeting. I can't say any more other than ask you a question: have you ever been to Lima or Ollantaytambo?"

She leaned back in her chair, started laughing, and said, "I see you are up to your old tricks. I thought of you when I was shopping at Barnes and Nobles and saw a copy of *The Adventures of Tom Sawyer*. Being around you requires that one must always be on his or her toes and expect to be had, one way or the other. Okay, I've said my piece. Now tell me, what it is that you need?"

Ashley reached down into the bag she generally carries, extracted a small note pad, and said, "Get started, señor Keshaw. Your secretary is ready."

Fifteen minutes later, she closed her pad and said, "Now, tell me about the juicy stuff and, more specifically, about that little hint or question you so effortlessly threw at me."

"I had almost forgotten what a good listener you are. Eric will play a key role in both phases in Lima and Ollantaytambo. Your silence is essential. Any more info will have to come from Allie Lea; other than that, let's get started. My first task is to make reservations for tomorrow's farewell party at the Mucho Grande restaurant. *Besos,* señora, *besos* (kisses)!"

As I slowly edged away, Ashley stood there with her hands on her hips, and said, "You didn't have to handcuff me to get me to agree to participate in another of your wild and exciting projects."

I borrowed Allie Lea's wagon and made tracks for the Mucho Grande. Surprisingly, I ran into Ahau and Elena. They seem to generate a crowd wherever they go, but when he spotted me, he motioned me to follow. He and Elena were on their way to the centuries-old church to participate in a friend's wedding.

He said, "Stick around, amigo. I won't be long." I settled down on one of the church steps that wasn't copal-encrusted and out of the sun's blazing rays. I wondered why he asked me to wait, but knowing Ahau, he rarely does anything without a purpose. The doors to the church were finally flung open, and the happy couple and their friends emerged doing high fives, ready to take on the world.

I looked for Ahau, but he was nowhere to be found. After working my way into the cool interior, I saw him sitting in a pew, and he said, "I have been so busy that I haven't had any time to spend with you. I know you have a lot on your plate as well, so I'll be brief. I'm aware of what you wish to accomplish.

"Without going into any further details, carefully consider your actions. Acahuana is growing into the leadership role Espiritius had expected. His mountain Inca respect and protect him. I cannot say the same for the Inca that live and work throughout Machu Picchu's sacred valley. Once they become aware of your intentions, they will look with suspicion on your venture. Their beloved Saba Inca, Pachacuti, in addition to being their most famous emperor, was considered a God and savior. That he was removed from mother earth six hundred years ago doesn't mean his remains are not being looked after. Be on guard. Otherwise, you or members of your archaeological group may find how unfriendly and deadly their mountains can be.

"Should you find what you seek and run into trouble, I recommend you have an escape or survival plan. Unless someone in your group is familiar with those mountains, you'll readily understand why they make such an excellent place for one just to disappear. I must go. Elena has to get home; she is cooking up a surprise for Allie Lea. *Adios* amigo. See you at the meeting."

Chapter 6

* * *

To Comprehend Mortality Is to Appreciate the True Meaning of Life

*D*riving back to señor Urgar's, I harkened back to Ahau's warning and wondered who in our group could develop and handle such a plan? I was so lost in thought that I almost hit a cow that was blocking the road. After a good bit of pounding on the steering wheel and using many Marine Corps expressions, the owner finally got the sonofabitch to move.

Despite the distraction, I knew I had a candidate in the person of Red O'Shaun, our VP in charge of research and development. The toys and gizmos he developed were responsible for helping us out of many previous tight situations. I hoped this project would be no different. The trick will be to get him away from Anna, his protective strong-willed Russian wife, long enough to properly explain the role I hoped he would play in our new project. Oh, well, such are the challenges of life.

Señor Urgar's great room was packed to the gills. There was a hush throughout as everyone was patiently awaiting Allie Lea's announcement. The rumor mill had been working overtime and I doubted if Allie Lea's remarks would come as a complete surprise.

She didn't disappoint them! When she said, "For openers, let's start with the special dinner we will be hosting at the Mucho Grande tomorrow night.

We wish to show our appreciation and love for our wonderful hosts, so don't be late. Any questions, see my main hombre, Ryan.

"The second part of my news has to do with a change of plans regarding our flight. Be prepared to board our bus on Tuesday, not Wednesday."

This brought a buzz and obviously most thought Allie Lea made a mistake. It didn't take long for several hands to wave.

"You heard right: Tuesday. I don't think any of you will want to miss our flight as our new destination is Lima, Peru, and not Dulles International. I just received approval to test some drones in partnership with the Larco Museum. If all goes as expected, there will be another project waiting in the wings.

"At this point, I don't expect to answer or speculate on any project that has yet to come to fruition. If this change in plans does not jibe with what you initially agreed upon, see Ryan. He will arrange transportation for you to Dulles."

That brought out several hoots, and one plucky person said, "You must be kidding. Miss out on the trip of a lifetime? Not on your life. I'm calling our babysitter and make sure she understands we will be delayed." The applause filled the room.

Allie Lea closed by saying, "Ollantaytambo and Machu Picchu are our ultimate destinations.

"It would be prudent for us to do a little bit of web surfing and familiarize ourselves with Lima, its surroundings, and customs. Señor Rafael will be our point man in charge of analytics in Lima, Ollyantambo, and Machu Picchu. Sara is our point person in charge of logistics. My principal role will be that of an observer and arbitrator, should it come to that.

"Señor Rafael and Sara have my absolute confidence. Señor Ryan is my minder, my confidant, and go-to guy."

That started the tittering and the finger pointing. At this point, Allie Lea turned, blew me a big kiss, and mimed, "Gotcha!" I returned the favor, gave her a sweeping bow, and intoned, "Yes, milady." Allie Lea then turned the delirious attendees loose, and they descended on Sara, Rafael, and Allie Lea.

I walked past the lectern, and as I did so, I saw I had a visitor. Doubtful was following me, despite my thinking that everything was peaches and cream.

I knew that at some point I would have to deal with Ahau and Catherine's warnings that were firmly pressed into my subconsciousness.

I was deep in thought when up walked Ashley who said, "If I didn't know better, I believe Doubtful is visiting you. Ryan, say it isn't so. Tell me that your thoughts or premonitions don't include me or Eric. I've have learned when you worry, others better take heed. You seem to have that sixth sense that says danger is at hand or just around the next mountain."

Her remarks completely blindsided me. I could only say no and then I saw a tear run down her cheek when she said, "Ryan, I'll never forget I owe you my life due to your quick thinking and unselfishness. I didn't mean to intrude into your private thoughts. Ignore my remarks, and let's join the rest; maybe some of their merriment will rub off on both of us." She gave me a kiss, took my hand, and pulled me into the throng.

Lord have mercy; I hoped that Allie Lea didn't observe my reaction. I wondered how I get myself in such predicaments, and, more importantly, how do I get out of this set of circumstances—without losing my cool? I looked behind me expecting to see Doubtful, but instead Jim made my radar. He laughingly said, "With this new turn of events, I have enough for either an extra-large book or two smaller ones." Jim gave me a friendly slap on the back and said, "Stay lucky ole buddy!"

Dammit all to hell! Why do so many of my friends take my skills for granted? That luck thing, if that is what they wish to call it, comes about only after a good bit of thought, planning, and perseverance. Thank goodness I'm not a big drinking man; otherwise, I'd get plastered and just vegetate. I heard Allie Lea's familiar, "Yoo-hoo" and when she saw me scrunched up on the far corner of the veranda, she exclaimed, "What in the hell are you doing out here all by yourself?"

I smiled and asked, "Can't a fellow have a few minutes of peace and quiet without everyone asking, 'Anything wrong?'"

She retorted, "Peace and quiet, my ass. I can spot your feeling-sorry mood a mile off."

Her remarks so pissed me off that I replied, "You don't know the half of it; get off my back." I huffed off looking for Rafael and Sara; I knew Doubtful wouldn't find a home there!

Later that night Allie Lea prodded me and said, "Here is my peace offering, and it comes with all my love and understanding." She then placed her tiara on my pillow and that was that.

Monday is one of those days I call, go-to-hell days because everything that could go wrong, did. Everyone was packing for Tuesday's flight, mailing home the things that they didn't think they'd need; in short, everyone was walking on eggs.

After talking Allie Lea into taking a swim, she invited Ken and Lynne to join us, which turned out to be very fortuitous, in that it gave me time to talk with Ken. I decided to play it straight up and asked, "Ken are you interested in a jaunt or two along the Urubamba River in Peru?" I didn't divulge the real reason for asking.

He gave me a big smile. "I'm game for any exploring you have in mind. I guess the real reason for asking has to do with my mom and dad. I'm capable of making my own decisions in life other than the need for money, which should be eliminated when I graduate."

A little bell went off that served to remind me to explain some of the possible pitfalls he or we might encounter. I thought what the heck? I'm dealing with a young, strong, smart man who is capable of making his own decisions. "I wanted to be sure that I made you aware we encountered some trying times on our last two excavations and have faced a dangerous situation or two."

He charged right back. "After living in Cairo for several years, my father and I often faced mobs of angry people who would have gladly torn off our faces when given the opportunity. I doubt we will encounter such trials in this part of the world. Like I said, I'm game and up to any challenge thrown at me. I am six foot three and 210 pounds, and the people in this part of the world are considerably smaller. Believe me, I am capable of holding my own, so count me in."

Lynne heard Ken's last words and said, "Ken, go easy.

"Dad, don't even think of roping Ken into one of your seemingly innocent ventures."

"Ken, before you commit, let me give you a few facts which Dad failed to mention; then you can talk about being counted in or not."

Allie Lea stood there looking baffled and forcefully said, "Lynne, I just came in on the tail end of your dad's conversation. You should be aware that any and all assignments have to be approved by me prior to participating in any part of this operation."

I didn't dare say anything as the mother lion was on the prowl. I didn't want any of her affections to drop on yours truly. I took the only way out and asked, "Ken, would you like to see Urgar's beach and the cavern behind the waterfall?"

He replied, "Lead on, McDuff." I won't say we moved in great haste, but we moved with alacrity.

Lynne made no move to join us, but I heard her say, "Mom, I let my emotions override my judgment. I had no business in that conversation."

She continued, "I'm aware you and Dad have had several close calls. However, Ken has had no experience in these types of excavations. I'll apologize to Dad and make Ken aware my remarks were off base. I promise not to interfere in any way in your business decisions. I'm old enough to know better, but my feelings toward Ken are pretty strong, and I don't want anything unfortunate to happen to him at this early stage of our relationship."

Allie Lea gave Lynne a hug and said, "We all have to learn, and sometimes it's painful, to say the least, but that is what life is all about—compromise, love, and understanding. Go get those two *hombres* and remind them it's time to make tracks for Mucho Grande and a night of fun and memories."

The dinner and the party was everything one could hope for. The owner saw to it that an astounding array of dishes kept coming and that the beer flowed like water. When it came time for dessert, he dimmed the lights and joined the waiters in singing (can you imagine?) the sentimental favorite "Auld Lang Syne" in Spanish. With a great deal of pomp and circumstance, the musical *grande* dessert was served, and did they ever make it a memorable occasion!

Midnight came and the party slowed as several said, "We have to get a few winks before boarding the 8:30 bus." I stayed until everyone was gone and signed the tab at 2:00 am. I didn't check the billing, but I made sure I included a 25 percent tip. I was that tired.

The owner dropped me off at señor Urgar's *estancia,* and I collapsed for the next five hours in a blissful sleep; then it was off to the races. You can bet I didn't load up on beer. I had no intention of being one of those anxious ones who unceremoniously had to ask the driver to pull off—quickly.

Breakfast was a quiet affair as most of us were dreading those narrow, treacherous, winding roads and the flight to Lima. However, Judy, Jim Leachy's wife, had gotten the gals together and they decided to present Marjua and each of her crew a gift that's well received all over the globe—Pesos, soles, quetzals, dollars, and other money in one form or another!

Allie Lea made sure I acknowledged this act of gratitude when she said, "Unexpected rewards show that acts of kindness, such as Judy's are indeed welcome. I presume you left the owner and his crew a plump service reward."

I smiled. "A 25 percent reward. How's that for gratitude?"

She gulped. "I didn't mean that plump!"

As our bus rolled into the La Aurora airport, I glimpsed the Smithsonian's jet parked at the executive terminal; it was surrounded by eight or nine maintenance guys. Jim Leachy groused, "I see those guys are a bit late in completing their 'go' checks. I wonder why it's taken them so long. Obviously, they had plenty of advance notice and time enough to make sure all checks were completed prior to our departure."

His wife, Judy, remarked, "Jim, give it a rest. All I hope is that the maintenance crew hasn't gone through a cutback or an expense reduction program in the past few days."

The baggage handlers knew what they were doing and they quickly stowed our luggage. Our flight crew signaled to the stragglers and motioned it was time to board. As Judy was boarding, I gave her a big grin and a thumbs-up sign. She giggled and responded, saying, "Señor Ryan, one must take advantage of each opportunity whenever it presents itself."

We were airborne in short order, and upon reaching our climbing altitude, the captain announced, "Radar tells us we are in for a smooth, on-time flight. Stay buckled up. I'm happy to report the bottled water made it, but the food didn't. It seems as though there was a mixup concerning another jet whose destination was also Lima. I fail to see how their five passengers will have the capacity to eat the food that was scheduled for our flight's sixteen passengers! Over and out."

His remarks brought a round of snickers and a few groans.

An hour into our flight, Allie Lea announced, "We will be working with a small drone manufacturing company in Ollantaytambo. Its role is to furnish the Larco and Smithsonian museums with a number of test drones. If the testing is successful, we will then seek approval from the proper authorities to expand our search.

"Inadvertent discussions regarding our goals will cause us problems. Eventually, this information will be public knowledge, but by then we should be well along in our testing, not to mention our overall goals. Should we be successful, looters, robbers, local treasure hunters, archaeologists, and the media will descend on us like a horde of locusts. Of course, they, too, will be seeking Pachacutie's supposed hidden wealth.

"Work assignments will be passed out tomorrow in the Larco's second floor conference room. We will be staying, for a short spell, at the Casa Inca, a small boutique hotel in the Miraflores district. According to Ryan, it's a delightful, well-run, small hotel, close to the beach, and great eating. As a special tip to the ladies, the Larcomar shopping center is within walking distance. Lima is home to Rafael and Sara; I'm sure they'll be happy to discuss, as well as answer, your questions, plus the do's and dont's of this great city. Rafael, any other instructions that I have overlooked?"

He smiled and announced, "Transportation is waiting. We will be using taxi metro cabs that are waiting at Terminal A. If you look to your left, you'll see they are ready to carry you and your luggage to our hotel. Señor Ryan is right; you will be very pleased with the accommodations. I wish to issue a word of warning: if you venture forth anywhere in this city, make sure you do not visit outside of the downtown area without an escort or guide.

"Lima is ringed with shanty settlements and, unfortunately, most of the occupants are poor and with little or no means of support. This is not an area you wish to visit for any reason. First timers often ask about the fog that seems to hang around the perimeter of the city. It is called the *garua* and normally doesn't affect the metro area. Many consider the *garua* a mystery because

Lima is flanked by a tropical desert. However, the *garua* is our seasonal fog and drizzle, and it's generally taken for granted.

"I don't recommend the displaying of jewelry when you are out and about. Casa Inca has plenty of safety deposit boxes. As to eating what, in the USA we call street food, be careful. Not all vendors are as sanitary as they should be. If you don't see it washed or thoroughly cooked, no matter how tantalizing, avoid it."

At this point, several hands were raised, and Red was first in asking, "How about the restaurants and directions to the museum?"

Rafael responded, "Ryan is a good source for places to eat. I'm sure he'll be happy to share his knowledge of the eateries located in El Centro, which is the center of Lima. The Larco Museum is housed in an eighteenth-century mansion built over the ruins of a seventh-century pre-Columbian pyramid. Our Inca museum gallery is the finest Inca collection in the world, specializing in genuine highland pre-Columbian artifacts.

"As a matter of interest, our cafe is also located in an old Chateau immediately adjacent to the museum and the food is *maravilloso*!

"Now to the museum's directions. It is but a short ten-minute walk and is located on Avenue Bolivar. For those who are not into a fitness regime, there is always a metro taxi close by."

Our metro taxi drivers wasted no time in loading our luggage. Check-in was quick, and several of our ladies said, "Let's take a stroll and see what that shopping center Sara was touting has to offer."

Allie Lea hung back and said, "Ryan and I are going to check out the beach."

I remarked, "If you think the water was cold at Urgar's, this is several times colder. So forget it."

She replied, "It's not the beach I plan to check out."

I looked perplexed and asked, "What's causing you such anxiety?"

"I wish to go to the museum."

I replied, "You what? We haven't been in our room for more than thirty minutes. Had no food for the last three hours, yet you want to go to the museum."

Then the light bulb went on and I got the picture. She said, "I wondered how long it would take you to get it. I'm disappointed that RK wasn't at the airport to greet us and, like any mother, I want to know our son is okay."

I wasn't about to get caught in that trap so I replied (tongue-in-cheek), "Since the whereabouts of our son is of the utmost importance, let's grab one of those metros, as time is, obviously, of the essence."

She looked daggers at me. "If you were a mother, which you aren't, you'd understand."

I remembered the great food at the cafe and said, "You'll see things a bit differently after you talk with RK, and we have some good food under our belts."

She said, "You're a bit late with that sweet talk, and at times, like now, you are acting like a smart-ass. Let's go."

It took all of five minutes for our metro to reach the museum, and guess who was sitting on the entrance steps?

Acahuana and RK were pointing and laughing at us. I wondered what prompted their outburst, so I asked, "What's up guys?"

RK gave his mom a big hug. "Mom, I guess you thought I'd be at the airport to greet you and I would have, except for the lack of forty dollars to pay the taxi metro guy. Acahuana and I figured you'd hotfoot it over to the museum as soon as possible to check on your darling! We have been waiting almost two hours and we're hungry."

Allie Lea's shoulders slumped, and she asked, "Couldn't you have borrowed a few dollars from señor Diego? After all, he runs the museum. I'm sure he would have helped you out."

RK laughed. "Señor Diego is on location at Machu Picchu, so we were stuck. Ever since we arrived, we have been hard at work in Larco's basement dusting and tagging a bunch of old stuff, including a few ancient paintings. After we eat, you might like to take a look at what we have done. Even though we have no idea of their value, we think some are pretty astounding."

I said, "Allie Lea, let's hit the Cafe. They serve outstanding food and take credit cards. You did bring yours, didn't you?"

RK said, "Dad, you always ask: why is it you always get in hot water! It's a wonder mom is as patient and forgiving as she is. Let's go. I know a shortcut to the Cafe."

As we made our way into the Cafe, Allie Lea remarked, "This is one of the most gorgeous restaurants I've ever seen. The flowers and the settings are a riot of color, and I could spend several hours examining these works of nature. I hope the food lives up to, what I believe will be, a most enjoyable start to our trip."

The señorita who was waiting on us overheard Allie Lea's remarks. "Better señora, better."

Acahuana asked, "Would you like me to recommend something from the menu"?

We closed our menus. "We're in your hands. While you are at it, please explain the purpose of this oblong vessel next to our table."

He grinned. "That vessel is known as a *Pacha Amanca* and is an earth oven. Don't touch it, as it is very hot. Lean over it and you'll notice a distinctive baking aroma. Food cooked this way is delicious, and the spices enhance the taste of whatever you select. *Almuerzo* is the term for our lunch and, in Lima, this is our main meal.

"Providing you are a lover of beef, I heartily recommend the *Loma Saltado*. This is beef tenderloin that has been marinated and supported with a host of spices and vegetables that are now cooking in the earth oven.

"If you are extra hungry, order the *sopa* of the day, which is a hearty soup, and is known as 'peasant food.' It is served only on Mondays throughout the restaurants in Lima. Another of the special soups that is a great favorite is the *shambar* soup; it consists of pork rinds, wheat, beans, green onions, and toasted corn.

"I notice you're eyeing those freshly baked loaves of white bread. All white bread baked in Peru is fortified with extra lard, butter, or shortening. The cuisine of Lima is known as fusion cuisine and has a strong creole influence due to our indigenous population. So what's everyone having?"

"The beef!"

When it came to desserts, Allie Lea insisted on having crêpes *dulce de leche*. When we were leaving, several members of our crew straggled in and asked, "How's the food?"

Allie Lea said, "Heavenly!"

On the way to the gardens, I reminded her of tomorrow's meeting. She snapped back with, "Why do you think I would overlook such an important task? While we are on the subject, do you have any additional thoughts you think I have overlooked?"

RK caught this bit of byplay and mimed, "Way to go, Mom!"

After admiring the museum's gardens, we cautiously made our way down the museum's three flights of stairs to Acahuana and RK's work station. I readily understood why they were eager to get this job over and done with. Despite the minimal lighting, the place was like a prison, and was it ever dusty! Artifacts and paintings were everywhere and space was at a premium. I thought a sale was indeed long overdue. It was obvious the boys had done a remarkable job. We were rummaging through a stack of paintings when RK said, "Dad, you won't find the painting I thought might interest you on this floor. It's on the upper part of the basement, along with all of the other objects we have cleaned and tagged. Come on, I'll show you."

"You mean there's more to this foreboding part of the museum?"

"Yep, a whole bunch more. We had to clean a space and provide a relatively dust-free area for the completed works, which are awaiting Sara's inspection and pricing. She has the knowledge and experience, and señor Diego trusts her judgment. Acahuana and I are betting a lucky member of mom's crew will be assigned to help and give her company. Otherwise, she may find her job to be somewhat spooky, unless she has another experienced person to work with. Allie Lea had already started toward the part of the museum where RK had parked the painting until we had a chance to look at it. After catching up with her, I remarked, "No doubt, Ashley will be your person *de jour* to work with Sara. Two lady tigers working together and no male supervision. That's a hoot!"

Allie Lea responded in a desultory manner, "Why must you always be so sexist? Still, as much as I hate to admit it, you're right. However, I think they will get along nicely. Sara and Ashley are top flight archaeologists. They will certainly enjoy examining a part of history that only a few ever dream about, let alone see.

"Don't forget Sara's expertise is with the Maya; Ashley's speciality is the Inca with a minor in the Maya civilization. Both of their talents will prove to be invaluable. Ashley has indicated she's not interested in any wild goose chases you dream up. So, put that in your pipe and smoke it. That's all the advice Dr. Keshaw has to offer, for now."

Chapter 7

* * *

Meet Felipe Guamán Poma de Ayala

I put my arm around RK and asked, "Why are you're being so persistent regarding that damn painting? I'm not in the mood to buy any painting—unless it was a self-portrait painted by Marilyn Monroe in the altogether—and certainly not one painted several hundred years ago and of all things, the Andes."

RK said, "Dad, I'm not pushing the painting, but I know how you like offbeat things. I thought this might pique your interest. Acahuana told me it was painted by the famous Inca historian and artist Felipe Guamán Poma de Ayala four hundred years ago.

"He titled it simply *The Andes.* The name surely fits, but for what reason? In our spare time, Acahuana and I did considerable research looking for an answer. We guessed he chose to honor the Andes, which the Inca consider God's gift to man. From all I have read, Machu Picchu and its awesome construction is reputed to be the seventh wonder of the world. Oh well, each to his own. Let's go! All this talking has made me thirsty. Dad, you coming?"

"Go ahead. Your mom and I wish to take a few minutes to examine *The Andes.* We'll meet you on the front steps. Here's a Ben Franklin; you guys earned your keep today."

RK looked at Acahuana and commented, "What did I tell you, mister Inca leader? Mom, I can generally figure out, but, Dad, that's another matter.

Mom is great at keeping him on track. The interesting part is that Dad is happy with that arrangement. As Dad said, 'We earned our keep today;' an ice cold Inka Cola is just what the doctor ordered, provided we can sit on the museum's steps and enjoy watching the señoritas."

We were deep into our watching when Acahuana asked, "Dude, do you think your mom will be interested in taking us along when they begin the drone testing? How about asking her if it's a possibility? I realize she'll discuss it with your dad, but that's okay. He's a fair guy, and maybe they will see fit to include us. One day in the future I will be my people's leader; when that day comes, I will seek to unite other Inca tribes, helping them to have a larger say in the governing of our nation. I realize it's just a dream, but dreams often come true, provided someone is there to nudge them along."

RK sat quietly before asking, "Amigo, señor leader, ruler-to-be, have you discussed any of these dreams with señor Rafael or anyone else? If you haven't, I have a suggestion: learn all that you can at that super-powered university you are attending. When it's your turn and time to lead, introduce your ideas a few at a time and when you are recognized as a leader, they'll support your dreams and ideas. I recommend you move slowly, bide your time, build a circle of friends who are thinkers and doers, but avoid politicians and lawyers!"

Acahuana looked thoughtfully at RK, and in a show of friendship, clasped RK by the shoulder and said, "Good advice amigo. You are my first circle friend, and I'm certain we will be friends for life. Here come your dad and mom. I wonder what he thought of the painting."

RK began laughing. "Dad, from the look on your face, I can tell that you have zero interest in buying that painting. If I am correct then, I have a proposition for you. How about lending me some money so I can buy it and make it the first painting of the collection I plan to start?"

Allie Lea almost turned purple trying to keep from laughing out loud. "Darling, he's got you there. He used you as a straw horse, trusting you wouldn't be interested thus clearing the path for himself. Evidently, some of those classes he's taking at college are paying off, or maybe he has been observing how you handle things."

I replied, "Either it's the altitude or that I am in need of a rest. If I understood your mother correctly, you and she expect me to shell out x number of dollars to buy that damn painting."

"Dad, that about sums it up. I'll set it aside, so it won't be included in the museum sale. I'll make señor Rafael aware of my intention. Now, if you give me your credit card numbers, that will seal the deal. I'll add the price in later."

"If you want it that bad, then the painting is yours. I'll adjust your spending allowance until its paid for."

"I'll be a sonofabitch. Dad, I thought you'd give it to me out of the goodness of your heart. While we are at it, I presume Acahuana and I will be joining the expedition when you leave for Machu Picchu. His being Inca might prove to be a needed asset."

I replied, "We'll think about it and talk with you tomorrow. Do you mind if your mother and I leave while we still have the clothes on our backs? Otherwise, we may raise an eyebrow or two for being like the emperor who walked the streets without any clothes."

We slowly made our way to the Inca Casa, and she remarked, "I'd like to forget it all and just enjoy some peace and quiet, at least for a few hours, if that's okay with you? However, I have a question that's been in the back of my mind since you agreed to pay for that painting."

With that said, I knew Doubtful would soon make an unwanted entrance. Sure enough, he was trotting along with us hoping to be acknowledged.

"When RK asked you to loan him the money for the painting, why did you give in so easily? It's not like you; it is so out of character."

I thought for a moment and replied, "The Inca Casa has good food, and since tonight will be warm and the skies clear, we can eat on our terrace. After that, a good night's sleep is just what we need."

Allie Lea looked questioningly when she said, "Ryan Keshaw, your sidestep is showing. Quit waffling and get to the point. I'm dying to hear how you plan to excuse or rationalize your actions."

I replied, "I don't know why I gave in so easily. The more I observed the detail on that painting, the more interested I became and, as I said, why, I don't know. Perhaps it was because it is a striking painting of the mountains that surround Machu Picchu and a memento of what I hope will be a successful venture. Despite it belonging to RK, it would still be in the family. I forgot to ask him if he noticed those small black dots or smudges on the mountain south of Machu Picchu. Had it not been for them, I would have purchased it for myself."

Allie Lea replied, "Why don't you ask him about them? Let's put that damn painting behind us and work on the assignments for tomorrow's meeting. After all, it's show time for one Ryan Keshaw, with or without Doubtful's help. By the time we finish dinner and work out the assignments, we'll be too pooped to pop. Speaking of Doubtful, until now he has been pretty scarce, and I hope he stays put and keeps out of my way. I'll arrange for room or patio service. Anything special you'd like to have in addition to dessert?"

"No, order whatever you wish and make it for two."

"I'll take a quick shower; and did you say we were eating on our patio? It looks like a glorious night, and if after dinner, we're both tired, the meeting assignments will wait. Okay? By the way, I just remembered we should have invited RK and Acahuana to share dinner with us."

"Allie Lea, ease up. I gave RK enough money for dinner and a night at one of their favorite hot spots. I don't think dinner with the 'fogies' was uppermost in their thoughts. You better hurry; our food will be here in a few minutes, or did you have something else in mind?

She stepped into the shower, giggling and murmured, "Some things never change!"

After a good night's sleep, we joined the rest of our crowd who were busily chomping down on the casa's great breakfast buffet. There was an air of anticipation wending its way throughout the room; everyone was envisioning how Allie Lea planned to use their skills and what their assignment would entail in Ollantaytambo.

The meeting got off to a welcome start when Allie Lea said, "This meeting will be brief; hold your questions until the end. Sara and Ashley have been cataloging and valuing the Larco's objects they deem worthy of the sale. Once they have completed their assignment, they'll join us."

"Eric is the expert we will defer to when it comes to the testing and programming of the drones. Drone command center is located on the second floor of the hotel La Casona de Yucay in Ollantaytambo. I've been told this is one neat hotel, and it's where we will be staying. It's a short walk to the center of the town and the train station to Machu Picchu. Titan Aerospace is providing the test drones. The drones are programmed to stay aloft for minimal periods of time and will be carrying some new state-of-the-art sensing devices. Our use of their drones will be confined to mapping the Sacred Valley of the Incas at heights of five hundred feet or less.

"Unlike the USA, Peru has as yet to issue regulations pertaining to the use of, or the heights, that drones can fly. Upon the meeting's conclusion, stop by the desk and pick up your kit containing directions, hotel instructions, and, most important of all, your assignments in this operation.

"Our jet is scheduled to leave Jorge Chavez Airport tomorrow at noon sharp. Should anyone be inclined to stay over an extra day, the expenses you incur will be on you. Bus service is available, and I understand it takes eighteen hours to make the trip.

"As to reserving a ticket on the train, they are hard to get and require a nearly impossible advance reservation. The trains run twice daily and handle four hundred passengers per trip. It would have been nice to have had an extra day or two to enjoy this beautiful city. However, we have a lot to look forward to, and now it's back to work, planning for what I hope will be a successful exploration."

Many scurried away, heading for the beach, cold water or not. I guess getting a tan must have been their main objective. Then I wondered, how many had an adequate supply of sun tan lotion, as the sun's rays during this time of day were hot as hell.

I saw Ken and Lynne making their way to where Allie Lea and Ashley were discussing who knows what. After observing Ashley's animated gesturing, I guessed she was trying to make a case for leaving with the rest of us. I had to grin when I thought, good luck on that. I knew she wasn't about to change the Iron Butterfly's (beautiful on the outside, but tough as steel on the inside) decision. When Ken and Lynne caught the drift of Allie Lea's tone, they did an abrupt about-face and motioned me to follow.

When I caught up with them, I asked, "What's bothering the two of you? When I first saw you, I thought you were going to talk with Allie Lea. What changed your mind?"

"When Mom's talking business, I know better than to hang around. I noticed you stayed out of firing range. Whatever they were talking about must have been serious; Ashley is on the verge of tears. Care to give us novices your thoughts?"

I am not the fastest cat on the block, but I know when it's time to retreat and wait for the cooling off period. "Speaking of that, here comes your mom. I would think carefully as to what you wish her to do or approve."

"Darling, I see we are off to a good start, and speaking of a good start, Lynne has a question for you. I'd stay, but I need to find Eric and discuss a thought or two. After I finish my business, I'll meet up with you, and if possible, take a spin on one of those three-wheelers along the beach."

She grinned and said, "Chicken."

I got the hell out of there before I stepped into trouble.

I finally found Eric in the bar with Rafael, Jim, and Red. I asked, "What gives, fellows?"

Jim replied, "We're making bets on who draws the short end of the stick when you ask for volunteers for the treks that appear to be in the offing."

"Well, who won?"

Red spoke up and said, "I guess I'm the lucky one. I can't wait to tell Anna. Of course, as far as she knows, the treks you have in mind are nothing more than little hikes along the mountain trails."

"Hey guys, you're taking a lot for granted. If Eric's mapping doesn't show promise, there won't be any treks, hikes, or otherwise."

Jim took issue with my remarks, saying, "If anyone in their right minds thought that this exploration would be anything but successful, they would have to be slightly loco. This is a costly exploration. Knowing you as I do, I'd say you believe the odds of success are at least fifty-fifty; otherwise, you wouldn't be risking the Smithsonian's money and Allie Lea's job. Each of us is prepared to look after you and the newcomers so we, or you, don't fuck it up! How's that for brotherly love, señor Keshaw?"

The look on my face said it all; and I replied, "Fellows, I quit wearing diapers quite some time ago. I appreciate your help, but give me a break: Don't bring up the subject again. Allie Lea is on pins and needles as it is. By the way Jim, you mentioned that you had a special stake in this venture. To which special stake are you referring?"

He laughed. "I thought you'd never ask—my third book."

"Just where and when do I come in on the royalty part of *our* venture?"

He gave a short grunt and said, "Huh?"

After spending a few minutes with Eric, he reminded me that Ashley is overly sensitive when the subject of treks or explorations comes up. "She is worried that something unfortunate will happen and she wouldn't be there to look after me. I told her the worst that could happen would be if I got in the way of one of the drones taking off or landing.

"Ryan, her escapade in the Maya's sacrificial cavern scarred her memory. So I'm pretty careful of what I say or do when I'm around and the subject of field trips comes up. I'm really looking forward to the testing of drones for this and others' explorations that follow. Drones are a step into the future and the future is now. I expect to play a major a part in the development, testing, and using of this new toy. Who knows, we may get lucky and exceed your dreams!"

A question suddenly popped into my mind. "Eric, what guarantee do we have that Titan Aerospace will not share our findings with anyone else, verbal or otherwise?"

He looked puzzled and replied, "I'll be damned if I know. Legal was responsible for handling such questions, but I'll get on it as quickly as I can and give them a buzz. I'm sure our people haven't overlooked such an important point. Regardless, I'll ask that they e-mail me a copy of our agreement prior to our starting any field work."

I gave him a pat of encouragement and made my way to our room as I decided a short siesta was in order.

A short while later, I felt Allie Lea tugging on my big toe and saying, "Get up sleepyhead; señor Diego is back in town and we're on for dinner. He wishes to know where things stand and asked if Sara and Rafael could also be invited. Darling, I have been talking nonstop the whole day, and a tiny, much-needed rest is in the cards for yours truly. We are to meet them at the museum at seven thirty. Tell me how your day went. Speaking of dinner, I hope it won't be one of those four-or-more-course jobs. I'm ready for an early all night snooze."

I remarked, "No doubt, you and Ashley were discussing something other than the flowers and the lovely weather when I saw you chatting, or was it something more than two women chatting?"

"You know damn well what we were discussing. I noticed you didn't come to my rescue and get me off the hot seat."

I grinned. "When you earn the big bucks, you earn the hot seat that goes with it. I wouldn't be too concerned. Ashley will get over it, and in three days she'll be joining us. Other than that, what else did you learn today?"

"A big, fat nothing. Do you think we can go as we are? I'm too tired to get all gussied up. I wonder if he is taking us to the museum's Cafe? The food there was luscious, and I would like to try one of those oven-by-our-seats dinners. Whatta you think?"

I replied, "In addition to it being nearby, perhaps he'll pick up the cost of dinner. I don't think it will matter what we wear other than it being clean, no patches, and no stains. After all, señor Diego runs the damn deal, and if he showed up in his skivvies, no one would say a word."

She replied, "Must you be so base?"

"No, I'm just being a realist." I thought I'd pull Allie Lea's chain, so I said, "Since Sara and Rafael will be joining us, I'll bet they'll be dressed to the nines. Maybe I'd better rush out and rent a tux; after all, this is the era of social and political correctness."

"Ryan, why do you do this? You know I have a million things pressing on me. Here I am counting on you to relieve some of those pressures, and all of a sudden you come up with a cockamamie scenario that is meant to rile me up. Give it a rest! I'm going as I am. Does that satisfy your devilish nature? When I think of it, you wouldn't know social correctness if it walked up and gave you a kiss, which I am going to do to satisfy your latent desires. We've screwed around long enough, so get ready, and instead of a taxi, why don't we take a leisurely stroll to what, I perceive, will be a most pleasant evening?

Upon entering the Larco, one of the cleaning señoras pointed and said, "Cafe, señora and señor." We carefully wended our way through the museum's gardens. One couldn't but help inhale the wonderful fragrances that permeated the area. Señor Diego joined us in the part of the gardens that was growing orchids and he had in tow Rafael and Sara. We learned two things: growing orchids was his lifelong passion and that he had invited two other couples to join us.

Allie Lea looked at me and softly said, "Damn, there goes our leisurely dinner. That means no ducking out early, so let's make the best of it. Our patience will be tested and let's pray there isn't too much business talk so we can get out of here at a decent hour."

"Hello everyone. Señor Diego, your Cafe's reputation has made the rounds. Ryan and I are looking forward to trying some of the oven specialties."

I smiled and whispered to Allie Lea, "Fat chance of us leaving early, and how do you propose I handle a check that will be considerably more than I anticipated?"

She looked at me as she pulled her ear.

I grinned and mimed, "I get it."

Señor Diego motioned to Allie Lea and said, "This seat is for you. Your señor can sit by Rafael."

I thought, the old fox has something to sell and he knows who the power broker is and it obviously isn't me. However, he announced, "This is not a business meeting. I hope we can talk about other things, such as the Inca Emperor who oversaw the planning and construction of Machu Picchu and the hope you have of finding his mummy and burial vault!"

I damn near fell out of my chair when he said that. I wondered who or what was his source of information. I sure as hell knew I hadn't divulged our plans.

Allie Lea looked helplessly at me as if to say, didn't he just say this wasn't to be a business meeting. After scanning the crowd, I discovered the answer.

Acahuana and RK were avoiding eye contact with everyone but the floor. Thank goodness the waiter came to take our order. I realized señor Diego's words couldn't go unanswered.

Looking directly at Acahuana and RK, I said, "Señor Diego, your sources are very accurate. Should our drone test prove successful, we will turn our attention to seeking Emperor Pachacuti's remains and his final resting place. We haven't discussed in detail what we call phase two with our associates. The last thing we wish to do is to alert the authorities and the citizens about our intentions prior to a successful phase one. However, should you have any other questions, my wife or I will happily discuss them with you."

I glanced at Allie Lea, and she had her ever-present Kleenex and swiped it across her brow. Lynne caught her motion and began to giggle. Señor Diego set the tone for the rest of the meal when he said, "In my opening remarks, I mentioned no business and I'm the one who cast the first stone. Since many of our dishes are Creole in origin, I would like to say bon appétit and good health to each of you."

RK got up to go to the restroom and, in doing so, tapped me on my shoulder and remarked, "Dad, I see you didn't forget to bring your dancing shoes. Thanks for removing the guilt load from Acahuana and me."

The rest of the night went well and proved to be a blowout evening where everyone let their hair down. With one exception, señor Diego cornered me and said, "I'm led to believe your son has taken a liking to a certain ancient painting."

I smiled. "We are still in the negotiation stage as to who pays and the terms."

Señor Diego continued, "RK believes its value is diminished by the spots or smudges on one of the mountains. However, I wish to make it a present for all the help he has given the Larco and Rafael."

I was flabbergasted and, without thinking, said, "Señor Diego, my son doesn't know squat when it comes to valuing a painting, let alone an ancient one such as *The Andes.*

"The real meaning of those six or seven smudges will remain unknown until someone comes forward with a plausible explanation that holds up to the light of day, something that has been lacking for the past four hundred years. Only then will the true value of the painting be known. However, your offer is most gracious. After our business is concluded, I would like to consider exercising an option to purchase it for a price upon which we both can agree."

He pulled at his goatee, extended his hand, and said, "Señor Keshaw, that's a fair bargain. I will ask your young son to place the painting in my special vault so that it cannot be sold or misplaced until such time as you are ready to make a decision."

I looked at my genuine Mickey Mouse watch, saw that it was 11:30, and remarked, "Allie Lea, like Cinderella, your slipper comes off at midnight, and the dawn will follow quicker than you imagine. After I pay the check, let's bid these fine people adieu and thank them for a wonderful evening."

I bowed, shook Señor Diego's hand, and then we were off for the fluffy clouds that awaited us. On our way to the motel, Allie Lea said, "Nice move, 'Mr Got Rocks.'"

Our phone rang promptly at 7:00 a.m. The first words I heard were, "This is the dumb ass that raised the stupid question. No one discussed our means of transportation of getting to the airport. I have been elected to raise the question for the rest of our crew, so don't hang up.

"Jim, rent a car, walk, run, or take a taxi. Make an executive decision! I need another fifteen minutes' thinking of how I can properly reward you for phoning at such an early hour."

I heard him laughing and then he hung up.

Allie Lea asked, "Who was that calling at such an hour?

"You don't want to know. If it happens once more, I'm going to borrow a shot gun and fill his ass with buckshot."

She laughingly said, "At least I know it was not one of the fairer sex. I thought it might have been Ashley, but then, I remembered she's working with Sara. That lets them out. Darling, on second thought, my response to you should have been 'it figures.' Now let's get dressed, eat a bite or two, and prepare ourselves for a great adventure."

The plane ride was a short hour-and-a-half and was it ever bumpy! When I looked out from my window seat, all I could see were mountains, mountains,

mountains. Our landing was okay, but the thing that occupied everyone was the thought they would be able to spend time in Cuzco, the Inca's capital city of centuries ago.

However, Allie Lea dispelled that notion when she pointed and said, "That lovely, antique-looking bus, parked beside our plane is our two-hour magic carpet to Ollantaytambo. This would be an opportune time for those who need to visit the airport restroom as our bus is nonstop. For those who are wondering, the word 'restroom' is singular and not plural. As you can see, this airport and its amenities are somewhat limited."

From the back of the room, another cluck asked, "Several of us are willing to pitch in and pay for a car rental. Would that be okay?"

Rafael jumped in and said, "Sure, but you'd have a problem with logistics. The nearest car rental is at the Lima airport which is 785 miles from here."

When I heard his response, I howled.

He continued, "There are four ways to get to Ollantaytambo: the first is walking, the second is by taxi, the third is by train, and the fourth and last option is by our bus. Despite it not looking as slick as some of the other buses, it runs and the driver is highly experienced and has an enviable safety record, which you will come to appreciate. Other than that, I recommend everyone grab a seat. Our schedule calls for us to leave in twenty minutes.

Allie Lea pulled me aside and said, "I thought Rafael handled the transportation issue very well. Who brought up the car rental idea? I was on my way into the restroom and I didn't see who asked it. It is pretty obvious that person hasn't traveled to any great extent in what many would call a third-world country."

I replied, "If you think I'm going to get dragged into a catfight, you have another think coming. Besides, what that person or persons said is not important. Rafael handled it very well, and his answer, for all intents and purposes, will forestall such future thoughtlessness. Now, if you don't mind, I see that the restroom crowd has thinned out. Adios, señora."

After everyone was aboard and settled in their seats, Allie Lea announced, "Tomorrow begins phase one, which Ryan now calls our *Mummy Hunt*. The Titan Aerospace techies hope to have the first of several drones in the air no later than the day after tomorrow. The balance of the day and tomorrow are yours to enjoy. Don't be fooled by that gorgeous sunlit sky and those fleecy clouds; it gets downright cold when the sun begins to set and sinks below the horizon.

"Starting Wednesday, our work begins in earnest and that means short exploration hikes or treks, so come prepared. This off time will give our bodies a chance to adjust to the altitude. Altitude sickness is no joke and can be serious. Pay attention to what your body is telling you. Unlike our previous exploration, any backup that's needed will fall on our shoulders, so let's make sure we look after each other. Our hotel will prepare lunch boxes; pick them up before you move to your assigned route, along with the ever- important water bottles.

"I'm sure we all plan to visit Machu Picchu. Remember there is no vehicle road between our hotel and that wonder. You do have a choice: you can either hoof the four miles or buy a thirty-five buck round-trip train ticket. Entrance into Machu Picchu also requires a ticket, and the prices vary. You can expense a train ticket and a one-day pass to Machu Picchu. Our hotel has set up a Smithsonian concierge desk for any help or information you need.

"As a final thought, there will be an after-dinner briefing on Tuesday. I must interject a note of caution, and it has to do with your personal safety. We are not sure how the local Incas will react to the drones we will be using. Many Inca believe they are small gods and are fearful of them.

"Be careful, and travel in pairs. Jim Leachy is our security guru. Should anyone probe or ask you direct questions about our operation, let Jim know. I've heard several of you using the term 'Mummy Hunt,' which is an inside joke Ryan dreamed up by Ryan. I don't recommend using it in public places. I see that we have arrived at our home away from home. Stay safe, everyone!"

At check-in, Lynne asked, "Mom what's in mind for Ken and me other than freeloading and enjoying the sights?"

Allie Lea gave a big grin. "Your dad has a task or two in mind, which I think you'll enjoy and consider worthwhile."

Lynne said, "I'll bet the task or two he has in mind will be geared to keeping us out of his and your hair. Well, something is better than nothing.

I notice the hotel has a great-looking spa and outdoor pool. In the meantime, Ken and I will just chill. If you and Dad care to have a bit of fun, why don't you join Ken and me for dinner? Perhaps the oracle will divulge a hint or two of the plans he has in mind for us. Ken, do you wish to add to what I have said?"

He gave a Cheshire-cat grin. "Now's as good a time as any for me to put in my two cents. Allie Lea, you might make Ryan and Eric aware I am somewhat versed in drone handling. I took a couple of drone technology courses at Georgetown. I'd consider it a privilege to work with Ryan and Eric and maybe my knowledge and limited experience will come in handy."

Allie Lea stood there stunned, to say the least, and in a measured response replied, "What a welcome bit of information! Dinner will include Eric and, no doubt, a chagrined Ryan Keshaw."

She then turned to Lynne and asked, "By chance, were you aware of Ken's hidden talents?"

"Yes, mom! And before you ask, I didn't mention anything about it because no one pays much, or any, attention to Ken or me. I guess everyone thinks we're just a couple of faces in the crowd doing a good bit of freeloading."

I managed to hear the tag end of Lynne's conversation, so I asked, "Just who is freeloading and why?

Allie Lea said, "The so-called freeloaders have some great information that should make you and Eric very happy."

I know I looked puzzled when I said, "Run that by me again."

Allie Lea said, "Mister Oracle, I believe it best we discuss this information over the dinner table. Now, let's see if this hotel lives up to its reputation. I'm dying to take a warm, leisurely bath. What are you doing rummaging through my things? If it's the tiara you're searching for, don't waste your time. After all, I need my big man to be primed and ready to take on any problems that come our way."

I threw out a lazy zinger saying, "For your information, I was looking for that new book you picked up at the airport in Lima."

Chapter 8

* * *

To the Inca, Mommies and Mummies Are Often One and the Same

"Since when did you become interested in King Tut and the new slant that's making the archaeological rounds dealing with his demise?"

"Young lady, I thought I should enlighten myself and brush up on mummies and the latest knowledge that's available. I learned that the Inca mummify their deceased rulers as well as their wives and then hid their remains.

"If what I have read is true, it means not only will we be searching for Pachacuti and his wife's remains, but other Inca rulers' mummies as well. You can well believe those remains are being cared for by someone who can keep a secret."

Allie Lea gave a yelp as she stepped out of the shower. She exclaimed, "Damn, I stubbed my toe. Ryan, your service is needed—hand me one of those big fluffy towels."

I couldn't resist leering and saying, "Now why would I do that?"

She ignored my response, stamped her foot, and said, "I'm sure you realize the danger that your thoughts conjure up! Should what you believe come true, then this project will take an ugly turn. Our people could well be in harm's way if your thoughts make their way into the public spotlight."

"Allie Lea, don't go jumping off the deep end. I was just musing and thinking about the what ifs. I guess my thoughts seem crazy, so let's drop it. Where might I ask is your tiara? I've looked high and low for it. By chance you aren't pulling a Lysistrata on me, are you?"

"Why would you think that, lover boy? Turn out the light; I'm tired, and I'm dreading sleeping after hearing your latest news flash. I often wonder why it is that many of your musings or thoughts tend to become unpleasant realities. Our safety net is pretty thin, and should anything happen to you, I'd have a hard time functioning."

I raised my head from my pillow, pulled her over, gave her a kiss, and said, "I think the reverse is more realistic."

Sleep for me was no problem. However, Allie Lea twisted and turned all night long.

After a good soaking, I stepped out of the shower and observed my old friend, Doubtful sitting patiently waiting for me. All I could say was "Hells bells and cockle shells" and then hastily dressed. Allie Lea had already made her way to the hotel dining room.

Our crew chattered throughout the meal, all but Eric. He was on an emotional high, and when he uttered the words, "We need to talk," Allie Lea asked him to sit with us. I immediately thought, uh oh, something's gone wrong. Eric held a folder that he was continually squeezing and then handed it to me saying, "This contains the parameters and routes I've programmed into the drone's memories. I need your approval to set everything into motion for tomorrow's test.

"I spoke with Ashley last night. They plan to complete their tasks in a day or two and be ready to join us and take on another 'meaty' (joke) task. She's bringing something for you, but didn't say what it was."

After hearing Eric's ideas, Allie Lea heaved a sigh of relief.

Eric sensed her mood change and said, "Ryan, it's time to get this show on the road."

I replied, "I need a few minutes to go over your notes. Meet me outside the lobby in about thirty minutes."

After checking Eric's calculations, I hotfooted it to the hotel's parking area and found the Larco's crossover vehicle all primed for our venture. However, several of our crew decided that they, too, would like to join the party.

As we pulled out, Eric explained, "I presume everyone is interested in a rundown on what we hope to accomplish. Okay here goes, The drones are programmed to fly no higher than five hundred feet and begin filming when they reach the Urubamba River. They will continue on southeast to southwest, which is the beginning of what the Inca call their sacred valley. As the drones make their sweeps, they will do so in tightly planned quadrants. This makes for easier analysis, as well as controlling expense factors which are appreciated by the 'suits.'"

Ken asked, "Eric, what do you hope to prove if the area the drones scan is mostly grassy, rock-filled terrain? Am I missing something?"

"Good question. Our flights tomorrow are mostly acclimation flights. For now, I haven't targeted any specific areas that warrant closer inspection. After we have completed our scan of the entire area, our objectives will no doubt change. Thursday's flights will be much more tricky, as we will be using three drones to scan the entire area surrounding and including Machu Picchu. I understand several of our crew will provide us with feedback on the response of the tourists and the local Inca to the three drones buzzing around this magnificent structure. It's hard to believe Machu Picchu is situated almost three thousand vertical feet above the Urubamba River.

"The drones will be doing a lot of dipping and diving, which may cause a bit of unease on the part of the tourists and local Inca. Here's another thing to be aware of: despite the drones looking much like a model plane, believe me they aren't. Their motors and propellers are powerful and they are capable of slicing any part of your body. Today's flight time will not exceed thirty-five minutes, which, I suspect, will cause one to wonder why spend so much money for such short periods of flight time.

"The answer is pretty simple: these little babies are daytime scouts that can scan objects or areas in less time possible than if you had to hoof it. They get into areas that are both dangerous or hostile without endangering lives. Like the commercial says, 'They're worth it.'"

RK asked, "I was under the impression that several of us would be involved in doing a ground inspection, or has that been called off?"

"That's out of my area; I suggest you to talk with Ryan about that."

We heard a steady thump, thump of a helicopter entering the valley flying between the mountain peaks of Huayna Picchu (Young Mountain) and Machu Picchu (Old Mountain). The 'copter was laboring due to the thin air. I noticed a good-sized crate swaying wildly below it, as the 'copter neared the open-launch area. It didn't take us long to get the hell out of the way where the pilot planned to drop off his load. In addition to that, those swirling blades were creating a dust storm full of small pebbles and stinging debris.

Red wasn't the least bit bothered by the situation unfolding, as he yelled, "Don't worry folks. This is a little surprise you will appreciate."

He motioned to a tall, angular, well-muscled Inca standing by his side and pointed to the lines dangling below the crate. Four other Inca materialized and each of them grabbed one of the lines and gently eased the crate onto the ground.

The 'copter pilot reeled in the four guide ropes and, with a wave, he dipsy-doodled his vehicle in a show of friendship and then climbed disappearing into the opening between the two mountains. I figured he didn't wish to tarry and he was in a hurry to get out of these mountains. The weather in this area is often iffy and changes without warning. One thing for sure: I want no part in flying or taking a passenger ride among these forlorn, high peaks for any reason. Red went to work with a crowbar and began opening the large crate, which contained a bright, shiny, three-wheel all-terrain vehicle. He asked, "Would you like to take it for an inaugural spin?"

"Red, perhaps another time. Why don't you offer our young studs that privilege?"

The tall, sinewy Inca showed up carrying a large can of gas and proceeded to fill her up. Red pointed to Acahuana, Ken, and RK, and said, "She's all yours; just bring it back in one piece in drivable condition." Smiling, he added, "Like mom used to say: 'Be home before dark.'"

"Oh, yes, I almost forgot, should you get lost, this baby is equipped with an onboard GPS system. Be sure and park it in our designated area at the hotel."

With that said, they climbed in and roared off and were soon out of sight.

Red turned and said, "I want you to meet my new Inca assistant Atoc. He comes highly recommended and will be responsible for maintaining our supplies and overseeing the local Inca that will be needed should this project go forward."

I shook his hand and said, "Glad to have you aboard, Atoc." He then introduced his four companions and said, "Good workers, good trackers, big help."

Meanwhile, Allie Lea joined our little group, and when she heard the words good trackers, she asked Atoc, "What do you mean good trackers? Did señor Red mention that we were going to need good trackers?"

Atoc stood mute; finally, Allie Lea asked, "Do you speak English? If not, we will be unable to converse, and we will be forced to seek an Inca who speaks English."

Red was steaming as he walked over to where Atoc and his four Inca friends were standing. And, in no uncertain terms, reminded Atoc that the señora is boss and in charge. "Don't you or your friends forget it. Now, answer the señora's question or leave and take your friends with you."

Atoc was obviously highly pissed at this turn of events. He stood stock still glowering, but his four amigos backed away and began walking toward town. He realized he'd lost his authority as well as a considerable degree of face. Despite all that, he refused to capitulate and Allie Lea turned to Red and said, "You know what to do."

Red wasted no time in bracing Atoc and said, "We don't want to see you or your four amigos in this area now or in the future. Furthermore, I plan to inform the police that you are an undesirable hombre and have been banned from any part of the Smithsonian's operation."

That got Atoc's attention, and he replied, "No need bring in police, we go, cause no trouble." With that, he began to lope along to catch up with his followers.

Allie Lea smiled when she said, "Red, I think you handled that problem very well. My thanks to you. Ryan, you were mighty quiet during this forceful interchange. Has the cat got your tongue?"

I nodded yes. I thought it best that I keep my true feelings to myself until I had the time to sit down with Rafael and Acahuana and do a bit of brain-storming concerning one Mr. Atoc. A quick look at Allie Lea said I'd better answer if I knew what was good for me. So I replied, "I think Red deserves a medal for his handling of the situation. Until we know more about Atoc and his crew, my guess is he is trouble. I have a question for Red: where are you going to find the men that will be needed to hump and carry our stuff?"

He replied, "That will be no problem. The drone company we're using has a steady stream of Inca looking for work and their attitudes are nothing like the ones I just got rid of. Why did you ask?"

"Oh, I had a momentary thought that it might be difficult to find loyal workers. Especially so, when they become aware of our true mission; other than that, nothing.

"Red, what would you think of having a group dinner to celebrate Sara and Ashley's home-coming? The señoras will keep the conversation from be-ing boring. How about pulling Rafael aside for a few words? I'd also like you to be a part of that conversation."

I added "Oh, what the hell, I forgot about Jim Leachy. How about invit-ing him as well? After all, his help will be in great demand if things take an unexpected turn. Before you leave, I'd like you to know if there is an explora-tion group, your presence would be most welcome."

That stopped Red in his tracks, and he forcefully exclaimed, "I don't re-member that being a part of my job description, and I sure as hell don't plan to volunteer for any assignment that has all the earmarks of danger. Who gave you this cockamamie idea? Before your idea gets legs, count me out. Breathing and enjoying life is a habit I've learned to appreciate."

"Your handling of the Atoc situation impressed Allie Lea. How about that? When it comes down to our exploring, I need to know that the person next to me will have my back. It's as simple as that. I had no idea that your reaction would be so forceful. So, it's back to the drawing board. However, I'd appreciate you keeping our conversation private. By the way, the terrain vehicle was an excellent idea and one that we will no doubt find very useful."

Allie Lea broke up our little tête-à-tête when she said, "Oh look, our drone is coming in for a landing. Eric tells me the people from Titan Aerospace are a joy to work with. One of the key projects they're working on is the development of outfitting a drone that is able to operate at night using some new infrared techniques. Titan, despite being a small company, is blessed with a bench of sharp individuals, which, no doubt, is why Facebook gobbled them up.

"Ryan, it's been a long day, and I'm hungry. The thought of a group dinner doesn't thrill me, but as you say, onward and upward."

"Honey, postpone your so-called state dinner until tomorrow night. We have a perfect excuse; I can say the analyzing of our drones' results is taking more time than anticipated. Don't sweat it. I'll post a notice on the electronic billboard and then you're home free.

"In the meantime, I'll grab Rafael and get his take on Atoc. I guess my body is having a hard time adjusting to the extreme altitude changes. After we eat, I plan to sink down between those crisply starched sheets and sleep for the next week or so. Do you think the shower can handle the two of us?"

"Ryan, I'm in the mood for privacy. How about dinner in our room? I don't care what you order just as long as there is a luscious dessert or two and remember, I said dinner!"

"Princess, your genie will do as you wish. From the sound of things, I guess there isn't a need for me to polish your tiara tonight. I caught that look of disdain, and the answer is obviously no, but I had to give it the old college try.

"Speaking of the college try, did you know the Inca ruler Pachacuti is given credit for fathering three hundred children in his lifetime and lived to be 103 years of age? All I can say is his genes must have been on steroids; speaking of Pachacuti, he assumed the mantle of leadership when he was a mere lad of twenty-two. Can you imagine that he was one of the longest ruling Incas ever? Incredible!

"I wonder what our country would be like if there wasn't a presidential time limit. Unless he or she could walk on water, I shudder to think of what our political landscape would be like.

"Get your shower. I'm off to announce the rescheduling of tonight's meeting and then the shower. The rumor mill will crank out a thousand-and-one reasons about what we have in mind. Ha, ha, and they'll all be wrong."

I returned twenty minutes later, and Allie Lea pointed to the serving table on our patio, which was loaded with what appeared to be a feast. Allie Lea, resplendent in her new turquoise robe, took one look and asked, "How many others did you invite to share this little repast? There's enough food to last us for several days. I think they must have a culinary expert working in the kitchen: each entree is a work of art. On the chance you didn't know the names of these delicacies, I asked our server to give me an idea of their names and tell us what's in them."

The server replied, "Señora, this one is *Loma Saltado* and is stir-fried beef spiced with an Asian accent and cooked in an earth oven, which is nothing but a hole in the ground; the food is cooked when hot rocks are placed around the top of the dish chosen. The other dish is known as *Arroz con Moriscos* and is a seafood dish (generally shrimp) richly flavored with rice as are many Peruvians' favorite foods. The shrimp is marinated in a secret mixture, which includes dark beer and grilled in special ovens.

"Peruvians love their desserts and these two are favorites. That one on the left is a jelly roll stuffed with *dulce de leche*. The other, nearest to your plate, are homemade crepes also filled with *dulce de leche*. I decided we didn't need any wine, and when that wonderful coffee hits our taste buds, that's all the liquid we need."

She grinned and asked, "Why only two desserts? I thought you were going to get an extra one for me."

"They're both for you! Tomorrow is shaping up as a long, decision-making ordeal. A sugar high tonight means little sleep, and that I can do without. Now would be a good time to get on the horn and invite Ken's father to join us. Assuming our reasoning is correct, we need to deal with the Peruvian authorities. Many of the local Inca are scared silly of the drones, and when it becomes apparent we will be looking for the remains of Pachacuti, they will jump right out of their skins. On a lighter note, the authorities who provide police protection for the visitors at Machu Picchu have an ongoing non-publicized problem.

"It seems that a number of visitors like to have their picture taken while running around Machu Picchu bare-assed naked. Naturally, Cuzco's and Machu Picchu's Director of Culture are not happy with any situation that causes them to increase and pay for extra surveillance. Here is another interesting tidbit of information straight from our front desk manager. The officers are in no hurry to perform their duties as many of the lawbreakers are young and nubile, something that the police are not!"

Our dinner was all that anyone could expect: good food and warm conversation without any interruptions. That is, until I upset the apple cart by saying, "I hope your talk is well in hand; I won't have time to help polish it."

When Allie Lea puckered her lips, I knew it was time to switch topics and quickly. "I don't know about you, but I'm beginning to feel great. Maybe it's the rarefied air. I don't have my usual aches or pains, my energy level is now okay, and I haven't gained an ounce. I'm glad you suggested a private dinner—it's nice not having someone always at one's elbow. I must say dinner was outstanding, and now it's bedtime. Perhaps you haven't noticed my staring, but that is one stunning, revealing robe. Would I be correct in assuming that other than the robe, you are, in the buff? This expedition doesn't have a minister of culture does it?"

"Go to sleep! You're right, tomorrow will require all our energy."

Breakfast was wild. We hardly had our first bite when Eric deposited himself in an empty seat. Even though he saw we were trying to get a bite or two into our mouths, he blurted out, "Success on the first try. I can't wait to show you the results."

Allie Lea smiled and said, "Eric we certainly are interested in your findings, but please, can we eat our breakfast and then meet you in the command post?"

He blushed and remarked, "Sorry about that. Whenever you are ready."

We finished the rest of our breakfast in peace and then started to walk to the command central. I felt a hand on my shoulder and Rafael said, "I need to talk with you about a problem in the making."

We went back to our partially obscured table, and Allie Lea said, "Rafael, we are all ears."

He replied, "I know I'm taking Eric's time and that he has some good news for you, but right now, the techies will keep him busy. What I have to talk about should be discussed with others in our group, and it has to do with Atoc. Red did the right thing in dismissing him.

"When the announcement is made that the Smithsonian and the Larco museums will be seeking Pachacuti's burial site, it will bring out emotions, many of which will be unfavorable.

"The drones themselves are bad enough; they are looked upon by many Inca as flying gods named *Pishtaku*. They are supposed to be supernatural beings who kill many of their victims for sacrifices and sell their fat to be made into soap. They terrify the Inca because they connect them with the flying gods.

"As to Atoc, his name stands for *Huahuqui*; in Quechua, it means supernatural guardian or brother or fox. He is the leader of a secret group of the local Inca. Most Inca walk softly when he's around and make sure his wishes are met. He, no doubt, will figure in your operation, but I have no knowledge of why or when. Beware, warn your people that this man is dangerous and should be avoided whenever possible."

Rafael continued, "Señora, prior to speaking, I recommend you exclude any who are not directly connected with our project. Alert señor Leachy that Atoc and his followers may brew up a bit of trouble. Now I must go.

"The 'copter bringing Sara is expected to arrive shortly, and we don't dare be late. I am meeting up with Eric as señora Ashley is also a passenger. If Eric missed her arrival because of a meeting, it would not be in our best interest as his señora can, at times, tend to be outspoken.

"I almost forgot—I just received a text from señor Diego alerting me that another drone technician has been assigned to the project and will arrive today with señoras Sara and Ashley. He asked that we give this person free range when it comes to the testing of the drones."

Allie Lea said, "Another fly in the ointment and no doubt an extra layer of needless, time-consuming bureaucracy. Do we know anything about this person?"

Rafael said, "Only that whoever this mystery person is, is Facebook's manager of advanced drone studies, and that tells me whoever it is, has some special drone knowledge."

I asked, "Why in the hell is Facebook sending such a drone expert when they have no interest or part in this operation?"

Allie Lea quietly answered, "I just received a text from Jim Hamilton asking me to extend every courtesy to the Facebook representative and that more information would follow as he would be in the office tomorrow. This person obviously has firepower and protocol says I should personally welcome señorita or señor x. By the time we return, it will be lunchtime and a perfect occasion to introduce the new person to the members of our group. Rafael, I presume you and Eric still plan to meet your wives? If so, I'll ask our hotel's concierge if we can use their limo for a bit, and Acahuana will be my designated driver and welcoming Inca."

About that time, Eric came trotting along and said, "Señor Rafael, sorry for being late. Ryan, let's get together right after lunch. Allie Lea, I presume you will attend as well. Based on the information yesterday's drone flight collected, it may be best to adjust our plans."

I replied, "Eric our plans might change due to the arrival of a señorita or señor drone expert from the great information company that is known as Facebook. Now you know as much as we do. However, I suspect you'll have the full story after you meet the helicopter."

Allie Lea stood with her hands on her hips, remarking to no one in particular, "And to think I thought this exploration would be without intrigue or danger! I only hope I'm right. I see you found Acahuana, and he was, no doubt, at the pool since he was in his bathing suit. How did you know where to find him and on such short notice?"

I looked at Allie Lea and asked, "Have you been out to the pool lately? When a fine physical specimen such as Acahuana makes an appearance, the word gets out and the señoritas decide it's a beautiful day to work on their tan. So, sussing out his whereabouts wasn't any great feat. Oh, yes, RK was helping him keep score, and I thought it only proper to invite him to go along with you."

She angrily retorted, "You did what? This is not supposed to be a social excursion. I planned to use the return trip to learn all I could about this person. RK's presence makes that impossible."

With that, she threw the folder she was carrying at me.

I often sense when there is a change in her attitude or when a storm is brewing, but, I couldn't believe what happened! She gave me a kiss on the ear and whispered, "Things may get out of control these next few days, and we will be quite busy putting out fires; hence, my outburst. Despite that, I'm looking forward to the peace and quiet of our room where I can put my plans and your ideas on paper. I'll be prepared when Jim calls me, and I'll ask him to explain his reasoning when he approved this new person, among other things.

"Before things get too far out of whack, I'll ask the hotel maître d' to pack us a lunch basket for tomorrow's excursion. Ryan, exploring the Inca's Sacred Valley of the Sun sounds so inviting that I wish we could throw caution and business to the wind and go right now. Remind me to get a blanket or two from our room. Maybe you could find a bit of straw for our so-called terrain vehicle. *Capish*?"

I replied, "No straw, but I'll think of something. By the way, when does Ken's father arrive and is he bringing his wife?"

She nodded yes. "He arrives in Cuzco tomorrow afternoon along with his wife, Barbara. I am counting on her archaeological skills to help if we ever get close to finding that rascal Pachacuti's final resting place. The only other qualified archaeologists are Ashley, Sara, and myself. Let's not forget Sara is pregnant, and we don't know how much longer she will be able to work. Why are you suddenly concerned? Is Doubtful making an unannounced visit?"

I said, "Not to change the subject, but I was remembering how cold it gets after the sun dips below the horizon. We may not make it back before dark, but we'll be here before your talk. Be sure you bring an extra jacket. I'll bet everyone will think we're nuts when they find out we took a lovers' day off, when, in reality, we will be accomplishing some old-fashioned exploring."

She looked very apprehensive and asked, "I thought this was to be a pleasure jaunt and here you go throwing a monkey wrench into my thoughts. What's your ulterior motive for this outing, Mr. Holmes?"

"If you must know, I believe we can combine business with pleasure and look for any signs that tie into those maddening six words: *Puric, Sinchi, Huaca, Chullpa, Yacara,* and *Tocco.* Oh dear, I nearly forgot about them being the catalyst for this expedition. I'm open to a refresher course, Mr. Keshaw."

"Okay, here goes: *Puric* stands for head of family, *Sinchi* leader, *Huaca* sacred archaeological site, *Chullpa* burial vault, *Yacara* soothsayer, and *Tocco* cave. The meanings of the words are very iffy, but they're all we have to go on until we examine the results of our drone's flight. So what the hell; let's enjoy the next six hours as we take in the majesty, the beauty, and grandeur of the Inca's Sacred Valley.

"We'll start with the Urubamba River and work our way back to the drone launching site. Along the route, we'll find a nice secluded spot and let nature take her course. So buckle up and hang on; the ride will be anything but smooth. I don't want to waste any time getting there."

It wasn't long before we arrived at the gorge that housed the Urubamba, and when we were stretching our legs, Allie Lea said, "It's hard to believe this valley or plain is three thousand feet above the river. It gives me the shivers when I look up at those towering mountains and realize how forbidding and hostile they really are. Why would anyone pick this area as their burial or resting spot is beyond me."

I replied, "You are probably right, and the drone's results may well prove your point. Care to take a look at what is almost a sheer drop to the river below?"

"Not on your life! Let's get away from here; I'm hungry. I don't want you to show some of that daring you have exhibited in the past. I'd rather have a live partner and not some fond memories of a dead husband who pushed the envelope too far. You don't have anything to prove to me, so fire up this unusual machine and find us a nice picnic place."

As we were buckling up, I noticed a glint or reflection coming from one of the trails that wound around the lower part of the mountain adjacent to us. I thought nothing of it; I believed it was a reflection of the mountain's mineral content. We carefully scouted the path, looking for anomalies that fit those six words; either we were too inexperienced or we were moving too fast to make an accurate judgment. I saw a nice hillock that rose up to meet us and I said, "We have arrived at nirvana, so let's break out the food and the blankets."

Allie Lea looked puzzled and asked, "You mean we have to climb that hill just to eat? Get real; I'm for parking right here, as I have no intention of busting my ass just for a special look down a valley we just left behind."

I laughed. "Okay, candy ass, this is as good a spot as we'll find. I thought that ledge would give us a little more privacy. That is, if it's privacy we are seeking."

She replied, "I can see for miles, and for your information, our vehicle affords us all the privacy we need."

I again saw that flicker or reflection of light, only this time it was closer. When I thought about it, I realized someone was keeping tabs on our progress. Allie Lea got busy spreading a blanket and then opened our lunch boxes. I asked, "Honey, why does the food taste so different from our outings back home? Maybe it's the altitude, the freshness of the food, or it's that we don't have to prepare it ourselves. Any comments, madam chef?"

I again saw the reflection and knew it was something other than the mineral content in the nearby mountain. With a bit of urgency, I gently squeezed her arm and said, "We're being tracked. Do nothing out of the ordinary. Take your time in getting something out of our vehicle, and then glance over your left shoulder. See if you can pick up what looks to be a reflection coming from the mountain just to your left."

She got up, shook herself as if to get rid of any stray crumbs and without showing any emotion, she said, "Yes, I see what you mean. Why would anyone in their right mind be interested in our taking a little trip and picnic on such a beautiful day?"

I realized that little reflection effectively killed any hopes of extraordinary action along the amorous vein. So I cheerfully said, "I know your heart wouldn't be in anything but packing our gear and making tracks for home. I plan to talk with Jim Leachy about this, and we should proceed as if nothing has happened."

Allie Lea asked, "You have any idea who it was and why they were so interested in what we were doing?"

"Yep, I do. I'll put my money on it being Atoc and or his followers, although I can't prove it. As far as I know, I'm unaware of any laws he or they have broken. The person or persons responsible for our being tracked have done us a great favor."

Allie Lea exclaimed, "What in the hell do you mean someone has done us a favor?"

"Darling, I am more determined than ever to suss out whoever feels it necessary to keep tabs on our movements. However, we must be on the right track toward finding Pachacuti's remains. The closer we get to the truth, the more active Atoc and his crew will become, and now that they have tipped their hand we'll be ready for them."

When we pulled into our parking space, Allie Lea said, "Brrr, it's gotten chilly all of a sudden; let's get inside. I'm going to have a glass of wine, warm my backside, and then face the reality of what I plan to present tonight. You know, I'm counting on you to help fill in the blanks."

I replied, "I must get with Eric and go over the first day's findings; they just might become the cornerstone of your talk. Now that Ashley is on board you can count on her to have opinions. I admit she's a clear thinker and, at times, her suggestions run counter to what others are thinking."

Allie Lea smiled. "The bar is a welcome sight, and the warmth that fire gives off is mighty compelling."

After ordering, I gave Eric a buzz to invite him and Ashley to join us, and wouldn't you know it? Ashley answered the phone! True to form, she asked, "And how is our intrepid risk taker fairing?"

I had to smile even thought her remarks riled me. I asked if she and Eric would meet us for drinks in the bar?

She quietly said, "Eric has had a full day and is resting. Could you set our get-together for tomorrow?"

"Ashley, it's important. Allie Lea wishes to talk with Eric before tonight's meeting."

She replied, "What meeting? I wasn't aware of any meeting, and Eric surely hasn't mentioned it."

"Ashley, wake him, and if he needs encouragement, tell him this is a command request and for him to get his butt in gear and meet with us in the next fifteen minutes in the bar."

She said, "You don't have to get all snarky about it. Why were you beating around the bush? We'll be there, so cool your jets, big guy!"

I no sooner hung up when I heard the cry, "Fire!"

Allie Lea and I sprinted for the door and headed for the parking lot where a spiral of smoke surrounded our vehicle. A large crowd had gathered, and Red and Jim were standing with their hands on their hips looking disgustedly at the fire that enveloped our all terrain vehicle.

The hotel staff was doing its best to move any other vehicles out of the path of the fire. Someone found a garden hose to wet down the other cars. The fire was over almost as quickly as it started. One of the hotel guests remarked that the fire had the earmarks of arson: it burned too quickly, which pointed to someone using an accelerant.

I asked this individual if he any experience in fires and he replied, "Thirty-five years in fire recovery investigations for a company in northern Virginia. Have you notified the police? I rather imagine they are very zealous in making sure nothing interferes with slowing the daily crowds wishing to see Machu Picchu. Are you the owner of the vehicle?"

"I am, but I am not sure about the question of insurance. The good news is that the hotel staff moved very quickly to contain the blaze and no one was hurt."

He replied, "I don't know what line of work you're in, but I would look very carefully at anyone with whom you had contact with since your arrival. Fires almost never start in this area; too many people depend on the flow of tourist dollars. I would think this was a grudge fire and whoever was responsible for it meant it to be a lesson to you or someone in your group."

I replied, "Thank you for your input. I have a pretty good idea who is responsible for starting this fire. I'll get in touch with the local police as quickly as possible and let them take over. They, no doubt, will bring this matter to the attention of the government officials in Cuzco. It's obvious we need to step up our security measures and that we will do."

I thanked him for his insights. Allie Lea joined the tail end of the conversation and spoke with the couple. She extended an invitation for them to take part in a special, no-expense tour the Smithsonian conducts for VIPs whenever they were in the DC area.

On that note, we turned away; Ashley, Eric, and one good-looking, young señorita dressed to the nines had been quietly standing by observing the goings on when Eric said, "I guess someone must have hit a nerve, and this project just got a bit dicier. Allie Lea, I would like to introduce you to Denise Williams, the newest addition to our growing group."

Allie Lea extended her hand to the petite young lady and welcomed her to Ollytaytambo. "This is Ryan Keshaw, my husband and go-to-guy for just about everything."

I noticed both women were shivering and remarked, "If we are going to stand here, it won't be for long as it gets pretty cold, and the hotel bar is warm and cozy. Shall we?"

On the way into the bar, Allie Lea whispered, "I agree with you. Her blouse is pretty thin, cut low, and her outfit simply stunning. Do you think she brought some outdoor designer, work gear, and you, no doubt, were worried that the little, sweet thing might freeze?"

All I said was, "Meow," which earned me a swift kick.

Allie Lea introduced Denise to several of our crew, and then the two of them made their way to the lobby and a corner where they could talk uninterrupted. Allie Lea said, "I hope you didn't get the wrong impression when we were introduced. I wish to clear the air; I suspect we will be working together before our job is completed."

Denise replied, "I am here working under the auspices of Titan Aerospace. I realize my abrupt entrance was totally unexpected, all caused by a foul-up in our travel department. Please understand I, in no way, will get in your hair. My role is one of an observer working for Facebook on loan to Titan Aerospace and to provide your operation with assistance should you request it.

"Your husband was right; I was about to freeze my buns off. By the time, they located me I was short on time. I had but an hour and a half to pack and get to the airport in Albuquerque. My choice of clothes could have been better, but I'll survive."

Allie remarked, "We better get back. Otherwise, my people will wonder why we are taking so long."

Denise nervously asked, "Should I call you Allie Lea or Dr. Keshaw?"

"Of course, Allie Lea. Occasionally, I get out of sorts, and then I address the person I am dealing with as Mister or Ms. Tomorrow we can spend time catching you up on all that's going on and the problems we have encountered. I find it interesting you represent Facebook which is primarily an open information company, and this project is anything but. Get warm, make yourself comfortable, and talk with our people as much as you like. When I return, we can have a drink, and I'll get the concierge to alert you.

As she turned to walk away, Denise asked, "Would I be out of line if I asked you a couple of questions?"

Allie tensed up. "Not at all."

Denise then asked, "After work, what does a gal do for fun? Provided that striking young man sitting at the table near the door is single, I'd like to know his name. He appears to be a most interesting, handsome individual."

Allie Lea laughed and said, "Let me introduce you to Acahuana."

When Acahuana was introduced to Denise, he kissed her hand, smiled, and turned on the charm.

I said, "Folks, the fire was set as a diversion to get our focus off of our main objective. Any scouting other than with the drones will have to be done in pairs and carefully monitored. Little, if any, consideration should be given regarding the burned-out vehicle other than we will have to hoof and hump our stuff when it comes to any sight excavations."

Allie Lea replied, "Since when did you become a protectionist? What damage can Atoc do, other than find subtle ways to promote fear in all who are connected with this project?"

I said, "Oh, he'll think of something, and it won't be as lame as starting a vehicle fire. It would be prudent to ask Steve to sniff around and try to get a handle on Atoc. Like, how or where he earns his money and who he works for. The officials in Cuzco would be very interested if his activities interfered with the flow of tourists and their soles. Remember when Red told Atoc he planned to make a report to the police? He broke his silence long enough to say there would be no more trouble. We certainly need to keep an eye on him and his activities, especially so when we announce we will be seeking to discover the remains of Pachacuti. That, my dear, is when the real trouble will begin."

Allie Lea smirked when she said, "Run that last thought by me again, because I suspect a problem might show itself earlier than we expect."

I know I looked puzzled when Allie Lea made that remark and I asked, "You mean of a pleasant sort, don't you? If Acahuana and that fashion plate Denise hit it off, you won't hear a peep from any of the wives."

Chapter 9

* * *

The Cavalry Makes a Timely Appearance

Allie Lea smiled and said, "Steve and Barbara's arrival completely slipped my mind. How about accompanying me to meet them? You can bring him up to speed and give me a chance to get to know Barbara. Steve will be quite valuable in representing us to the politicians in Cuzco. His former ambassador status will carry a great deal of weight in the discussions. So, for us it's a win-win situation."

I said, "Allie Lea, after getting them set up at the hotel, I have a pressing duty, and what I learn will, no doubt, impact your remarks at tonight's meeting."

"And, just what is that pressing duty that you haven't discussed with me?"

"It's Eric and his drone report. I can't wait to learn the results."

"Oh! That's one meeting I can do without. I get lost in the technical aspects when he gets going. I realize I'll have to get more familiar with all this new technology. However, all I need tonight is an executive summary, and I'm counting on you to give me just that."

Eric was in command central going over the results of yesterday's flight, and he grinned and said, "I wondered how long it would take us to get together. Let's move to a more private area nearby where we can talk without interruption. I'll shorten my remarks; I don't wish to miss dinner: the food here is outstanding."

I no sooner settled back when Eric remarked, "Our drone's results were simply amazing and what a time-saver it proved to be.

"We programmed the drone to conduct a sweep, beginning with the landing area east of the Urubamba. To make sure we didn't miss anything, we divided the area into quadrants using the parameters you gave us. The experts examined the results, looking for anything unusual. The areas they were particularly interested in were the footpaths beginning at the base of the mountain adjacent to Machu Picchu; from all indications this signals unexplored caves. We can now rule out all of the other areas our drone was asked to scan. The experts at Titan agree with my reasoning. However, they came up with another idea for us to consider. They suggested launching three drones over a one-hour time frame, which, they say, will ultimately save us and them time and money. How about that?

"We would program them to scan the area where the Urubamba makes a sharp horseshoe turn and continues to the end of the Sacred Valley, which is some five miles. For what it's worth, this is the area where we might strike pay dirt. It will be interesting to gauge the reaction of the tourists at Machu Picchu, as well as the local folks seeing and hearing three drones in the air simultaneously.

"They'll create quite a racket when the sound reverberates off these mountain walls. Technically speaking, we only requested permission to test one drone. I never considered that we would be able to get three in the air at once."

"Eric, I believe your deductions are spot on. After talking with several of the people at the hotel, they indicated that there are a number of caves along the area we should scan. Steve Hookway, the former ambassador, informed me he will be making the trip to Cuzco to meet with the Peruvian Minister and his staff. Hopefully, he will be successful. As to the question of making three launches, I'm not so sure. However, unless you hear anything to the contrary after tonight's meeting, go ahead and launch. If the local officials register a complaint, we'll give them assurances we will not in the future violate their air space without their prior approval. By the by, what would be the times, dates and duration of this grand launching? This information will be high on Allie Lea's priority list."

Eric shook his head and said, "Both good questions. The launching would take place tomorrow morning as quickly as the mists burn off. The length of the flights will be anywhere from forty-five to seventy minutes. I'd give you a more definitive time frame, but we are in the hands of Mother Nature and have to wait until she is ready."

"Eric, keep this matter between us until after Allie Lea's talk tonight. Also, be on guard at the launching. Alert your friends at Titan Aerospace of the possibility that Atoc or his followers might try to gum up the works. The fact that you will launch three drones within such a short space of time will cause them a great amount of anguish. Once they learn our true objective, all bets are off.

"By the way, how is Ashley faring? That was a mindless job she and Sara had at the Larco. I'm glad she and Sara hit it off so well. Her archaeological knowledge and understanding of the Inca will be needed, and soon."

Eric paused and asked, "How does this Facebook manager fit into our plans? I guess I'm confused regarding her involvement or role she will play and does her presence diminish my part in this project?"

"Eric, I, too, am in the dark regarding the question you have raised. Allie Lea is getting with her tonight, and as soon as she lets me know, I'll be talking with you. But, this much I know, her presence in no way affects or diminishes your position. The more I think about it, the more I agree with the three-drone launching. While we are on the subject, I'd like to know what's so important that the flight level be five hundred feet or less? Those three drones will sound like all hell has broken loose due to the sound echoing off the canyon walls. Talk about people being upset!"

He replied, "The experts insist that five hundred or no less than four hundred feet are optimum heights. At these heights, the drones won't have to battle the strong upper air currents that swirl around these mountains and there is less chance of them being blown off course. The one thing that they and we don't wish happening is to have a drone end up crashing into one of those imposing canyon walls. Also, we are mindful of the noise these drones will make, so our launch window will be between 8:00 and 8:30 am.

"Ryan, this is an early-rise community; the launch will be over and done with before they realize what all the commotion is about. Ken's father should be able to get approval for us to continue our operation. Our connections say the big shots in Cuzco can be real assholes, and they often delay or draw out approval times. I can't believe they would shut us down, especially since we are, in my estimation, on the verge of a real breakthrough. Plus the fact they will, no doubt, be happy to bank the extra fees our project will generate."

I gave Eric a big smile and asked, "Just when did you have such an epiphany? You haven't been to Damascus lately have you?"

"No, but during my research, I came across an interesting anomaly that got my attention."

"And just what is this earth-shattering observation?"

"One of the areas is dotted with caves and they face Machu Picchu!"

I immediately asked, "Have you shared this information with anyone outside of yours truly?"

"Yes, Ashley! She understands the need for privacy."

"How about the people at Titan Aerospace?"

"I don't make it a habit of discussing our project with outsiders. The techies at Aerospace will be instructed that one of the drones is to be programmed to make several passes over a particular area. I didn't give them any reason for my request. Oh yes, the other drones will be programmed to scan and include in their sweeps the footpaths and how worn they appear to be. The aerospace techies have installed a special scanning program that allows streaming. I don't plan to miss that!"

"Eric, you have really done your homework! Allie Lea will be pleased when she learns of your efforts and the drones' ability to shorten the time and money spent on location."

"Ryan, as quickly as the drones return, I'll be pretty busy for the next two days analyzing the raw data and preparing a report devoid of the technical jargon. The experts at Titan will give me a preliminary reading of their observations. Ashley realizes I'll be pretty scarce during that time. She expects to do a lot of sightseeing and exploring at Machu Picchu. I might have to pull an all-nighter, and the moment I have anything worthwhile, you and Allie Lea will be the first to know. See ya."

Upon entering, the hotel manager handed us a message; it was from the local police. They wished to discuss the matter of our burned vehicle and asked that we meet tomorrow at 9:30 a.m., and if that time was not convenient, to call and set another time.

Allie Lea said, "Darling, your public is calling, and if you don't wish to attend the launching, I'll carry the flag. I think it important that the police know the facts, and maybe you'll be able to get a better handle on this Atoc fellow."

As I was sitting on the edge of the bed unlacing my shoes, it hit me: I realized I had just received an order from your highness and it didn't include my attending the launching.

She came over, planted a big kiss on my forehead, and said, "Need I say any more?"

She then skipped into the bathroom all the while closing the door. I replied, "Some things never change." Then I saw my old companion, Doubtful, parked on my side of the bed, wagging his tale.

After grabbing a quick shower, she said, "You better hurry—we have to discuss Eric's recommendations and eat dinner. It might be a good idea if you skip the shower; we have only an hour and fifteen minutes before our meeting begins."

"How about a better idea? I'll sum up Eric's recommendations while we eat dinner?

That way we don't have to answer a zillion questions and be interrupted nonstop. How's that for a plan?" Of course, I didn't tell her that Doubtful has made an entrance.

She gleefully replied, "Works for me. You do the ordering while I put together a few of the key points."

I ordered dinner and began explaining Eric's ideas. She agreed with the majority of them, and then she laid out her game plan. I couldn't find fault with her reasoning. She surprised me, saying, "Why don't you cover what you just discussed with me? I can handle the summation, using your key points as well. That way, we're sure to cover the waterfront. By the way, this steak is one of the best I've ever had; I want you to know I'm eating only one dessert."

I decided to add a bit of levity into the conversation. "A couple of days ago, I noticed you were having trouble getting into your new bathing suit. In my opinion, you'd look good even if you gained another ten pounds."

She replied, "You are joking, aren't you? Another ten pounds and I'd stop eating. If I gained all that extra weight, you would have a fit."

I grinned and asked, "And what makes you say that?"

"I'd have to buy a new wardrobe and that would interfere with your dreams of buying that hot new car you have in mind."

"You're right, one dessert is enough, despite the fact your sweet spots still look plenty okay. Perhaps after the meeting, we can celebrate my stumbling across your tiara."

"Good luck on that, lover boy! I have a get-together scheduled with our Miss Denise. It's time to face the music, so get ready to go into your famous dance routine."

The meeting room was very comfortable and, as Allie Lea says, "cozy." Husbands and wives alike were in an anticipatory mood, but I wondered if the same mood would be evident after we concluded our talks. I discussed Eric's plans and that we would launch three drones instead of the usual one. I extended an invitation to anyone who wished to observe this event. On a scale of one to ten this fact might have registered a three. Their ears perked up when I brought up the subject of staying safe and my upcoming visit to the local police station. When I mentioned Atoc and the vehicle fire, there was a noticeable shifting and squirming. I was giving them information they didn't wish to hear. I left the really big news for Allie Lea, then moved away from the podium, and sat down.

Allie Lea asked all the señoras and their señors who are not involved in the launch to visit Machu Picchu and observe the tourists' reaction to the drones. She then introduced Barbara, outlined her credentials, and told the assemblage that Steve, her husband, is in Cuzco speaking with the authorities.

"He will stress the fact that both the Smithsonian and the Larco museum are partners seeking the final resting place of the Inca's greatest *Sapa Inca,* who among his many other accomplishments, designed, and supervised the construction of Machu Picchu."

There was a sharp intake from the attendees after they grasped the actual meaning of her words, as it means an extended period of time in Ollytaytambo and work would begin in earnest.

"I have asked Jim Leachy to select two teams to do the actual field work. This area can be dangerous and I don't expect any heroics. Red will be passing out some small GPS units, and if you are not aware of their use, they are global positioning devices and they work anywhere in the world, provided they have an unobstructed view of the satellites in the heavens above.

"When you are searching underground or in caves, they don't work. Should you run into trouble, use it and, for heaven's sake, don't lose the one assigned to you. We don't carry spares. Should you lose yours, it would behoove you to stay close to your buddy. Otherwise, if you get lost or separated from your group, we may not find you for days. If at all!"

Those remarks got everyone's attention, in addition to a bunch of snickers from the audience and certainly less grousing.

She introduced Denise, outlining her credentials as manager of Facebook's drone division on loan to Titan Aerospace. She is a graduate of Ohio University in Athens, Ohio, which is known as a research university, and is heavily into drone research and the impact these flying devices will have on society in general. She comes well qualified; her degree is in electronics with an accent on drone technology and Allie Lea said that we should get to know her.

I cut off a short guffaw and thought Acahuana was well on the track to that aim. Allie Lea looked daggers at me without missing a beat.

She closed, saying it would help if everyone did a little research on the *Sapa Inca* whose name was Pachacuti. "Pick up one of the booklets at the table by the door; they are quite interesting. Eric, Ryan, and I are open to any questions, as long as you understand the drinks are on you."

That brought groans and a flurry of questions.

Ashley managed to corner me. "You are still a great dancer, huh? Letting Allie Lea take the role as the heavy, shame on you."

I replied, "Ashley, other than tweaking my chain, what else do you have on your mind?"

She laughed. "Oh crap, you always see right through me. You're right, I brought you a little something, but I forgot and left it in my room."

"Ashley, you know I abhor mysteries. Can't you give me a hint, even a little one as to what it is?

"Ryan, I see Eric, and he is beckoning, catch you tomorrow. "

I asked myself why is it Ashley always revels in the fact she gets under my skin? And she doesn't even work at it. I stomped off, headed for the bar, and asked for a Scotch on the rocks, something I rarely ever drink. I understand why Doubtful made his appearance. If the past is any indicator, I knew that tomorrow I had better be prepared for trouble. I decided to duck out and get a nice warm shower and chill, but that was not to be.

Allie Lea cornered me just as I was about to make it out the door, "Why are you leaving early? Isn't that a Scotch rocks you're drinking, and has Doubtful made an entrance? I thought you would like to sit in on my talk with Denise."

"Sweetheart, a nice warm shower and a few extra winks is all that I need. Tomorrow will be a full and early day, beginning with my visit to the police station. As for your meeting with Miss Denise, I think you'll have to stand in line as Acahuana and RK have her boxed in."

"You wouldn't by chance be trying to con me, would you? And have you spoken with Ashley? She was looking for you. Ah ha, I now understand your problem. You spoke with Ashley, and she got your goat and Doubtful is back for another visit. After I finish my obligations, I'll join you, and then Dr Allie's magic fingers will do their thing and sleep will come quickly."

Allie Lea was up bright and early, as she didn't plan to miss the drone launching. After a quick breakfast, we headed out. My visit to the police station was anything but rewarding. They were vague about how quickly they would start their investigation regarding the fire.

Also, when I brought up the name Atoc, the atmosphere visibly changed. The officer with whom I was dealing was hesitant about cooperating. After fluffing off my feelings regarding Atoc, I was so pissed off at his lame response I got up and started out the door. As a parting shot, I retorted, "I plan to file this report with the police in Cuzco. Perhaps they will show more interest and concern in my employer's problems than you have exhibited."

Like a shot, he came out of his chair and said, "Perhaps I misunderstood you. As a show of concern, I will assign one of my best men to work with you and help solve your problem. He will be available this afternoon; he is out working on a *pequeño* problem we are having at Machu Picchu."

I told him where he could find Jim Leachy and that he is vice-president-in-charge-of-safety for our *hombres* and señoras, and as a matter interest, it would be wise if someone kept an eye on Atoc and his followers.

"And, why is that señor?"

"As you well know, he is a troublemaker and the leader of a secret group that operates out of Ollantaytambo and the surrounding areas. Furthermore, when he realizes the Smithsonian and the Larco museum have joined hands to seek the burial place of Pachacuti and that we are using drones to help speed our efforts, he will not be a happy hombre. So be prepared, *adios amigo.*"

I felt I wasted two hours with an asshole who planned to do nothing toward solving our fire problem, other than provide us with a window-dressing cowboy. I headed for the launch area, despite being late to observe what I thought would be an exciting moment. Well, it did prove to be an exciting moment. The drones came roaring in, and the handlers gently eased them to their assigned landing spots. I noticed there were only two drones. I pulled Eric aside and asked, "Where is the number two drone? Is there a problem?"

He worriedly answered, "Yes, and the technicians are trying to pinpoint the exact location. The number two drone was mapping the middle area, east of the Urubamba River facing Machu Picchu. It would be a good idea to talk with our people who visited that shrine and see if they noticed anything out of the norm. For what it's worth, the Titan technicians remarked that the missing drone was the one programmed to stream its findings.

"After a cursory 'look see,' they deduced what they saw was abnormal foot traffic. We must find that drone and learn why it went down. It appears the weather was cooperative: no fog, no heavy winds, and yet it remains a mystery."

Eric interrupted saying, "This was that particular drone's second pass at that area. We are not sure of the exact height it was flying, but we think it was a bit less than two hundred feet. It's very possible it crashed into one of the canyon walls. I made the changes in the drone's flight level; I felt it important we film a regression of that area and that's how the technicians came up with the heavy foot-pattern scenario. "

Allie Lea, Jim, and Red joined our conversation along with Rafael and Sara, and almost to a person they asked, "Where is the second drone?"

I said, "You tell us!"

Rafael asked, "Is it lost, crashed, or has it possibly been knocked or shot down?"

Everyone's mouth dropped open when Rafael asked, "Was it knocked or shot down?"

Allie Lea responded, "I surely hope not. As we speak, Ryan is assembling a crew to search for the downed drone, and, hopefully, locate it before the locals find and destroy the black box each of them carries."

Sara announced, "I'm ready and willing to go. Despite my being three months pregnant, you might need my mountain climbing skills. Ashley and I have been jogging each morning and we're in great shape!"

She patted her stomach and said, "Rafael don't worry, honey. I'll be okay, and I won't take any unnecessary risks. I had enough of that on Ryan's last escapade."

Ken and RK wandered in on the scene and volunteered to be a part of the search party. RK said, "Sara's right: you may need some extra muscle if her mountain climbing skills come into play."

Lynne piped up and asked, "What about me? Don't I rate a spot on this expedition?"

By now the demise of the drone had made the rounds. I announced the search party will leave immediately after lunch and they will take enough supplies for an overnight. The men will muscle the four-wheel-drive excavation buggy.

Allie Lea remarked, "Lynne may have inherited some of your daredevil tendencies, so look after her, and don't let her get in harm's way. How do you feel about Sara's volunteering?"

I replied, "Having worked with Sara, we pretty much know each other's capabilities. As to the pregnancy question, that's between her and Rafael. Should he be against her performing, then she will have to sit this one out. Eat a good lunch everyone, and let's hope for a quick find and that the drone simply malfunctioned and crashed into one of the mountains."

I asked all who were participating to assemble for an indoctrination session before they ate lunch. I made a mental checklist of what I knew would be needed and stressed the fact that one of the most important aspects of any trek was to have comfortable walking shoes or boots.

"Most important of all, if someone has an emergency or gets sick, help will be a long time in coming. Other than that, we meet here and get on our way."

While we were eating lunch, Allie Lea asked, "Don't you think you laid it on a little heavy regarding the sickness thing?"

"Allie Lea, what we are attempting won't be a picnic. If anyone has a problem with what I said, they should come forth, not when we are into the hard part of our venture.

"Personally, I believe that the drone didn't malfunction. We won't be the only people looking for it. There are others who would destroy it out of plain old fear. The most dangerous seekers are those who don't want the finger pointed at them for shooting it down. Our little trek will be anything but peaches and cream."

I set a brisk pace for the first hour, and when we stopped for a break, Sara asked, "What's the big hurry? I didn't realize we were preparing for the Olympics, and that drone isn't going any place. So how about slowing it down a bit, Mr. Hard Ass?"

"Sara, there's a reason for my pushing so hard. I don't, for one minute, believe the drone malfunctioned. Whoever took it down is as interested in finding it as we are. According to the coordinates where the drone was functioning before it disappeared off the screens, is about another mile. If, indeed, it was shot down, then the person or persons is not adverse to using a gun to get their way. Accordingly, we need to double our awareness. RK, you will be our scout who brings up the rear. Watch for any signs that we are being followed or watched."

"I'll take the point and do the same. Sara, you, Lynne, and Ken start scouring the nearby mountain, particularly along the crags, cracks, and crevices, and see if you can spot the drone. The drone is painted a fire engine red and should be easy to spot. Also, it was flying less than two hundred feet and should be somewhere along the lower part of the mountain."

Ken asked, "If we spot it, should we sing out?"

"No, just catch up with me, and in normal conversation, alert me as to where you saw it, without pointing. If we are being watched or followed, I don't want to give someone else the chance to get their hands on the drone before we do."

We had proceeded almost three-quarters of a mile when Sara stumbled. After I picked her up, she winked, gave me a big smile, and said, "I spotted the sonofabitch, and we are almost on top of it. So what do we do now, Mr Hot Shot?"

I gave her a light buss, a big hug, and said, "Great work Sara. Okay, everybody this is where we make camp. It will be dark in another hour, and we don't need to stumble around without being able to see. Ken, you and Lynne see if you can scrounge up some wood and get a fire started. If you can't find enough, use the wood from our four-wheeled friend, and then we will eat. In the meantime, I plan to use the mobile that Denise gave me for just such an occasion."

She asked, "Why don't you use your cell phone instead of that bulky mobile?"

"Cell phones in this part of the world are often unreliable and tend to take spells of not working. Sara, give us a rundown on how you think we or you can go about retrieving that drone."

Darkness fell quickly, bringing with it a chill as the sun sunk behind the forbidding mountains. Everyone was in a state of elation and couldn't wait to hear what Sara had to say.

While we were eating, Sara said, "The drone is wedged in one of the crevices right above us about eighty or so feet high. One of the wings appears to have been torn off of it, wedging it into the crevice. It would be difficult to spot unless you were right on top of it. I was able to spot it, because sun's rays reflected off the drone's bright red aluminum covering."

She continued, "The bad news is, it will be most difficult to retrieve. Should we try to approach it from above, I would need another experienced handler, at least one hundred feet of rope, and climbing equipment. That would mean two of us climbing the mountain and me rappelling to where the drone is lodged. After that, make my way to ground zero. This is a very dangerous way to go, and I'm not prepared to take that risk by myself. If Rafael were here, it would be less of a problem."

I said, "Sara, we are on the horns of a dilemma. You're our resident mountain-climbing expert, and that said, what do you suggest we do? Somehow we must find a way to get to the drone before others come up with the same idea. Otherwise, we will arouse the curiosity of the backpacking early birds, causing them to wonder why we spent the night in such a location."

"I have another thought: send out our crew and ask them to search for a trail or path that leads to or near the crevice where the drone is wedged. After the sun dries the mountain facing us and a path is found, I'll make the climb. It will be a most difficult, but not an impossible climb. These are my only choices, unless you decide to leave the drone planted right where it is and let some lucky soul stumble across it at some time in the future."

I replied, "Sara climbing by yourself is much too risky. If Rafael were here to assist you, I'd say yes in a minute, but I have another idea. At the crack of dawn, I'll ask our trekkers to alert Rafael and let him know he is needed. They should make it in an hour or less. The return trip shouldn't take as long, providing they use Larco's SUV. Since we're not going anywhere, I'll give them the mobile phone just in case they get intro trouble.

"In the meantime, let's all get a good night's rest. Tomorrow we should go about our duties, just as if nothing has happened, and for goodness' sake, don't stare or point out the location of the drone. Now, Mrs. Sara, how does that plan strike you?"

"I'll sleep better! Be sure they remind Rafael to bring our mountain-climbing equipment."

I thought Sara's quick acceptance meant the climb was risker than she cared to admit, but she had the good judgment to let it pass, at least for now. Despite having a warm and toasty sleeping bag, I was cold and spent most of the night tossing and turning. The gang was up well before sunrise and they, too, had a hard time sleeping.

Sara said, "There's nothing like a hot cup of coffee and a bun or two to get my motor running."

Ken stretched his big frame and said, "We ought to leave as soon as possible before the backpackers, the tourists, and Atoc get wind of what we have discovered."

RK, Ken, and Lynne loped off, carrying their mugs of hot coffee and several buns. As they departed, Ken mused, "I don't know if it's the mountain air or what that makes this coffee taste so good. Ryan, I didn't forget the mobile; it's in my backpack, and, hopefully, we don't run into any trouble."

The sun slowly rose above the mountains, and suddenly it was warm, and, poof, the mist disappeared.

Sara asked, "Ryan, why don't you and I do a little reconnoitering and see what we can find?"

"I'm game, but if it comes to climbing or scrambling up one of those animal trails, count me out."

Sara quizzically asked, "I thought it was underground exploring that you couldn't handle."

"Sara, call it what you may, but as I've gotten older, I find that I am more risk averse and unwilling to put myself in harm's way as we did on our last venture in that Maya temple in Guatemala."

She replied, "I haven't forgotten you saved my life on our last outing and I am in your debt. I'll do my damnedest to make sure nothing happens to you. So, let's get started."

As we were making our way up the mountain trail, Sara abruptly stopped and said, "Ryan, I think this is the trail that will lead us to the drone and, unless my eyes are fooling me, there is an hombre watching us. Take a quick look and tell me if I am nuts or I am hallucinating."

I scanned the area. "Sara, your mind or the altitude is playing tricks on you. I don't see anyone, but I do see a well-traveled trail."

"Ryan, I damn well saw either an hombre or something else moving toward us."

"Sara, this is a good space for us to take a break. We accomplished our objective and we know how to get at the drone. I'll round up a couple of our hands, wait for Rafael, and then as you said, 'get that sonofabitchin drone.'"

Twenty minutes later, Sara said, "Get off your duff; we're not going to wait for the others. The trail is pretty wide, well-traveled, and a good place to start. You'll appreciate its gentle rise as it makes its way up the mountain."

We had gone some five hundred feet when I heard a thunderous click of hooves and Sara screamed, "Hug the mountain and stand perfectly still—it's only a llama!"

I looked up and, lo and behold, a llama was charging down the trail and he was on a mission; his nostrils were flaring and he obviously expected us to get out of his way, pronto! I glued myself to the mountain all the while praying the llama had enough room to get past me without clipping me with his heels. Before I could blink, he snorted and zipped by me.

Sara yelled, "We're okay; llamas are friendly."

I replied, "So you say! I'm going to sit right here and take a water-and-sandwich break."

After a bit, Sara said, "Let's move out and see how far up the trail we can go before the going gets rough and the trail narrows."

I carefully made my way another fifty yards, never looking down for fear of pitching forward into space. Sara then paused. "This is where the train stops. The going is getting more precarious, and from here on in, the trail would test an experienced mountaineer. If we go any further and you had to turn around, you might find it rather daunting and at this point, it's a seventy-foot drop to the canyon floor. So, why don't we call it quits and wait for the gang?"

I cautiously asked, "How in the hell am I supposed to turn around without losing it and ending up in tomorrow's obituaries?"

She replied, "Backtracking is easier than going up, and here's how we do it. Press yourself close to the mountain wall, don't look down, stand perfectly still, and watch out for the scree."

"Sara, my understanding of mountaineering lingo is anything but strong. What in the hell is scree, and why is it important at this stage of the game?"

"Dear me, I thought everyone, but everyone, knew what and why scree is so important."

"Sara, skip the geography lesson and help me get down this damn path—alive."

"Ryan, you are one impatient so and so. Take it easy, and don't talk so much. I work best when I can hear myself think."

She then pulled a chipping hammer and a couple of pitons from her pack and began driving them into the rock face. After she was satisfied, she opened her jacket, uncoiled a long nylon rope, which she had wrapped around her midsection and which she then attached to the pitons. She exclaimed, "Ryan, my friend, you're fortunate that I am an experienced mountaineer and that I came prepared. This is your parachute." She wrapped a couple of feet of it around me and said, "If you lose your balance or begin to fall, for God's sake, don't let go of this rope."

By now I wasn't sure of what I was supposed to do, but I sure as hell did as she said. I looked down and saw that the rope didn't quite reach the ground, so I asked, "Sara, how am I supposed to keep from dropping the rest of the way?"

She laughingly said, "Do what you were taught in tumbling class. Just before you hit the ground, make like a ball and start rolling!"

"Sara, you must be kidding. The thought of that fall scares the piss out of me, let alone the possibility of breaking my neck."

She replied, "The rope is some seven feet short of the ground, and a fall from that distance won't kill you. Ryan, you have one of two choices: if you don't make one pretty soon, we will both be embarrassed; I have to pee, too. I'd rather do it somewhere other than on a mountain trail with you watching."

I asked, "Who said I'd watch?"

"Get real! You couldn't turn around if your life depended on it. You men!"

"Sara, is there another choice?"

"Sure, all you have to do is slowly inch your way back down the trail. This is a slower option, but whichever you choose, don't let go of that rope. Do you understand what I'm saying?"

"I'll take the second choice. Here goes nothing." I cautiously began to work my way down the trail. Surprisingly, as I gained more confidence, my progress increased.

A few minutes later, Sara sang out, "You're doing just fine, and guess what? In another twenty feet, the trail widens, and then you are home free. But hurry, my urge is greater than ever."

I laughed. "Sara, you are not the Lone Ranger. I wish I hadn't drunk that third cup of coffee. When I reach the part of the path or trail where I can turn around, I'll make a promise that my rock climbing days are over, now and forever."

Sara passed me and breathing hard said, "I just might make it, but I'll give you dibs on second place."

"Sara, before you bail out, tell me what is scree?"

"Ryan, do me a favor: have a seat. I'll be back in a few minutes and teacher will then explain the importance of knowing all about scree. Now, get out of this pregnant woman's way before you and I are embarrassed."

As I sat there, I realized my knees were actually trembling from all the exertion. My moment of solitude was broken when I heard someone yell out, "Dad, are you all right, and what are you doing sitting there on the ground, and where is Sara?"

I looked up and saw RK, Ken, Allison, Allie Lea, Rafael, and Denise climbing out of the Larco's all-terrain vehicle, and I asked, "Who drove?"

Denise stepped forward and said, "Me. Do you have a problem with that? I'm like the rest. Why are you sitting on the ground? Are you ill?"

"No, I'm sitting here waiting for you."

About that time, Sara made her appearance and she said, "There are some bushes just down the trail; you can have your dibs now."

Allie Lea broke into a big smile. "Ryan, it happens to all of us." The rest of the crew turned away, each trying to keep from laughing. I knew this wasn't the time or place to stand on ceremony, so I made a beeline for those bushes.

When I joined our crew, Denise said, "From the looks of things, we're attracting a great deal of attention from the tourists at Machu Picchu. I recommend we get this over with as soon as possible. Now where is that drone?"

I wondered how they got here so fast, despite my seeing the all-terrain vehicle. About then Allie Lea stepped forward and asked, "Don't I even rate a kiss, let alone a how are you? You owe Denise a vote of thanks for her skillful maneuvering that got us here in jig time."

I shook Denise's hand and asked, "What's with the box you're carrying?"

"This is what we use to retrieve downed or lost drones. Let me show you what I mean."

She punched a couple of buttons, and without any warning, the stuck drone emitted a high shrill sound.

"Sara, I understand you are the one with mountaineering skills. Let's do a bit of climbing; we are on a tight schedule—our rescue drone will soon be arriving."

She turned to Rafael and said, "Your company would be appreciated if you are up for it."

Rafael looked at Sara and asked, "How difficult is the climb and would I be a hindrance or a help?"

She took a moment to reply. "Darling husband, I don't wish to trample on your manly pride, but Denise and I can handle it, provided she isn't fearful of heights."

That said, she took Denise's hand, walked her over to the trail, and said, "I presume heights don't bother you."

She nodded, "I'm your gal, despite the thought we have a difficult climb in store. From the looks of things, the trail we have to traverse is an ancient walking trail, and I need a heads-up as we move upward.

Sara said, "The first part is okay; the second part downright dangerous; it narrows, is some seventy to eighty feet to good old *terra firma*, and requires mountaineering skills. Are you sure you're still game?"

Chapter 10

* * *

Novices Need Not Apply

"Heights don't bother me," Denise replied. "Since I am the one with the box that controls the drone, I must be within fifty feet of where it's stuck to make it work. This special drone has a flight time of forty to fifty minutes, and the clock is ticking. Time's a wasting, so let's get started."

Lynne went over to her mom and said, "I'd like to try it. I'm not afraid of heights, and now's as good as any for me to learn."

Allie Lea then asked Sara whether it would be okay if she went only as far as where the path narrows and no more.

Sara intervened and asked, "Promise?"

Lynne replied, "promise," and with that, she took off running.

Ken remarked, "I hope she knows what she's in for. I took a class in college that was supposed to teach us about rappelling, its dangers, and all the things necessary to survive. I did well in the class until we went on a field trip!

"I quickly learned they don't teach the most important thing of all, and that, my friends, is courage, which you need in abundance. Particularly so when you are swinging with only the pitons and those special ropes to keep you alive if you begin to fall. At that point, things come into focus rather quickly. I am not a coward, but I know my strengths and limitations. Climbing or mountaineering is not one of them."

I thought, *that's comforting information.* I only wish he had spoken up sooner. I looked at Allie Lea to get her reaction.

She walked over and said, "Sara told me about your little bout with the heights. I'm glad she pounded those pitons deep into the mountain face so they wouldn't pull out at a critical moment. That, my loving husband, may be our little girl's safety net should she falter or get into trouble. That's why I didn't say anything."

About then we heard a whirring noise, and, as if by magic, flying over Machu Picchu was a large drone. The wing span was enormous, and it looked as if it was dancing on the wind. All the tourists were pointing to this strange, ugly flying object.

In the meantime, Denise, Sara, and Rafael had worked their way to within twenty feet of the downed drone. Denise appeared to be fiddling with the dials, and then the large rescue drone responded by flying in lazy circles. I then noticed a large, mean-looking hook attached to its underbelly. Our group gathered near where the safety rope swung, and RK remarked, "I wonder how she plans to get that drone out of the crevice."

Ken chimed in, saying, "It will take a good bit of power to pull it out and that hook looks rather formidable. I dare say the drone will be in one piece when that hook digs into its thin aluminum skin."

It took an agonizing three passes before Denise was able to maneuver the rescue drone into a proper position to hook onto the downed drone.

She said, "I just hope the recording box hasn't been damaged to the point of being unusable. We should learn a good bit from it."

"Yeah, like should we go forth, or do we shut down this venture, pack up, and go home?" I challenged with a hint of sarcasm.

That brought several questioning looks.

Allie Lea was pretty strident when she said, "Any decision as to packing up and going home would be premature. After we have all the facts, I'll be the one making that decision."

I asked, "Speaking of that, where is Acahuana? I would have thought he wouldn't have missed this show for all the tea in China and spending time with Denise."

Allie Lea replied, "I got caught up in the moment and forgot to tell you."
"Tell me what?"

"Steve was able to convince the officials in Cuzco to extend our project for four more months. He brought up the question of our vehicle fire and that we suspected the culprits to be Atoc and his followers. His contact informed him they had a file on Atoc and considered him to be an agitator who uses strong-arm tactics to get his way. The contact promised to have a talk with the resident police and ask them to keep an eye on Atoc. So far, Atoc has done nothing to harm the flow of tourists' soles. Should that happen, he would understand why our jails have earned a reputation for being a most inhospitable place to spend one's time. Getting back to Acahuana, he wanted to mingle with the local Inca without our being underfoot."

"I doubt the locals realize they were conversing with their future leader. I suspect his job would have been more pleasurable had Denise been able to accompany him."

Allie Lea pulled me aside and said, "Listen, Buster, it's time for you to get off this Denise kick. I realize she is an attractive young lady and a quick study. If she and Acuhana hit it off, that's life and none of your damn business. From all that I have observed, she is a talented, driven individual who is not interested in married men. Are we clear?"

I replied, "Perfectly!"

She then gave me a kiss. "In case you have forgotten, we belong to each other! Oh look! She has hooked onto the downed drone. It shouldn't be long before she knows if the black box was damaged."

A shout went up from the tourists at Machu Picchu who had been following the drone's every move as it rose majestically, turned, and headed for home with the downed drone firmly attached to the rescue drone's underbelly. About that time, Rafael, Sara and Denise came scrambling down the trail full of excitement and elation.

Whatever it was, they weren't sharing it with anyone, as most were interested in Denise and the drone, so their moment of excitement went unnoticed. Despite that, Sara took Allie Lea's arm and whispered, "Rafael and I stumbled onto something very important. Let's go into town and try one of the local bistros where privacy won't be a problem. The majority of our crew eats here at the hotel, so our chances of running into one of them are slight."

Allie Lea said, "Ask Ryan not to make any plans until I have a quick talk with him also. Let me know how Lynne performed. Did she take any wild chances and push the envelope more than she promised? Ken was supposed to keep a close eye on her and make sure she didn't take any foolish chances."

Ken smiled and told Allie Lea, "I believe she is now aware of the dangers that heights impose, and without experienced help nearby, she could be in serious trouble. I doubt she'll be eager to volunteer anytime soon for future mountain climbing. She learned a valuable lesson: this can be a cruel world if you don't know what you are doing. One other thing, your daughter is not wanting or needing is courage."

While everyone was packing, Rafael reminded us of Smokey's motto, "What you brought in goes out with you."

We had a good laugh and then faced the problem of who gets to ride and who gets to walk. Allie Lea made that decision for us. "Denise and the señoras ride plus baggage; you strong, virile hombres get to work off any extra flab by hoofing it."

Denise finished tying the baggage to the vehicle's roof carrier and then said, "Surprise, we have room for two lucky ones."

Rafael said, "Ryan and I need to catch up, so we'll walk."

Ken responded, "My six-foot-three frame will take up too much room, so I'll walk with these two experts and learn what they have on their minds. RK, it looks like you drew the lucky straw."

Allie Lea asked, "Denise, was the mapping impaired or less than usable? I'm dying to know."

"It may take a while, but this much I know, my cursory examination says the drone was shot down; it didn't fly into that mountain all on its own."

Allie Lea said, "Denise, don't pull out just yet. It is important that I bring Ryan up to speed."

She yelled, "Yoo-hoo," and I came strolling back and asked, "Just what does my queen desire?"

"I need a few minutes of your time." She then told him of her conversation with Denise.

I replied, "I thought as much. I'll discuss the findings with Rafael. Dollars to doughnuts, Atoc is our man, and all we need to do is catch him or his hombres in the act. Why don't you ask Denise to head on back, so she and Eric can get started analyzing the drone's results?"

She motioned for Denise to move out and away she went. We conducted an on-the-spot-walking pow-wow concerning Atoc and his habits.

"I don't think we need to be overly concerned about his activities during the daylight hours; after hours are his favorite times to operate. We should have alerted Denise to keep the doors to the tech area locked during the nighttime hours. If there is anything of value belonging to us, put it in the Titan's safe.

"Also, we should alert the hotel staff to be on the lookout for any prowlers and make sure the exit doors cannot be opened from the outside. Then, get with Jim and Red and bring them up to speed. Jim is a pro in this area and he may have some additional thoughts."

Rafael took Denise's remarks in stride, but Ken was beside himself when he said, "Hot damn, I guess just like in the movies—we're the guys wearing white hats."

We laughed and I said, "Pick up the pace. The sun will crawl behind that mountain they call, 'Old Machu Picchu' in about an hour-and-a-half, and the temperature will drop like a rock, and all of our cold weather gear is now on its way back to the hotel."

We had been walking at a brisk pace for the better part of an hour, and in another hour we should be safe and sound in the company of others. I asked Rafael if he would like to tell me what it was that so excited Sara and why she didn't wish to discuss it back at our camp area.

"I wondered how long it would take you to get around to that subject. The suspense must be killing you, and to be perfectly honest with you, she didn't discuss it with me either.

"All she would say when we were working our way down that narrow trail was, 'Ryan and Allie Lea are going to be very happy when I tell them what

I found and Ashley gives Ryan the little surprise present she's been keeping locked in her suitcase.'"

"Well, señor what do you make of Sara's remarks?"

"Whatever it is, you can bet it's important. Otherwise, she would have spilled the beans. There's another thing that bothers me, and that's Denise's assessment that the drone was shot down. Yet no one has come forth who witnessed or heard the reverberations that a firearm would make. And why was the drone flying such a low pattern? Obviously, its speed had been throttled back and the person who fired the gun had to be a crack shot.

"All the violence thus far has been toward objects and none toward any of our crew. I suspect all these tactics were meant to serve as a warning and intended to scare us off. The closer we get to our goal, the more dangerous it will get. Our goal must be much closer than I first thought. I have an idea or two that just might smoke them out. But first, I want to hear what Eric and his techies have come up with."

"Ryan, I'd like to know what goes on in that head of yours. You're always a step or two ahead of me."

Before he could say any more, our rescue vehicle made its way over the horizon.

On the way back, Ken offered this thought: "If the others are going to use guns, shouldn't we as well?"

I quickly retorted, "No guns, no time, for no reason. Allie Lea would have a hemorrhage if I or you brought up that subject! Should it come to that, we will let the local police handle any problems that call for the use of firearms. Besides, there are a host of other ways or roadblocks that our so-called 'friends' could use to hinder our progress."

Ken gave a big smile when he said, "I walked right into that one, didn't I? You can bet your sweet ass I won't broach that subject again. Despite being on several previous excavations, this one tops all the others for suspense and we're just getting to the juicy part. Wow!"

Away we roared, and I remarked to Red, "You have hidden talents that we must use more often; you are a first-class wheel man."

He smiled. "Don't we all?" The rest of the trip was, at times, rough and rocky, and we tried to grab a few z's for we knew what lay ahead of us.

No sooner had I settled back in my seat, when I saw Doubtful sitting beside me and he wasn't smiling. My imaginary friend rarely brought good news and I knew we were in for some trying if not dangerous times. I tried to ignore his presence, but I couldn't shake the feeling that danger was lurking just around the corner.

Allie Lea and the gang were there to greet us, all of whom were seeking information. Eric, grinning like a Cheshire cat, shook my hand and said, "The black box and film were unharmed, and just maybe we stumbled onto some valuable information."

I backed out of the circle and said, "I need to get out of these hot, sweaty clothes and take a long, hot shower. Afterwards, we can meet in the bar, and then I'll answer any questions."

Sara and Ashley pressed forward, and Sara asked, "Mr. Smart Guy, got a minute? The word 'scree' stands for a thin, slippery covering often found on mountain trails. Many experienced climbers do what they call 'scree skiing' as they descend rocky slopes. It's a quick, but often dangerous way to descend."

"Thank you, Sara. I will treasure that knowledge for years to come."

Those remarks earned me a quick thumb of the nose. I noticed the bulky package Ashley was carrying, which she then presented to me saying, "This is an early Christmas present. I think you'll find it interesting."

Allie Lea sidled up to me and remarked, "Before this goes any further and after you examine your surprise, what do you think of my setting up a private buffet dinner for the members of our crew and Titan's techies? Today is a gold star day, and I don't want everyone's efforts to go unnoticed."

I planted a big kiss on her ear. "Way to go girl; thanks for coming to my rescue. Just so you know, that climb came close to doing me in. Be sure the manager gives us the larger conference room."

She replied, "Can do. I'll get Anna to spread the word."

I finally made it to our bedroom and the shower when I heard a knock on the door. I hastily put on my shorts, grabbed one of the hotel robes, and heard Allie Lea talking with Sara and Rafael. Of all things, she was inviting them to stay.

I stormed into the room, angry as hell!

Sara coyly said, "I recall seeing you in less clothes than those you are wearing. Don't let our presence bother you. Maybe you don't remember our little escapade at the Mayan temple."

I couldn't let her remarks go unchallenged, so I worked up a big smile and said, "I vaguely remember."

Allie Lea gently closed the door, trying hard to suppress her giggles.

Sara asked, "Only vaguely?"

I managed to get out of that trap by asking, "Okay, friends, what's on your mind that couldn't wait until tonight?"

Sara smirked when she said, "Get dressed; your other guests will be here shortly. In the meantime, we'll make ourselves comfortable and talk with Allie Lea."

"Are you sure you didn't sell tickets for this occasion?"

After dressing, I saw that our other visitors, Ashley and Eric, had arrived.

Ashley kicked off our little talkfest asking, "Have you looked at my present?"

I asked, "Just when do you think I have had time to do anything, let alone look at what I don't know?"

"Señor Ryan, it's just as well. Sara and I will now put on our dog-and-pony show, so make yourself comfortable on the bed and we'll get started."

"Allie Lea, do you know anything about this, or are you in the dark as well?"

Sara answered. "This is new for her as well. Where is that package? We need it as a prop?"

I had put it under our bed and felt like a fool getting down on my hands and knees to retrieve it, which prompted Ashley to ask, "I wonder how long that would have lain there before seeing the light of day?" When she was unwrapping it, Sara reminded us she had observed something that may shed light on where Pachacuti is buried. Now that got our attention big time.

I exclaimed, "For goodness sake, what is it?"

Ashley reminded us that she and Sara had the job of cataloging the objects the Larco Museum intended to sell.

"That original oil painting *by Felipe Guamán Poma de Ayala* and titled *The Andes i*n which you had no great interest possibly holds the key to our goal."

With that, she unrolled the picture, and it was a black-and-white copy of the artist's rendition.

"If I heard correctly, you weren't all shot in the ass with it after you noticed several small smudges since you felt they destroyed the illusion and the painting's value."

I asked, "Ashley, why go over plowed ground? I studied that painting until I was blue in the face. Why I asked to have it set aside, I don't know. The only reason I decided to purchase it was RK's interest in buying it for his collection, as if he had a collection. Everyone has to start somewhere, and speaking of that, where is this conversation headed?"

Sara jumped in and said, "Okay, smart ass, here is the bottom line. Those eight so-called smudges are anything but. They are openings that have been chiseled out of the rock and the surrounding crevices. They were made to look like exactly what someone wanted them to resemble, natural rock formations, and these two are genuine Inca trapezoidal openings.

"That's why our royal friend's tomb hasn't been found these last six hundred years. That mountain is forbidding enough, and all the experts dismissed those small openings, or crevices, as natural erosion because of time and never gave them a second thought."

I thought Sara was carried away with hopeful thoughts and I had to say, "Sara is it possible you are overstating what you have observed?"

Allie Lea said, "Ryan, Sara is an experienced archaeologist; don't be so quick to dismiss or judge her observations. After all, it wouldn't be too hard to prove her remarks."

Sara quickly retorted, "I have further proof. Ashley's archaeological studies included the study of the Maya and Inca and I wanted to get her opinion. That's why I was reluctant to tell you what I believed to be a significant observation."

She then turned to Ashley who had been silently drawing on the large pad and said, "It's your show Ashley."

Ashley held up the sketch she had drawn and pointed out saying, "These are Incan windows; notice the difference between them and other construction. The lintels have been carefully shaped and fitted into the opening, making them appear to look like they are part of the mountain."

She continued, "The Inca were the only race in South America who used this type of construction. Without proper examination, I cannot explain the window's purpose other than to let in light. If you asked me to take a guess, I'd have to say one thing is clear: the Inca wouldn't have wasted all that time and energy for no reason, unless they were hiding something of great value. Take a look at this photocopy and tell me what you see."

Rafael walked to where Ashley was holding the picture and exclaimed, "There are several other openings I completely overlooked. Sara, my darling, you have been vindicated. Señor Ryan, it's time for you to take center stage and round up a crew to examine what could be an archaeological find of a lifetime."

Allie Lea groaned. "Oh Lordy! What have we let ourselves in for?"

When she said that, Sara and Ashley went into hysterics, and Ashley said, "Señora, that is why they pay you the big bucks. When it comes to chumming up the working assignments, remember, no underground excavations for me, and Sara is pregnant. Other than that, we are all yours to do as you wish and command. Any orders, Ms. boss?"

It was Allie Lea's turn to be amused, and she inquired, "Old intrepid explorer, exactly what are your plans? I'd like to hear what you have in mind."

"Well, since I had all of a half an hour to think on the subject, I do have a plan or two, and the first part of my plan involves Eric."

He then entered the fray, saying, "Ryan, I'll do a lot of things for you, but rock climbing, heights, and underground exploring are not any of them. I am the Smithsonian's technical expert and the only one you have on the scene who can handle your IT needs."

"Eric, you're right. Get with your drone experts, set up a night flight for each of the next three days, and make sure they are equipped with infrared-vision capabilities. I don't know how long these drones are capable of staying airborne, but I want several passes built into their coordinates.

"We need to have a clear scan of those damn holes and the path that leads to where the drone was shot down. Don't share this information with any of our gang. That's all for now. Stay tuned; other orders will be forth coming after Allie Lea approves them."

Allie Lea said, "My approval is dependent on the information I receive and, thus far, our sources have proven to be extremely accurate. But and there is always a but, I'd say we are entering a fluid information period and we shouldn't relax our efforts. Anyone have a problem with that? Don't forget tonight's buffet."

Eric was the first to bolt out of the room, but on his way out I cornered him and asked, "What's the hurry?"

"I must alert the Titan people, so we can make our first flight tonight."

"Eric, I think our plans and the flights will keep until tomorrow. Have a good time tonight, and thank Ashley for her contribution; tell her I bow to her wishes."

"Ryan, she will appreciate the consideration. I doubt she mentioned she still has occasional nightmares whenever she dwells on what went on in the Temple of the Two Jaguars. She is slowly working out her problem, but she isn't there yet."

"Eric, I wasn't aware that she was still reliving those nightmares. Let her know she can talk with me anytime. I realize she went through several harrowing experiences, and I'll do anything that will bring her out on the other side. Please let her know my feelings and that I am available."

Allie Lea said, "These extra night flights are expensive and they will knock the hell out of my budget. So, fess up!"

"Call it a hunch or intuition. These flights will tell us a lot.

"Sara reminded us the footpath was well worn and it led to nowhere, except to where the drone was found. Unless I miss my guess, our intruders will lead us to a cave or opening that will possibly point the way to Pachacuti's final resting place.

"The reason for the consecutive night flights is to catch any intruders who act under cover of darkness to complete their mission. They will, no doubt, think that their actions will go unnoticed after the first night's flight. Provided I'm right, someone had better begin planning how we can safely traverse that very narrow path without getting killed.

"Sara, you and Rafael should scout around and look for an additional path and or another way or entrance into the cave and what's the safest way down, other than that narrow path. When Atoc and his followers get what we're about, you can bet your sweet ass they will do anything to booby trap the entrance."

Unbeknownst to us, Steve and Barbara had been standing nearby taking in our conversation. Steve walked over, put his arm around me, and said, "It might be wise if you had a few more numbers in case protection is needed. Barbara and I have had extensive experience in working digs throughout the world, and if your friends would like a little company, we're available."

Without any hesitation, Rafael said, "We welcome your company. Señor Ryan, as you suggested, Sara and I will get together whatever mountain climbing gear will be needed, in addition to doing a bit of scouting."

As they were walking away, I shouted, "Don't skip dinner unless you are ready to tell the gang where you are going and why."

Barbara gave Allie Lea a hug. "It's good to get back in the harness once more. Thanks for giving us the opportunity to be useful."

I asked, "Why the hurry?"

Steve grinned asked, "Have you forgotten packing is a woman thing?"

Allie put her arm around me and said, "You should have been born a spider! The web you wove was so compelling Sara and Rafael had no choice but to accept. What other thoughts do you have swirling around in that noggin of yours that possibly might be of interest to the head of this expedition?"

"As if you didn't know. However, I'll make you a trade?"

"Ryan Keshaw, what in the world are you talking about?"

"Dig out your tiara and then I'll tell you all about it."

"I should have known. I keep forgetting what is uppermost in your list of dream wishes. Okay, after we have eaten, showered, and are safely in our lovely room with the covers pulled up around us, you're on. How does that grab you?"

"Let's eat fast! We had a delicious dinner and a most memorable night; need I say more?"

Tonight the little private meeting room was packed to the gills, and everyone was anxiously waiting to hear what she had to say. After the tables had been cleared and the entrance door closed, Allie Lea handed Lynne a sign, which she promptly hung on the door knob; it read, "Private meeting, guests no."

She got off the meeting with a bang when she said, "Sara deserves special recognition for her bravery, so, Sara come on up here and tell us all about your accomplishments."

Her story was brief and to the point. Surprisingly, she opened the floor to questions, and after fifteen minutes, Allie Lea remarked that Sara would be available for any additional questions as soon as the session ended.

Eric came forward, gave his version of how the drones had been used and said that there would be another flight or two in the near future. He dropped a pearl that stunned everyone when he added, "Titan experts definitely state the drone was shot down and the culprit hit it with three shots."

A few of the wives immediately grasped the impact of the shooting and were heard to say this idyllic adventure had taken on a whole different meaning, and how do we protect ourselves, and is it safe to walk around Ollantaytambo?

I knew Allie Lea didn't want to handle this hot potato, so I said, "Folks, I don't think we have anything to fear at this time. Trouble will come after we send in a search team looking for ancient Inca artifacts. So far, the culprits have confined their activities to physical objects."

"Speaking of sending in a team, I will lead a group of four or five hearty souls. If you are interested, see me after the meeting; don't be bashful and step right up. Oh yes, I almost forgot, if you wish to volunteer, you must not have a fear of high places. Other than that, goodnight."

Ashley pressed forward and said, "Good luck in finding two or three prospects, let alone four or five lucky souls. You know I'll be rooting for you." She vanished into the crowd, leaving me standing there tongue-tied.

Anna and Red wandered over, and Red said, "Against my better half's judgment, I'd like to be your first volunteer."

I smiled and asked, "Anna, are you okay with his decision?"

She remarked, "Like the good wife that I am, I'm happy with his decision. My delightful redhead told me he thinks you might be in need of a resourceful individual before this thing is all over."

"Red, welcome aboard; it's good to have you. I hope you bring your bag of tricks; I rather believe you may be right." Then I got a real surprise.

Steve and Barbara asked, "Filled your quota yet? If not, we would like to volunteer. You will be getting a couple of experienced archaeological persons who may prove to be valuable assets."

"Of course, I'll be glad to have you as members of the team. However, your six-foot- three height may prove to be a tight fit if we have to traverse any of the caves."

He replied, "Close places and tight spots were my stock in trade, and Barbara is five foot two and fit as anyone can be. She is the one with the archaeological degree, in addition to being a first-class environmental lawyer.

I had to grin when I said, "The two of you will make a good fit. Welcome!"

Sara waved and yelled, "Count me in! I have to use the bathroom, so don't wander off."

Rafael told us wild horses won't change her mind and "Goodness knows, I've tried."

"Rafael, if you remember, we were lucky the last time. Sara will be happy with what I have in mind for her provided you're okay with her doing a little mountain climbing?"

Sara and Allie Lea finished their little chat and Allie Lea said, "By the looks on your faces, I can tell you've been plotting."

"Plotting no; exploring a few ideas and thoughts, yes!"

Sara said, "When you take a congenial approach, it's time for us to grab our wallets and take what you say with a grain of salt. In short, how do you plan to screw Rafael and me?"

I responded, "Sara, that's downright mean for you to harbor such thoughts. I have a great plan for both of you, and it involves minimal risk. How does that sound?"

"Ryan, cut the bullshit. Tell us the cold hard facts, then we'll see if what you propose is doable." She then asked Allie Lea, "Are you in on this charade?"

"Sara, you have my word this is the first that Ryan has discussed it with anyone!"

Sara thought for a moment and added, "Should that be the case, we're all ears. If you haven't heard of it, then I know he wouldn't put a half-baked idea on the table if he thought you'd throw cold water on it."

"Sara, you always did have a way with words."

"Here's my plan: You climb or use the path to the crevice where you spotted the drone, then continue on to the first opening. Then take some of those life-saving pitons and string three or four of them as close to the opening as possible. Make sure they will hold during repeated usage."

"Sara, how many feet do you estimate it is from the ground to the opening?"

"I'd say seventy to eighty-five feet, maybe a bit more. Where are you going with this?"

"Okay, here's the tricky part. Is it possible to fit an iron bar into the opening?"

"Ryan, of course it's possible, given enough time and materials. I suppose your next question will be, can I attach a rope to the bar long enough to reach the ground?"

"Sara, you are thinking like a champ. You know we may have a sore need for a safety valve and this is it."

"Ryan, I'm past the kiss-up stage; just get to the point before you drive me and everyone else nuts."

"Well, it's a fact that Atoc and his band of thugs operate only at night, and I doubt they will see or even notice the pitons or the rope dangling in the darkness. Rafael, while you are in town, pick up a couple of safety harnesses, one of which Sara will put in place, and then we'll see how feasible our plan is?"

Rafael blinked and asked, "Ryan, just to whom were you replying when you said, 'Our plan'?

Chapter 11

* * *

Space Walking Is for Astronauts

"Rafael, it's pretty clear where Ryan is going with 'our plan,'" Sara answered. "The only question I have relates to the size of the opening. We don't know for certain if it's large enough for a person to wiggle through and whether that individual has the nerve necessary to strap himself or herself into a safety harness while suspended in space.

"Your volunteers must have an astronaut's capabilities and an insurance policy that includes unusual peril coverage; you are asking an awful lot of your friends."

Allie Lea nodded in agreement saying, "Sara, why don't you and Rafael put your heads together and see if you can come up with a simpler plan? Eric has the drone scheduled for night flights tomorrow, Wednesday, and Thursday. Without a workable plan in place, we don't go forward. The safety harness is almost a given! I only hope it doesn't scare the living pee out of those who have to use it.

"Rafael, there is an outdoor store in town where the backpackers fill their last-minute needs. I'm sure they'll have whatever extra equipment you need, in addition to some long climbing rope and plenty of pitons. The ATV is reserved to carry your equipment and a couple of volunteers who will give you a hand setting up camp. A word of caution, you'll arouse plenty of attention when the Machu Picchu tourists see you scaling that mountain as they will want to know what's happening. So be prepared and remember this has to be a daylight operation."

It was then that Acahuana came rushing up and said, "I hope you saved a spot for me. I spent more time than I anticipated talking with the locals. Señor Ryan, my time was well spent. I understand you asked for five volunteers, and I'm number five! Such a venture should have a genuine Inca working in harmony for what I believe will be a great discovery."

"Allie Lea, the quota is filled and they all volunteered."

RK was hanging in the background, so I nudged Allie Lea and said, "Here comes a problem, and it's yours to solve. I'm off to see one wizard who goes by the name of Jim Leachy. I plan to spend time with him and make him aware of our plans and the part he will play in this adventure. You might keep in mind he is slight of stature without an ounce of fat on him."

Allie Lea asked, "What's that got to do with the price of tea in China? Is there something else you forgot to tell me or are you still hatching an overall plan?"

"Bingo! You nailed it! Rest assured you'll be the first to know when or if I put it all together. Have you noticed the volunteers are slim and fit except for yours truly? I should have shed a few pounds, but it's a little late for that. But, what the hell! It is what it is."

"RK, Lynne, Ken, and Ashley were over in a corner of the bar commiserating. I suggested that Allie Lea give them a part to play and not sic them on me. She threw her hands in the air and asked why is it that I get all the poopy jobs? I wish, just once, it would be my turn to lead the parade and not follow the elephants, cleaning up their messes.

"Speaking of that, what do you plan to do in case Atoc shows his hand? Not knowing what he has in mind makes it difficult to do other than guess or go all out on a supposing spree. We'll know more when we get the results of the late night flights.

"I just spoke with Acahuana and he gave me an earful about our *señor* Atoc. His Quechua name is *Huahuqui*. In your language, it means he is a supernatural guardian or brother and is connected to Pishtaku, who is also considered a supernatural being and is also known as one that kills Incas and sells their fat to make sacrifices or to be made into soap. He and his gang apparently have little income, but they never seem to want for anything. Regular Inca steer clear of him and want no part of him or his gang.

"Many of the townspeople wonder how he lives and they are not exactly sure where he lives. In fact, he is rarely seen in public during the daytime and occasionally at night. A rumor making the rounds is that you fired Atoc, causing him to lose much face. The townspeople believe, given the opportunity, Atoc, sooner or later will extract a measure of revenge. Your redhead had better watch his step and make sure he doesn't plan any nocturnal visits into town.

I thought about Acahuana's remarks and said, "Red isn't a babe in the woods and can take care of himself in a fair fight, which, unfortunately, is anything but what he would get. I'll alert him when his wife Anna isn't around. He'll be prepared."

Allie Lea was frantically waving, trying to get my attention, and then I saw Eric and Ashley talking with her. I thanked Acahuana for his information and told him the day after tomorrow would be our jumping off day.

He did a little dance and replied, "For *mucho* luck."

Allie Lea couldn't wait to tell me of our drone's night flight, but she said, "Eric I don't want to steal your thunder, so why don't you tell him about what the drone filmed?"

He broke into a big grin and recapped the findings. He showed us the films and explained that on the first pass it would appear we found nothing, but, he added, "Take a look down here in the lower left hand corner. What do you see?"

I shook my head. "Beats the hell out of me. Rather than keeping everyone in suspense, why don't you tell us?"

Eric said, "Those dark shapes at the beginning of the path are very unusual, and while it would appear they mean nothing, the camera saw otherwise. The Titan people had loaded the drone with a new type of infrared sensing equipment, and as you can see, it has the resolution of a daylight shot. Good call huh? Because of the extra technical and infrared sensing requirements, the drone's flight time was severely limited to a maximum of forty to forty-five minutes.

"The other drones will be programed to make another pass some twenty minutes later. They will zero in on the path, making sure that what we were seeing wasn't an animal, but possibly a human. Although I don't know what anyone would be doing out at that time of night and on that rough trail!"

I shook his hand. "Eric, you and your tech buddies have earned, at my expense, a round of drinks."

Ashley asked, "Allie Lea, did I hear Ryan right? You mean he's buying drinks for our crowd?"

Ashley pulled Eric aside and said, "Now would be the time to hit Allie Lea up for a raise."

Eric said, "Ashley, must you be so crass? Have you forgotten I am well paid? I love my job and I wouldn't jeopardize it for anything. If what I've discovered helps us and the Smithsonian, Allie Lea won't forget it. I presume you know we could never be able to afford such a trip on our own. So, bury that thought and forget you ever raised it. Now let's take advantage of Ryan's offer and see what exciting things the morrow will bring."

Ashley took off running in the direction of the woman's restroom. Eric stood there not knowing what to say or what to do. A few minutes later, she emerged, face in place, and smiling as she took Eric's arm. "I am a doofus! Forgive me and forget I ever brought up the subject. I know better than to bring up the subject of money at a time like this. I just read that protracted and less-than-harmonious discussions of money are among the major reasons leading to divorce among the millennials.

Meanwhile, I rescued Allie Lea from the hangers-on and said, "The moon is out and it looks like a beautiful night for a stroll to see the sights in Ollantaytambo, which should take all of fifteen minutes, unless we stop for a drink at a place they call El Bar. I think you will be blown away by what Acahuana learned from our people as well as the townspeople, courtesy of one Acahuana. I'll be back in a jiffy; don't get involved in another of your chats. I don't wish to share my thoughts with anyone else."

She smiled. "My, oh my! Am I going to be involved in a clandestine plot? It's not like you to suggest a late night stroll. I'm chilly despite my jacket;

couldn't we have the same conversation in the hotel's cozy, warm bar? In case you are interested, my tiara is sitting on your pillow!"

"Well, well, maybe that cozy bar is just what the doctor ordered."

Allie Lea nodded. "I thought that would change your mind!"

She pointed to a secluded table, ordered a couple of beers, and asked, "Romeo, what's on your mind other than a tryst with your lover?"

"I think I've pieced it all together. I previously thought we might bump into Atoc and his followers making their nocturnal forays, but based on what Eric showed us, it no longer matters for I now know where they are, and that they, unknowingly, will lead us to the entrance of the cave. As to his reason for Atoc making these nightly pilgrimages, who knows?

"Tomorrow's drone flights should provide us with the additional information we need to begin, in earnest, the hunt for Pachacuti's burial chambers. Surprisingly, the answer to that question has been staring us in the face. Remember, Pachacuti had a great love for Machu Picchu and didn't wish to be separated from it, even in death. I'll bet his remains are somewhere in one of those caves close to the Urubamba River facing Machu Picchu.

"As to those eight holes, I believe I know what purpose they serve. The mountain face and those holes catch the early morning rays, filling the cave with streams of sunlight if only for short periods of time. Somehow those beams must illuminate Pachacuti's remains. Here's the rub: should my reasoning prove correct, getting in will be easy, but getting out not so easy! One thing I know for sure is that the place will be full of hidden traps.

"When Atoc becomes aware that we have found and entered the cave, he will make it his business to see that we don't get out—alive. Which means we must have a backup plan, and that's where Sara and Rafael come in. My plan might not work, for it hinges on our ability to squeeze through that small opening.

"But that's something we'll face if it comes to that. Each of our intrepid adventurers must understand when they clear that opening, they will be dangling in space, hopefully, for a short period of time. Even so, it will require a strong stomach and a good dose of courage. Otherwise, the harness is a good idea, and I'm sure it will be okay. If push comes to shove, it's the best I could come up with. At least, it's worth a chance. Perhaps Sara and Rafael have come up with a better plan. Now to the really difficult part!"

"Ryan, I wish you would quit sending chills up and down my spine. Based on what I've heard, I am not sure we should go forward. How do we get across to our volunteers just how dangerous this mission could really be? I insist they understand they have the option of going or not going, with no hard feelings. I wondered what was your reasoning for making one of the conditions they must be slim of stature. If that's so, I don't believe you qualify as the mission leader. It appears you are a mite or two over what I categorize as being slim."

I replied, "Damn it all, I knew you would get around to that sooner or later. I'll admit to being ten or so pounds beyond what you consider as being slim. However, if I rule myself out, who would you get to assume the role of an experienced leader who is used to getting out of scrapes?"

No sooner had I uttered those words when I sensed Doubtful's presence, and he wasn't smiling. I got the feeling that this project was going to end very badly for someone, and then a question flashed through my mind: would this possibly be my last mission?

That night Allie Lea and I spent most of the night hashing and rehashing our options and plans we thought would work. Our first objective was to bring together our volunteers and brace them for what could happen.

The next objective was to bring in Rafael and Sara and ask them to explain to us what we would need in the way of help should things go awry and see if they came up with a better 'rescue' plan. I asked Allie Lea if she had any idea about what to do with the other working members of our group and whether we should include Denise in any of our plans.

She replied, "I'll ask Jim Leachy to make himself, RK, and Ken available in case a rope rescue comes into play. We will need their muscle. Lynne can be in charge of keeping order and making sure that the tourists or backpackers don't get in the way. I suspect before this thing is over and the word gets around, it will be a real problem.

"As to Denise, I suspect she will be happy to help in any way she can, providing Acahuana is free. I'll bet you didn't know they have been seeing the sights—what there are—and I believe they are planning an excursion to Cuzco whenever they have a free weekend."

"Allie Lea, how in the hell do you know that?"

"A little birdie told me!"

"I'll bet the little birdie was Sara. I wonder if Denise knows Acahuana is one of our volunteers and his free time will be somewhat restricted. Maybe you could get her to be our sixth volunteer. I'm sure they would both appreciate that, and the fact she only weighs 117 pounds is an added plus."

Before Allie Lea could respond to my bit of humor, I jokingly remarked, "Knowing Lynne, I suspect she will have an MP armband for each of her crew!"

At three a.m. we were both exhausted and hungry. I called room service, only to learn the cooks don't arrive until five a.m. I asked them to let me cook up a couple of eggs and some bacon. But the word was no.

Allie Lea said, "Don't say it; I know you believe you were screwed again. Get in bed; at least, we can grab a couple hours' sleep. And would you tell me why you are getting in bed fully clothed?"

"Let's put it this way: if I sleep in my clothes, I can squeeze in an extra hour of bliss. Does that answer your question?"

She shook her head. "Sometimes I believe I married a man who is within a hair of being nuts."

"Okay, you win. I'm off to slumber land and if you're smart, we can make that journey together!"

We slept until (if you can believe it) until nine-thirty a.m., only to be jarred out of our sleep by an incessant pounding on the door. Allie Lea hastily put on her robe, found her way to the door, and saw Sara and Rafael holding two trays, loaded down with sausage, eggs, three large pancakes, and two jugs of hot coffee.

Rafael said, "The breakfast was Sara's idea. It was my idea to wake you late. I figured you were in need of all the beauty sleep you could get. You will be happy to know Sara came up with a twist or wrinkle that might make your plan a bit safer."

Allie Lea said, "Give me a moment or two to freshen up, and after a few swallows of that delightful smelling coffee, I'll be ready to take on the day."

With that, I rolled out of the bed fully clothed. Sara started laughing and asked, "When did you take to sleeping in your clothes?"

Allie Lea smiled and replied, "You don't want to know. If you did know, you might question his sanity. Why don't we talk while we eat? Make yourselves comfortable in those lounge chairs, and we will be all ears about how you're going to solve our escape problem."

Rafael paused for a moment and replied, "Ryan's plan is a good one, but a couple of additions will make it even better and safer. Sara came up with the idea of placing extra pitons in stair-step fashion and add an extra length buckler, a carabiner (locking device), and most important of all, a safety harness that easily attaches to a special climbing rope.

Allie Lea nodded. "How in the hell will anyone be able to take advantage of this method of escape?"

I grinned. "Simple, issue personal safety harnesses. This method of escape is anything but perfect. When one is faced with being saved by a rope or not getting out alive, I believe one's choice will be to put on the safety harness, get through that hole, and hold onto the rope for dear life while being lowered to safety.

She said, "Well, that settles my question. Let's pray it doesn't come to that. Our next move is to get the volunteers together and lay out what they might possibly encounter and the dangers they may face. The unknown part of this operation is how we respond to Atoc and his gang should they accost us. He has proven to be a very unreasonable man; his response will be anything but pleasant. Jim, RK, and Ken will provide the ground muscle. Red placed a can of mace in each of the volunteer's packs and that should help deter any violence. Any questions? If not, let's round up our volunteers, so we can get this distasteful part of the business behind us."

Sara asked to join us for lunch. "I'm developing a case of first-day nerves. Perhaps a good, quiet lunch will help me overcome my problems."

After lunch, I popped off saying, "Allie Lea, if our volunteers change their mind, I am prepared to go solo."

You should have seen the jaws drop, and I knew I screwed up big time.

Allie Lea glared at me saying, "Mister hip shooter, I have a few questions. Just when did you get the crazy idea that you would go alone if you had to? I don't remember our discussing that matter in the last day or so. I will not cotton to anyone going solo and that's that!"

Going solo just flew right out the window. Believe it or not, I heaved a sigh of relief. I sure wasn't all shot in the ass committing to a venture that was looking more dangerous by the day. I looked around for Doubtful and he had disappeared. How about that?

My quiet reverie was interrupted by Rafael who announced, "It's all set—the volunteers will be here at three o'clock."

Allie Lea seconded that, and for lunch she ate two desserts. I made a crack about our volunteers trying to squeeze through any of the eight holes. She got the message and looked daggers at me and I quietly slid out of the picture. I knew my Sphinx act had better be working if I knew what was good for me.

Three o'clock came and with it, an anxious group of people. Allie Lea made the motion we move our meeting outdoors. She said, "It's a warm, beautiful day. Why not hold our little meeting over by the spa? There was a dash for the big lounge chairs. After everyone was seated, she began by saying, "The topics you hear discussed are considered privileged information. If our plans are openly discussed, they may put this mission in a good bit of trouble."

She continued, "Hold your questions until the end of our discussion. We'll answer as many as time permits. If anyone needs to freshen up, now's the time."

A mad dash ensued. I had to laugh when I reminded Allie Lea how quickly a bit of tension can affect our plumbing system. She ignored my comments and asked Sara to explain the role she and Rafael will play.

After demonstrating the proper use of how to use the harness, she switched to an explanation of the significance of the eight holes that dot the lower face of the mountain.

"Each of you who have volunteered may realize the use of the safety harness will be your only path to safety. The difficult part of this operation will be making it out of one of those eight holes and attaching yourself to the safety rope and harness. This is a neat, but doable trick that requires a considerable amount of courage. Once you attach yourself to the safety harness, you will be lowered down the face of the mountain.

"A rescue of this type should be considered only after all other escape routes have been explored and ruled out. Don't let what I've said throw you; the items covered are relatively safe. For the volunteers, a word of caution: don't forget to keep at hand your rescue harness. You never know when the need will arise. On that sobering note, I believe it's Ryan's turn to wow you."

It became eerily quiet as I approached the lectern; then I realized everyone was busy absorbing Sara's sobering remarks. I nervously dropped my papers, and when I stooped to pick them up, there was Doubtful. I knew I was in for a difficult time. I had little or no news that would make our gang anything but happy.

I took the plunge. "The plans discussed today are flexible and subject to change depending on how events transpire."

After outlining the dangers, I threw out a lifeline when I said, "Should any one of you choose not to participate, see me at the conclusion of this meeting."

There were several gasps and a couple of oh's when I offered the volunteers the option of backing out. Judging from their response, I realized my remarks were anything but what was expected.

"Lynne will be in charge of crowd control. Remember, it's important you not give out any information other than saying we are conducting mountain climbing and rappelling training exercises. We shouldn't have any trouble with the police. Steve visited the police station in Olly and dropped off a copy of our governmental permit. The officer in charge, Rondo, assured Steve his officers would provide assistance should the need arise.

"What I said about my plans being flexible is the unvarnished truth. Any of our plans are subject to change as we are awaiting the results of a late-night drone flight."

That brought a murmur of expectation along with a question.

Red said, "A break would be appreciated, and for those interested, a chance to examine some of the items in each of the safety kits."

Everyone finally got settled in their seats, and with a large cup of coffee and a muffin in each hand, Red approached the lectern saying, "One of the most valuable items in each kit is this miniature camera. It has been outfitted with an infrared sensing device and operates in low or no light with amazing results. Each comes with a chip that is capable of taking two hundred shots. Pretty neat huh?"

He held up a softball-sized GPS and remarked, "This is the latest whiz-bang GPS. However, it will not work in underground areas. Despite that, I packed one in Ryan's and Steve's kits on the premise they are ones who are most likely to have the need."

I had to challenge that statement. "Red, how did you arrive at that prescient conclusion?"

He blushed and said, "That possible conclusion has to do with extra *avoirdupois!*"

The silence was deafening.

He continued, "Each of the volunteers will find in their kit six bottles of water, heavy duty flashlights, a set of spare batteries, eight juice boxes, and a lightweight thermal blanket, not to mention several cans of survival food and assorted sandwiches. Each of the packs weighs approximately thirty pounds. If any of you wish additional sandwiches, get them today. Any questions?"

Someone in the back yelled, "Red, are you planning on an extended stay? Thirty pounds for a one-day venture sounds like overkill to me."

Red hesitated before answering and slowly remarked, "I've been on several such ventures and found it's better to prepare for the worst rather than suffer because those in charge didn't properly prepare for the unexpected."

That brought another round of silence and no more questions. I realized it was wrap-up time and I closed, saying, "Providing we make a significant discovery, you can bet on the Peruvian ministry declaring our findings national treasures, and they will then take over. In addition to that, when it becomes the news that we have made a significant discovery, archaeologists, looters, tourists and the media will descend like locusts. That's why silence is so important. Rain or shine, the balloon goes up bright and early Thursday morning. RK is today's wheel man. The first group leaves at 7:30 a.m. and includes Sara, Rafael, and the ton of equipment they require, plus any of the volunteers, provided they can find any extra space.

"I'd like to remind everyone we owe a vote of thanks to Sara for finding the entrance to what we believe holds the key to our success. Providing our plan works, we'll be out and home in time for tomorrow's dinner. Meeting adjourned."

Sara came tripping up to the lectern and whispered in my ear, "You didn't by chance guild the lily did you? Carrying thirty pounds up that bitchin' trail is anything but easy!

"Where the trail narrows, they will be under a good bit of stress. This part of the trip is by no means a walk in the park—it's downright dangerous. Everyone better keep their fingers crossed."

By then Rafael joined us, and I knew I had to respond to Sara's remarks. So I decided to wing it. "Sara, you are 100 percent correct. I felt I had to interject a bit of hope in this operation, and this was the time to do it. What I said was accurate; the only part I left out were the 'what ifs' and this was not the time or place for speculation. Satisfied?"

Before anything further was said, Ashley joined us and asked, "Ryan, was your speech one of those 'peachy keen' jewels you save for situations just such as this? You were so inspiring that you made me almost wish I had volunteered. But then I said, 'Nah, not on your life!'"

Her remarks broke up the tension that had been building, and before I knew it, she threw her arms around me, gave me a buss and said, "The thought of entering another cave and once again experiencing the horrors of the Maya sacrificial chamber, I know I'd freak out. I wish you and your team luck. Eric and I will say a prayer for your group."

When she turned to walk away, she asked, "Is your partner Doubtful around?" She giggled and gave the V-for-victory sign.

Allie Lea observed our antics, and after giving her a weak smile, I blew her a feathery kiss. She slowly made her way to where I was standing, took my hand, and asked, "Politicking, are we?"

I was saved from giving her a sarcastic retort by Eric who yelled "Got-em."

After much huffing and puffing, coupled with an iced margarita, he tapped on the folder and asked, "Can we go where it less crowded?"

I asked Eric, "What's got you in such a dither? I've never seen you so worked up."

We pulled up our chairs and prepared to hear what I presumed would be earthshaking news.

Allie Lea asked to be excused for a quick pit stop and said, "Don't you dare start without me."

She returned and said, "Whew, I'm glad that's over."

She saw the look of embarrassment on Eric's face and hastily said, "I was referring to the meeting."

He turned red and then said, "Take a look at these films; they were taken on our drone's second pass. Ryan, your hunch was right. Look closely and you can see five people making their way down the trail on the mountain face. Based on this additional information, the cave in question, no doubt, holds the answers to what you are seeking. Obviously, these individuals were carrying heavy sacks of some sort or the other. Navigating that trail, with only the moon to guide them, is something I wouldn't wish to do. Where the trail narrows is apparently the danger point for anyone climbing or descending. The volunteers should be made aware of this before they take one step up or down, but that's up to you."

"Eric, you have confirmed my suspicions and provided me with a most valuable piece of information."

Allie Lea interjected with a question, "Maybe you would like to share this 'gem' with the rest of us, if that's not asking too much?"

I stepped in and said, "Eric's information means we must be in and out before Atoc and his gang make their nightly foray. Otherwise, we'll be in real trouble, the likes of which might mean we would be trapped in the cave for quite some time or maybe, heaven forbid, forever.

"Once we're in the cave, Atoc may well have the means to seal the entrance and leave us to figure out how to get out before our food and water run out. As to another entrance or exit, I don't think one exists; we haven't discovered any evidence that says otherwise. At that point, our remaining safety valve is getting through one of those holes and depends on Sara and Rafael to spring us."

Looking at Allie Lea, I joked, "Perhaps I shouldn't have eaten so many of those crab cakes and charbroiled shrimp over the last three or four months."

Puzzled, Eric asked, "Allie Lea what is he talking about?"

Allie Lea shrugged her shoulders. "It's just an inside joke and a bit of gallows humor."

Eric said, "Huh," realized he was on thin ice, and changed the subject.

Allie Lea said, "Eric, our talk today is not for publication today or tomorrow. Okay?"

"You're the boss, and since your name is on my paycheck, your wish is my command. It's been a while since I've eaten. Ashley will be glad to know I'm back and hungry."

The rest of the day was a blur, and the only peace Allie Lea and I got was in our bedroom. I said, "Honey, I guess that do-not-disturb sign kept others away, except for Lynne and RK."

Lynne asked, "What are you doing here holed up in your room? Everyone is wondering if you are okay, and is everything still on for tomorrow?"

Allie Lea laughed. "Darling, we won't have that private dinner after all. Okay kids, what else is on your mind? I know you didn't just drop by to know if tomorrow is a go or not."

Lynne said, "RK and I feel neglected and the bullshit job you assigned us is something any asshole could do. What gives? After all, we are part of the family aren't we?"

I responded with a little more vigor than needed when I retorted, "Since when were you two anointed ? Family or no family, what gives you the right to expect preferred treatment? Your mother is running a business, and the decisions she makes are not open for questioning.

"Take a look at the facts: neither of you have any experience in working in such a dangerous environment. Lynne, despite your gutsy performance, it was abundantly clear you need additional training. RK you are a strong, young man, short on experience. I wonder how many volunteers would step forward and willingly put their lives in such an inexperienced person's hands? I know I wouldn't!"

Despite Lynne's sobbing and RK's hanging his head, Allie Lea said, "I've changed my mind., Why don't we have an old-fashioned family dinner without worrying about tomorrow or who does what? Kids, give us a few minutes to change and meet us in the dinning room."

With that, she pulled them close, gave them a big hug and kiss, and remarked, "There will come a time when you will be ready to accept the challenge your father just gave you, so scoot!"

I looked questioningly at her highness and asked, "Is this to be a formal dinner? If it is, I didn't bring my tux!"

She marched over to the closet and pulled out a stunning turquoise cocktail dress.

I guess my jaw dropped and I asked, "Just where and when did you buy such a jewel?"

"Oh, I just picked it up the day before we left. I thought it only proper that I have a little something extra to celebrate our discovery."

"I presume you also brought your crystal ball for this celebration. I love the dress, and I only hope your intuition is right. By the way, how much did this filmy inspiration cost?"

She took a good look and asked, "Have you taken a look at your shirt lately? I think it looks a bit grungy. You don't have a celebration shirt, by chance, do you?"

I repeated my question, "How much did that killer dress cost?"

She replied, "The answer to that question would be better discussed on our way home."

I knew there was no way in hell she was going to tell me the cost of that dress. At least, not while we are here in Peru. My stomach began rumbling, bringing with it pangs of hunger and dinner was a good way to let off the steam that's been building. Who knows, this may be our last family dinner. Tomorrow and a successful excavation are not a given, and I intend to make the most of what's left of today. Doubtful had disappeared and that, my friend, was a good omen.

Wednesday arrived and the first of our crew departed, right on schedule, bringing with it a noticeable charge in the air. And adrenaline was flowing along with everyone's apprehension. It seemed as though it was only minutes since RK pulled out with everyone waving goodbye, but here he was ready for another load. I intoned, "RK, if you break an axle or burn up the motor setting a speed record, you will be grounded for life."

"Ease up, Dad, I know where the ruts are, and for your information, this baby is equipped with four-wheel drive."

He yelled out, "The Andes taxi is now taking on passengers and I'm ready to transport those responsible for setting up the campsite. I'll get the volunteers on my next trip. See ya!"

Allie Lea mused, "Ryan, I guess you and I are the cow's tail. Did you plan it that way?"

"As a matter fact, I did. I thought you would be going with the other volunteers. You seemed eager to get started. I was, until I realized it's not such a good idea to start in the middle of the day. I didn't think it wise for us to be caught in the cave after dark. Atoc will be watching our every move, and if we begin our climb early in the morning, there is less chance he will know it. Since we are RK's only and last passengers, I think I'll ask him to stop in town and find a place that sells candy bars. I'm feeling the need for some quick energy."

"Ryan, it isn't like you to need quick energy this early in the morning. What gives?"

"I guess all the hustling, the shortened sleep time, and erratic eating have taken its toll."

It didn't take RK long to find a sweets store and when he came out, he was carrying a large box of assorted bars.

"Dad, business was slow; the old guy managing the store said, 'Buy box, I give good deal.' So here you are; they should last you a long time."

"That damn box of candy just adds weight, and frankly I don't see the need."

Then another thought crossed my mind that said, Don't be so hasty; after all, the box weighs less than a pound. Little did I realize we would be thankful for the decision I grudgingly made about such an insignificant matter.

Surprise, surprise! Lynne and her crew had organized our campsite and were ready for business. A crowd of tourists as well as those on Machu Picchu gathered at the site where Sara and Rafael were busily driving the pitons into the face of the mountain.

Sara waved and Rafael told us she would be finished in another hour and everything had gone well.

She yelled, "Send up one of the iron bars along with one of the safety harnesses. I'm ready to attach them. I had a good look at the indentations and I think that one of them is usable. Either way, I'm going to hook up an additional harness just in case one doesn't work. I'm not sure I can safely reach the second opening, but I'll give it a try."

Steve waved and said, "Great leader, we're ready to go, so how about it?"

I asked Lynne to round up the remaining volunteers. We walked toward the Urubamba River away from the gathering crowd watching Sara and Rafael perform their high wire act. I explained why I had thought it best that we get an early start tomorrow morning. They agreed, and that was that. Just before darkness fell, Sara fitted the last harness in place and quietly rappelled her way down the face of the sheer cliff. Everyone heaved a sigh of relief.

Red asked, "Allie Lea, do you have a moment? I have an idea that's worth considering."

"Red, we welcome any of your ideas. What's on your mind? Since we have postponed our venture until tomorrow, it might be a good idea to post a guard. If Atoc works best at night, and he sees that we haven't posted a guard, he might be inclined to try and dissuade or force us to cancel tomorrow's venture."

Allie Lea said, "Excellent idea, Red! Who do you suggest we post for guard duty?"

He threw his hands in the air and said, "I didn't see that one coming. I presume you expect me to set up a schedule and notify the patrol volunteers."

Allie Lea said, "As usual, your prescience is right on target."

She turned to Ryan and asked, "I presume your sleeping bag is large enough for two?"

The night passed without any further incidents. Atoc and his gang were notably absent. I commented, "Campfire eating isn't half bad," and the conversations took our minds off of what we were facing. Barbara was full of herself, bubbling over with excitement. She told all of the volunteers that under Sara's supervision, she had made the climb early this afternoon, and that the whole procedure had worked very well and had gone off without a hitch.

The big day arrived and shortly after a hasty breakfast, the volunteers and I began that long trudge up the treacherous trail. I set a deliberate, slow pace and I damn sure didn't look down. Otherwise, I might have thrown in the towel. Acahuana, like most young studs, groused a bit saying, "At this pace, we'll never get there before dark."

Barbara replied, saying, "Acahuana, if Ryan picked up the pace, there would be one less archaeological volunteer who's experience and knowledge may be needed. This damn kit is giving me fits, and if you like, I will gladly allow you to carry mine."

Acahuana changed the subject and made the rest of the climb, in silence.

We made steady progress until we came to the part of the trail that narrowed precipitously, and I yelled, "Break time!" We didn't waste any time in shedding our thirty-pound loads. Quite a crowd had gathered to watch us make the climb; Red raised his hand in a victory salute and, in return, received a round of applause. After taking a long swig of water, Steve looked at the narrowing trail and asked, "How about letting me go first? I've had a good bit of experience in working my way through tight spots."

I agreed. "If anyone has a problem, chuck your pack, and don't try to move; just hug the mountain. The safety rope is in place, and don't be ashamed if you have to yell for help, and remember to lock your legs around it and hold on tight. Sara will then lower you to the ground. Heroes often reach the ground at a higher than anticipated speed."

Red said, "Steve, you go ahead."

Red then cautiously moved forward himself and made it without any problems. Barbara began her climb and we held our collective breaths as she haltingly made her way to safety. I was friggin' glad she was a fitness creature and could handle the thirty-pound pack, despite her five-foot-one stature. I needn't have worried for she was one formidable gal.

She cupped her hands and yelled, "It doesn't pay to misjudge the power of a determined woman!"

The on-the-ground onlookers applauded and someone yelled, "Out of sight, girl!"

Acahuana turned to me and said, "If she can do it, then so can I."

I remarked, "Acahuana, this isn't a speed or endurance trial. It's all about surviving, so go slow, and take it easy."

Halfway home, a few of the rocks shifted and went cascading down the cliff face. It's a good thing that Acahuana was a strong, young Inca, who wasn't afraid of heights; he slowly backed down the trail and yelled, "I'm okay. I'm going to wait a minute or so until I know the rocks have finished moving further, narrowing the path. I'm doing as you said: hugging the mountain. You might alert our rope people to get the safety rope a bit closer, just in case I slip and fall."

The rest of us stood anxiously by, then we heard him say, "Señor Ryan, try to avoid the part of the path where I had trouble; it's very unstable, so as you said to me, 'Go slow and you'll make it.' I'm within sight of the cave's entrance, and despite my not fearing heights, I wouldn't recommend you look down more than absolutely necessary."

All I could think of was, 'Oh crap,' I'm on a short leash and the supposed leader of this venture. What was needed was a helicopter or a wider path to go with my courage. The courage I've got; the helicopter I don't. It was time to get my ass in gear, and as we said in the Marines, 'Move out.' After making it to the cave's entrance, I said, "This space is getting pretty crowded."

I then put my hands on Acahuana's shoulder, saying, "You are the reigning Inca, and it is only fitting you be the first, to hopefully visit Pachacuti's final resting place."

By now the sun was in its full glory, and what a sight it made; it was as though we had stepped into another world. The sun streamed in through the eight holes and lit up the interior like a Roman candle; over in the corner was an unbelievable sight.

Nature had hollowed out this humongous cave over the eons of time, gouging out the rock to where the cavern itself was some nine or ten feet high. Its overall length was about the size of half a basketball court. I noticed several alcoves surrounding what appeared to be tunnels or leading to what or where I don't know. Time and a constant supply of rushing water had transformed the interior of the cave into a multicolored-stone wonderland.

It was as if we had entered an underground cathedral where silence and majesty reigned. If this cave proved to be Pachacuti's final resting spot, he chose well. Standing off in a far corner was a large golden palanquin that glittered in the sunlight. It was surrounded by boxes and boxes of precious stones, emeralds, and nuggets of gold arrayed in long tables that were decorated in Inca designs. I spotted a series of small tables, embellished in gold that held, of all things, fresh food and beverages. We were so overwhelmed that we were speechless until Acahuana went over to examine their contents. Before he could take another step, I, in a fit of anxiety, yelled "Stop! Don't move another foot! Walk backward toward us in the dusty tracks you just made. Otherwise, you may not live much longer. Being so adventurous could prove to be your demise!"

Acahuana, bewildered, asked, "What did I do that was wrong?"

I ruffled his hair and said, "My fault; I should have explained the do's and dont's that often spell the difference between survival or death when excavating ancient Maya or Inca pyramids or underground caves.

"They usually build in cleverly designed traps, pits of death, and myriads of other ways to ensnare the inexperienced, their enemies, and looters. Their goal was to ensure that their departed ancestors or rulers made their way through the underworld well prepared to live on the other side in comfort and that their every desire be met."

After delivering those words of wisdom, I noticed the other members of the team looking longly at the narrow entrance of the cave. In fact, Steve made the observation that the large boulder at the entrance to the cave was anything but stable, and it wouldn't take much to move it, thus blocking the cave's entrance.

Now, that got everyone's attention, and Red asked, "Where do we start and how long do you think will we be here? People, we are here on an archaeological search, and that means taking as many photos as possible, but moving any of these precious objects for anything but examinations, go slow. Tomorrow, we'll get our two other Inca experts to examine what we have discovered. I'm sure they will come up with a working plan of how we should proceed."

Barbara took the initiative and calmly remarked, "I was under the impression our goal was to find the remains of Pachacuti and, in doing so, not fall prey to any of the Inca's traps."

"Barbara, if we are lucky, his remains will be lingering in one of the other caverns ringing this cave, and that I can assure you, will take a bunch of time. But before we do any exploring, our IT genius Red will have to conduct a sweep of the caverns. He will pinpoint the locations of any traps. The rest of us will begin a photo shoot. Anyone care to hazard a guess as to what our photos would bring if we decide to offer them on the web?"

Red answered, "Okay, so now I am a mine-sweeper, but before assuming the responsibility for such a heavy task, I am in need of a comfort break, after which, I will be ready to eat a bite or two before we lose the daylight. Then If the light holds, I will conduct a lifesaving sweep; otherwise, I will conduct the sweep at the first light tomorrow. Any objections?"

I noticed that not one of our crew got up to stray away into the dark recess of the cave.

Later, Steve, and Barbara quietly took the initiative and moved out of our tight little circle. When they returned, Steve remarked, "It will soon be pitch dark. How about calling it quits for the day? If we leave right now, navigating that path is tough enough in the daylight, let alone in the dark, even if we don't have to hump our survival packs. I vote we get some food in our bellies and a good night's rest and wait for the sunrise."

Chapter 12

* * *

That Wasn't an Earthquake—
It Was Dynamite

*B*efore I could answer, there was a thunderous crash, followed by a
cracking sound and then a steady cascade of rocks and boulders that
effectively sealed the cave's entrance. Steve yelled, "Stay put! Don't anyone
move! Wait for the aftershock that always follows an earthquake."

After a long period of silence, Red said, "I think we can safely move
around."

He then cautiously picked his way to what was once the cave's entrance.
After a cursory examination, he shook his head. "From the looks of things,
there is no way we can dislodge these mothers without some serious moving
equipment."

As he turned to join the rest of us, a more powerful cracking noise shat-
tered the stillness, and even more stones and boulders further blocked the entrance. The dust was almost overwhelming. I yelled, "Everybody, cover your
face!" and grabbed my survival blanket as did the others.

Steve asked, "How did you know to do that?"

"Simple, Mr. Ambassador. I don't believe what we just experienced was an
earthquake! The loud sound that moved all those rocks and boulders was the
result of an explosive charge, no doubt, set off by Atoc."

After taking stock, I asked, "Everyone okay? If so, let's see what we can do to move enough stones and make a path big enough for us to crawl through."

As hard as we tried, it was to no avail. Those stones were there, and there they were going to stay, until hell freezes over or an experienced crew of removal specialists are found.

Steve made himself comfortable and said, "In Egypt, they would say we have a 'sticky wicket' on our hands. The trick is how do we get out of this mess? That very large boulder at the entrance of this cave evidently moved and triggered the additional collapse, thus further lessening any chances we may have had of using it as our exit."

He faced our group. "Short of a miracle, I seriously doubt if anyone will be using that exit for some time to come."

I said, "Our goal is to find an alternate way out, and if my thinker is working correctly, we should give consideration to using the safety harness as our way to freedom. My genuine Mickey Mouse watch tells me it is 2:35 a.m., and it will remain pitch-dark for the next four hours."

I shook my thermal blanket and that sent the dust flying. After looking around, I found a comfortable spot and said, "I don't know about the rest of you, but I'm going to get in a few Zs. I recommend you do the same. There isn't much we can do until it becomes light. Right now, things look pretty bleak, but after a few hours of sleep, things will look better and we can work on an escape plan."

Our sleep was interrupted by a deep voice that echoed throughout the cave saying, "You hoped to find Pachacuti's remains! Well, you've found them! A lot of good it will do you! He has been asleep for hundreds of years. You and your group will soon join him when your food and water run out. Be aware of the surprises that are in store for you.

"The only entrance to his tomb has, unfortunately, been closed. Few, if any, of your amigos camped out below heard the small explosion. I trust that none of your people were harmed by the shifting of rocks. Their and your death will be slow and painful, as it should be, for you have violated sacred Inca space. We leave you now, adios, señor!"

Barbara remarked, "At least, we know we can communicate with our people courtesy of Atoc and his warning. I'm going to sleep in our lovely air-conditioned palace."

It got so quiet you could hear everyone breathe; then, we heard a shrill, piercing scream, followed by a dull thud.

Acahuana calmly remarked, "I believe a member of Atoc's crew found the path more slippery than he expected. I wonder how Atoc will explain his companion's death and our disappearance to the police."

Shortly after Atoc's friend plunged to his death, we heard a jumble of voices just outside of our now blocked entrance.

Barbara asked, "What's that all about?"

Acahuana said, "One of Atoc's hombres evidently found the part of the path that was unstable and, in doing so, he further dislodged some of those broken stones and is now visiting his ancestors before his soul begins to forever wander the underworld as a non-person."

Speaking in Quechua, he shouted, "Atoc, you are, no doubt, trapped much the same as we are. Was it your right-hand man who fell to his death, all because he was unable to keep his footing? The police have been notified and you know what that means. A long stretch in the jail in Cuzco. You will be an old man before your sentence time runs out. No women, no *chichi*, and no freedom!

"Perhaps, your followers will be allowed to join you if they don't first shorten your life."

Acahuana sat down and I asked, "Right-hand man and we have notified the police? Where did that come from?"

"I didn't see any harm in saying that. I decided to put a little fear and doubt in him and his followers; that's why I spoke in my native tongue. It's almost daybreak and time to work on an escape plan."

I only hope he is right. I looked around for Doubtful, but it was too dark to see him. I knew he was lurking in the darkness—taking it all in.

Red announced, "We better take it easy on the food and water; we don't know how long we will be here."

Daylight began to stream in, and I made my way to the golden palanquin where I started to examine it when Red asked, "Are you thinking what I am thinking?"

I couldn't help laughing when I said, "Yep. Let's see if we can move this monster."

Steve figured out what we had in mind and joined our lifting and moving party. His six-foot-three frame and muscle were deeply appreciated. After a great deal of effort, we were finally able to scoot the palanquin to where it was directly under the overhead escape hole.

We turned it on its side and in the process snapped its short legs into place. After testing it for stability, I motioned to Barbara, did a little bow, and said, "Pretty ladies first."

She looked at me as if I was nuts, saying, "I don't suppose you expect me to stand on that monstrous creation, jump the remaining five feet, grab onto that safety bar, and pull myself to safety. Or have you forgotten, I'm only five-feet-one inch tall?"

Red answered, "Barbara, all you have to do is stand on your husband's broad shoulders, pull yourself up to the opening, and fasten yourself to the safety harness. The rest of us will steady Steve as you make your way through the opening near our former entrance. After that, it should be a piece of cake. Sara and Rafael will be manning the safety ropes and guide you down."

I thought for a moment and hesitantly said, "There is a slight problem, and it should be easily rectified provided Eric's on the job."

Barbara asked, "What in the world does Eric have to do with any of this? I thought he was the drone expert working out of the command center in our hotel."

Red asked Steve to dig into his kit and give him his baseball-sized GPS. He then handed it to Barbara and said, "Put this in one of your cargo pants pockets, and when you reach the outside, yell like hell, hold this jewel up and expose it to daylight. Then, gently pass, not throw, it back to us.

"Hopefully, Eric or one of the Titan's techies are watching their screens. Once the GPS triangulates the satellite signals, they should spot the response and alert Allie Lea who, in turn, will alert her mountaineering crew that someone needs rescuing.

"Sara and Rafael will know what to do, as well as notifying the police. I say 'notifying the police' for Rafael will, no doubt, spot Atoc and his hombres who are trapped just as we are. I don't think they are in for a pleasant encounter. Are you ready, Barbara?"

"Give me a minute; I'm having a problem with my harness. Okay, I'm ready."

As she began her climb, she said, "Steve, I love you darling. Don't take any unnecessary chances and stay close to Ryan. He'll figure out something."

She squeezed the iron bar that was wedged into the hole as she attached her harness to the rappelling rope, all the while dangling in space. "Help! Help! Help!" she screamed, hoping to attraction the attention of the ground crew.

She then felt a tug on the rope and a voice said, "You've done the hard part; now relax, and let us do our part."

Allie Lea watched with apprehension as Rafael haltingly lowered Barbara to the ground and eased her out of the harness. Barbara promptly fainted.

Ken quickly doused her, using one of his water bottles, and then said, "Mom, relax; you're safe." She looked somewhat bewildered and said, "Watch for the others."

Several of the crew besieged her with questions, but Allie Lea intervened. "We need to get Barbara to bed and let her rest."

RK made her a makeshift cot in the SUV and then zoomed off.

Steve and I made an executive decision and selected Red as our next escapee, despite his insistence that we take Acahuana. Before hoisting Red on Steve's shoulders, I whispered, "Red, soft pedal our position; it's apparent that Steve and I will be stuck in this hellhole for some time to come. Get with Jim and see what can be done to move enough of those stones blocking the cave's entrance to where we can squeeze through. Getting Acahuana up on Steve's shoulders will take some doing due to his weight.

"Tell Sara not to be in too much of a hurry rescuing Atoc and his gang. I hope they rot in hell! Steve and I will begin looking for another exit, but I don't hold much hope for that. You can never tell, though, whether something may turn up. Good luck old friend."

I hoisted Red onto Steve's shoulders, and before I could count to ten, he had steadied himself, gave a strong leap, and up he popped out of our stone prison. After locking himself into the safety harness, he wrapped his arms around the rope and slowly began his way to life and freedom.

We motioned to Acahuana. "Put on your safety harness; it's your turn."

He looked defiantly at us. "I'm not going; I'm going to take my chances and stay with you."

"Acahuana, Steve is getting tired, my energy is running out, and it will take a good bit of luck for me to hoist you upon Steve's shoulders. Your grand-father would say a live Inca is better than one who will no longer walk this earth. So, move over here and stop trying to be a martyr. Your people need to see you as a strong, brave Inca leader."

He started climbing, and as he did so, the palanquin lurched, and slowly started to give way.

I yelled, "Acahuana, jump now! Grasp that iron bar—it's your only chance! There won't be another."

He gave a mighty leap, swung on the now creaking bar, and made his way up and out of the opening onto the harness, amid a great deal of clapping and cheering from the watchers at Machu Picchu, the crowd assembled at the base of the mountain, and our campsite.

Allie Lea approached Acahuana and asked, "Is it possible for either of our men to make it out the same way just as you did?"

"No, señora. They are too large to get through the hole, and the means they used to gain enough height to reach the bar is broken. I'm afraid they will be there for some time until the rocks are removed.

"Señor Ryan told me they are going to look for an another entrance, but that will take time due to the numerous alcoves they have to search. He thinks they have enough food and water to last three more days. He also told me to tell you he loves you and not to worry as 'the bad penny always shows up.'"

Allie Lea broke down in a sea of tears. It was good Lynne was there to console her saying, "Dad has been in worse situations than this. At least we know where he is and he's mentally and physically okay."

Allie Lea hesitated a bit and said, "Lynne, Jim and Red are working on a rescue plan. Why don't you walk over to what we call the command tent and talk with them? Better still, give me your arm and we will go there together."

Ashley and Sara wandered off to themselves and, without thinking, Ashley asked the unthinkable, "Was anything of note discovered before your world collapsed?"

Sara grimaced and said to no one in particular, "The only person who would have the gall to ask Allie Lea that question would be Ashley."

Denise arrived and upon seeing Acahuana ran to him, embraced him, and whispered, "Thank goodness my hero is safe."

And, for good measure, she planted a big kiss on him.

Ashley turned to Sara. "At least romance still exists. Now back to business. Come to think of it, none of those rescued have spoken about what they did or didn't find. I find that rather odd. Perhaps they made a pact not to discuss their findings until they were all safe and on the ground with us."

Ashley asked, "How are you going to get those ill-meaning sons of bitches off that little perch? I'll bet they froze their collective asses having to stay there all night."

Sara replied, "Getting them off will be very difficult; they don't have a safety harness. If I can get the rope close enough, they will have to grab and hold on until they reach the ground. If they lose their courage, they surely won't, anytime, be rock or mountain climbing in this world."

Allie Lea uncharacteristically said, "I hope those bastards froze their balls off, but on second thought, maybe that's too good for them."

Ashley seconded that motion and asked, "Wouldn't it be best to wait for Rondo, the police captain, and his officers? It would be not a good idea to have Atoc and his followers running amuck; there is no telling the damage they would do."

A few minutes later, the police van rolled into sight, and Rondo demonstrated why he is the police captain. It took all of five minutes for him and his crew to clear out the sightseers and backpackers. Allie Lea then told him about the situation and led him to where Rafael and Sara had started their rescue efforts.

He said, "Bring those hombres down very slowly; I don't want my men having to deal with more than one of these criminals at a time. It wouldn't be difficult for any of them to disappear into the crowds."

Rondo motioned to his officers. "Get the net; the rest of you be ready in case one of the hombres decides to jump when they are close enough to the ground.

Pay particular attention when their leader is brought down. Atoc knows he will be facing a long jail sentence for a string of crimes we have known about, but couldn't prove were his work. He wouldn't hesitate to injure or kill if anyone got in his way."

The rescue mission began and, wouldn't you know it, guess who came first? Atoc. The officer who was responsible for getting the net unfolded told Allie Lea, "Like spider web, no escape."

Jim Leachy's wife, Judy, turned to Anna and in a saucy exchange asked, "Do you think that would work in our house when the kids get out of hand?"

She laughed. "Just kidding, just kidding."

Jim overheard her retort and gave her an angry stare. She danced up to him, planted a sweet kiss on his cheek, patted his ass, and ended what could have been a contentious situation. The police had literally wrapped up Atoc in the net. He did nothing but glower as the officers shoved him in the police wagon. The rest of the hombres made it down the safety rope without any further incident. They were a disconsolate and a whipped bunch.

They knew the future they were facing was anything but good. Then a strange thing happened: when the last of the hombres was on the ground, he motioned to Sara and gave her thanks for helping to save his life. Sara smiled. "*Gracias,*" and before he was extended the opportunity to climb aboard and join his friends, he asked, "Does señora plan to use rope again?"

Sara was dumbfounded. "*Sí.* Why do you ask?"

He patted his rather large stomach, held up two fingers, and then pointed to Sara, now holding up one finger. Not understanding his actions, she called to one of the officers, explained the situation, and asked him to translate, but she first wanted to know the prisoner's name.

The officer asked the prisoner his name, and he replied, "I am known as Mojo." The rest of the conversation was conducted in Mojo's native Quechua tongue, the officer acting as the interpreter.

Mojo said, "I weigh two hundred pounds. When señora lowered me, I heard cracking sound at head of what you call the safety rope. I believe you will have a problem if hombre is my weight. The rope is tired and won't last much longer."

He bowed, shook her hand, and with his head held high, climbed aboard the police van.

As the van pulled out, Sara wondered, could he be right? Regardless, I am going to heed his warning. I'll do a proper inspection as soon as I deliver these supplies, but in the meantime I'll keep it quiet; there's no need to get anyone else worked up.

Red and Jim approached Rondo and asked, "Did anyone report that one of Atoc's gang fell to his death when they were trying to make their escape?"

Rondo shouted when he asked, "Death, what death?"

He immediately strode over to the police van and asked, "Did one of your hombres visit the underworld before his time?"

One of the prisoners replied, "*Si*, señor captain," and pointed to where his friend had fallen.

The captain rushed to the spot and discovered Atoc's brother's twisted, mangled body lying behind one of the numerous boulders that dot the landscape. It was obvious Atoc's brother had suffered a broken neck when he hit the ground. Rondo was bristling when he said, "Withholding information regarding a death is taken very seriously. Why was this not reported as soon as someone knew of this man's death?"

RK said, "We didn't hear him scream; we were in bed. We heard a noise; we thought it was the scream of an animal."

Rondo scratched his head. "Why was he out that late and on such a treacherous path?"

Allie stiffened her back. "Why don't you ask Atoc why he deliberately blocked the entrance to the cave? Captain, the Smithsonian and the Larco have written permission granted by your country's Minister of Antiquities in Cuzco to explore this area in search of Pachacuti's final resting place. Our lawyer has a copy of the agreement."

"And where is this lawyer?"

"He is trapped in the cave with another man, my husband. We hope you have some ideas about how the rocks or boulders can be moved, so we can get them out.

After thinking a bit, he asked, "Why haven't you rescued the two remaining señors in the same manner? It would appear to me that your method was successful for the others."

Sara sighed. "They are too large!"

He looked astounded and in stern tones said, "Señora this is not the time for games or jokes; explain what you mean when you say they were too large."

"Captain, both of those men are simply too large to fit into the rescue exit. Before you leap to the conclusion that they are fat, forget it. Tall yes, fat not so much!"

"Señora, I was merely trying to assess the situation. I must tell you we do not have the equipment in Ollyantambo to deal with such circumstances. I'll notify my minister in Cuzco and ask his help. It will take at least four or five days before we can get a crane to handle the height where they are trapped. To ask my men to scale the mountain would be most dangerous and, without the proper equipment, impossible.

Allie Lea and Sara started to walk away when Rondo said, "A minute señoras. How is it that you knew that one of the hombres fell to his death? I do not understand why this is the first I've heard of it."

"Julie, one of my people, discovered the body when she went for her early morning jog. She came back running and screaming, 'There's a dead person lying several yards from Jim's tent.' That type of news makes the rounds pretty quickly. Don't you think?"

She continued, "I knew you had been alerted about our problem and saw no reason to bother you, as you were, no doubt, on your way. Now, if you don't mind, I have a bigger problem that needs solving, and that is the rescue of my husband and his friend Steve."

Rondo tipped his hat to her. "We'll be in touch."

Allie Lea asked Lynne to round up the rest of the crew and meet at the base of the entrance to the cave.

After assembling the crew, she said, "Several of you have probably wondered what went on in the cave before Atoc's blast destroyed our entrance and exit. The volunteers have been asked to refrain discussing any part of our operation.

"These artifacts are what archaeologists, looters, and bandits dream about, and in many cases, kill for. The pictures are being held in Titan's photo lab. Eric has been asked to make sure the information these photos contain does not, in any way, become the latest hot stove topic. When Ryan and Steve return, you'll have the opportunity to talk with our volunteers and examine their findings. Until then keep a lid on it.

"Now, the bad news: Rondo has informed me the rescue team and equipment will not arrive for several days. Jim and Red are working on a rescue plan, but they don't hold much hope of putting it into action before tomorrow. They are now in town seeking a generator, a jackhammer, and enough high-pressure hoses that will reach the cave; both men are well. In addition to seeking another way out, they're exploring the tunnels that ring the cave, looking for anything having to do with Pachacuti's remains. However, our and their number one priority remains the same: their rescue!

"When the news breaks that there has been a death in the area, it will draw spectators, reporters, and tv and radio personnel, in addition to the unsavory characters who, like sharks, just seem to show up. Many will speculate we have made a 'find' and that there are ancients or antiquities they can steal, regardless of the circumstances. RK and Acahuana will soon return with enough potluck dinners for everyone. A good, hot dinner will go a long way toward helping everyone relax. Bon appétit!"

Halfway through the meal, one of the police came running and exclaiming, "Señora, señora, come quickly. Trouble, big trouble!!"

The diners rose as one and followed the messenger. The area was lit by a series of floodlights, and Rondo was busily examining the contents of a large gunny sack. After completing his investigation, he addressed the assembled crowd saying, "not murder. The reason this hombre fell to his death was because the load he was carrying was simply too heavy. When he tried to shift it, he lost his balance. Many people have seen what happened and will question what the hombre was hauling.

"As to the contents of this sack, I can assure you, I, and I, alone will examine its contents and put under lock and key in our station."

With that said, out went the spotlights, but not before Rondo announced, "This is a crime scene and the area is closed."

He asked Allie Lea to follow him to his office where they could examine, in private, the astounding artifacts.

"Señora, for now, it is not in our best interest to divulge these contents. Should I be asked, I will simply say the findings are considered police evidence and will be presented at the man's trial. The trial date will be flexible. Other than that, for the time being, there is nothing else we can do here."

"Captain, your offer is appreciated.

"Would it be too much of an imposition to meet tomorrow morning at your office? I will bring my Inca archaeologist; her findings will be kept private until we are ready to release the information concerning this find."

"Señora, I have no problem with you bringing your Inca expert. I must inform my minister of the death of one of the looters as well as the capture of the four other looters. He will, no doubt, wish to see and question their leader. The subject of what caused Atoc's brother's death will be his number one challenge."

Allie Lea said, "Your point is well taken. Perhaps we can change our meeting to later this afternoon, say around four p.m. The only question is where?"

"Very well, señora. My office will ensure our privacy. I will see to that. *Mañana* señora."

Allie Lea wasted no time in running down Ashley and informing her of the day's happenings who said, "Up to now, I have felt like an extra thumb. I am thrilled at the opportunity to examine a piece of history that has been dormant for over four hundred years. Does anyone else know about the 'find' and our meeting?"

"Only Rondo, the police captain; I trust him not to to talk for the next two days!

"Be ready to leave in the next hour, and for heaven's sake, don't bring anything other than a notepad. Anything else might spook our dear captain. In case anyone should ask where you're going, say: 'To examine the latest drone's results.'

"Once we reach the hotel, I must call Jim Hamilton and dazzle him with our success. No doubt, he will be over the moon. When it comes to raising money for future explorations, there is nothing like a successful exploration. As he often says, 'Get the donors while the iron is hot.' I would like to spend a few minutes with Sara and Rafael and see what advice they have. I suspect that any outside help will be a long time in coming.

"Oh goodness, I see that Sara is beginning that dangerous climb and her backpack is bulging. Rafael, why is she doing this? Couldn't you stop her? I was under the impression one of the prisoners warned her the iron bar and the rope might be a problem."

"Allie Lea, when Sara makes up her mind to do a thing, she becomes single-minded of purpose. She tested the rope and decided it was good for several more climbs, but in the interest of safety, she told me she will replace it after this trip.

"She doesn't plan to end up splattered all over the landscape as she is looking forward to the joy of being a parent. However, she often forgets she's pregnant and needs to take less chances. I see she has reached her objective."

"Senor Rafael, how did you find out they needed anything? I thought we were unable to communicate with them."

"They gave a note to señora Barbara. Is there a problem?"

"No problem, I'm happy Sara is able to handle such a load. I'm sure the supplies she's carrying will be greatly appreciated."

The noise level dropped to zero as everyone held their breath watching Sara unhook herself from her harness. A moment later, all hell broke loose when Sara gave a loud shriek, yelling, "Oh no! Dear Lord!" And then she disappeared from view.

Her scream was followed by Ryan shouting, "She's okay; we caught her. The extra weight and the explosion caused the rock to crumble, forcing the iron bar to work its way loose. That's why the safety rope and harness came tumbling down with her. Regardless, she's okay and when things settle down, we'll resume the search for another exit. My voice is going, due to my hollering. We'll talk tomorrow at about this time and hopefully have some good news."

After listening to Ryan from down below, Allie Lea went over to Rafael. "I'm going to push Jim and Red to hurry up with their rescue plan. I feel the situation has become more urgent. Señor Rafael, I have a question for you: when the iron bar worked itself loose, did it enlarge the hole enough so that everyone could get out?"

"Señora, the hole was large enough for Sara as she is, what you say, 'petite.' I don't think you would classify the señors as petite. It would be a mistake to consider this as a future means of escape. I am not experienced enough to attempt such a climb. Perhaps one of the rescue amigos will be skilled in such climbing. Even if I were able, there is no assurance I could enlarge the hole or attach the safety rope."

Allie Lea and Ashley went to the four-wheeler to talk with RK. After they made him aware of the latest, he said, "I'm sorry, Mom, I didn't know. But, don't worry Dad's a survivor. I'm sure he'll figure out something, just give him time."

The approaching dusk created a surreal picture of the surrounding Andes, bringing with it a somber attitude for those who decided to stay and camp out.

Jim pulled the guards aside and said, "Our nemesis and his henchmen are safely in jail, so we can rest easy tonight."

His thoughts and reasoning turned out to be a little out of kilter, but that's life.

Meanwhile, inside the cave, Steve and Sara were beavering away working on a rescue plan.

Finally, Sara said, "It's late; let's give it up for the night. I have had a traumatic day and I'm not thinking clearly. Besides we need to conserve what little battery power we have. If I have to get up in the night, don't be alarmed; remember, I'm expecting."

Steve said, "You're right. We can't accomplish anything in the darkness. Maybe tomorrow we'll get lucky. Goodnight, everyone."

Midway through the night, Ryan tapped Steve on the shoulder and asked, "Did you hear anything or was I just imagining I heard someone or something moving?"

"Yeah, it was Allie Lea telling you to get your ass in gear, so that the Smithsonian could get the word out that a historic discovery had occurred under their auspices."

Sara groggily answered, "Ryan, it was me. Can I go back to sleep or do you want a running commentary?"

Steve snickered and said, "Goodnight again, mother hen."

Morning came with a bang as the sunlight streamed in through the eight holes of our cell. This was the first time we were able to examine the treasures the Inca had accumulated. If one believes the journey and the afterworld are one and the same, having a goodly store of gold and jewels insures a great measure of happiness and power for many eons.

No doubt, the rulers expect to be well-cared for throughout the afterlife, and they didn't expect to be at a loss for caretakers if this supply of gold and jewels means anything.

Sara was her usual bouncy self and asked, "Which comes first? Seeking another exit or examining these goodies?"

I said, "Without a doubt, seeking another exit is the first order of the day. Thanks to you, we are good for another three to four days. After that, we're in trouble. I recommend we ration our water and go easy on the sandwiches, canned meats, and candy bars. While you and Steve were sleeping, I looked for several rocks that will come in very handy. They will be our means of communicating to the outside world."

Sara stood there with hands on her hips, lips puckered, and announced, "As the reigning queen of this Inca cavern, I hereby acknowledge, that you,

Merlin, conjure up another method of escape because rocks sure as hell won't get it."

Steve commented, "Ah, I see that you are a King Arthur fan; perchance, you ask Merlin to include an order for ham and eggs and a steaming pot of coffee for breakfast. Can you handle that Merlin?"

I didn't wish to show my pique, so I remarked, "You're both right. Now let's eat."

After eating, I rummaged around and found a dog-eared note pad and a pencil at the bottom of my kit and made a few notes for Allie Lea. I then asked, "Anyone like to add a few comments before I tie and hurl this missile into outer space?"

Sara looked perplexed. "I remember in the dim past Allie Lea telling me you played ball when you were in the Marines. Do you honestly believe you can throw that rock through that hole in the ceiling?"

"Why not? Don't you think it's worth a shot? My only worry is, will the cord wrapping stay intact and not flutter off into God knows where!"

"Provided you are successful, how do you plan to keep it from bouncing off the noggin of one of our crew or even worse a spectator?"

I said, "It may take a few practice throws, but remember the old adage, 'Practice makes perfect.' If you step back a foot or so, I will do my imitation of Greg Maddox. Sara, for your information, he was a most successful pitcher for the Atlanta Braves. As to the problem of zonking anyone, I suggest we yell, 'incoming!' After that, it's every person for themselves!"

She replied, "If we were under different circumstances, I'd give you a swift kick in the ass. Even I have heard of Greg Maddox and that he had pinpoint accuracy, but no fast ball. So there! Let's get with the program."

We stood under the opening and waited for a response."

It was not long when Allie Lea answered, "Got it. After we interpret your notes, we'll get back to you. How do you like the bullhorn? It was Jim's idea."

I shouted, "Can they come up with another idea? We are running short of caverns and tunnels to explore. I imagine the folks visiting Machu Picchu can hear everything we say. Go easy on the information that affects us and your efforts to get us out of this damn trap. It wouldn't surprise me if the song 'Send in the Clowns' makes a comeback. Be careful, thirty!"

Sara asked, "What does thirty mean? Is it a code the two of you have cooked up?"

I smiled. "The numeral thirty at the end of a story or memo was a reporter or writer's way of saying 'I'm done,' or 'That's the end of the story for now.' The use of thirty in this day and time is dated, but you're right! Allie Lea and I have used it many times. It's easy to remember and I hate having to remember a slew of passwords. Well, gang, it's work time. Before we do much moving around, we must conduct another sweep and see if we can pinpoint any traps we may have missed on our first pass."

Steve remarked, "I'm in the dark; we don't have any sweeping equipment. Merlin, do you plan to conjure up this needed piece of equipment?"

"Steve, the only way I know is that we scout around, look for a staff or a piece of wood, and if we don't find any, we'll use our eyes and hands. First, we begin by dividing the cave into quadrants and do a systematic probe of each area. It's a crude and dangerous way to find trouble; unless either of you have a better way, we shouldn't waste any more of the daylight hours."

Sara decided to take the third cavern and do a floor search. The first two we explored were what we expected: they led to blind ends. The third not only narrowed to a blind end, but at its end, the Inca had dug a 'Pit of Death,' measuring approximately twelve by ten feet. Those clever devils had covered the pit with rushes and a light sprinkling of soil that blended in perfectly with the rest of the cavern floor. I would have loved to examine this pit and see how many visitors had met their demise through the years.

Steve remarked, "I encountered similar traps when Barbara and I were working on a dig in Egypt. The difference between the two is that in Egypt, the unwary were entombed never again to see light. This method of torture is different; the victims have a longer time to adjust their thoughts as life slowly ebbs from their earthly bodies."

Sara smirked when she uttered, "Aren't we just the essence of joy and happiness? I'm going to take a look at the food on that exquisite table next to the palanquin; it looks so inviting. I guess this is what Atoc and his gang brings as a tribute to Pachacuti."

I motioned for Sara to stop and not move a muscle, and as calmly as possible said, "Sara, back away from that table, and don't even think of touching any of that food. You are in a dangerous situation, and because of your lack of weight, the trap hasn't been sprung."

Glaring, she hesitated. "Why is it you are always giving the orders? These ears of corn are so appealing and they don't weigh very much and the ears look so fresh!"

"Sara, if you wish to live long enough to see tomorrow, do as I say, and for God's sake, quit questioning and arguing! If you don't do as I say, Rafael will find himself without a wife!"

"Ryan you are scaring the living hell out of me! Against my better judgment, I'll inch my way to where you and Steve are standing no matter how ridiculous it may look. If you are pulling my chain, you'll find that I have a long memory."

She no sooner uttered those words when she began to slide into the pit. Steve was the closest to her. He grabbed her hands and effortlessly pulled her up and out of harm's way.

I said, "Sara, this is your lucky day, thanks to Steve. Had he not been in a position to yank you to safety, you would have suffered a fate you wouldn't wish on your worst enemy. At the bottom of the pit, a dozen or so sharpened sticks had been sunk upright just waiting to impale their next victim, causing a slow agonizing death."

Sara took one look, gave me a bear hug, and promptly collapsed to the ground tearfully saying, "I'm sorry, I'll never doubt you again, please forgive me! Steve, had you not been there to haul my dumb ass out of trouble, Rafael would have been without his wife and our child-to-be.

Steve took one look at the pit. "Maybe you can return the favor one day in the future."

Sara scanned the pit and exclaimed, "What a horrible way to die and to think I almost didn't heed your warning! Ryan, that's twice you saved my life.

Rafael has often told me I need to practice listening. He'll be glad to know as of now I am a full-fledged listener!"

I couldn't help laughing when I replied, "Wanna bet?"

I noticed her tears were really flowing. I put my arm around her and gave her a squeeze. "It's better you found that little Inca surprise when you had someone to help you, instead of an unsuspecting or novice archaeologist.

"Let's get back to searching those tunnels off to the right. I doubt the Inca built in any other surprises in this part of the cavern. But first I have a task to perform."

I walked to the other side of the table holding what seemed to be food that positively glistened. I realized this is what Atoc and his gang worked on each night. I then did something I know any good archaeologist would never do. I picked up a couple of pieces of corn, and after closely examining them, I began to laugh and handed them to Steve to examine. Sara wouldn't touch them.

I remarked, "Sara, these two pieces of corn are worth a fortune. The reason they're glistening is pretty simple. The kernels have been shaped to simulate a person's natural teeth. They are solid gold and each kernel has been sewn into an ear of corn. I remember reading that the average ear of corn is made up of eight to twelve hundred kernels.

"How's that for a bit of illuminating information? At the time, I was researching the Inca and came across this piece of information that I thought was totally unimportant. I don't wish to be a killjoy, but I wonder how many of these treasures will ultimately make their way to a museum. Until they are in a museum's hands, someone will have to stand guard 24/7; otherwise, they will vanish."

We then examined all but one of the remaining tunnels without any luck; they too led to dead ends.

After a meager dinner, Steve commented, "We have become a pretty despondent group, and unless we shake this feeling, things are not going to get better. We are running low on food and water, and those extra batteries have just about had it. I find it difficult to think safety and freedom are just a few feet away, and there isn't a damn thing we can do to help free ourselves. We need to rid ourselves of the cobwebs and get a good night's sleep, and in the meantime put on our collective thinking caps, and tomorrow see what percolates."

I said, "Everything looks better in the daylight; your idea of brainstorming makes sense. Sara, you have been strangely quiet. What's bugging you?"

"I have been worrying about being pregnant, and if I don't make it, this little girl I'm carrying won't ever see the light of day."

"You mean you're feeling sorry for yourself, don't you? That's nonsense; you are going to make it. So buck up! Remember, each day is like a deposit at the bank, and you have many deposits yet to make. Mountaineers are made of tough stuff, and since we survived our West Virginia upbringing, we can survive anything. Let's go to sleep folks."

Chapter 13

* * *

Things that Go Swish in the Night

I had just settled down and started to drift off when I felt a gentle nudge, and Steve whispered, "Did you hear that swishing sound? It sounded like it was a person dragging their feet."

I asked, "Do you think it was one of Atoc's crew? If that's what you heard, then it's good news."

Steve sat up. "Ryan, you're right. A good night's sleep is what we all need. As to it being 'good news,' I vaguely remember Atoc or one of his crew pulling the plug on the entrance to this cave. I suspect they would have anything but good wishes for us."

We listened very carefully, but the sound was not repeated. Steve said, "Whatever or whoever it was is gone. Tomorrow night I plan to sleep with one of the cans of mace close beside me. I realize this small can won't afford much of a deterrent, but we don't have any other means of protection. How about it, Ryan? Let's keep this little episode to ourselves. Sara doesn't need to handle the thoughts of another person in this cave; she might freak out. Good idea that mace; maybe now I can get back to sleep."

The next morning's breakfast found Sara in a chipper mood. Steve and I looked at each other and wondered "Who gave her a happiness pill?" After making ourselves comfortable, our first topic of conversation had to do with Allie Lea's lack of communication. I said, "She must have a sound reason for not being in touch. Sara, how about writing her a note? And I'll once more do my Greg Maddox imitation."

She replied, "Should I include in your note a request for a couple more cans of mace?" She then broke out laughing. "Don't you boys just hate when you are bested by a wisp of a woman such as myself?"

I blushed after hearing Sara's remarks and said, "I'll be, go to hell, you were listening all the time. Why didn't you say something?"

"I didn't want to interfere in the big men's talk and I needed sleep. I knew this bit of information would ultimately come up, so what was the hurry? I guess the rest of our brain-storming session will be centered about who and how did someone get into this cave, and how do we come up with an answer to those two questions? It's your serve gentlemen."

Steve answered, "I too have a wisp of a woman who, like Sara, is not above giving me a piece of her mind when the occasion presents itself. I may, at times, resent it, but then that's what it takes to make a good marriage. How about it, Ryan?"

"Mr. Ambassador, I'll take the fifth on that one. I believe it's time for us to get at our problem and, hopefully, our opportunity. Sara let's hear your thoughts."

She replied, "We need to know if our supposed invader is a human or an animal, and then set our own trap accordingly. It would help if we knew the reason for its being here, and then look for other exits or entrances. Of course, this is all conjecture on my part. Who wants to go next?"

Steve answered saying, "I couldn't have said it better myself, and I expect Ryan agrees. Am I correct in my assumption, señor Keshaw?"

Before I could answer, we heard Allie Lea calling on a bullhorn. Her news was anything but encouraging.

"The idea that Red and Jim Leachy came up with was a bummer. They had thought of getting a jackhammer expert to crack the rock surrounding the entrance. When they talked to the hombre whose job it is to work the jackhammer, he remarked, 'Too dangerous, do not have equipment.' In short, all he said was, '*nada señors, nada!*'

"I believe he's right because Jim offered him more money, and all he said was 'Nada' and he walked away. On the orders of the Minister of Antiquities, the Peruvian rescue crew is being assembled and will leave tomorrow. I don't think they'll set any speed records. Knowing the roads and the fact they have to drive four hundred fifty miles, we'll be lucky if they get here the day after tomorrow. We have another problem: the area is swarming with people. The news of what's happening has spread like wildfire.

"Jim is also working on a plan with Rondo, our friendly police captain, to contain their movement. He believes it is best to cordon off the area around our campsite. He means to make it difficult for anyone to attempt to climb or scale the eighty or ninety feet to the cave entrance, especially without any equipment, unless they are in a hurry to leave this planet.

"How is everyone doing? Anyone come up with an idea of how you can get out of there? Oh yes, how are your food and water holding out? Give me a shout about the same time tomorrow. Here's Barbara and Rafael who wish to say a few words."

I closed our conversation by shouting, "Look for another Greg Maddox special. Remember, silence is golden."

Sara asked, "What the hell was that all about?"

"Just a thought I didn't wish to share with that mob of tourists. How about getting a pencil and paper and answer her questions? Tell her our food will run out tomorrow, and water, maybe, in another three days. You might add this as a postscript: make sure Eric is on the job and that he stays alert, this for your eyes only, and the same for Eric."

Steve came alive when he heard me add a postscript and asked, "Ryan this is not the time or place to keep secrets from each other. What's so important about Eric staying alert? He no longer has to oversee the drone flights. What do you know that we don't?"

Sara chimed in. "Ryan, I'm for anything that gets us out of this prison, and I'm running low on optimism."

I said, "Guys, I have come up with a half-baked idea, but I need more time to think it through. The last thing I want to do is to give you a sense of false hope. The sun is setting, and there isn't much we can accomplish in the dark; we need to save our flashlights for genuine emergencies. I'll have my idea fleshed out by morning. Okay?"

Sara took center stage when she announced, "I, too, have a plan, and it won't have to wait until morning. Any one interested? If I am right, then each of us will be mighty happy."

Steve shook her hand and said, "In for a penny, in for a pound. Let's hear it señora!"

She curtsied and asked, "Do either of you have a piece of underwear that you can do without? If so, get it quickly; we have but a few minutes of light left.

"Guys, don't be bashful. I'm very familiar with men's underwear. After all, I am married, and many's the time I have to pick up after Rafael."

She giggled when she added, "Daily. Here's my plan: During my college archaeological training, one of the animals we studied lives in the Andes. It is my belief we had a nocturnal visit from a puma, which is known to be unkind to humans, and he was sussing out the territory.

"I say puma because other mountain cats are much smaller, and their feet are heavily padded, so that they make little noise when they are on the trail of their prey. I believe he or she will return seeking whatever it is that has a human smell.

"Steve, you and Ryan move or scoot that palanquin and turn it on its side, so it's just beyond the pit of death. Our undies will lead our visitor to the trap that I am skillfully camouflaging. The palanquin will be our shield should 'it' not take the bait. If that turns out to be the case, we'll have to depend on the mace to make him think twice before attacking us. If these protective measures work out, we'll be happy or at least alive come tomorrow morning.

"As they say in the mountains of West Virginia, are you 'fer or agin'? Tempus fugit."

With that, she picked up the undies and placed them, so they led right up to edge of the pit.

"Okay boys, move your ass and hump that palanquin right over here. I'd do it myself, but I don't have enough muscle power."

As we were hoisting and dragging the palanquin, I asked, "Where would you like us to place this friggin,' heavy, golden chariot?"

She then casually picked up her bedding, unrolled it, and placed it directly behind the palanquin.

We looked at her questionably.

She smiled, saying, "We girls have to look out for ourselves. Anyone have a problem with that?"

Steve looked at me and asked, "Do you think there is enough room for our bedrolls?"

I broke into a laugh. "Steve, I think you asked the wrong question."

He replied, "How so?"

The proper question should have been, "Do you think she'll let us?"

The next two hours I did nothing but fidget, toss, and turn. I finally drifted off. Just before dawn, I heard a movement of some sort and I nudged Steve and asked, "Did you hear anything?"

I didn't waste anytime getting my canister of mace out of my kit.

Steve replied, "You bet I heard it and I believe it's an animal. I just hope it isn't a puma. They are large, know no fear, and when hungry, attack and kill humans."

Our intruder then let go with a prolonged snarl and a deep guttural roar as it ripped our underwear to shreds. It sensed our presence and prepared to spring. That was its undoing. The cover over the trap gave way, and it was immediately impaled. We determined the 'it' was a she just as she let out a piercing scream of agony and lay there thrashing about, and after a while, her cries slowly diminished.

We stood there frozen in utter disbelief as to what we had done.

Finally, Sara asked, "Is it over?"

We approached the pit and confirmed it was indeed a female puma; and what a beauty she was. Sara started crying and asked, "Why couldn't it have ended another way?"

"Sara, it was her or us. Take a seat and listen how Merlin plans to successfully end our little escapade. I can now tell you about my plan because it depended on an ending in this fashion. There is no time to waste. Our friend, no doubt, has a mate and that mate will come looking for his partner. My plan should work, provided we are long gone before he discovers his mate's demise and that we're out of here before darkness sets in. Steve, get our GPSs, as they will play an important role in our getting out of here. The puma must have made her entrance from one of two tunnels, thanks to Sara's placement of our underwear. This is how I hope it will play out.

"Roll one of the GPSs into the tunnel on the left and listen for the sound it makes as it rolls along. Two, Steve, clocks the length of time that he can hear it roll for each tunnel. Three, Sara and I will be the listeners, and when we no longer hear it rolling, we tell Steve. If my idea works, one of the two tunnels will lead to the outside. Hopefully, the GPS's rolling will not be impeded by a stone or a blockage of some sort.

"I'm banking on our friend, the dead Puma, to show us the way to freedom. After all, she got in and must use the same pathway to get back out."

The bullhorn sounded and I yelled, "We're busy. Tell Eric we said 'Hello' and that our GPS is working just fine. Over and out."

My two partners looked perplexed and asked, "What about the rest of your plan?"

"All in good time, my Huckleberry friends, all in good time! Now, let's get started. Steve you have the honors, roll your GPS down the tunnel on the left, and Sara roll yours down the other tunnel after Steve tabulates the time on tunnel one."

We listened intently for fifty to sixty-seconds, then the sound died away.

Sara stepped up, hoisted her ball, gave it a powerful thrust, and as she released it, she said, "Go all the way, you sweet thing."

This time we heard the GPS rolling along and after what seemed an eternity, the sound faded into nothing, its time was seventy-four seconds.

I remarked, "That cinches it! Sara's ball rolled further and that means we go to Plan C."

Steve asked, "Now what in the blue blazes is Plan C?"

"The acid test!"

Sara pensively said, "I have a feeling I'm not going to like what our dear leader has in mind *for me.*"

"Sara, Sara, I've thought of a way to take the risk out of what we must attempt. Our food is running out, and we barely have enough water to last until tomorrow, not to mention the possibility that we may be Mr. Puma's next target and that we have used up most of our mace."

Steve replied, "I like that part where you said you have taken out the risk!"

"All right, let's don't quibble; here's the deal. Sara, put on your mountaineering jacket, pants, and boots, and lace your boots up good and tight. Where are your gloves? It is imperative that you wear them. They are gonna take a beating as well as protecting your pinkies. Steve, help me move those coils of climbing rope to the number two tunnel and scrounge up her chipping hammer. Sara, the hardest part of your trip is that you might need to break up a stone or two. The tunnel was large enough to accommodate our puma, and based on that knowledge, your trip should go well."

"Whoa there, Mr. horsey! I don't remember being asked to perform a miracle. I gather you want me to crawl headfirst into the unknown. My question becomes obvious, why me? I have a problem with tight spaces in fact they scare the pee out of me. Have either of you got any ideas about how I can keep from going nuts because of my fear of closed-in places? If so, I'd love to know how I can overcome my claustrophobic self, particularly at a time such as this."

"Sara, despite your pregnancy, I'm guessing you weigh little more than, say one hundred twenty pounds and that qualifies you for the opportunity of a lifetime. I see you shaking your head no, but hear me out before you make up your mind. We wrap part of the rope around your ankles, and as you move downward, the rope plays out and becomes your lifeline to safety. Should you run into trouble, pulling you back will be a cinch, all because of your low weight. Ms. Priss, I'm sure you now understand why you are the logical choice for this once-in-a-lifetime adventure. "

"Ryan Keshaw, that is pure bullshit and you know it!

"I would have been more receptive had you said, 'Sara, it's you or no one; the risk is heavy, and we've run out of options! However, there is another option: do nothing or stay and take what I believe to be a dwindling chance of us getting out of here—alive.'"

Sara began to cry. "Ryan Keshaw, you always have a way with words. You know I'll go even if it kills me!"

Steve had been silent throughout, but then he went over to Sara, picked her up and said, "No wonder Rafael walks around with a smile."

He gave her an extra squeeze and then gently lowered her to the ground.

I looked at Sara. "We'll look for another way. I realize I pushed too hard."

She replied, "You numbskull, you know I'll do it. I was just venting my fears."

I quietly said, "Thank you Sara. Once you have gained your freedom, and if you believe our size won't be an impediment, walk or crawl a few feet up the tunnel and yell as loud as possible the word 'go.' We won't need the rope; neither Steve nor I will have the strength to pull the other back up the tunnel. So how about it? Are still you game?"

"Ryan, I am almost scared beyond belief. I understand your logic, and even I believe your plan has a chance of working. The one reason I'm willing to give it a try is the thought that if I get into trouble you and Steve will be able to pull me back to safety. So, let's go before I chicken out and change my mind. For luck, I would appreciate a hug from each of you big apes."

"Sara, keep mum about this new escape route. I'm pretty sure Allie Lea understood my message and should be standing by awaiting your successful exit. Try to blend in, stash your mountain climbing gear, and make yourself as inconspicuous as possible. Otherwise, you'll be inundated by all sorts of people who will have a million questions beginning with: how did you find your way out and what about the others?"

As she made her way into the tunnel, she turned and blew a kiss saying, "Tell Rafael I love him." The darkness of the tunnel then swallowed her up.

Steve whispered, "Ryan, there goes one plucky girl and our only hope. I don't believe you told her the truth about the food. You know it's all gone, and we have but one small bottle of water between us. I don't need to tell you that we are in a world of hurt if that tunnel is too small for either of us."

"You're right. I didn't tell her the truth. I thought she might back out and be unwilling to navigate the tunnel. Had she known the facts regarding our food and water supply and we had to pull her back, I hate to say it, but we would be truly fucked. If she makes it and signals a 'no,' then we'll go back to plan B, whatever that is, but let's not give up—at least not yet!"

"Ryan, she's moving slowly, but the ropes are still playing out. I figure she will reach the outside wall within the next forty minutes or so. What's plan B?

I don't recall us discussing any such thing. Is what you have in mind one of your pull-it-out-of-your ass things?"

I replied, "Something like that! Hey, take a look at this! The ropes have gone limp. That means she's not moving. I hope and pray she isn't stuck or that claustrophobia has caused her to panic."

"Ryan, I think if she was going to panic, it would have happened much earlier in the game. I'll bet she has encountered some rocks or stones and is using her chipping hammer to fracture or break them apart. Barbara and I have participated in several digs in Egypt and Guatemala these last eight years. We've encountered some dicey times, but this one tops them all.

"I daresay we'll think long and hard before agreeing to participate in another dig or exploration. Yipe, the rope has started to move!!"

"Steve, little victories often lead to greater accomplishments."

From the way we yelled and high-fived each other, you would think we had just won the Super Bowl. No matter, the news from Sara was nothing but good. She was now moving forward and at a more rapid pace than before.

"Steve, she must have sighted the opening, and it's giving her an extra burst of adrenalin.

"I hope her voice is strong enough for us to hear."

The ropes stopped moving and we stood there in utter disbelief, not saying a word and, in unison, gently laid them on the floor of the cave. Twenty or so minutes later, one of the ropes moved in a jerking fashion and we both grabbed it and tugged on it as hard as possible.

When we first started pulling on it, the rope moved very slowly and then it gathered speed, causing it to pop back out of the tunnel, unceremoniously dumping both of us on our asses. A white cloth was wrapped and tied to the end of the rope.

We hurriedly untied the cloth and read the note. "Sorry, fellows, it took so long. I ran into several obstacles. I had to chip a few stones that I knew would cause you trouble. I damn near gave up and pulled on the rope several times. My problem manifested itself in excess perspiration of a sort. Exiting the tunnel proved to be most difficult. The exit was filled with several rows of thorny bushes, and I didn't have anything, but my little chipping hammer, so I did the unthinkable: I knocked down a number of the bushes, so that I could squeeze through.

"It's no wonder we didn't see this exit, as it has a dense grove of thorny bushes and several shrubs protecting the opening. I was lucky that Lynne was patrolling the area near the exit. When she spotted me whacking those damn bushes, she used her cell to call our crew. They came running!!"

Sara saw Rafael, grabbed him, gave him a mighty hug, smothered him with kisses, and remarked, "I am a mess! My hairs the pits; my jacket and pants are in shreds; and my hands are in sore need of attention. My poor gloves just weren't up to the task, and if you get close enough and are downwind, you will understand why I really need a shower and a clean everything. Oh me! Allie Lea, here I am running off at the mouth when I should be telling you the Rover boys are fine."

Allie Lea asked, "Can they make it through the tunnel without getting stuck?"

Sara said, "Getting through the tunnel was the easy part; why I didn't panic, I'll never know. The intense darkness, the seeming closeness of the walls, and having to remove several rocks made me forget everything else. On several occasions, I came within an ace of tugging on the ropes, asking the guys to pull me back. When I was oh-so-close to panicking, I knew I had a couple of heroes who would haul me (if it came to that) back to safety and that, my friends, was what kept me pushing forward.

"As to your question, the answer is, yes. They must be prepared to pace themselves, despite the heavy perspiration their bodies will generate. Use your horn to make them aware there will be a couple of tight spots, and when they reach them, they are halfway home.

"These two spots require intense panic control. The trip should take no more than forty minutes. Allie Lea, why don't you make your way into the cave and let 'em have it?"

She smiled, hugged Sara, and said, "Thanks for being so considerate."

Allie Lea carefully made her way through the thicket and crawled into the entrance and repeated the words, "Go, go, go!"

The sound of the bullhorn was deafening as it reverberated and bounced off the tunnel and caves walls, but we got the message. "Steve, old friend, it's your turn to make several people happy. After you make it out, give me the signal, and I'll be hot on your heels. Before you depart, take a good look, and remember what we have accomplished: something that others will only dream of, but we will have lived it."

He changed back into his regular garb and said, "I've changed my mind and wish to go last; my family will have to wait for their big guy. However, before we go, let's do something that many archaeologists wish they had the opportunity to do. We should each take one of those golden apples and an ear or two of corn for our museums to analyze and place on display, just in case."

I asked, "And why do you think that, and what's the deal with the, 'Just in case'?"

"Didn't the captain say these artifacts would be targets if not placed in safekeeping?"

I thought for a moment, and we raised the ears of corn, exclaiming, "For the museums!"

Steve then said, "Okay, I'll go now, and I guess I'd better get on my heavy duds."

I reminded him not to forget to tie one end of that rope around one of his ankles. "If you run into trouble, I'll think of a way to help you.

"So, get a move on. I don't wish to crawl through this tunnel after daylight. It wouldn't surprised me if our now departed puma's mate doesn't come looking for his female companion; that's something I couldn't handle. After this is all over, I think it only fitting that we hold a special survivors' dinner and I'll pay. How about that, my friend?"

Steve slowly ambled to the tunnel entrance. "I'm not claustrophobic, but the darkness of that tunnel bothers me no little bit. I don't know how Sara summoned up the courage to be the first to try and crawl her way to what she hoped was safety."

I remarked, "Sara is a young lady of many talents, but on several occasions she has been known to get under my skin and annoy the hell out of me. The problem is she's right more often than wrong, hence my irritation. Despite her tramping all over my manly pride, she is first-rate and has proven to be a valuable asset. Rafael is fortunate he chose her for his wife. Enough of this maudlin stuff. Are you going or are you just going to sit there and rot?"

"I'm going, but don't push me. I am slowly working up the courage to take the plunge into the unknown."

After sitting there for a couple of minutes, he said, "I've completed my analysis of the situation, and based on Sara's trip, I believe I'll make it. I should make the cave's entrance no later than thirty-five minutes, barring any unforeseen complications. I'll be the first to greet you when you exit the tunnel; that is, unless you decide you'd rather stay in this homey abode."

With that, he dropped to all fours, gave a couple of growls, and began his descent. I sat on the cave floor watching every movement of the rope. The rope played out without any jerks, and if I didn't know better, I would swear he was moving much faster than did Sara.

He had been gone almost eighteen minutes when my old friend Doubtful made his appearance. My immediate reaction was, oh shit I'm headed for trouble, but where? I didn't have long to wait. I became aware of a series of low moaning sounds that kept getting stronger and they really spooked me.

I picked up Steve's can of mace and flashlight and cautiously examined the trap where the puma had fallen. Somehow, she had extricated herself from the stake that had impaled her and she was attempting to climb out of her prison. Her bleeding had ceased, and despite her wounds, she was still a force to be reckoned with. Her resurgence made up my mind: it was time to move and quickly.

I couldn't wait for Steve to give me a shout. Despite that, I gathered up our packs and dragged them over to the tunnel entrance. Unlike the others, I backed into the tunnel and then, using the packs, blocked the entrance. The only thing I carried was that can of mace. Going into the tunnel feet first meant my progress would be slower than going head first. I knew the puma would climb out sooner or later, and those packs and her wounds hopefully would slow her down.

If that happens, I prayed my can of mace would stop her and last long enough for me to reach the tunnel entrance. I was so preoccupied with those thoughts I forgot I was claustrophobic. I kept watching and listening for a sign of her and concentrating on making time.

I was at what I thought to be the halfway mark when I heard and felt a sound so loud that it frightened me. All I could understand was the word "go." That was music to my ears. I redoubled my efforts after I passed the two tight areas Sara warned us about. I was sweating like there was no tomorrow and I stopped to get my breath.

For some strange reason, I began to laugh when I heard a familiar voice shout, "Is my lover about to return to me and the land of the living and is he ready for a triumphal entry? If not, you better get ready, be graceful, and no grumping. A great many of our crew told me they have been praying for your safety."

Before I knew it, Allie Lea had me in a bear hug and gave me a lingering kiss.

An instant later, we heard a great roar followed by a lingering snarl. That damn puma, despite her wounds, had somehow clawed her way out of that pit of death. She was charging down the tunnel like a freight train, scaring the living hell out of everyone who was desperately scampering to get out of the way. This two hundred pounds of coiled steel wanted no part of us. She was frantically working her way out of the thorn bushes and shrubs surrounding the entrance and then she high-tailed it to safety.

After taking a moment to reflect, I asked myself a question, was it the prayers or dumb luck that saw me through? Either way, I felt fortunate things turned out as they did.

Steve casually walked up and shook my hand. "I wasn't the first, but you know how I feel; thank you."

RK had thoughtfully brought our RV as close to the entrance as possible, and the survivors and their wives piled in, but not before Rondo our friendly police captain made a statement. "My congratulations on the timely escape. The hombres from Cuzco will be here tomorrow and start clearing the way to the cave's entrance. Señora, we have a problem that needs fixing. Did you not find an abundance of ancient Inca artifacts, and didn't your señors find another entrance? I'm asking my officers to rock and concrete the new entrance; otherwise, what you found would disappear in front of our very eyes. I will post a twenty-four-hour guard at this entrance, and he will be instructed not to leave this post until he hears from me. Okay?"

She said, "Captain Rondo, you are a quick thinker and a man of action. I will mention this when I talk with the Minister of Antiquities in Peru. May I call on you for another favor?"

"Certainly, señora, what is it you wish?"

"After your amigos have disposed of the stones that block the entrance and created a usable path, I would like my people to be among the first to view the Inca treasure since the Larco in Lima and the Smithsonian in Washington sponsored and paid for this excavation.

"Señora, I will personally see to it that your wishes are carried out. Word of your discovery has spread and many are coming to view such a find and are bringing, as you say, their tourist dollars."

He gave Allie Lea a snappy salute and RK shifted into four-wheel drive and took off.

After pulling into the hotel parking lot, Barbara said, "I don't know about anyone else, but I'm all for a slow shower and a long nap."

Everyone seconded her motion with the exception of Acahuana who said, "I'm pumped and ready for a look at Ollytaytambo. RK care to join me? Maybe we'll get lucky and meet some nice señoritas who also wish to see the sights."

"Great Inca leader, we'll shove off soon as I fill up this gas hog."

Allie Lea said, "Be home by midnight."

She then burst out laughing, full well knowing they roll up the streets in Ollytaytambo, what there are of them, well before midnight. She turned, facing me, and asked, "Mr. daring explorer, what is it you have in mind other than sex?"

"I'm for a hot shower, dinner in our room, and then to bed. These last two days have pulled a great deal of emotional and physical energy from this old bod, and I may sleep non-stop for the next twenty-four hours. Be sure and put out the *nada moleste* sign! After that, who knows?"

Doubtful was nowhere in sight. What a relief! I was so tired that Allie Lea had to pull off my clothes and help me into the shower. Meanwhile, they delivered our meal. I took a swig of coffee and immediately fell into bed.

Allie Lea remarked, "Sleep tight, darling, the food will keep."

She turned out the light and slid in *au naturel* beside me, but not before giving me a hug and a kiss saying, "Thank God, you made it and none for the worse."

The next morning, she was sitting at the desk busily doing her paperwork. About noon the phone rang and she said, "Ryan, as much as I hate to bother you, I have to take this call. I have been expecting to hear from Jim Hamilton. He's tried to get in touch with me for the past two days and he's getting a bit testy."

I took our pillows, gave a grunt, and disappeared under the covers, saying, "Invite him to visit us. Tell him he'd love the views from the walking trail up to the cave's entrance, providing he doesn't make too many missteps. Ha, ha!"

That earned me the finger. I made sure Allie Lea didn't see or hear me laughing; after all, she is my sleep partner, and that says a lot.

Two hours later, there was a rap on our door, and the next thing we knew Captain Rondo was asking, "Could he enter along with two of his deputies?" He was beaming from ear-to-ear and said, "I know your señor is tired as he has been through much, but I have news that couldn't wait. The rescue squad has made progress in clearing and rebuilding the trail that leads to the cave.

"Tomorrow, they will begin removing the rocks and large stones that are blocking the entrance that prevented your señor and his friends from making a timely exit out of what must have been a troubling experience. I wish to introduce my numero uno hombre who will guard the entrance to your outstanding discovery. I think it only fitting señora *t*hat you and those you select officially reopen it on the day after tomorrow. The Minister of Antiquities will also join you and your party and do what you *americanos* say, 'roll out the carpet!' including a special barbecue to celebrate this discovery. This find will generate a great deal of attention from the press and will bring our little town much attention and soles.

She replied, "Captain Rondo, I have but one reservation: the barbecue should be postponed for an extra day. That would give my chairman time to put together his travel and flight plans."

Captain Rondo threw his hands skyward and said, "Señora, our minister set the time and I dare not go against his wishes, unless I wish to be assigned to a less desirable district. Not to mention I would see my rank go flying out of one of our beautiful jail windows. Can you telephone your 'big man' and perhaps he will see it my minister's way?"

Allie Lea looked helplessly at me, and I tried to keep from laughing when I said, "Honey, I think my famous line is very appropriate at this point in the conversation."

Captain Rondo and his men looked perplexed and stood there shifting from one foot to the other, noticeably embarrassed, not knowing how they should respond to this strong-willed señora.

Finally, Allie Lea said, "I'll see what I can do and give you his answer shortly."

"*Gracias*, señora, *gracias!*"

He and his men set a record exiting our room, bowing every step of the way.

I jumped out of bed, dressed, and said, "I think some room reservations are in order before the news leaks about the big shindig. You may be pissed, but I wouldn't waste time in locating Jim Hamilton and extending him and his wife the invitation. It's different when the shoe is on the other foot, isn't it, dear?"

She replied, "Of course, Jim will jump at the chance to take a part in such an occasion. It's that I detest someone else calling the shots when we are funding this excavation. Our good captain knows damn well he left us with only one choice, and I am going to take it right now. Hand me my cell phone; it's under that pile of dirty clothes you left lying on your side of the bed."

I took a long, hot shower, and after stepping out of the water, Allie Lea flipped a towel to me. She was grinning ear-to-ear as she threw her panties on the bed and remarked, "I haven't had my shower; would you like to join me?"

I laughed and asked, "It went that well did it?" All the while, I lazily washed her back.

She giggled and replied, "Jim's on vacation in Paris. He told me he wouldn't sacrifice the food and sights of Paris for a twenty-four-hour flight to Lima for all the coffee in Peru. Using his words, he said, 'This is your baby; handle it with care and watch the expenses as your project is nearing the red line. *Au revoir, Mademoiselle.*'" He then hung up.

"My dear, he just gave you the keys to the candy store! Call the captain and let him know you have decided to handle the opening yourself. Remind him that should there be any additional changes, he should seek your approval prior to them being implemented."

"But, Ryan, he will lose face when I deliver that message."

"Allie Lea, it isn't his face he'll worry about; it's his ass! He'll be tickled pink when you advise him you can live with his plan. I'll call the front desk and inform them our plans have changed and they should cancel the reservations I just booked."

There was a light knock on the door and Sara said, "Time to come up for air, folks. Allie Lea, I need to talk with you, and if Ryan is decent, which he normally isn't, please open the door."

I opened the door and said, "Sara, I resent your remarks. I'm always decent, except when I'm in my own bed. Tell me where this bit of late-morning espionage emanates from; perhaps, I can dispel any misunderstandings that are making the rounds."

Allie Lea blushed. "I told her one night when we girls were letting our hair down and having an all-out discussion about our husbands and former acquaintances."

I replied, "I have suddenly developed a great taste for a bottle of *Cusqueña*, Peru's most popular beer, and a few chips. When you ladies finish your summit meeting, I'll be in the bar commiserating with the other male members of our group. Ta, ta!"

As I walked into the bar, a familiar group of guys beckoned me over, and Jim said, "You're just in time; we're holding a wake. Care to join us?"

I did a double take and asked, "Who's the lucky guy?"

Red shot back, "Who said it was a guy?"

"Fellows give me a break. I've been taken over the jumps more times than I care to admit, so cut the bullshit and tell me what this *faux* wake is all about."

Eric saluted the group. "My productive days are over, as well my useful-ness. Allie Lea would be within her rights to send me back to my job at the Smithsonian."

I laughed. "Eric, you've had more than enough to drink. If Ashley were to walk in here this minute, she would tie a knot in your tail the likes of which you have never seen. Guys, get some coffee, and, if necessary, pour it down our only drone expert's throat. Put him in the chair next to the bandstand and let him sleep it off. Hopefully, none of the gals and Ashley, in particular, find him in this condition.

"I'll square it with the manager to see that no one bothers him. I think he may approve of this Andrew Jackson I'm about to present him."

I motioned to the manager, and not only was he happy to meet Andrew Jackson, but he went the extra mile and had a couple of his hombres place a screen around Eric. This brought a round of applause from the other patrons who had gathered for their daily "picker-upper."

Walking to the pool and exercise area, Steve raised a sobering question when he stated, "Eric has a point. The majority of our work is finished; isn't it time for us to pack up and head back home?"

Fortunately, I didn't have to answer that question because Allie Lea waved to me and yelled, "Yoo-hoo, Ryan, can you spare a minute?"

I waved back, did an imitation of a hound dog howling, and trotted back to my now thoroughly pissed-off wife.

"Steve, we are about to receive our marching orders; get ready for an after-dinner meeting, which should prove to be very stimulating."

I reminded Red to look in on Eric.

Allie Lea said, "Let's take a walk, Mr. Smarty."

As we ambled along, the steam was still coming from her ears, and she asked, "Why is it you always expect to have the last word? Don't you know how ridiculous you are when you act like a teenager?

"As much as I hate to admit it, you correctly surmised there will be an after-dinner get-to-gather, everyone, including the wives, will be asked to at-tend. Those who don't come will find themselves on the first bus that rolls tomorrow. The ribbon cutting, scheduled for the day after tomorrow, will be orchestrated by Captain Rondo. Peru's Minister of Antiquities will be the head knocker, and our people must treat him accordingly. This is a serious occasion, and no half-assed remarks will be expected. We'll take our cues from Captain Rondo.

"Speaking of the good captain, he seems to have disappeared. I have tried to reach him, but no one knows his whereabouts. I hope his absence doesn't mean trouble is brewing. See if you can do a bit of scouting, and if you find him, let him know there are several who wish to converse with him. Don't forget to take Eric with you; the fresh air will do him a world of good!"

I couldn't believe how easy she was able to switch gears. I replied, "Okay," and let it go at that. Eric and I were making our way to Ollantaytambo when he said, "I fucked up, didn't I? How do I make amends?"

"Easy; shake it off and pray that Ashley doesn't see or hear about the so-called wake."

After looking high and low, our search came up with zip. It was if he had disappeared off the face of the earth. Our last stop was the police station an, d wouldn't you know it, it was locked with no sign of any officers or Rondo. It was getting close to dinner, and Eric had sobered up and all he wanted to do was sleep.

During the hour-long walk, Eric asked, "Do you think there will be any need for more drone flights?"

"Eric, I don't have the foggiest! Why do you ask?"

"The Titan engineers have developed an advanced model drone and indicated they would like to do a test run tonight, at no charge. This model is short on flight time—thirty to forty minutes—however, it is equipped with the latest infrared technology. Ryan, this would be a freebie. Why not give it a shot? You never know what it might bring to light."

"Eric, I probably will regret this, but, yes, give it a shot, but only on one condition."

"Great, I'll catch up with their lead techie and Denise and give them the good news. I may be a little late for dinner. What is the one condition that I'm not going to like?"

"Eric, I'm very serious when I ask that any information regarding this flight be confidential. By the way, what terrain do you suggest we scan?"

"The trail that leads to the cave and the cave entrance. If I spot anything out of the ordinary, I'll ask our aerospace handler to go in tight and slow. We will be using VGA, 575 square pixel technology. If anyone or anything is out there, we'll get it on high res."

"Eric, I'm at sea when you get into the technical aspects of your job. But go for it!"

The hotel's dinning room was too small to accommodate our crowd, so they moved us outdoors into the recreation area. They lit their outdoor torches, furnished ponchos to ward off the chill, and even sprang for a neat four–piece band and a singer to perform. I asked Allie Lea whose idea it was for this red carpet treatment.

"Sara's!"

I said, "I suppose this is one of her ideas when you girls were having another of your hair sessions?"

She replied, "Naughty, naughty, rover. It isn't polite to show your fangs."

The rest of the dinner was without incident and, for me, the high point was the dessert. I asked one of our waiters to tell me what it's called.

He smiled. "Señor, this is a very special Peruvian dessert; homemade *crêpes* are filled with *dulce de leche* and served with a bit of flame. The 'dules,' as we call them, are a sweet mixture of fresh fruits, which gives the crepe a special taste. Do you and your señor not like them?"

Allie Lea replied, "We think they are so special; I wonder if you could arrange to send a few to our room for a late-night snack."

"Most certainly, señora, most certainly!"

Allie Lea lowered her voice and whispered, "After a meal like that and the heavenly dessert, I need a nap, not a meeting. If I wander, be sure and nudge me back onto the trolley."

She welcomed everyone and said, "I see many of you brought your electronics, and that's okay. But do not share any of the information presented tonight until after the ribbon-cutting ceremony.

"Feel free to mingle with your fellow associates; ask them any questions you have in mind. The ceremony begins Thursday between two and three p.m. and is followed by a humongous barbecue. The dress of the day is country casual, whatever that means in this country. Ryan and I are the associate hosts. The guest of honor is Peru's Minister of Antiquities and his staff."

She continued, "Captain Rondo is in charge of organizing the affair, and a number of press and TV personnel will be present. They will be seeking information, and any tidbit you are willing to share just encourages them. Should you be questioned, you're on your own. Remember, you must be able to back up your story with facts.

"Pay attention, guys. I want to give you a name: Pearl Estrella. She's the top anchor for Station WKOG in Mexico City and is Mesoamerica's darling. She is resourceful, attractive, smart, does her homework, and will go to any length to get her story. Her station is known as the best in all of Mexico and their feeds include Peru, Argentina, and Guatemala. She and her crew will arrive late in the afternoon. That's all for now; enjoy the rest of this beautiful night."

While sitting beside me, Sara said, "I understand you don't approve of our hair sessions? When two people have as much in common as we do, getting along should be a breeze; so what's the problem?"

"Sara, don't make too much of my remarks. Allie Lea caught me at a bad time. I've got a problem or two that needs attention and my body is telling me to hit the sack. I can't make up my mind about whether to go skinny or sleep in what I'm wearing. Which do you suggest?"

She laughed. "I get it! This is your way of letting me know everything is okay with us. Your better half is concerned and has asked me to intercede. Gottcha, señor Keshaw!"

Several of the wives were gathered around Allie Lea, and Lynne was prevailing on her mom to approve a group tour of Machu Picchu and lunch in one of the picturesque, little taverns in Ollantaytambo.

However, that's one tour I intend to miss. I have couple of important things on my mind, involving Acahuana and Steve. After stopping to pick up a six-pack and chips, I began my search. It didn't take me long to find them. When I entered the drone center, Eric was holding court, giving Acahuana and Steve a brief overview of how the drones operate and what it takes to control them. Denise had quietly moved next to Acahuana intently listening to Eric's pitch. I later found out that our free flight tonight was her idea. She too was interested in the test drones' nighttime effectiveness. I wondered what other test equipment the drone was carrying.

When they saw me and the gifts I was carrying, Eric said, "Uh-oh, guys, I think our session just ended. Our maestro looks as if he is ready for a dress rehearsal. Why don't we move to the small conference room just down the hall? It will afford us more privacy."

"Eric, everyone else is at lunch. Would it be possible to scrounge up a sandwich or two to go with this beer? Then, we can hold our own picnic."

"Can do. I'll be back in a few minutes."

In the meantime, Denise had taken the initiative and ordered a patio takeout lunch. She said, "Ryan, I hope you don't mind my ordering lunch. Acahuana and I will be eating and lounging by the pool, and when you have finished your private meeting, give us a call. Do you think we will have time for a quick dip in this lovely pool?"

She giggled and said, "I'll take your silence as a yes." Then off they went.

I was left standing like a tongue-tied dunce, not knowing if I should smile or be angry. I came down to earth when I saw Steve tap Eric on the shoulder and say, "Another six-pack would be appreciated."

I added, "He will be gone for twenty to thirty minutes, giving us enough time to resolve what could be a dangerous situation."

Perplexed, they looked at me. "What in the hell are you talking about?"

"The ears of corn and apples we removed from Pachacuti's palanquin."

"Oh that!" Acahuana looked puzzled. "Why do you expect this to evolve into a dangerous situation?"

"I haven't discussed our actions with anyone, not even RK."

Steve chimed in. "Barbara and I haven't discussed any of what we found in the cave. We have been waiting for you to give us the high sign before we let anyone know of what we discovered."

I said, "Steve, it's time for you to put on your lawyer hat and read the fine print in the contract we have with the Antiquities Ministry in Cuzco. In the meantime, I'll alert Allie Lea and, on her behalf, thank each of you for keeping this under wraps. In the not-to-distant past, I distinctly remember this became an issue with the Guatemalan government. However, they were able to resolve their differences. After much haggling, they allowed the principals to keep a quarter of what was found, with one proviso: the items in question were to be available for display and not for sale. Hopefully, it will prove to be the same here."

I walked out of the Titan Aerospace Center a happy camper and for some reason I began to whistle "Don't Sit under the Apple Tree (With Anyone Else But Me)." Out of the corner of my eye, I saw Jim, Red, and Rafael approaching, and they too started whistling, only they were whistling "I'll Be Seeing You!"

"Okay guys, cut the bull, and why that particular song?"

"We have a problem, and we hate to intrude on your rare happy interlude. We are attempting to organize our part on tomorrow's program, but to do so, we must talk with Captain Rondo. But is he is nowhere to be found. We have looked high and low, even visiting the cave site but no luck. Why would he go underground at a time such as this? Any suggestions?"

"Hell no, I don't have a clue! Do whatever you see fit, and when you find him and if he gives you any guff, tell him to talk with me. The only reason we are cooperating with his unorthodox requests is because he works for Peru's Minister of Antiquities, who happens to be the guest of honor."

Red said, "Whistling often belies one's true feelings."

Jim then exclaimed, "I get it! Use the hammer, but first wrap it in velvet; that way it doesn't leave any marks. Wow!"

They walked off with Jim humming, "Don't Fence Me In."

I had a task that was anything but pleasant to perform. It was time to face the music and level with Allie Lea. I knew she would burn me a new one when she becomes aware that I kept information from her, and now, I have to grin and bear it. The perfect time to cover my tracks and make things okeydokey was after dinner. After all, everyone would be feeling warm and cozy and many chattering like magpies. No one would pay any attention to our conversation, provided Allie Lea didn't go bananas.

I smiled to myself and thought yep, I still got it as I walked by the pool. On the spur of the moment, I decided to take a quick dip. The only problem was I didn't have my suit with me. I looked around and saw that I had the pool and the recreation area all to myself, and I did the unthinkable: I shed my shoes, socks, and jeans, and dived in.

The water was warm and invigorating, and I felt like a million dollars. Then I heard a familiar voice ask, "Yoo-hoo, Ryan, are we in for a bit of skinny dipping, and would you like some company?"

Standing beside Allie Lea was Ashley, Sara, Barbara, and Lynne, who were laughing their guts out. I scrambled out of the pool and hustled over to where I left my clothes and said, as jauntily as possible, "The pool is all yours."

I made for our hotel room, embarrassed as ever, followed by a series of whistles and cat calls.

However, Allie Lea wasn't smiling. I decided there was no way I would brace Allie Lea and give the tiger in her a chance to take me on, at least not tonight. On second thought, I realized my question could wait, and because of my silence, she would not be put in a compromising position. Blue skies are often a little late in coming, but providing one has patience, they will come!

So, the fairer sex saw me in my jockey shorts; what's the big deal about that? I was now relishing the thought of a great dinner, a beer or two in front of a warm fire, and a good night's sleep. Well, I thought I earned it.

After answering too damn many questions, we gave up the ghost, bid everyone goodnight, and walked to our bedroom.

I had hopes of a quiet exit to La La land, but it was not to be. No sooner had I slid into in bed, when Allie Lea interrupted her nightly face cleansing ritual saying, "I noticed you didn't touch your corn. In fact, I wondered why you asked our waiter to remove it. I thought you love fresh corn smothered in butter. How about it, lover boy?"

"Allie Lea, I do love corn, but the altitude has affected my digestive system, corn, in particular, by giving me gas. Not wanting to burden you with such trivialities, I chose to give it up for the rest of this trip."

"Ryan Keshaw you are positively full of it! Why would you think I'd fall for such a line of bullshit is beyond belief. Especially since you didn't eat the corn because it reminded you of what was removed from the cave."

"Where did you get such a crazy idea?"

"Don't go into damage control when it's not needed. It so happens I agree with you. I don't want to know any of the actual details. If I don't know about them, I can withhold any decision until after everything is sorted out regarding the artifacts you discovered.

"For your further edification, Sara and I were sunning by the pool, near Steve and Barbara, and we overheard snatches of what transpired in the cave. After tonight's dinner, I put two and two together when you asked your waiter to take your corn away. Coupled with what we overheard, I was able to fill in the blanks."

I shrugged my shoulders and said, "I thought we were going to get a good night's sleep."

"Ryan, darling, I'm not angry; I just wish you had given me a heads-up. That's all. Turn out the light; we've got a big day tomorrow. By the way, Captain Rondo has finally surfaced. I wonder what he's been up to? Oh well, we'll find out tomorrow, presuming he shows."

When she said, "I presume he'll show," I snapped to attention and said, "My darling you raise a very interesting premise. Tomorrow may hold more surprises than we anticipate. I think I'll alert our guys and come up with Plan B just in case."

Allie Lea laughed and asked, "What happened to plan A?"

"I scrapped it when I realized you knew about the incidents in the cave."

After dozing for a short while, I felt her soft fingers running up and down my spine. I shook the sleep out of my eyes and smiled. "I presume this is a pleasure call."

"No, darling, this is an anxiety call. I can't sleep; all I have done is toss and turn. You have wakened the anxiety in me and I'm worried. What made you abruptly change your tune ? Has Doubtful made a belated appearance?"

"Yes, and I don't know why. I have the oddest feeling something is about to go boom, and I am unable to do anything about whatever it is. If it wasn't so late, I'd round up our guys and alert them that we may be in for a rough patch."

"Ryan Keshaw, it's almost four in the morning; come over here, and cuddle up. I need my Sir Galahad by my side to fight off any ugly things that come my way. On second thought, what if we're just chasing shadows and are dead wrong?"

I said, "That's a chance we have to take. If we are wrong, we'll have to live with it. Now, will you please go to sleep?"

Breakfast was a happy occasion. The majority of our group spent yesterday touring, hiking, and enjoying the pool. The gals got everyone together and presented me with, what there was of it, a good-looking thong bathing suit.

They insisted I model it, but I declined, and they called me a party pooper. However, I did hold it up and say, "This will just about fit Allie Lea. Maybe tonight she will hold a private modeling session—for yours truly!"

Chapter 14

* * *

Aces Always Beat Kings

I wondered how Allie Lea would react to my outlandish remarks, and all she said was, "Right." Our little pleasure session was interrupted by one of Captain Rondo's lieutenants who asked, "Where is señora in charge?"

Allie Lea raised her hand and motioned to the officer, who handed her an envelope and started to walk away when Allie Lea asked, "Where is your Captain?"

All he said was, "Read, señora. Our captain see you this afternoon at ceremony."

Everyone crowded around her saying, "Open it, open it."

She tore it open, scanned its contents, and read aloud its message, which said, "Minister unable to come; we go on without him. Signed Captain Rondo!"

Allie Lea stood there transfixed, saying, "Something has gone very wrong. Ryan, your intuition was spot on. I can't understand the Captain's logic in not personally delivering such a message."

She turned, facing the sea of inquiring faces and said, "Don't let the contents of this letter bother you. As far as we're concerned, the ceremony will take place as scheduled. I'd like to see Ryan, Jim, Steve, Red, and Rafael for a short meeting in the hotel's small conference room."

We were no sooner seated when she said, "Ryan, you are our master of intrigue. What do you think is going on? I find it hard to believe the minister would duck out at the last minute without contacting me and extending his apologies. He certainly loves publicity, and now is the perfect time for him to garner plenty of it. Whatever his reason, you can bet it does not bode well for the Smithsonian and the Larco. The floor is open. I need your thoughts. Steve, I'll start with you. Guys, let's keep it brief."

Steve scratched his head and replied, "Whatever his reason for not showing was with the express approval of someone who has a great deal of fire power or information. If we find out where that person or persons fit into the puzzle, we will then know the whys, and will be in a position to correct, what we perceive to be, a major problem."

Jim grinned. "Your ambassador experience is beginning to show. I couldn't add a word to your logic."

Red added, "I second what's been said. Ryan, it's your turn."

Allie Lea applauded after Red sat down and remarked, "Gentlemen, you have succeeded in accomplishing a rare feat, and that's putting my dear, sweet husband on the hot seat."

I grumped a bit and acknowledged Steve's expertise when I said, "You nailed it and so succinctly that it awakened a thought or two. It shouldn't take us long to gather some information that may prove to be very valuable since only two, maybe three, players are involved."

Allie Lea jumped into the conversation. "Is this Plan A or is it Plan B? Guys, that's a private joke between Ryan and me. Go ahead, darling, we are all ears."

"For everyone's information, this is Plan C. Plan B has been tucked away for use when needed, but right now, this is what we required: Steve, do your charming best and call the minister's office in Cuzco. See if you can dig up any information relating to his traveling plans and, if possible, who initiated this change of plans. I realize what I am asking is a long shot, but what the hell, maybe you'll get lucky.

"Red, you and Jim mosey out to the cave site, talk with the officers, and see what, if any, information you can pick up about the change in plans. Rafael, check at the jail: find out all you can about Rondo's background—personal and business—as well as his whereabouts these last three days. All scraps of information are welcome. Let's meet back here in say two hours. Good Luck!"

Jim added, "I'd be surprised if we obtain any new or useful information in such a short time frame."

"Well, any information is more than we have now. Go get 'em guys; time's a wasting!"

Allie Lea asked, "Where do you figure in this quest for information?"

I said, "As your favorite undercover agent, I plan to talk with several of the senior persons who run this hotel. I have a hunch the rock or rocks I'm about to turn over will give us some valuable insights into who is actually behind the throne pulling the strings and why."

"Ryan, I love you dearly, but there are times when I question your thought processes let alone your actions."

"Allie Lea, there are times I question not only my reasoning, but my sanity as well. Somehow, some way, I always seem to muddle through. Have faith. The picture we are about to paint will possibly surprise us all."

Allie Lea threw her arms around me and purred, "My tiara is polished and sitting on my night table!"

I gave her a big smile and said, "We have two hours before our amigos return."

She wasted no time in saying, "Get real. We'll need all our energy and wits to get through the day. Never fear; there will be other opportunities. Have you forgotten you have a task or two to complete? I wouldn't wish to get in the way of a man on a mission. In the meantime, I'm going to find Sara. I have an idea you and she might appreciate. Ta, ta."

Red and Jim were the first to report in and they were smiling. We sat and talked over a delightful libation and awaited the return of the others. Rafael was the last to return and Allie Lea said, "Okay, guys, let's have it."

"We uncovered some puzzling information. The guards at the beginning of the trail and the cave's entrance wouldn't say much other than, 'Captain's orders no enter unless he say so.' The entrance to the cave was sealed tight. A funny incident occurred when Pearl and her TV crew tried to set up their equipment.

"Regardless of how loud she yelled or how much she tried to intimidate the guards, she was not allowed entry to the cave. She is one unhappy, pissed off señora. In fact, the trail and the cave's entrance were closed to everyone and that included the media. Captain Rondo was nowhere in sight. That's it from us."

"Steve, you're next. My calls proved to be useless. Everyone with whom I spoke professed no knowledge about the minister's travel schedule. One of his aides did tell me the minister and his staff would be in their offices tomorrow afternoon. Rafael, I hope you had better luck."

Rafael smiled. "My visit to the police office proved to be very fruitful. Our captain in his youthful days was the local leader of the *Huahuqui*. They are best known as Inca guardians. During Rondo's early days, he was often in and out of trouble. Over time, he earned the reputation as one who settles problems working on the side of the law. Eventually, his good work led to his appointment to the police force and then captain by the minister with the approval of *el Presidente*."

Allie Lea interrupted saying, "There is your fire power. Rafael, is there more?"

"More, señora much more! I asked a young officer who was on duty which is the Captain's office and, on a hunch, I asked if it was locked and he said, 'Si.' I remember you saying Atoc's brother was carrying a rather heavy sack when he fell. When the captain placed it in his police vehicle, you asked what he was doing. I distinctly remember him saying he would keep it safe for you. Now comes the fun part, being that the captain was not available and the officer looked to be a 'greenie,' I thought I'd run a bluff.

"I pulled out my identification card that states I am president of the Larco Museum and requested that the young señor retrieve the package his captain has been holding for me. Astonishingly enough, he unlocked the captain's office door, and out he came carrying a large cloth sack and said, 'Here señor is your package.' I couldn't get out of that place fast enough. Thank goodness the captain was at the cave, making sure everything is ready for the ribbon-cutting ceremony."

We were thunderstruck. Then it hit us, and we couldn't stop laughing when the gravity of the situation sunk in.

Allie Lea said, "We must not break any laws, nor do I wish the bunch of us be given any jail sentence. That being said, where do we stand legally?"

Steve summed it up very well when he said, "My British friends taught me when it comes to solving a problem, if one moves too quickly, one often ends up with twisted knickers. Off the top of my head, I believe you're okay. Artifacts found on a dig most generally come under the heading of 'finders keepers' dictum; unless their permit says otherwise, they become the property of the museum sponsoring the dig or the Department of Antiquities. Technically speaking, the artifacts contained in that sack belong to the Smithsonian. When Captain Rondo finds that the sack of goodies is no longer in his possession, the *merde* will hit the fan."

Allie Lea shrugged her shoulders, sighed and said, "I have half a notion to give this sack to the Captain and be done with it. I can see nothing but trouble ahead. Any ideas on how we get this sack of history to the Larco without anyone being jailed, hurt, or hospitalized?"

There was a minute or two of complete silence and then I softly said, "I think I may have a solution to both of our problems."

Jim Leachy laughed. "I knew it, I just knew it! Let's hear what you have to say old friend. I've been wondering how I would end my book. I've had writer's block and no ideas for the past three weeks. I can't wait to hear what you have to say."

I knew what I was about to say would be treated with dismay by Jim and the others, but I had to make sure I had an ace in the hole, just in case I made a miscalculation. I thought I'd lighten the atmosphere, so I asked, "What in the hell is the title of this supposed book you are writing?"

He replied, "Why I thought you knew it's *Drones Over Machu Picchu.* How's that sound, guys? Ryan, I believe I got you off the trolley; let's hear what you have to say."

"At this point, it's in everyone's interest that I'm the only one who knows what I am proposing to do. The last thing we want to happen is to have the captain question and implicate you for your part in my sleight-of-hand operation. I don't plan to attend the opening ceremonies and I hope the captain doesn't ask my whereabouts. After I complete the first part of my mission, I'll show up and none will be the wiser. Red, if you will hand me that sack, I'll be on my way.

"Allie Lea, you'll have to trust me on this. If my plans work, our problems will float away and never be seen or heard from again. Wish me luck."

I threw the sack over my shoulder and made a beeline for Eric's office. One of the Titan's techies told me he was at the drone testing site working with some of his buddy experts.

He saw me coming and asked, "What's up and what's in that sack? And, no, I'm not attending the ceremonies. Ashley and I hashed out that problem, and if you're here to encourage me to attend, don't waste your time. I have more important things to do. Why haven't you returned my calls and messages? I have the results of our night drone flight, and after examining them, I knew you would come running when you knew what I discovered."

I replied, "Sorry, old friend. I've been putting out a few fires, but now you have my undivided attention. Can we go where we can have uninterrupted privacy?"

"Sure, let me grab one of the smaller drones, and let's make for the testing ground. The testing is done for the day, and the techies are off, so, we can have complete privacy. Here, let me have that sack, and I'll put it in the closet by the entrance."

I replied, "This sack goes where I go. If there happens to be a dolly close by, I'd be glad to transfer this heavy sonofabitch."

"Can do. There's a small dolly in the closet by the door; we use it when we ferry more than one drone at the same time. From the looks of things, I smell trouble and the way you have been lugging that sack around, I'd say it figures in our conversation."

"You're right! I'm anxious to hear what you have to say about that night flight."

Eric handed me an enlarged-sized film and asked me to tell him what I saw.

"If you need a glass, I've got one handy, but I don't think you'll need it."

"I see five figures carrying sacks similar to this one coming out of the entrance to the cave. It's obvious they hear the drone and have turned their faces toward the mountain. Am I seeing things or not? One of the individuals is a uniformed person, whom I suspect is Captain Rondo and the others are no doubt Atoc's hombres."

Eric looked puzzled and asked, "I'd like to know what was in those sacks and what were those men doing out at two a.m.?"

I smiled and said, "My boy, you just verified my thoughts. There will be no need for further drone testing. Could you and Ashley pack up your gear, including what's in this sack and be ready to leave on tomorrow's late morning train for Lima? Tomorrow afternoon, all hell will break loose and I'd just as soon the two of you be out of the line of fire.

"Make sure Ashley understands that your work is done here and both of you are making a normal departure. Once you are in Lima, go immediately to the Larco museum, señor Diego Fuentes will be expecting you. After arriving at the museum, ask Ashley to handle with care the items in this sack and to place them out of sight somewhere in the area she and Sara were working. No one other than señor Diego is to know of their presence. Call me after you have checked into the hotel."

I filled Eric in on the rest of my plans and what should happen once they were put in motion. In the meantime, I asked him to make me a second set of high-res prints of the latest drone flight, as they figured mightily in my plans.

"Ryan, this calls for a drink or two. I only hope things work out the way you think."

I reminded him, "Should you or Ashley be asked, by any official, the reason for your trip, just say that before being paid, you are required to make a full report to señor Diego Fuentes, president of the Larco museum. Other than that, say nothing. If you are pushed, show them a copy of one of the photos the drone took. They won't understand the technical aspect and that's about it. Are you up for this bit of espionage?"

"Hell yes!! I'll make the copies you requested. I presume you and everyone else will be making the ceremony. I'll take that sack and carefully pack it among all the rest of our IT gear. I wish I could stay and watch the fireworks, but Ashley will enjoy the extra days' shopping in Lima. See you there when this is all over."

I hustled back to our hotel, and a short while later, took one of the shuttles to the ceremony area. I couldn't believe the crowds. The shuttle driver spent most of the time weaving in and out of the crowds trying to avoid hitting anyone.

Following one of Pearl's TV crewmen, I found myself at the foot of the trail leading to the cave. The area was jam-packed with people, including those were watching from Machu Picchu. I was surprised to see that a festive tent had been erected at the base of the trail and not at the cave. Evidently, I missed the ribbon-cutting and I wondered why everyone was just milling around. I overheard one of the spectators say, "Honey, if you think I'm going to climb that narrow path without any means of support, you are nuts. Let's get out of here."

I had to agree with that wise man, but I knew Allie Lea was expecting me to show, so I shoved my fears aside and cautiously made my way forward. When I walked into that cavern, I was rendered speechless by what I saw. Despite the poor lighting, the place was empty with the exception of Pachacuti's litter, and it had been placed, as a cover, over the pit of death. Someone had repaired the broken litter support that was used to hoist Acahuana out of the cave. Pearl was standing close by with one of her camera men and was dabbing her eyes with a well-used tissue. I walked up and asked, "Pearl, what happened? Where are the artifacts?"

She put her head on my shoulder and began sobbing, all the while saying, "All gone, no show, disappeared. Someone took!"

The reason for the silence and the subdued atmosphere that engulfed the area was understandable. I searched for Allie Lea and saw her giving forth with some of the TV and press, and from the looks of her gestures, she was very, very angry. Standing off to one side was our good captain, professing to all who would listen how sorry he was for the Smithsonian coming up empty-handed.

Allie Lea gave me one of those where-in-the-hell-have-you-been looks that said get your butt over here and pull my bacon out of the fire. She introduced me to the group and whispered, "Okay, genie, let's see how you can extricate us out of this pile of crap."

Pearl had been standing nearby, and when she heard Allie Lea give me marching orders, she waved at her camera and light men. They immediately sprang into action and on came that infernal camera light.

Pearl, ever the consummate professional, jumped right in and told her audience, "WKOG and I will be right here to bring you the latest on this exciting story as it develops."

While Pearl was emoting, I pulled Allie Lea aside and asked, "Would you, by the wildest chance, happen to have a couple of the photos taken by one of the volunteers?

She replied, "No, but I believe Barbara does. Why in the name of goodness are you interested in a damn picture when our honor and veracity are being challenged?"

"Allie Lea, for once don't argue; get them and put them in the handbag you drag around. It is of the utmost importance that our good captain not be aware of what you are doing."

"Ryan, I know you have a plan that will get us out of the hole we're in, but, for heaven sake, at least give me an inkling of how you plan to go about it."

"Allie Lea, outside of Eric, I haven't brought anyone else other than you into what I have in store for the captain and his associates. I am operating on the fly, and because of that, the situation is very fluid, so bear with me. Everything will come to a head within the hour. I trust you are prepared to say and play your part. We must show Captain Rondo a united front, and that means no crying, hesitating, or asking him for help."

She replied, "I'd walk through fire before I showed that asshole any emotion, other than what you expect. Does that satisfy you?"

I've always said, "'When women are locked and loaded, they present a formidable force.' I'm going to enjoy watching and listening to what should be an interesting repartee."

The attendees that made the earlier dangerous ascent assumed there wasn't anything else going on, and there was nothing more to learn, so they began to filter out the cave's narrow entrance.

However, there was one who didn't move out; it was Captain Rondo. He was pissed to no end when he roared, "What the hell do you think you are doing? This is my country's territory. The only rights you have are those having to do with exploration, and since there is nothing further for you and your crew to explore, your permit is considered fulfilled."

I knew he was trying to goad me into a full scale argument, but that I would not allow. He didn't realize we held all the aces, and, equally, he was totally unaware that the full force of the facts was about to knock him for a loop. Our group of guys sensed we were in deep trouble, and despite that, they moved in, surrounding Allie Lea, the Captain, and me.

After a moment or two of nervous silence, I said, "Allie Lea, the Captain, and I need some quiet time together to discuss this embarrassing situation. How about it Captain?"

He retorted, "I don't see any reason why I should spend any more time listening to you or others of your group. As far as I am concerned, this place is now off limits to members of the press, your group, and that infernal TV señora and her equipment."

It was then he became aware of the red light and realized his remarks and demeanor were on their way, via satellite, to WKOG and its various feeds throughout Mesoamerica. He then made an abrupt 180, walked over, and put his arm around me, and said, "Señor, there is no need for us to be adversaries; let us go where we can discuss our differences in private."

"Okay, but I insist on the Smithsonian's vice president accompanying us. She is responsible for this operation that was approved by your Minister of Antiquities."

Our guys looked questioningly at me, and I gave them the thumbs-up sign. They too made their way out of the cavern's entrance.

Pearl asked, "Señor Ryan, should we pack up our gear?"

I put my arm around her and said, "Hell No!"

She surprised me when she said, "Please don't play with my head. I had enough trouble getting my office to approve, let alone pay, for this trip. Will it truly be worth my station's expense for me and my crew to stand by?"

I gave her a big smile. "By all means, stick around if you wish to cover a big exclusive story. I wouldn't be at all surprised to learn that our captain will be making an announcement that will create a great deal of interest through-out the Inca world. You'll love the buzz and the recognition this story will generate for you and your station. Comprendes, señora?"

"I'll stay! To show you my gratitude I'd like to buy you and your señora dinner. I understand your hotel has fabulous food plus an exquisite bar. I promise not to bring our cameras. Roga, my wonderful director, would be very unhappy if he wasn't invited."

"Of course, Roga is welcome. I have always enjoyed his company. He is one bright, witty señor, much like the *numero uno* TV anchor señora with whom he works. I must catch up with Allie Lea and the Captain. Wish me luck!"

She laughed and asked, "Have you consulted your famous crystal ball lately? Perhaps it will tell you. Luck you have, patience I'm not so sure! Good hunting, señor Keshaw!"

Her remarks stopped me in my tracks. I spun around and saw that she was making a twirling motion around her head and laughing. I nodded my head and gave her the V-for-victory sign.

The cavern had now emptied with the exception of Allie Lea, myself, and the captain, who continued his bombastic tirade saying, "I don't know what it is you are trying to pull, but I have had enough of your tricks. It's time for you and your people to leave; otherwise, I will have to arrest you."

Allie Lea asked, "On what charge captain?"

He replied, "Misleading the public, making false statements, the theft of many pieces of Inca treasurers and obstructing justice."

Allie Lea said, "Enough of this charade. As soon as we pack up our equip-ment, we will be on our way to meet with your president in Cuzco. On behalf of the Smithsonian, we plan to file charges against you and your minister based on the facts and evidence my señor has uncovered. Would you care to hear what we have found?"

She continued, "If not, we will be on our way, but not before we talk with WKOG's anchor person. She is anxiously awaiting our version of the facts regarding the events that have occurred on your watch. In fact, when our position becomes public knowledge, I'd be surprised if you and your minister were not required to stand trial for much the same charges you just presented us with. Oh, yes, in case you decide what you hear is not correct, señor Ryan has an extra copy of our findings for you and your cohorts. Darling, he's all yours."

"Captain, you became our prime suspect when we learned you are a member of the *Huahuqui* sect, both as a young man and as an adult. Research told us the word *Huahuqui* stands for supernatural guardian or brother and involves a select few Incas who are dedicated to looking after the empire's departed rulers.

"This explains your not moving on Atoc, a fellow member, as hard as you should have, had he not been a *Huahuqui*. By the way, what have you done with him? He certainly isn't in your jail as I thought he should be.

"Your eagerness to maintain control of the sack of 'ancients' that accompanied Atoc's brother in his unfortunate fall raised a red flag. Those 'ancients' have been legally transferred from your office and will remain safe until this matter has been settled. Take a look at these photos taken inside this very cavern. The fact that these artifacts are covered with dust indicate they have been there for many centuries. I understand precious stones and gold were an Inca ruler's after-life necessities, many of which we discovered, in addition to finding Pachacuti's golden palanquin that was used to carry him around. I have every confidence to believe his remains are close by. But that's a matter for another time. I see you repaired and moved his palanquin to warn others that a pit of death is nearby. Any thoughts, captain?"

"Yes, you have failed the same as many others to find our beloved emperor's remains. I will recommend that our government not issue permits for any future archaeological explorations within my jurisdiction that seek the same objective."

"Oh, I wouldn't say we failed. We have brought to light some of the most valuable Inca relics and culture known to date. Captain, you should spend a little time with yourself and ponder exactly how it is that you plan to hold back the dawn. Now, to the most damning piece of evidence. I have here a set of photos taken by one of our drones. Notice the time and the date these pictures were shot.

"Unless my eyes are deceiving me, I believe the first figure happens to be you and then your men carrying, what look to be, heavy sacks. In reality, you were looting ancient Inca treasurers."

He replied, "I repeat, 'I would never consider stealing a part of my country's history.'"

"I'm guessing you and your minister have cooked up some scheme or plan to bring dishonor to the Smithsonian and the Larco museums. Hence, the last-minute change in the minister's itinerary. Neither of you wanted him to appear as a 'dolt' by having him face an empty cavern. I'd like to hear how you plan to explain away that one.

"I notice you're not saying anything in defense of this hot potato. We now come to the last piece of the puzzle, and here is where you showed considerable initiative. I wondered why an inventive person such as yourself would hide a cache of valuables in such an obvious place. When you informed us that you were putting a twenty-four-hour guard on the hidden exit, that got my attention. You said you would have the exit sealed to keep out looters and thieves.

"Then it hit me! I was the one who provided you with a solution that wouldn't cause the raising of eyebrows. This, despite everyone wondering who was responsible for stealing such priceless artifacts. That really got me thinking. On impulse, I visited the location and spoke with your guard; my mission was to examine the exit and see if it had been sealed with cement. I saw that the exit had not, as of then, been touched. Two days later, before attending this pseudo-opening, I made it a point to see if the guard was still there and if any work had been done toward blocking the opening.

"And, indeed, the opening was now blocked, despite your guard being on duty. I rather suspect if one took the time and trouble to examine the exit and the cave in question, *voila,* they would, no doubt, find the missing Pachacuti artifacts. I have no doubt that Atoc, the same Atoc who was supposed to be safely ensconced in your jail, and his men, all members of the *Huahuqui* sect, assisted you in hiding Pachacuti's valuables."

I looked at Allie Lea, who stood there smiling, and winked, and whispered, "You just heard plans A and B. Plan C is on the way.

"Captain Rondo, what do you have to say for yourself?"

He stood as if rooted to the cavern floor; his usual ruddy complexion was ashen, and sweat was running off him in rivulets. Rondo finally threw up his hands and contritely asked, "How and what must I do to make right the wrongs I and my people have committed?"

Allie Lea sternly responded saying, "Perhaps a solution can be worked out, providing you are willing to accept the suggestions that señor Keshaw is about to propose. These suggestions will go a long way toward solving your problems. There can be no recriminations now or in the future on your or your government's part relating to our exploration. Need I go further? Ryan, now is the time for plan C."

The captain said, "Prior to my agreeing to anything, I must know the details of plan C. You already have me on the ropes, and I know when I'm beaten. Understand, I had no intention of stealing any part of my country's history. I merely meant to discourage future exploration and make sure no more drones would be used in my district. Prior to my actions, I discussed and received approval of my plans with my minister."

Allie Lea said, "Let's not bicker; either your minister agrees to our terms or not. These terms are not negotiable. If you and he want this mess to go away and return things to the status quo without anyone being the wiser, you have until tomorrow at noon to let us know your position. This conversation, both now and in the future, will be known only to the three of us, plus your minister. He must agree to our suggestions. Otherwise, we will bring this situation to the attention of *el presidente*, who will take a dim view of both you and your minister's actions."

"Si, I agree. I should have known better; let's hear what I know are bound to be difficult conditions."

"Okay, we are all on the same page. Use your bullhorn to announce the closing of the exhibition for the next seven days and that there will be a glorious reopening shortly afterwards. The reasons for closing the exhibition are the dangerous foot path, which needs widening, and the installation of a safety net. The cavern floor must be cleaned and proper lighting installed, in order for all who wish to see Pachacuti's treasures in all their glory.

She continued, "The minister to host the grand reopening with no excuses. He will acknowledge his Captain's foresight in securing such treasures. After an agreeable period of time, not to exceed six months, without any additional strings or requirements, fifty percent of the artifacts will be donated to the Larco and the Smithsonian's museums. The minister should give as his reasoning the fact these institutions bore the considerable expense of discovering such precious objects. Well, Captain do you think you can deliver on what I just discussed or do you wish to take your chances and ride out the storm?

"Before answering, you might consider the facts: meet our requests as outlined and all of this will go away. No unfavorable publicity, no loss of jobs and no jail terms. In fact, if you and your minister handle it properly, you might even come off as heroes who lived up to their Inca heritage. The decision is yours."

With that, she handed him a hastily scribbled outline of the terms, saying, "Just in case you or your minister forget what you are agreeing to."

Rondo hung his head as he acknowledged agreement to the terms. He said, "I tried to do what I thought was right and look what happened. I know I can speak for my minister as well as myself and pledge that we will meet your 'requests.'"

He brushed the perspiration from his brow, took off his jacket, and asked for a bottle of water, saying, "I'm dying of thirst!"

She then asked, "Captain Rondo, why didn't you just come out and ask us if we would be agreeable to move the artifacts? Or better still, think about what we could have accomplished had you been willing to work with us instead of working against us. Perhaps Atoc's criminal intent and greed influenced your thinking.

"Ryan, I believe we are done here. Anything we have forgotten? Damn, damn, damn, there is a small detail I forgot. Captain Rondo, since you are in such a giving mood, this little request should meet with your approval."

The captain asked, "What now? You have already gotten your pound of flesh. I know I'm stuck; let's hear how generous you expect me to be."

I said, "Remember that sack of artifacts that Atoc's brother was carrying before he made his final plunge? Which, I might add, you so obligingly kept in your office? It would only be fitting if you personally donate those Inca artifacts to Acahuana, who, one day in the not-too-distant future, will be the rightful leader of all Peru Inca. That's not too much to ask, is it?"

"Señor Ryan, you test my giving mood. Being that I have no choice, I will happily donate the artifacts you now have in your possession. I will acknowledge this gift at our grand reopening, with one request."

I thought here it comes. I steeled myself, expecting that his request might be a deal breaker.

I looked at Allie Lea, who puckered up her face, expecting the worst, said, "Let's hear it."

Rondo smiled. "This is my request: Do not think of any other archaeological excavations in the areas where I am police chief! I wish to retire healthy and enjoy living, despite my getting bald. You and your people bring anxiety to a whole new level, and I don't think my heart would stand a return visit."

Waving good-bye, he said, *"Adios amigos.* This now free man is off to make the announcement you requested and then talk with the señora who has the red eye."

I looked at Allie Lea, who had the damnedest smile one could imagine when she said, "Merlin, we need to visit our hotel room and dig up your crystal ball and ask it a question or two."

"Allie Lea, get real; we just scored a major victory, plenty of favorable publicity, no one hurt or injured, no loss of money, and a great discovery. What's not to like about that?"

She replied, "Yes, many good things have happened, but I have this nagging doubt that only your crystal ball can answer. Let's get out of here before the world comes tumbling in on us."

"Allie Lea, you're driving me crazy! What are the questions so bothering you?"

"Okay, Merlin, who won, us or Captain Rondo? With the exception of Atoc's brother's demise, did the captain manipulate us to achieve his and his country's objectives?"

When I answered, I couldn't help laughing, which made her so angry that she folded her arms, stamped her foot, and said, "Sara was right; you are one diabolical so and so. Now what do you think of that? But that doesn't mean I don't love you!"

I managed to keep a straight face when I said, "Darling, I believe you just inherited my old buddy Doubtful. Take good care of him."

I put my arm around her and said, "*Of course we won!!!*"

Chapter 15

* * *

The Present, the Past, and Time Are Our Daily Companions

RK Consulting has been going like a ball of fire these past five years, due mostly to my new partners, Lynne and Ken. The phones thus far have been silent, and despite the gloomy, rainy day, I felt pretty upbeat. I fixed myself a mug of hot steaming coffee, put my feet up on my desk, turned off the lights, and settled back into my executive lounger. The house was eerily quiet, and that was the catalyst for me to take a trip into the past despite Sara's admonitions.

Time flies, taking along with it a portion of the many memories that were once very vivid in our everyday lives. I remember Sara telling me it's the present that's important and we should leave the past where it belongs—in the past.

It's hard to believe it's been five years since we concluded our search for the remains of that most famous of Inca emperors, Pachacuti. I keep thinking we were within a hair of finding his burial place. The one thing that jogs my memory was Atoc's admonition when we were trapped in that cave. I don't know if he meant what he said immediately after he dynamited the entrance to the cave. Was it a bluff to induce fear or just plain hate for each of our volunteers?

Those thoughts dredged up a smile when I remembered he had been sentenced to serve twenty years at hard labor. Allie Lea pleaded for mercy for Mojo as a way of saying thank you for his act of kindness. The court agreed and gave him five years, which will be up the seventh of this December.

Acahuana kept tabs on Captain Rondo and, believe it or not, he has led an exemplary life these past five years. However, that in no way increases my desire to return to Machu Picchu. When we wish to view Machu Picchu, all we do is look in RK's room and view the painting for which I grudgingly paid four hundred dollars. Some bargain, huh?

Incidentally, RK is now attending Wharton's School of Business. He is managing his personal life, no drugs, and finances. Sweet young things are now on his radar. Allie Lea and I are thankful he's turning out to be a contributing member of society. As a reward, I gave him my old Volvo, along with the never-ending repairs for which older Volvos are famous.

The big news around our house is that Lynne and Ken are planning a February sweetheart wedding. They interested me in expanding my business and think I should move my office to Fourteenth Street in D.C. I wasted no time in vetoing that idea. I have no desire to be known as one of the fourteenth street consulting, connection-pedaling bandits.

Since Ken and Lynne are unable to fund or expense a new location, they decided it would be only fitting to work out of my office and, for the time being, live with us. Talk about bungee kids!!! Of course, all this has to be approved by her highness, as if that will be a problem! Wouldn't you know it? They expect to share equally in any income the firm generates. Allie Lea thought it only fair that we temporarily (I use the term loosely) give them a hand.

I didn't agree with her logic until she exclaimed, "You know how hard it is for young people to make it in today's work force. This is not the time for you to play the role of Scrooge."

I thought for a moment or two, mulling over her logic and then it came to me: logic is on the side of the person making the case, regardless of the facts. In short, I just heard the judge say case closed, next case.

Allison is in her second year at Duke. She hopes—make that "plans"—to become a biological engineer. She has good grades, is a clothes hound, and is learning that the money printing press will soon be shut down unless she improves her understanding of Ben Franklin. Most important of all, she inherited her mother's good looks and winsome ways. Plus, she is five foot four, which Allie Lea dearly wishes she was instead of being five foot one. I don't hesitate telling her that good things come in small packages, like diamonds, not that any of what I've said should be construed as a prelude to my visiting Tiffany's any time soon.

Allie Lea, as far as I can tell, is doing very well at the Smithsonian. She and Jim Hamilton have meshed very well with a minimum number of hiccups. Allie Lea has been asked to evaluate a possible dig deep in the heart of one of the jungles in Guatemala. At least for now, I'm staying out of the line of fire. I have no desire to go anywhere near that dangerous country. At the last count, excluding the countries in the Middle East, Guatemala is listed as the third most dangerous place to visit, work, or even think of going near, unless one has a shortened mortality wish.

Rafael and señor Diego are doing their best to find funding and keep the dream alive of finding Pachacuti's burial place. But so far they have yet to find anyone with deep enough pockets who share their same dreams. Sara gave birth to twin boys, and were it not for her being able to afford a nanny, she would go nuts. I happened to overhear a snippet or two of a recent conversation between Allie Lea and Sara. They were discussing Acahuana and his longing for Denise who is back working for Facebook at its Silicon Valley location.

Allie Lea told me Denise's reason for being assigned to Ollytaytambo was to conduct special drone tests having to do with 3-D imaging and the effects that retrogression had on the overall imaging, all of which was top secret. Despite her living in San Jose, she still has strong feelings for Acahuana. Allie Lea doubts the relationship will go beyond the friendship stage. I'm not so sure their relationship is dead in the water. Isn't love supposed to conquer all?

Rafael tells me Acahuana is spending more and more of his time with him and señor Diego, learning all he can about what makes a good leader. He continues to makes regular trips to his people's mountain lair, and I get the feeling it won't be long before he is handed the reins as Inca ruler and the authority that accompanies it. Unlike his father, he doesn't much care for Inka Cola.

Our relationship with Steve and Barbara has blossomed, and we have become fast friends. Steve has slimmed down and makes no secret that he would like to go on another excavation whenever and wherever the occasion arises. I doubt that will happen. Barbara is deeper than ever in the environmental world. Good for her; maybe she can someday give Allison some pointers.

Time has not dimmed or diminished our friendships in Mesoamerica. We text and talk with them, albeit on a somewhat irregular basis. Perhaps we'll get down there within the next year or two.

Catherine, Juma, and the twins visited us last year. We gave them the royal tour of D.C. and all that it has to offer, and to tell you the truth, I think we wore them out. Juma is now manager of the two temple exhibitions in Chichi. Catherine is in the midst of writing a book regarding the Smithsonian's excavations and her role as a Maya fortune teller. I wonder if it will be a tell-all. If so, I suspect her book will find a ready audience. She promised me the first copy. Oh yes, I've been told she still has a knockout figure. The more I think about it, the more I believe it might be time for Allie Lea and me to give serious consideration to a return visit. After all, we spent almost four years of our life there with some wonderful people.

The same can be said for those of us who continue to labor for the Smithsonian. It's kinda funny, but I get the feeling, despite the dangers and the hardships, the years we spent with our friends in Mesoamerica and Peru have indeed become our golden years. My reverie was broken when I heard Lynne and Ken stamping on our front porch. I was so wrapped up reminiscing I didn't realize it was pouring down rain and that it was well past six o'clock.

Lynne yelled out, "Anybody home? And why is the house so dark?"

She turned on the great room lights and saw me sitting in my office in the dark. She anxiously asked, "Dad, are you ill, and what's with the no lights? Mom will be home in a few minutes, and if she sees you sitting in the dark, she'll call the doctor and 911. Oh my golly, she's pulling into our driveway. Ken, let's get out of here before Mom hits the front porch. I just remembered you and I need to go to the gourmet Giant at Tyson's Corner and get some food for dinner, so move."

As they made for their car, Allie Lea opened the door and asked, "What's up guys?"

Ken gave her a big smile. "We're off to pick up a few delicacies from the gourmet Giant in Tyson's Corner. Anything special you'd like?"

She answered "no" and then said, "I thought it was Ryan's turn to put it all together. Evidently, he forgot we're having one of his favorite dinners: baked spaghetti, garlic toast, Caesar salad, and chocolate pudding. By the way, where is Ryan and why on this gloomy evening is the house so dark?"

Lynne said, "I guess our trip to the store is out, but Steve and I have a project that just came up, and we need to spend a few minutes online. Come on, Ken." They quickly vanished into their room.

I knew the jig was up, and I made my entrance as unobtrusively as possible saying, "Hi honey, traffic bad?"

She replied, "Not as bad as it's going to get if you don't tell me what's going on. As soon as I shed this rain-soaked coat and use the bathroom, you and I are going to have a summit meeting."

I knew I was about to face the full thrust of trouble, and like the matador, I must make my thrusts count.

I decided to go on the offensive and try to get by without really exposing my whole card, so I said, "Darling I'm not ill and I feel great. Yes, I was in my office sitting in the dark, relaxing and doing a bit of reminiscing and reliving many of our past experiences in Mesoamerica and Peru. What's the harm of that?"

Allie Lea retorted with a sudden intake of air and said, "Oh?"

$*\quad*\quad*$

Epilogue

I realized I'd carried the day, and despite that, I poured on the coal and replied, "The weatherman says this weekend is supposed to be warm and dry. How would you like to spend Saturday hiking and picnicking along the C & O canal? Think of it—no phones, no kids, no one else, and no one asking for this and that."

She threw her arms around me and said, "Wonderful, Romeo, just what I have been hoping for."

I looked perplexed. "Then it's a date."

She said, "I often wonder how you do it, but you must have read my mind. As to the rest of what you said, I realize it was pure baloney, designed to lead me in a nonsensical direction and a subject you're not ready to discuss."

She then called to Lynne and Ken. "Get ready for dinner."

They came charging down the stairs, and Lynne asked, "Mom, does this mean the storm has passed without the usual thunder and lightning and that you bought Dad's story?

"Dad, I remember Allison telling you a few years ago that miracles were in short supply in this house. Ken, you have just witnessed one of those rare occurrences. Amen!"

The meal and the conversation were very pleasant except for the thought that kept nagging at me. What did Allie Lea mean when she said, "Just what she had been hoping for"? I gave her a loving look and thought I'd see if she would be amenable to giving me an insight about what she meant.

All she did was give me a smug look and say, "Saturday."

Ken asked, "What's the big deal about Saturday? I don't remember either of you inviting Lynne and me to whatever it is you have planned."

Allie Lea smiled when she said, "Romeo has set up a picnic for Saturday and the invitations are closed. Just think, you'll have the entire house all to yourselves for most of the day. Isn't that right, Ryan?"

Lynne looked astounded and finally said, "I believe there is a conspiracy brewing, and I can't wait to hear the details. Does RK or Allison know?"

I mumbled, "The same also goes for me."

Allie Lea in all innocence asked, "Whose turn is it to clean up? And, no, they don't know."

I spent the early morning hours buying the goodies for our picnic, and then I announced, "The C & O walking path awaits."

Just like the weather man on channel 13 projected, the weather was beautiful. Allie Lea looked the part of Heidi, complete with a new purple backpack and she was raring to go.

We walked across the Cabin John Parkway and onto the canal's footpath. Before you knew it, we were joined by many others, who had the same idea, taking advantage of a great day and one of Georgetown's lesser known secrets. The leaves were, for the most part, still clinging tightly to the trees and their colors were spectacular. The Potomac River's flow was unhurried, a contrast to the chirping birds around us. Yet, we remained silent—it was if the Sphinx had control of our tongues.

Another mile saw us aimlessly ambling along, and as we passed the picnic and boathouse area, Allie Lea said, "This is a good spot. Let's stop here. I didn't eat much breakfast and, truth be told, I'm ready to eat and talk, provided you don't decide to stream the Mountaineers who are playing their arch rival, Pittsburgh."

I couldn't but help but smile when I said, "It's your nickel, and you're the one who called this little meeting. I hope you noticed that I didn't pump you or the kids for what I don't know, despite my curiosity.

She replied, "And for that, I'm grateful; now, let's eat."

I put my arm around her, zipped up her jacket, and then we dug in. I decided this was the moment to tell her that I too have a thought to pass on that is significant and important to our future health and happiness.

That really got her attention, and we ate the rest of our meal in contemplative silence until she said, "Allison will graduate from Scripps in three years; each of our kids will or should be on their own financially, and I think it's time for me to give thought to retiring in three more years!"

I quickly sat up, looked her straight in the eyes, and asked, "When and what prompted this monumental decision?"

I had no sooner asked those questions when she said, "I decided it was time to take the plunge when I first saw you crawling out of that cave at Machu Picchu. I damn near lost it that day. Right then, I said to myself, 'Old girl, you have given our kids, the Smithsonian, and you my all for the last twenty-five years. It's time you and I spend more quality time with each other in the remaining time allocated to each of us.' That's it, nothing else. Now, all that's left to do is for us to hash out the details and inform our kids and my coworkers when the time is right."

She then snuggled up to me, wrapped the extra blanket around herself, and giggled when she said, "I've shown you mine. Now, it's your turn to show me yours!"

I asked, "You didn't by chance bring your tiara, did you?"

She asked, "Do you think I always need my tiara?"

I replied, "You are the best person to answer that question."

She retorted, "Enough of this foolishness; let's hear what you have to say."

I said, "I don't understand why or how we both reached the same conclusion at about the same time. Pretty scary huh? I think the chain of events while we were seeking Pachacuti's remains weighed heavily on both of us, resulting in our thinking of our mortality."

"Ryan, you have echoed my feelings and thoughts. Frankly, I have been reluctant to bring them out in the open for fear of you thinking we are locked into a marriage headed for trouble."

I said, "Nothing of the sort. I think our premonitions are nature's way of saying slow down, you lucky people; it's time for you to start smelling the roses. As to our love affair, it doesn't and never has depended on your tiara or anything else except caring for each other. It will be dark before long, so, let's pack up and head back home."

"Ryan, when you lose your ability to dance, I'll know trouble and Doubtful are not far behind."

We packed up our things, and as we ambled along, Allie Lea asked, "How do you propose we handle this vexing question and how do we break it to the kids?"

"Simple, call a family council meeting and make it clear attendance is a must. No iPhones, no outside calls, and say that this is a fact-finding session that will, no doubt, take most of an afternoon."

"Darling, the stance we take and the answers we give must be objective despite how heated or contentious it may become. Above all that's good and holy, we must project togetherness and that any final decisions will be made with their and our best interests at heart. Don't forget to inform the kids, including Ken, that dinner is on us at Clyde's."

"My, oh, my, you must have given this a great deal of thought, and to think I was worried that our marriage was heading for trouble. You're right: we don't need anything as long as we have each other."

As we traversed the cobblestones at M street, I decided to go all the way and tell her of the poem that came to me while I was reminiscing yesterday. Prior to now, I have never explored writing poems. I wasn't sure how she would react, including her possibly thinking I'm sorta dopey. As I opened our front door, I said, "I have a surprise for you. Let's grab a cold beer, and I'll give you a first reading of a poem that came to me out of the blue while I was reminiscing yesterday. Are you interested?"

"You and a poem? This, I wouldn't miss for a million dollars!! Of course, I'm interested. But first, let's get rid of our outdoor togs, take a shower, and then open one of those expensive bottles of wine you have been hoarding. I'm first in the shower."

I joined her in the shower, and, for once, her tiara wasn't the main attraction. Thank goodness, the kids are out doing their thing and we have the great room all to ourselves. I uncorked the wine and said, "Buckle your seat belt and hold on tight. Here goes:

Are we going to the fair so high in the sky
Or go where we can see the monkeys
And watch them as they go swinging by,
Happily making their wishes known
With their red rumps for everyone to see
As they sit on their throne-a-high,
Chattering, squealing, oblivious to all
Not a visible care or worry except to dream
Of the pleasures that the morrow will bring.
Oh, if life was only that simple.
However faint, we learn to listen for that drumbeat—
At first the beat comes from afar, then without warning
Hastens as autumn makes its way.

The stage grows narrower as the wheel of life turns ever faster;
And we ask ourselves has it always been thus, or
Have we been sleeping only to find the earth's
And our internal clocks have been on fast forward?

Time, that linear mechanism, recognizes neither hopes or dreams
As it quietly sidesteps into the next dimension carrying with it
Our follies, our plans, our knowledge, our love, and from that
Caldron of fire, water, and despair, life will once more emerge.

Does this signal a new beginning or a beginning fraught with
Previous lives' scenarios? Do you think a thousand years from now
Mankind will be able to understand, let alone enjoy the fruits
Of the millenniums past?

I wonder!

She sat very still, dropped a tear or two, and said, "Ryan Keshaw, you have been hiding your light under a bushel. I am positively overwhelmed. And to think you have been hiding that talent under the cover of the 'ah shucks' routine you so frequently project. What name did you give your prize winning poem?"

"Allie Lea, I seriously doubt my poem will win any accolades; do me a favor and low key it. For grins, I'll run you a copy, and maybe you can provide a scintillating thought-provoking title."

She marched to where I was sitting, ruffled my hair, gently stroked my head, and replied, "That's easy."

She took my hand and said, "Come on, let's go upstairs."

I did a little jig. "Is your tiara possibly involved?"

She then held me tight and wickedly said, "I *wonder*."

Other books by Edward Curry

Temple of the Two Jaguars

2012: Maya End Date

2012:
A New Maya Nation Emerges

The Pink Bra Archaeologist

Edward Curry, the author and former West Virginian, now resides in Virginia Beach. He has three grown children: Lynne, Richard, and Gregory. This is his fifth fictional writing about the Maya and the Inca. He has written and produced nine agency-management videos as well as six insurance marketing books. He is currently working on a mystical, true-life adventure titled *Notes from Another Time and Place.*

www.ingramcontent.com/pod-product-compliance
Lightning Source LLC
Chambersburg PA
CBHW070336260626
47160CB00003B/1058